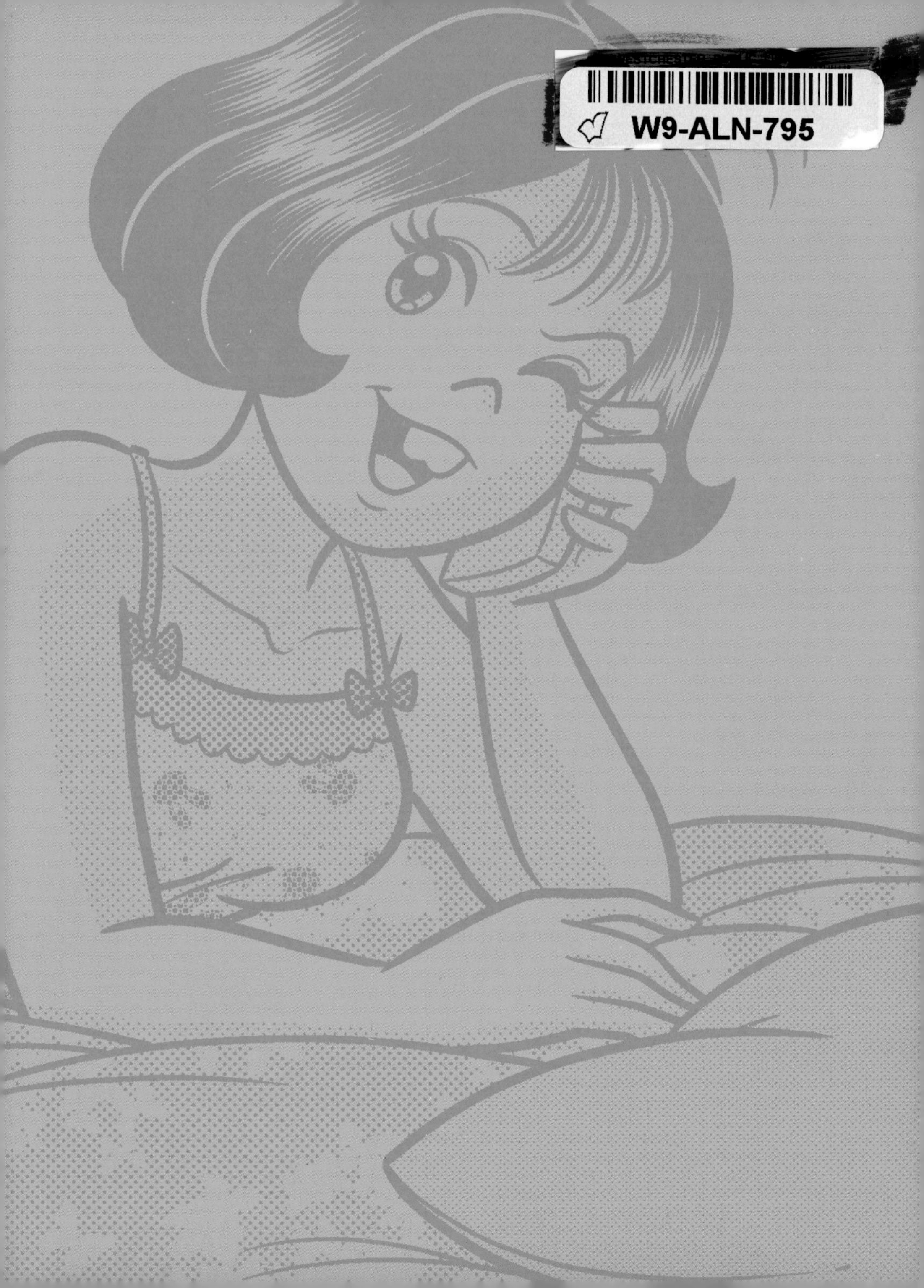

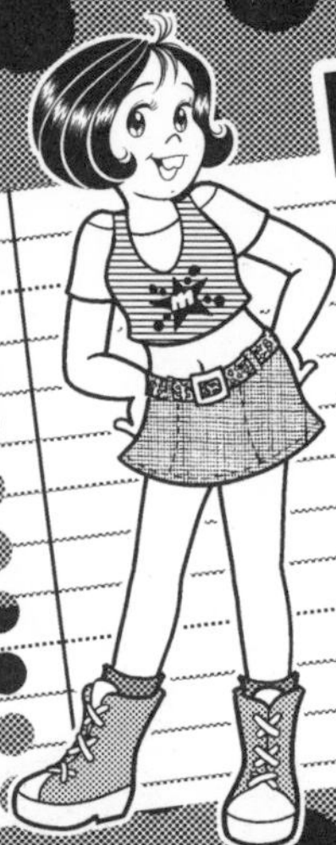

Monica

Monica is a sweet, happy, buck-toothed, teenage girl. When she was younger, she was known for being intolerant of disrespect and always stood up for her friends. That is, unless Jimmy-Five and Smudge would cause her trouble, then Monica would bash them with her favorite plush blue bunny, Samson! Still, occasionally, she does her classic bunny bashings as a teen, but has chilled out when it comes to Jimmy-Five, who has been catching her attention a lot more lately. Monica is the leader of the gang because of her honest and charismatic—and powerful—personality.

J-Five

Jimmy-Five, or J-Five, has always been picked on for his speech impediment. He used to lisp, which caused him to switch letters around, such as r's for w's, when he would speak. He has grown out of that as a teen, unless he's nervous, which typically happens around a certain girl. He also was picked on because of the five strands of hair he had on his head, which have all sort of filled out as a teen. Still, J-Five is sometimes made fun of for his hair, but he doesn't let it get to him as much anymore! When J-Five was young, he would often try to steal Monica's blue bunny from her and attempt to take over as leader of the gang with his questionable schemes. J-Five is no longer focused on being head of the gang as much as he's focused on being close with his friends, and closer to one friend in particular…

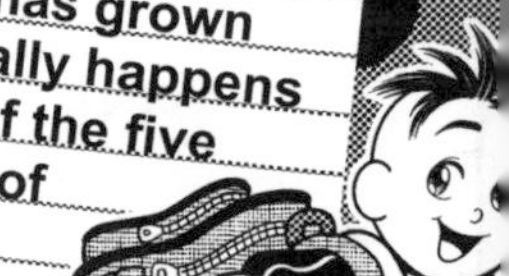

Smudge

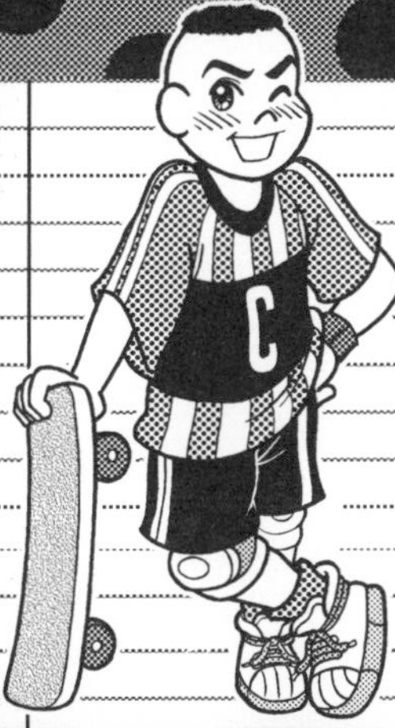

Smudge has never liked water and prefers his messy and dirty lifestyle over showers, rain, swimming, or even drinking water any day, but he's warmed up to taking showers as a teen… sort of. He cleans up sometimes mainly because the opinion of girls has started to matter to him, unlike when he was a kid. Smudge loves sports, especially skateboarding and soccer because of how radical they are. He also loves comics, and shares this love with his best friend, J-Five! Smudge is kind of the "handyman" of the gang, always helping his friends in times of need but typically also messing everything up.

Maggy

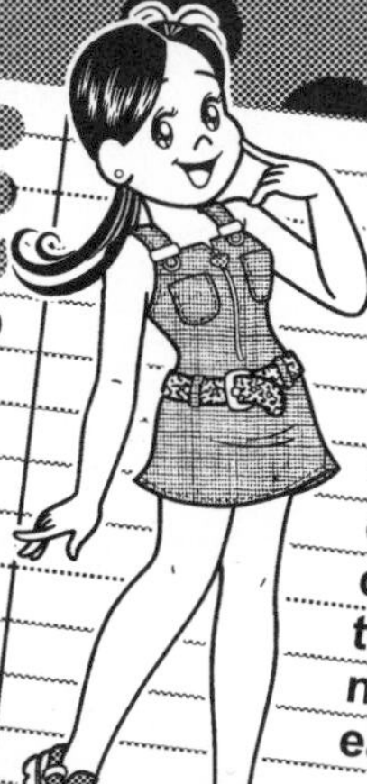

Maggy is Monica's best friend, always having her back and being there for her in good times and bad. Maggy is also a huge lover of cats. Maggy has always had a voracious appetite, mostly eating watermelons but never discriminating against any other food put in front of her. Maggy is more conscious of what she eats now… perhaps a little too much. She is virtually obsessed with proper nutrition, sports, and exercise instead of eating anything she sees.

Monica Adventures

#1 "Who Can Afford the Price of Friendship Today?!"

Characters, Story, and Illustration created by Mauricio de Sousa
DENNIS OYAFUSO, DIOGO NASCIMENTO—Cover Artists
MAURICIO DE SOUSA, MARINA TAKEDA E SOUSA, FLÁVIO TEIXEIRA DE JESUS—Script
JOSÉ APARECIDO CAVALCANTE, LINO PAES, ROBERTO M. PEREIRA—Pencils
MAURO SOUZA, ZAZO AGUILAR—Illustrations
CRISTINA H. ANDO, JAIME PODAVIN, TATIANA M. SANTOS, VIVIANE YAMABUCHI—Inks
CARLOS KINA—Lettering
A. MAURICIO SOUSA NETO, ANTÔNIO R. F. GUEDES, KAIO RENATO BRUDER—Finishes
JAE HYUNG WOO, MARCELO KINA, MARIA JÚLIA S. BELLUCCI—Colorists
MARIA DE FÁTIMA A. CLARO—Art Coordination
SANDRO ANTONIO DA SILVA—Script Supervisor
ALICE K. TAKEDA—Executive Director
SIDNEY GUSMAN—Editorial Planner
ÍVANA MELLO—Original editor
PECCAVI TRANSLATIONS—Original Translations

Special thanks to LOURDES GALIANO, RODRIGO PAIVA, MÔNICA SOUSA, and MAURICO DE SOUSA

MAURICIO DE SOUSA EDITORA

www.turmadamonica.com.br

JEFF WHITMAN—Editor, Production
KARR ANTUNES—Editorial Intern
JIM SALICRUP
Editor-in-Chief

Charmz is an imprint of Papercutz.

PB ISBN: 978-1-5458-0218-2
HC ISBN: 978-1-5458-0219-9

Printed in China
January 2019

Charmz books may be purchased for business or promotional use.
For information on bulk purchases please contact Macmillan
Corporate and Premium Sales Department at
(800) 221-7945 x5442

Distributed by Macmillan
First Charmz Printing

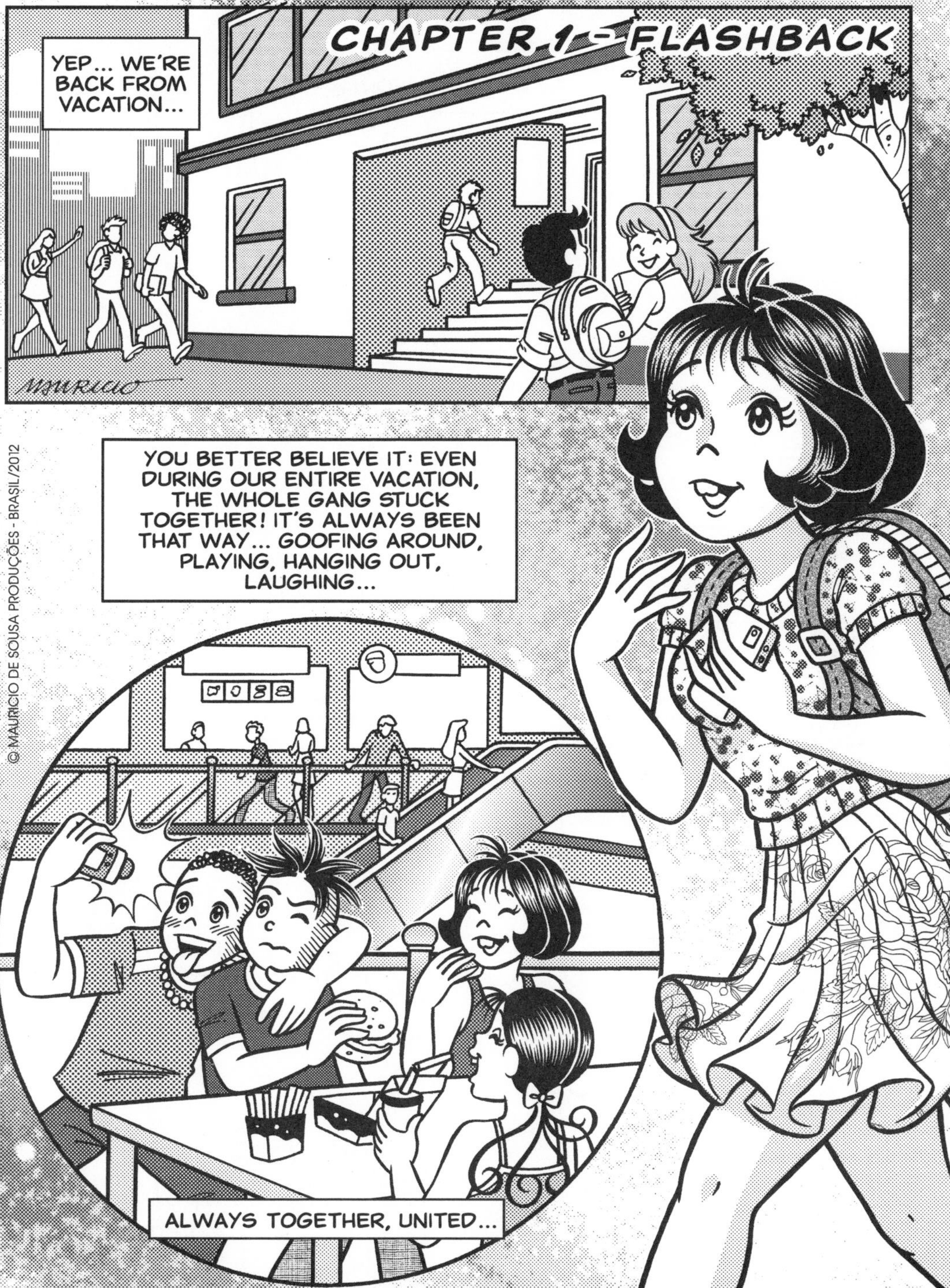
CHAPTER 1 - FLASHBACK
YEP... WE'RE BACK FROM VACATION...
MAURICIO
YOU BETTER BELIEVE IT: EVEN DURING OUR ENTIRE VACATION, THE WHOLE GANG STUCK TOGETHER! IT'S ALWAYS BEEN THAT WAY... GOOFING AROUND, PLAYING, HANGING OUT, LAUGHING...
ALWAYS TOGETHER, UNITED...

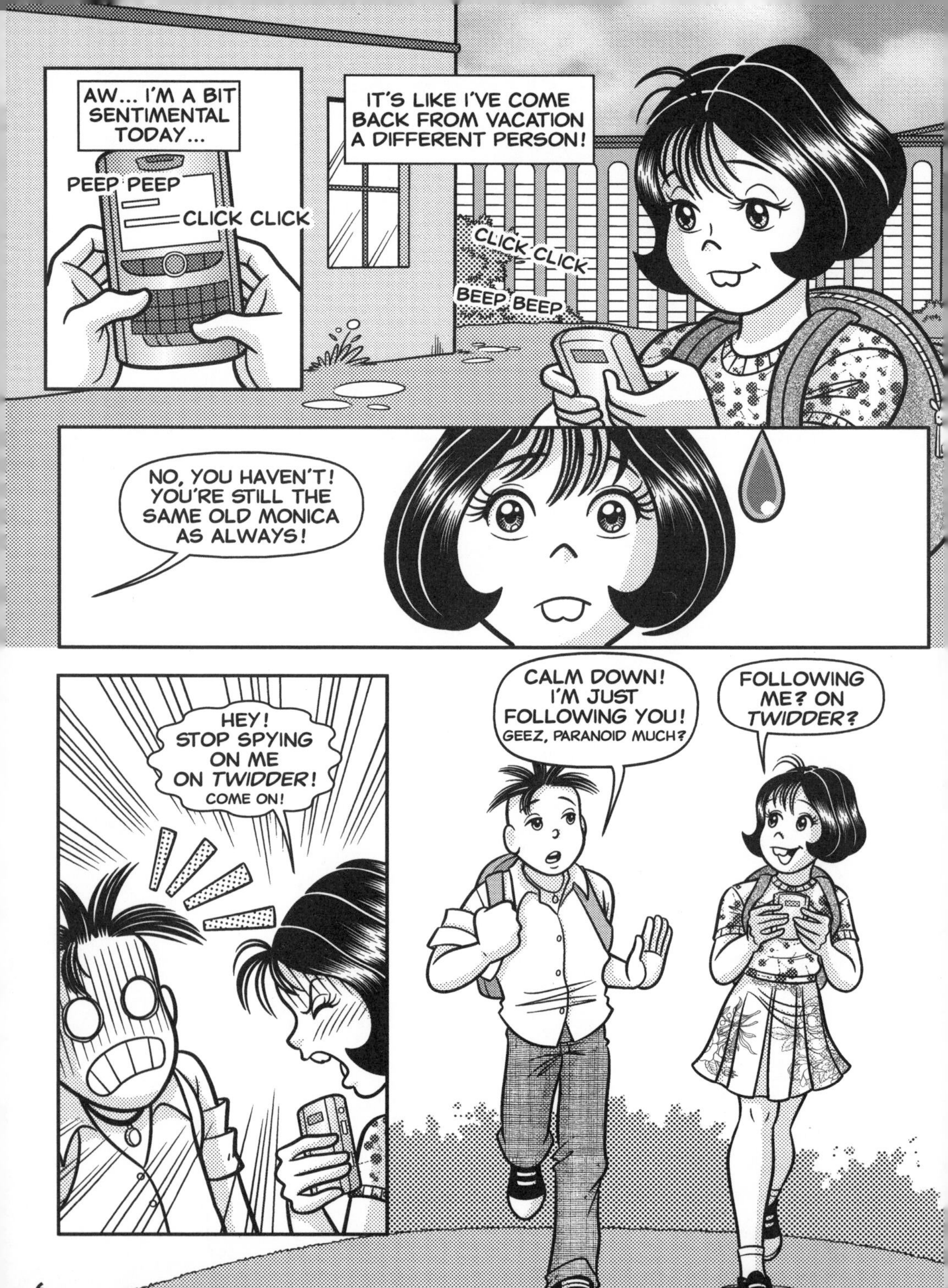
AW... I'M A BIT SENTIMENTAL TODAY...
PEEP PEEP
CLICK CLICK
IT'S LIKE I'VE COME BACK FROM VACATION A DIFFERENT PERSON!
CLICK CLICK
BEEP BEEP
NO, YOU HAVEN'T! YOU'RE STILL THE SAME OLD MONICA AS ALWAYS!
HEY! STOP SPYING ON ME ON *TWIDDER*! COME ON!
CALM DOWN! I'M JUST FOLLOWING YOU! GEEZ, PARANOID MUCH?
FOLLOWING ME? ON *TWIDDER*?

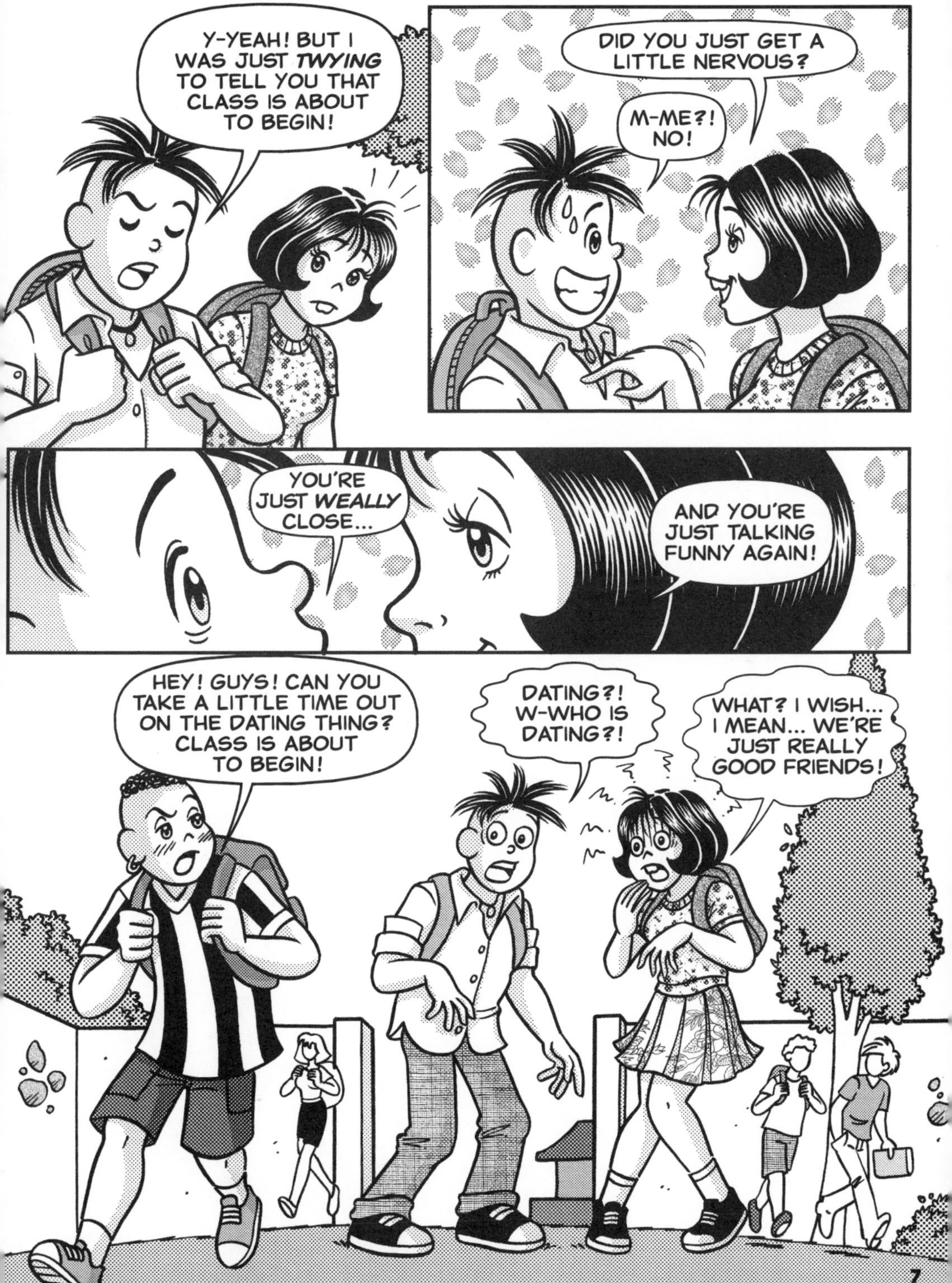
Y-YEAH! BUT I WAS JUST *TWYING* TO TELL YOU THAT CLASS IS ABOUT TO BEGIN!
DID YOU JUST GET A LITTLE NERVOUS?
M-ME?! NO!
YOU'RE JUST *WEALLY* CLOSE...
AND YOU'RE JUST TALKING FUNNY AGAIN!
HEY! GUYS! CAN YOU TAKE A LITTLE TIME OUT ON THE DATING THING? CLASS IS ABOUT TO BEGIN!
DATING?! W-WHO IS DATING?!
WHAT? I WISH... I MEAN... WE'RE JUST REALLY GOOD FRIENDS!

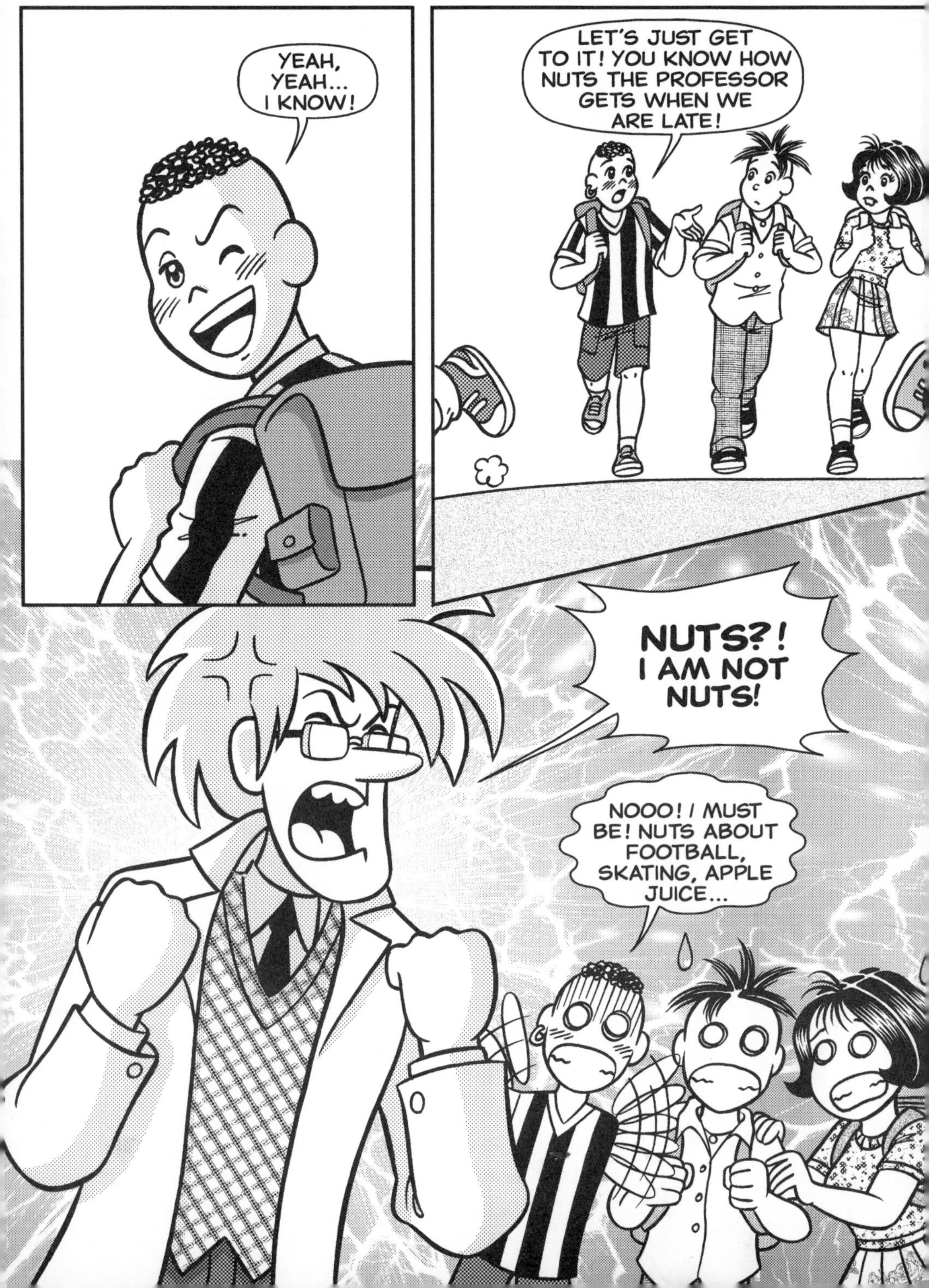
YEAH, YEAH... I KNOW!
LET'S JUST GET TO IT! YOU KNOW HOW NUTS THE PROFESSOR GETS WHEN WE ARE LATE!
NUTS?! I AM NOT NUTS!
NOOO! I MUST BE! NUTS ABOUT FOOTBALL, SKATING, APPLE JUICE...

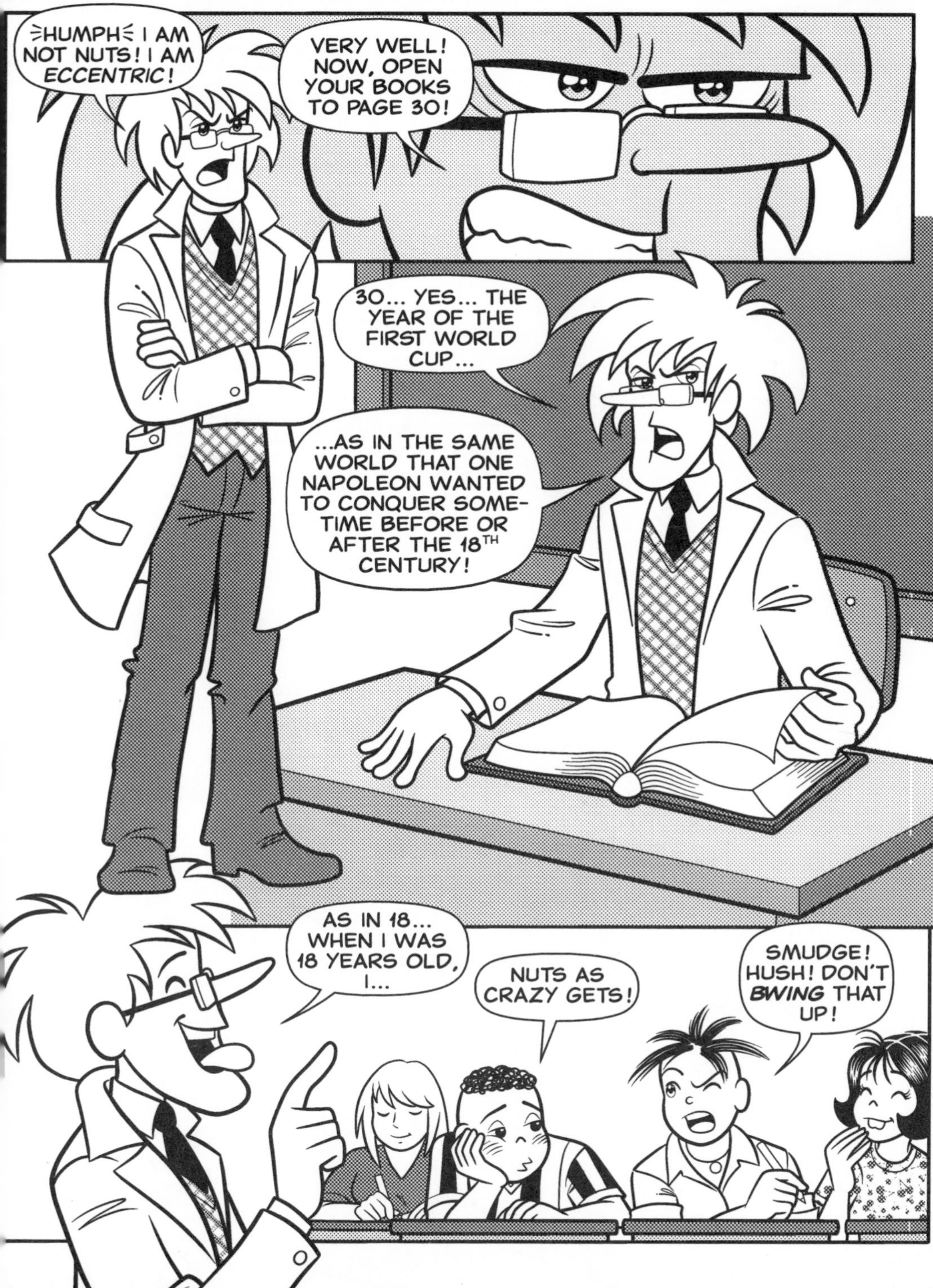

⋛HUMPH⋚ I AM NOT NUTS! I AM *ECCENTRIC*!
VERY WELL! NOW, OPEN YOUR BOOKS TO PAGE 30!
30... YES... THE YEAR OF THE FIRST WORLD CUP...
...AS IN THE SAME WORLD THAT ONE NAPOLEON WANTED TO CONQUER SOME-TIME BEFORE OR AFTER THE 18TH CENTURY!
AS IN 18... WHEN I WAS 18 YEARS OLD, I...
NUTS AS CRAZY GETS!
SMUDGE! HUSH! DON'T *BWING* THAT UP!

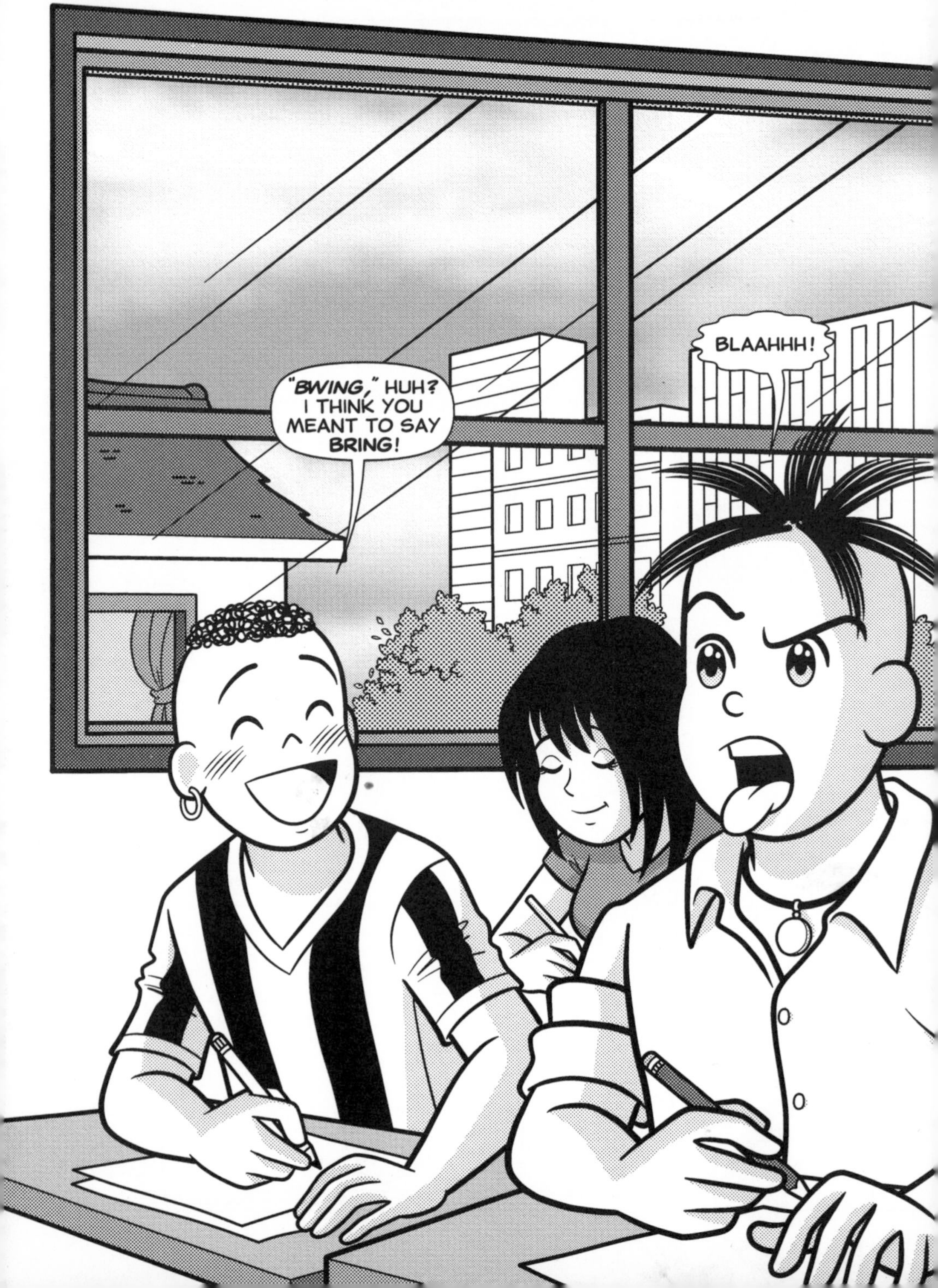
"*BWING,*" HUH? I THINK YOU MEANT TO SAY **BRING**!
BLAAHHH!

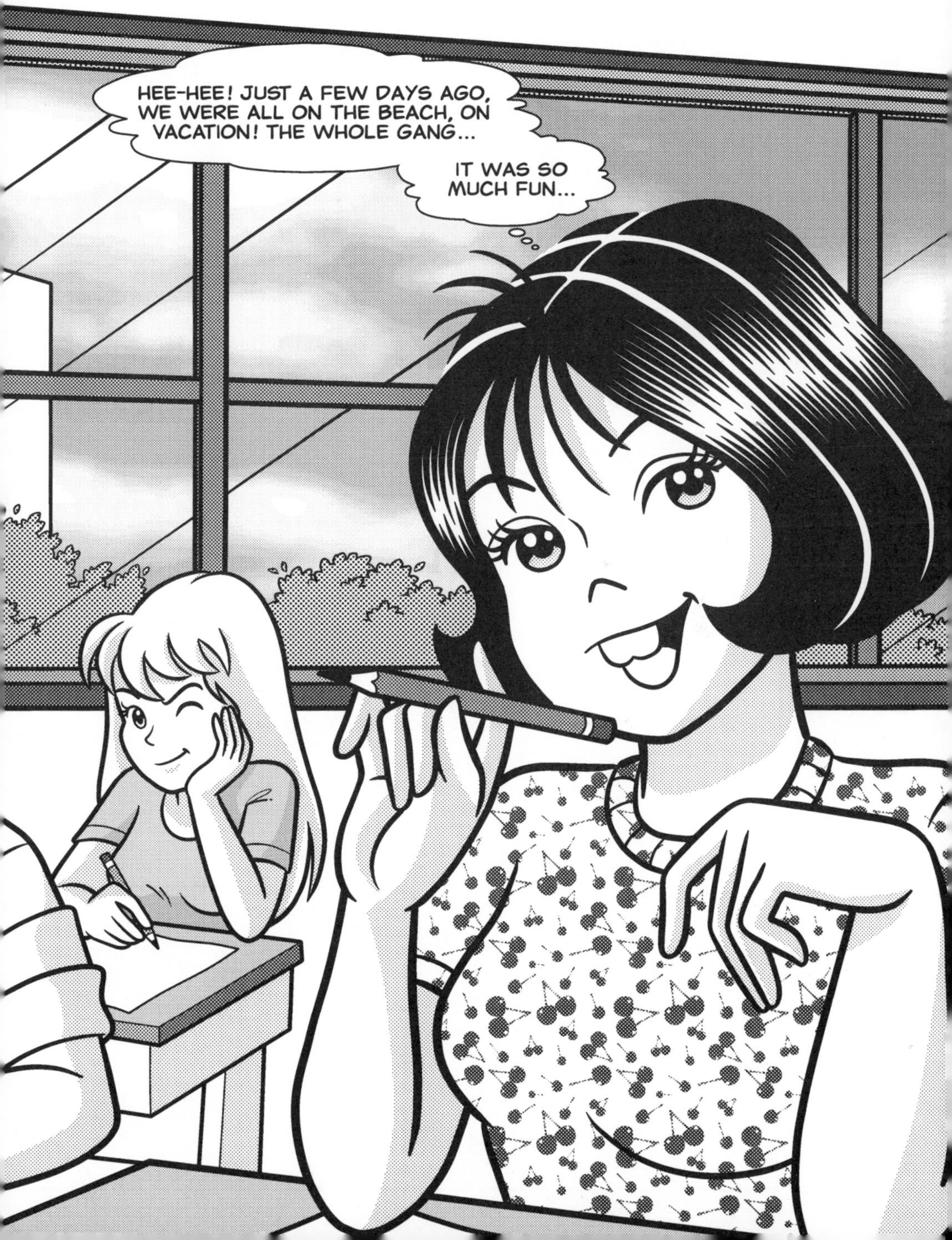
HEE-HEE! JUST A FEW DAYS AGO, WE WERE ALL ON THE BEACH, ON VACATION! THE WHOLE GANG...
IT WAS SO MUCH FUN...

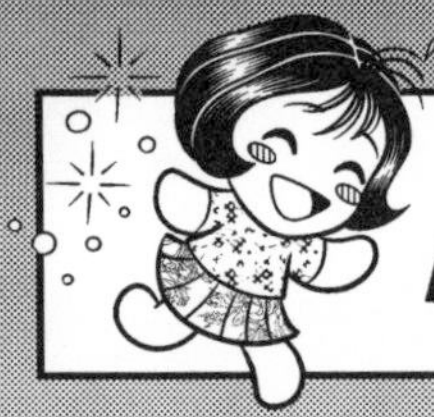

PAUSE FOR THE FLASHBACK

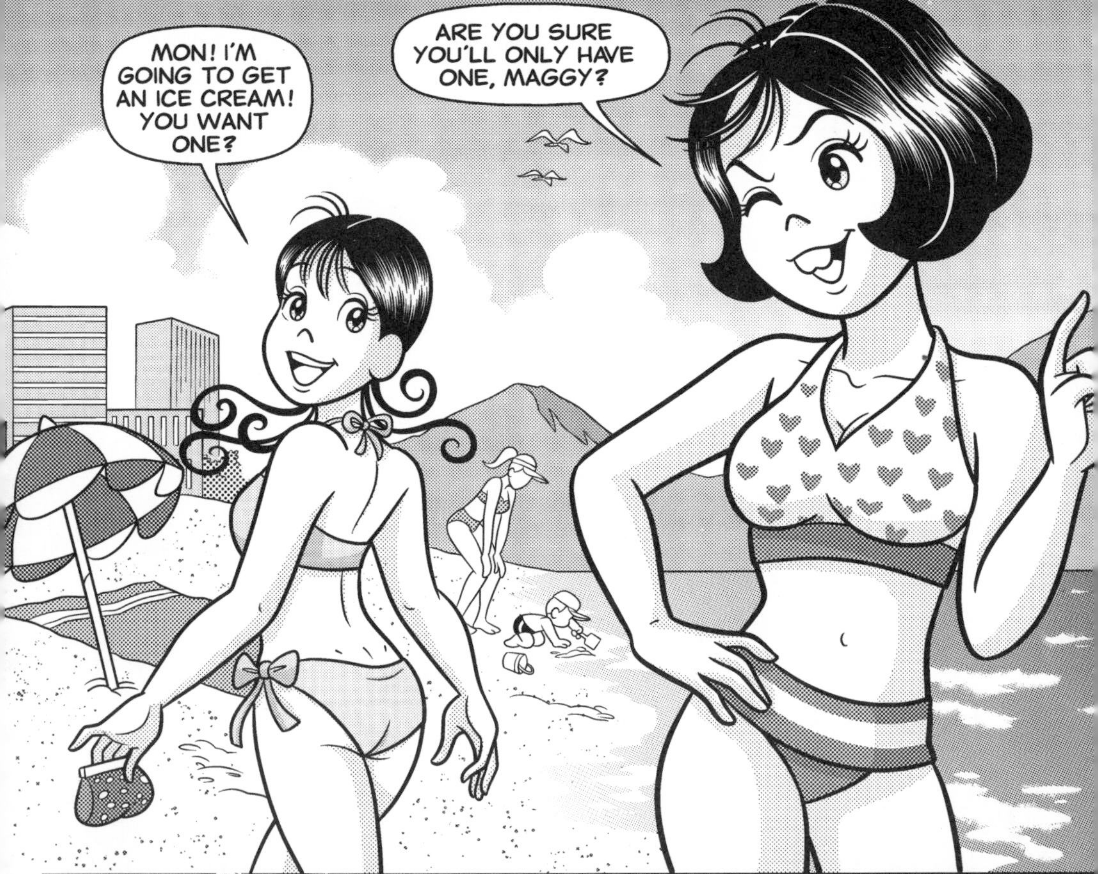
MON! I'M GOING TO GET AN ICE CREAM! YOU WANT ONE?
ARE YOU SURE YOU'LL ONLY HAVE ONE, MAGGY?

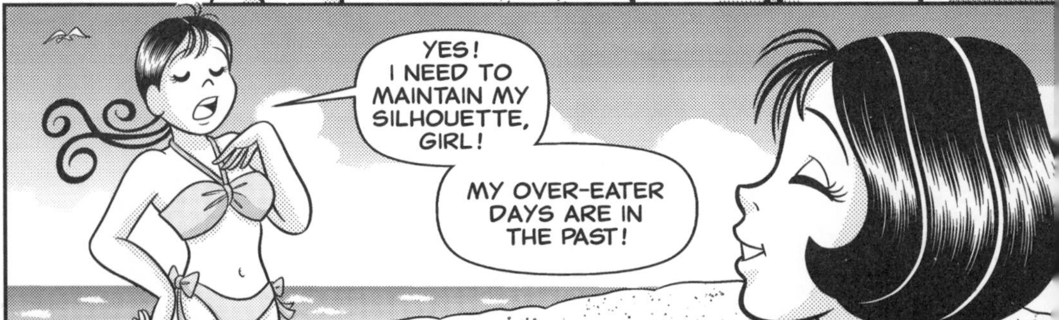
YES! I NEED TO MAINTAIN MY SILHOUETTE, GIRL!
MY OVER-EATER DAYS ARE IN THE PAST!

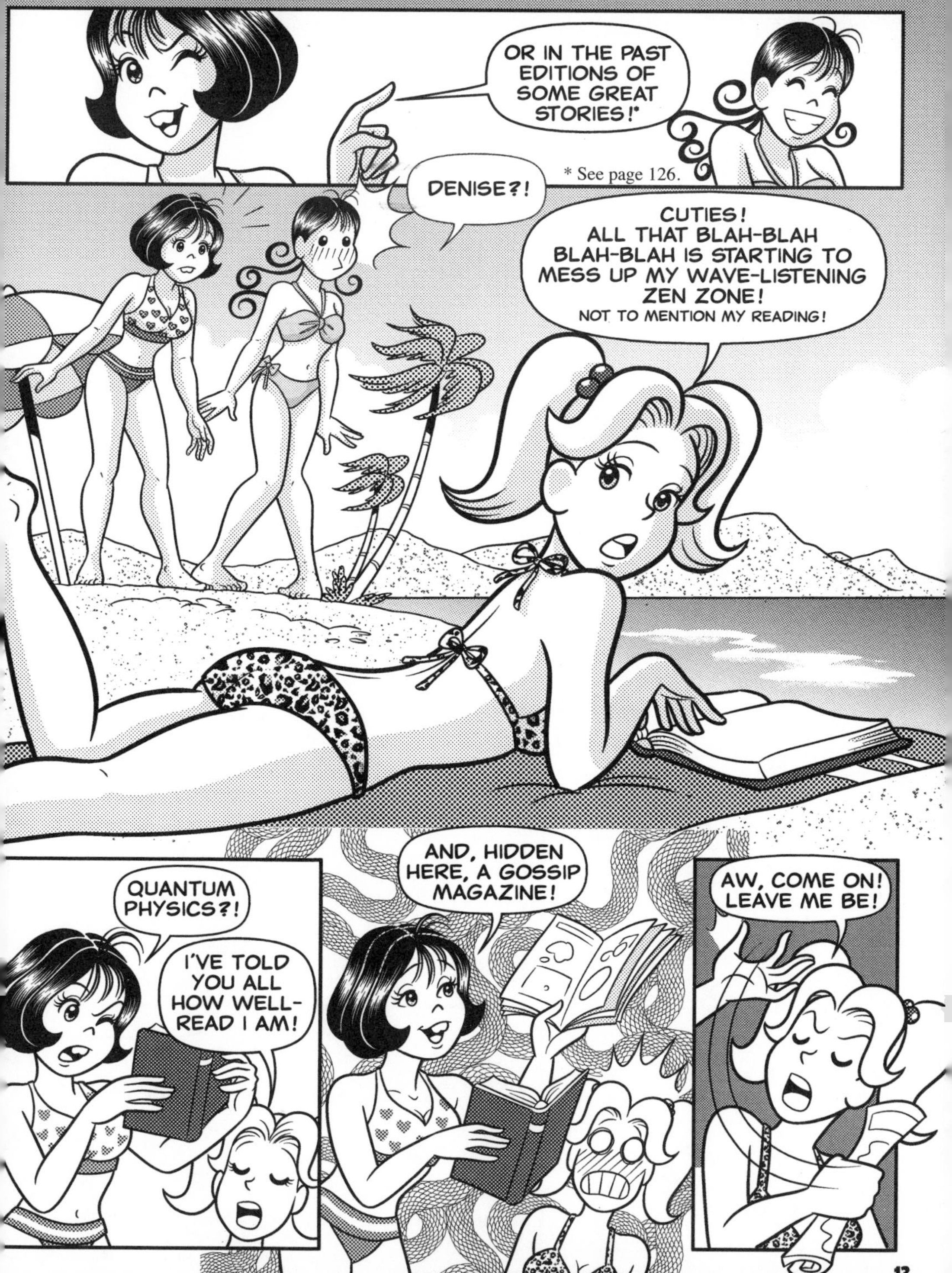
OR IN THE PAST EDITIONS OF SOME GREAT STORIES!*
* See page 126.
DENISE?!
CUTIES! ALL THAT BLAH-BLAH BLAH-BLAH IS STARTING TO MESS UP MY WAVE-LISTENING ZEN ZONE! NOT TO MENTION MY READING!
QUANTUM PHYSICS?!
I'VE TOLD YOU ALL HOW WELL-READ I AM!
AND, HIDDEN HERE, A GOSSIP MAGAZINE!
AW, COME ON! LEAVE ME BE!

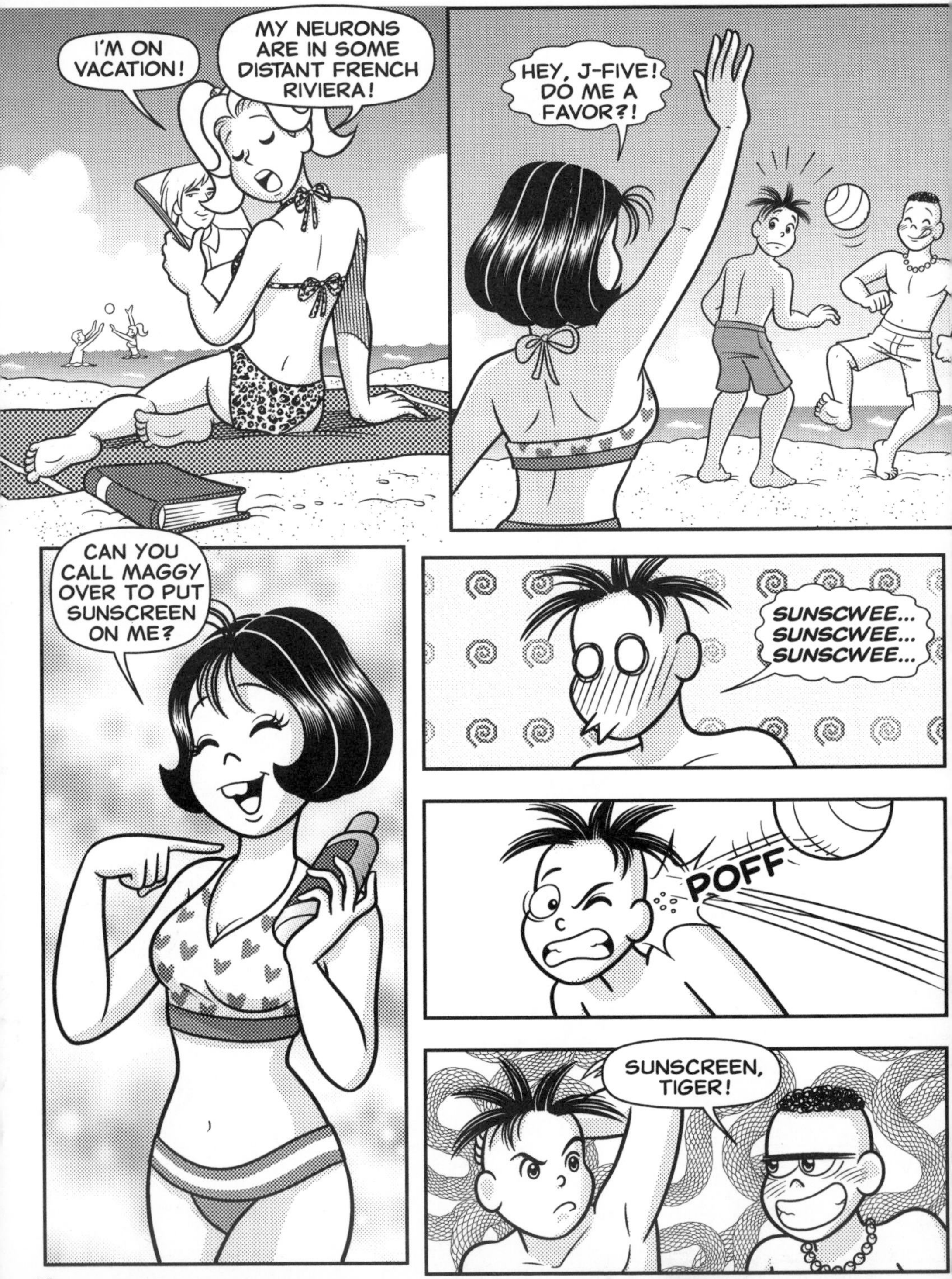
I'M ON VACATION!
MY NEURONS ARE IN SOME DISTANT FRENCH RIVIERA!
HEY, J-FIVE! DO ME A FAVOR?!
CAN YOU CALL MAGGY OVER TO PUT SUNSCREEN ON ME?
SUNSCWEE... SUNSCWEE... SUNSCWEE...
POFF
SUNSCREEN, TIGER!

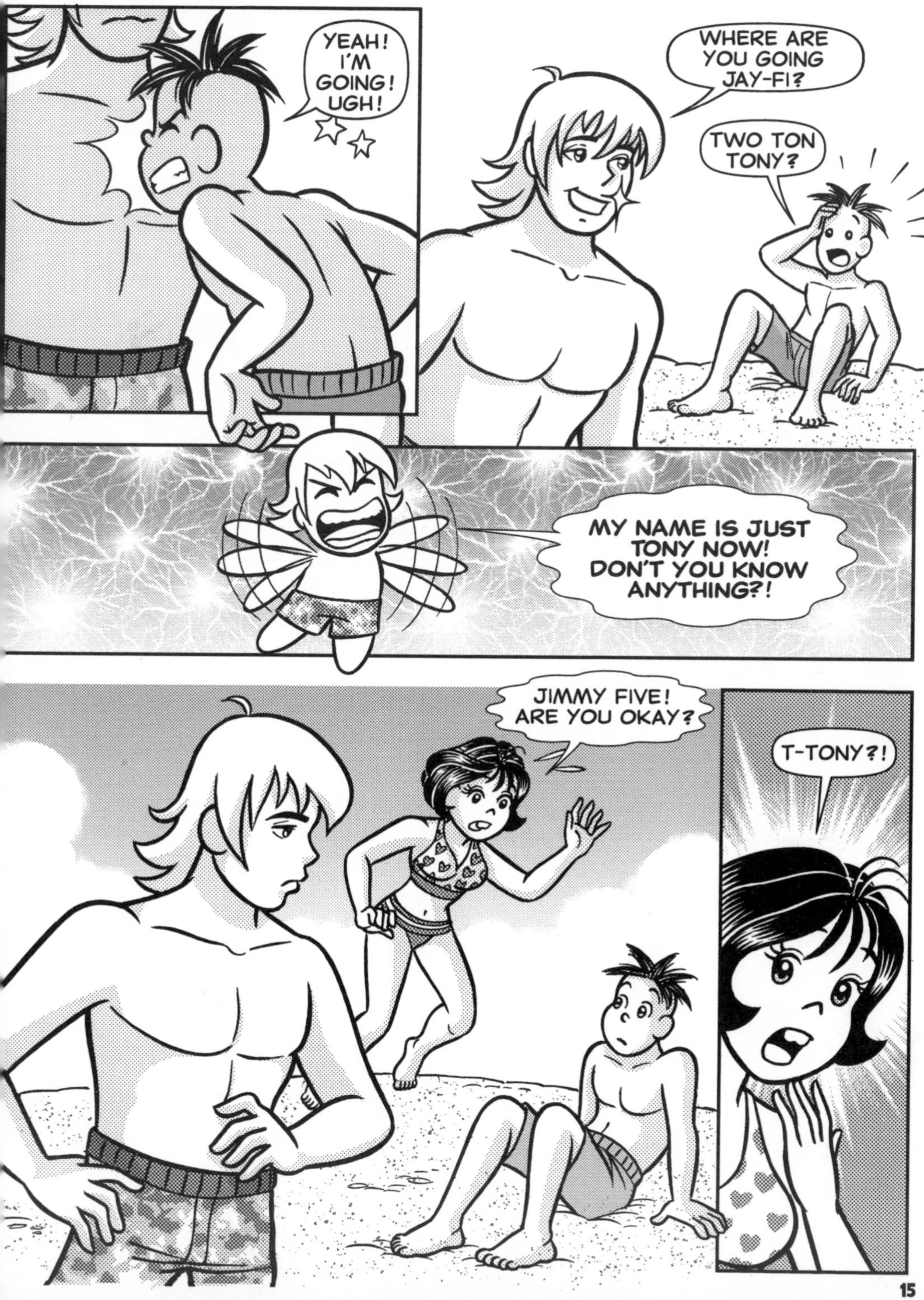
YEAH! I'M GOING! UGH!
WHERE ARE YOU GOING JAY-FI?
TWO TON TONY?
MY NAME IS JUST TONY NOW! DON'T YOU KNOW ANYTHING?!
JIMMY FIVE! ARE YOU OKAY?
T-TONY?!

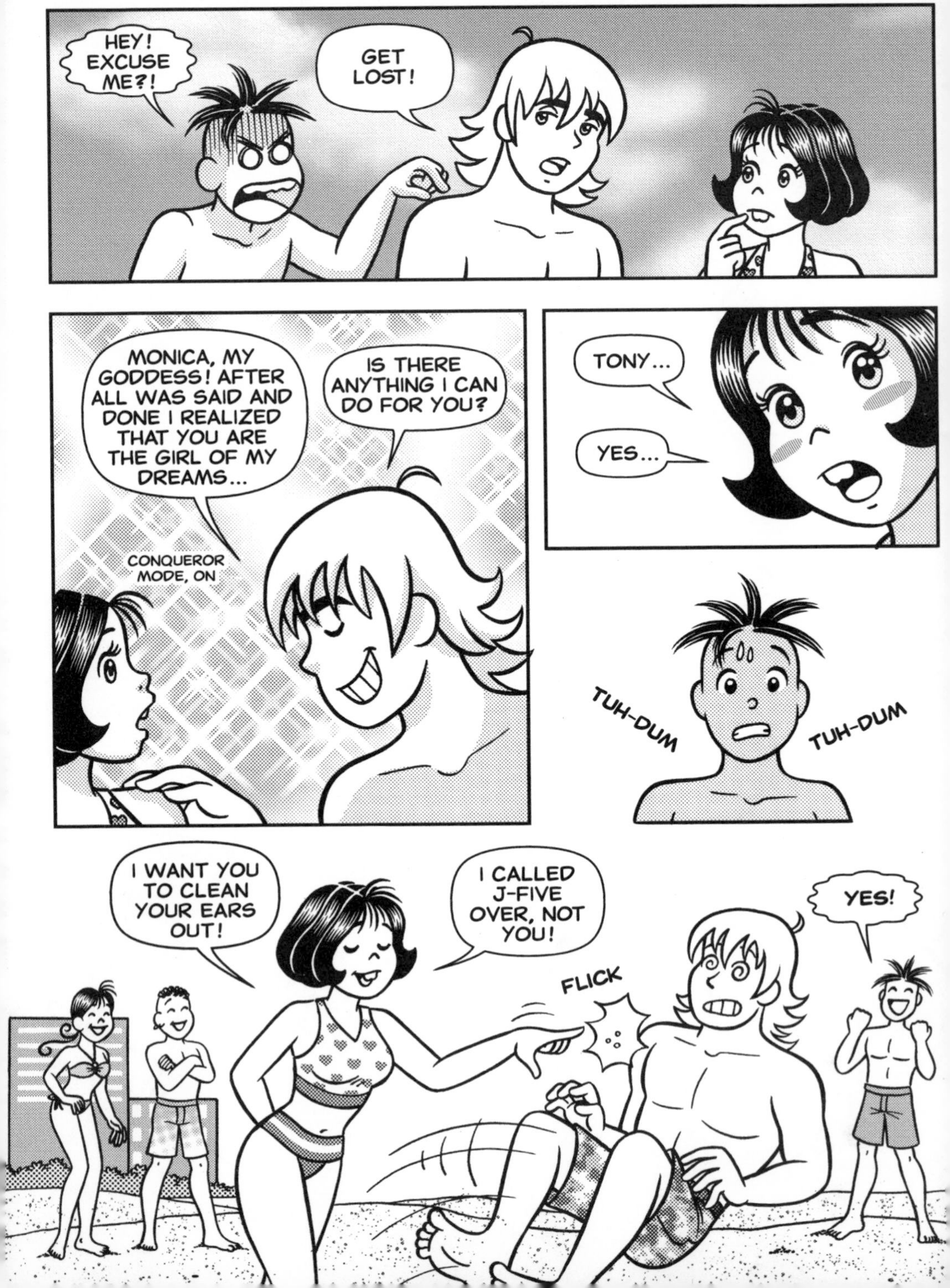
HEY! EXCUSE ME?!
GET LOST!
MONICA, MY GODDESS! AFTER ALL WAS SAID AND DONE I REALIZED THAT YOU ARE THE GIRL OF MY DREAMS...
CONQUEROR MODE, ON
IS THERE ANYTHING I CAN DO FOR YOU?
TONY...
YES...
TUH-DUM
TUH-DUM
I WANT YOU TO CLEAN YOUR EARS OUT!
I CALLED J-FIVE OVER, NOT YOU!
FLICK
YES!

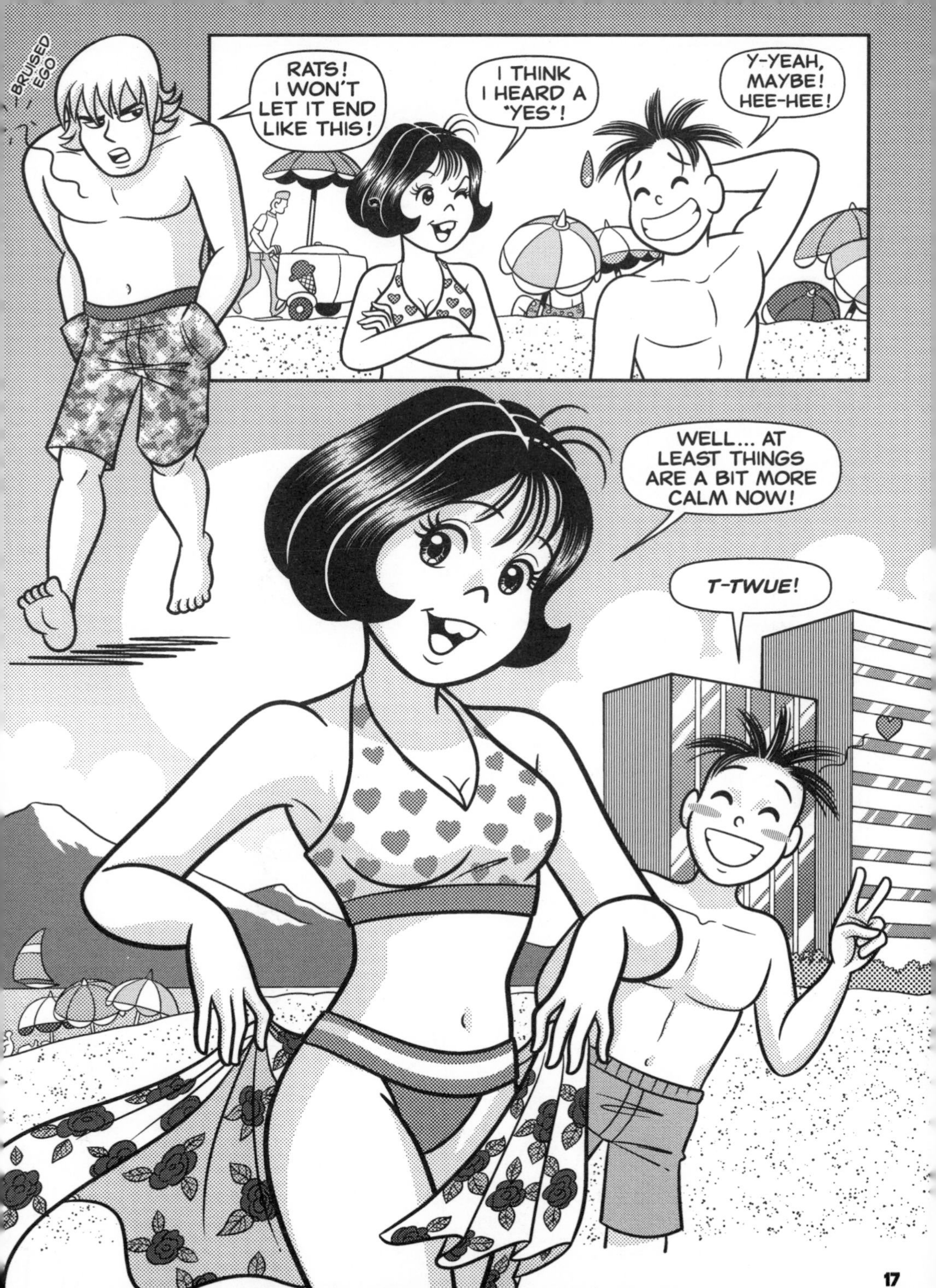
BRUISED EGO
RATS! I WON'T LET IT END LIKE THIS!
I THINK I HEARD A "YES"!
Y-YEAH, MAYBE! HEE-HEE!
WELL... AT LEAST THINGS ARE A BIT MORE CALM NOW!
T-TWUE!

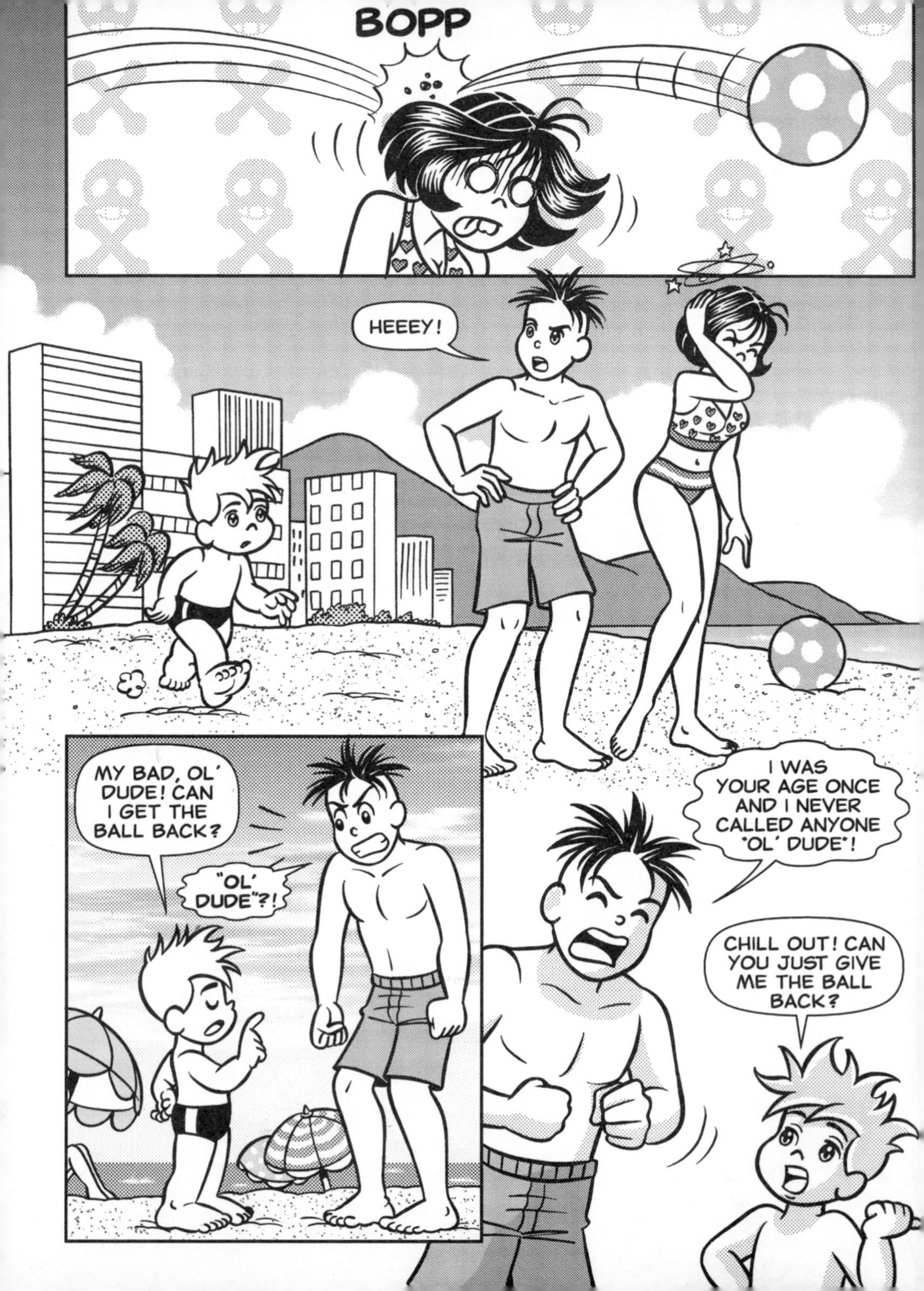
BOPP
HEEEY!
MY BAD, OL' DUDE! CAN I GET THE BALL BACK?
"OL' DUDE"?!
I WAS YOUR AGE ONCE AND I NEVER CALLED ANYONE "OL' DUDE"!
CHILL OUT! CAN YOU JUST GIVE ME THE BALL BACK?

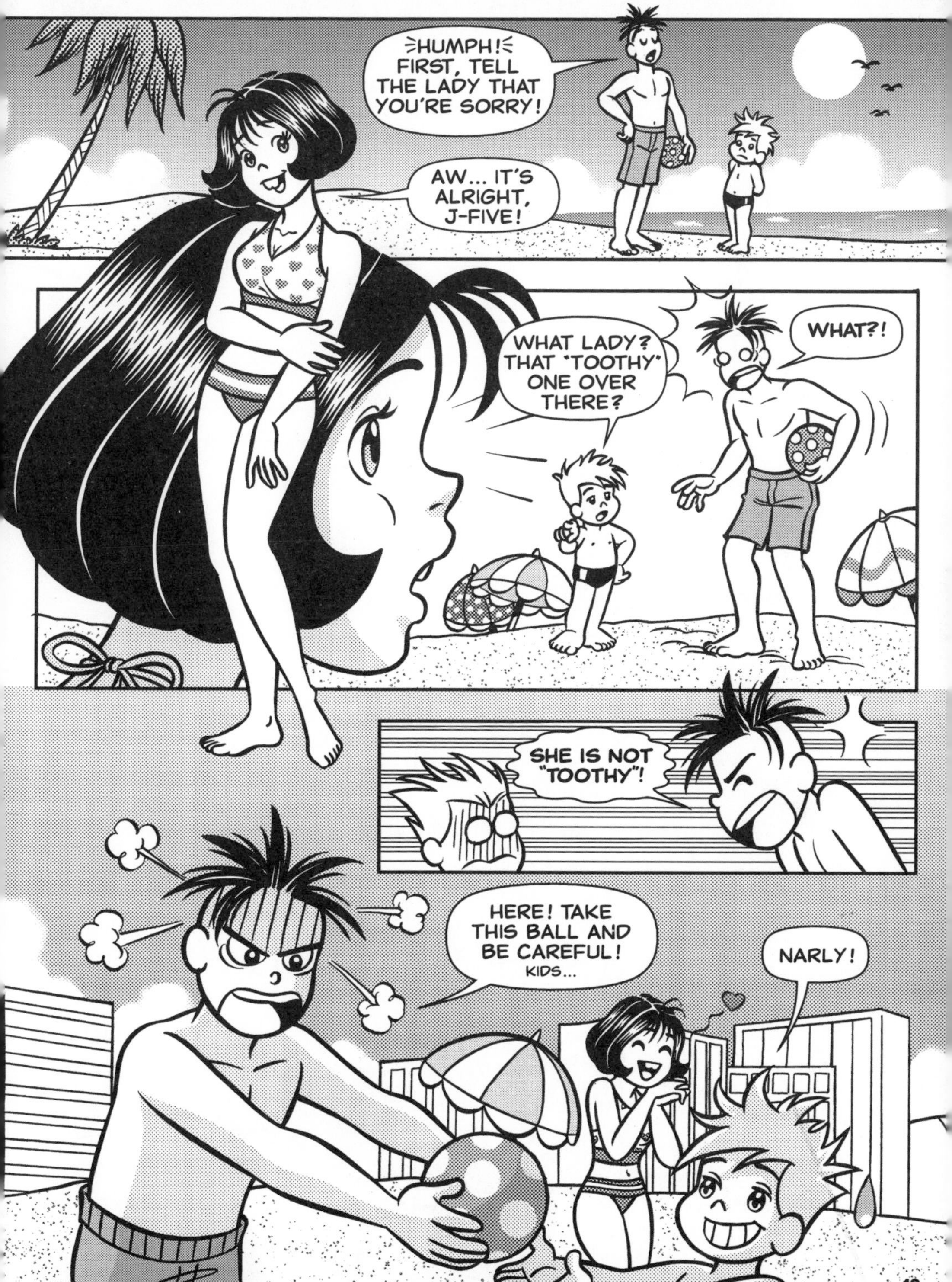

≷HUMPH!≶ FIRST, TELL THE LADY THAT YOU'RE SORRY!
AW... IT'S ALRIGHT, J-FIVE!
WHAT LADY? THAT "TOOTHY" ONE OVER THERE?
WHAT?!
SHE IS NOT "TOOTHY"!
WHAT?!
HERE! TAKE THIS BALL AND BE CAREFUL! KIDS...
NARLY!

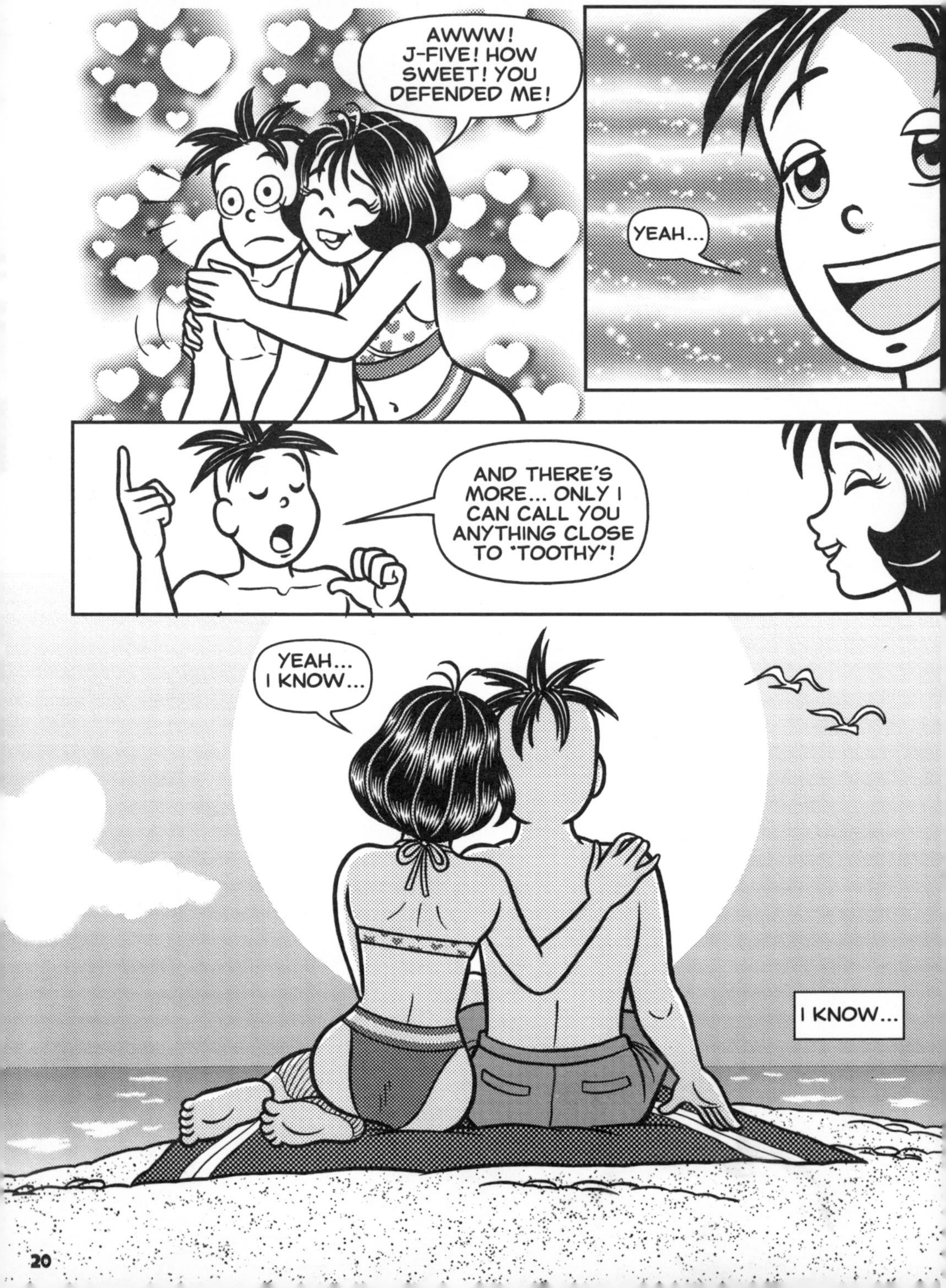
AWWW! J-FIVE! HOW SWEET! YOU DEFENDED ME!
YEAH...
AND THERE'S MORE... ONLY I CAN CALL YOU ANYTHING CLOSE TO "TOOTHY"!
YEAH... I KNOW...
I KNOW...

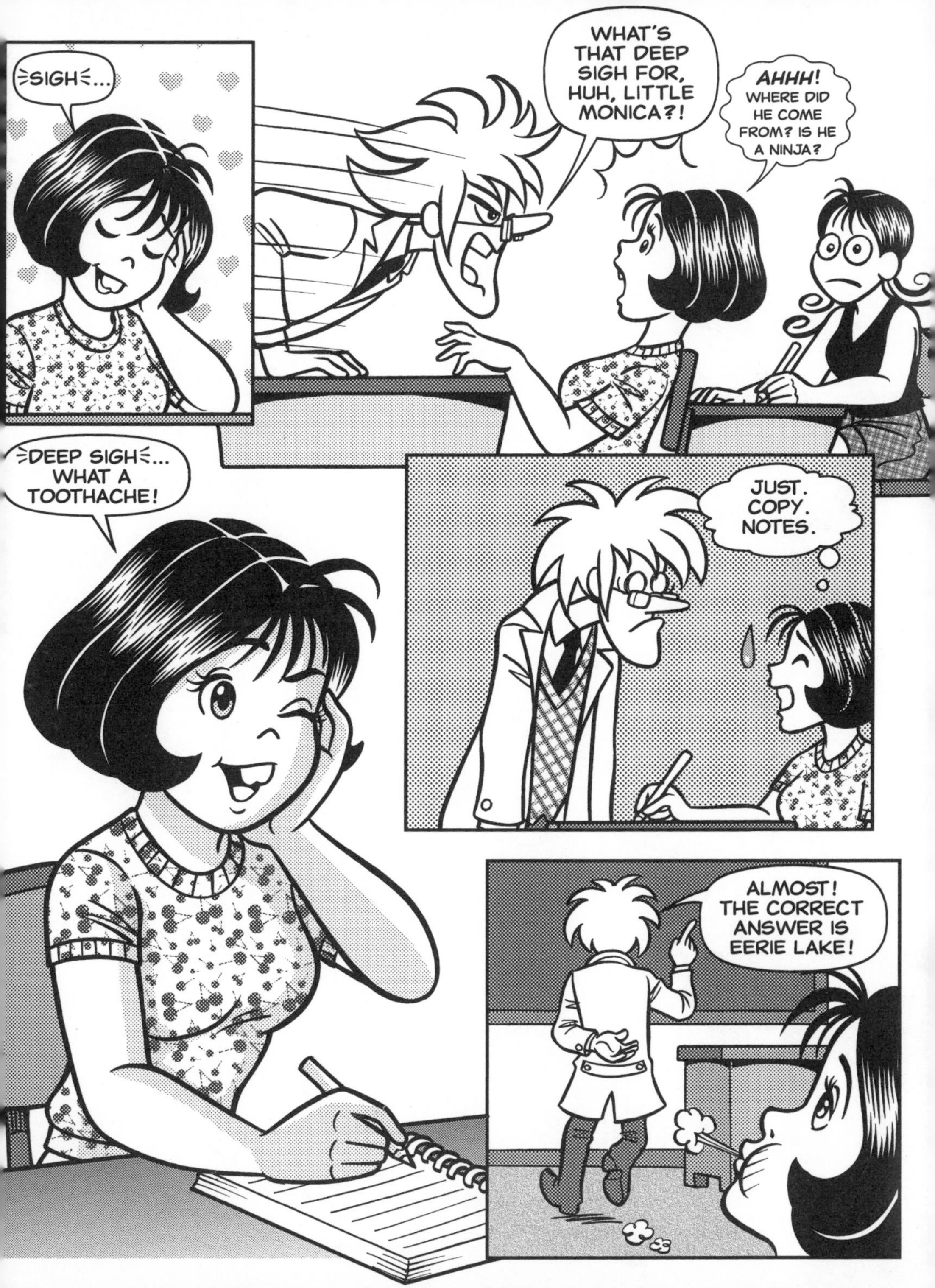

≡SIGH≡...
WHAT'S THAT DEEP SIGH FOR, HUH, LITTLE MONICA?!
AHHH! WHERE DID HE COME FROM? IS HE A NINJA?
≡DEEP SIGH≡... WHAT A TOOTHACHE!
JUST. COPY. NOTES.
ALMOST! THE CORRECT ANSWER IS EERIE LAKE!

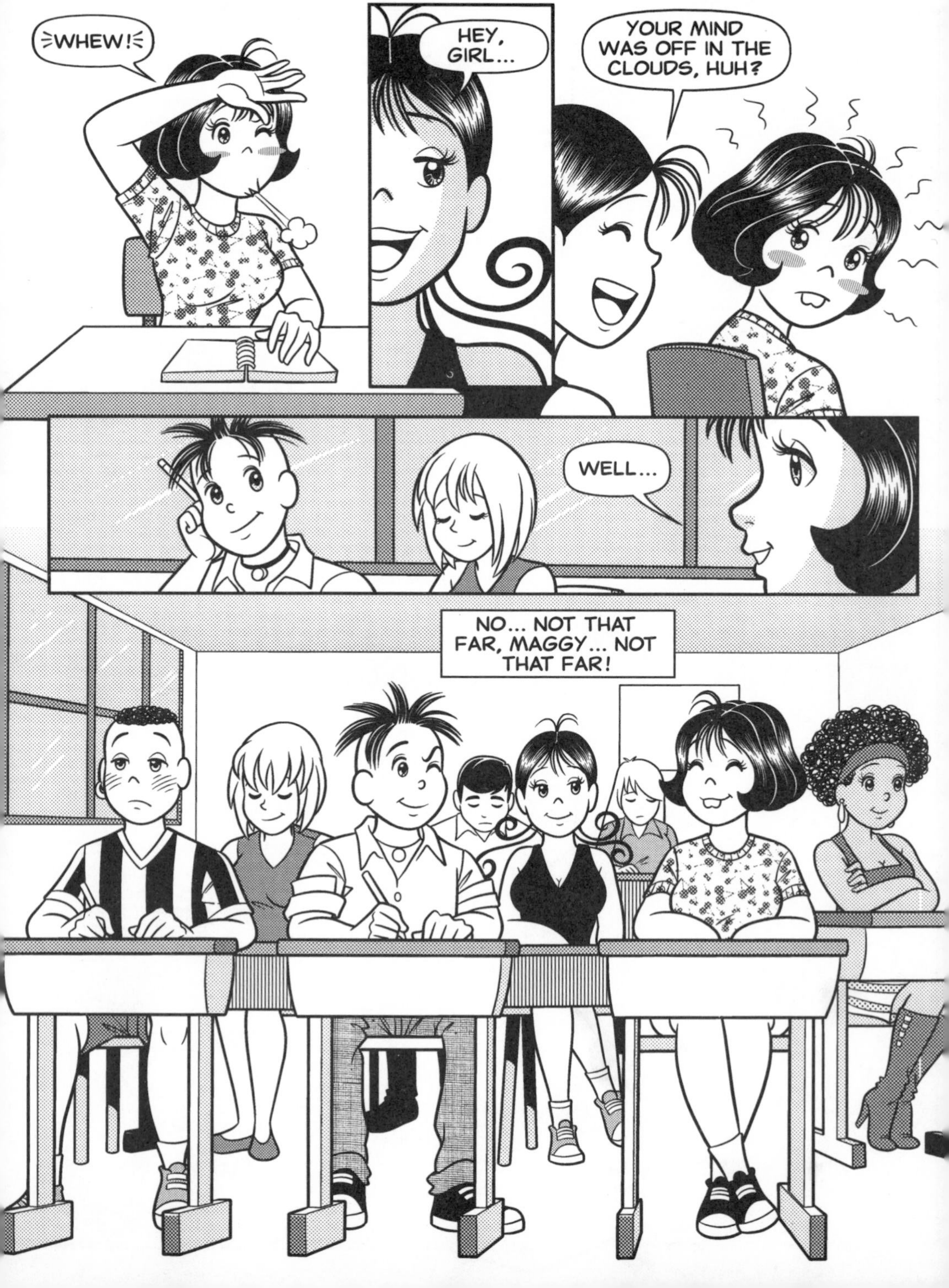
WHEW!
HEY, GIRL...
YOUR MIND WAS OFF IN THE CLOUDS, HUH?
WELL...
NO... NOT THAT FAR, MAGGY... NOT THAT FAR!

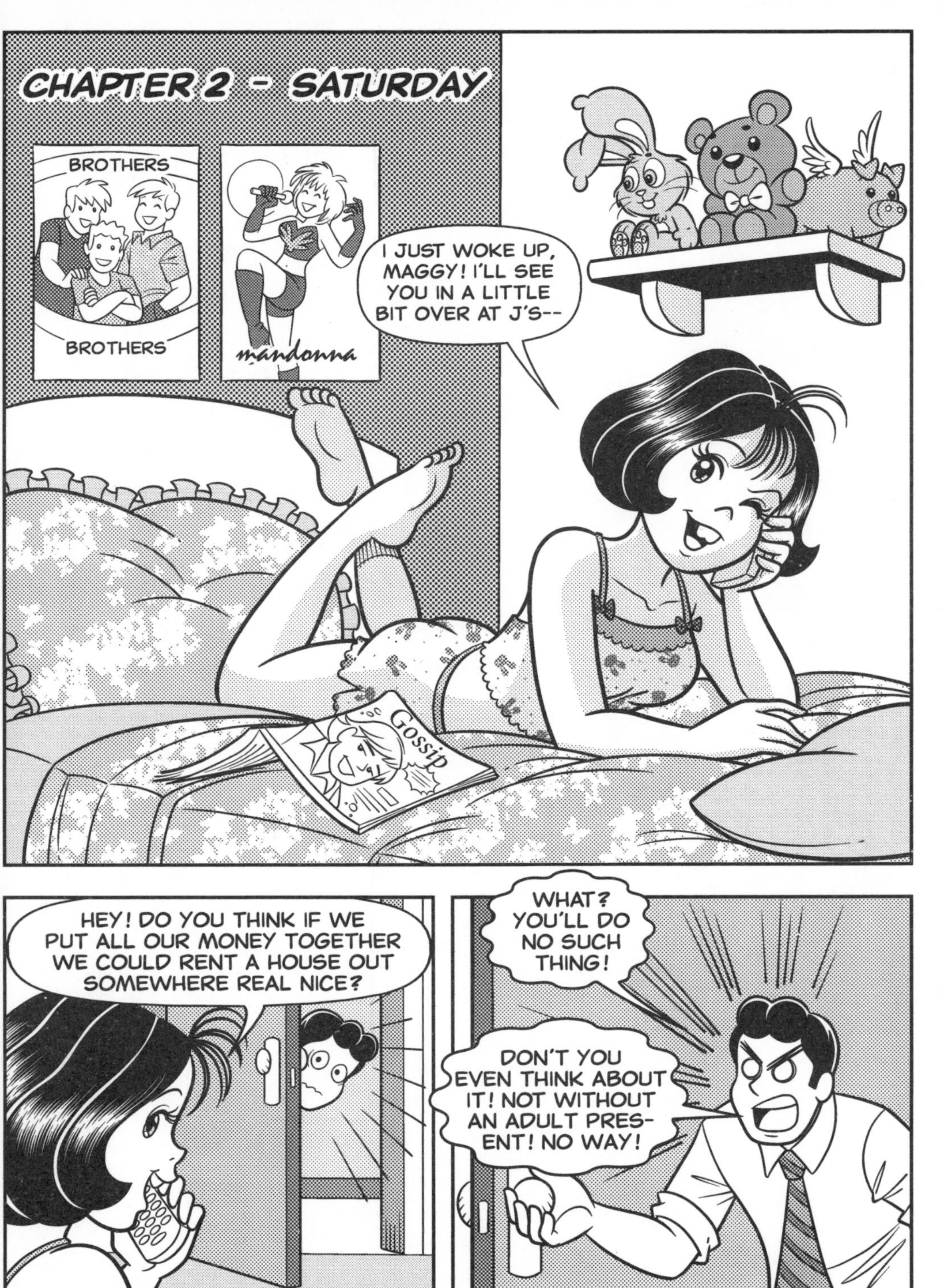
CHAPTER 2 - SATURDAY
BROTHERS
BROTHERS
mandonna
I JUST WOKE UP, MAGGY! I'LL SEE YOU IN A LITTLE BIT OVER AT J'S--
Gossip
HEY! DO YOU THINK IF WE PUT ALL OUR MONEY TOGETHER WE COULD RENT A HOUSE OUT SOMEWHERE REAL NICE?
WHAT? YOU'LL DO NO SUCH THING!
DON'T YOU EVEN THINK ABOUT IT! NOT WITHOUT AN ADULT PRES-ENT! NO WAY!

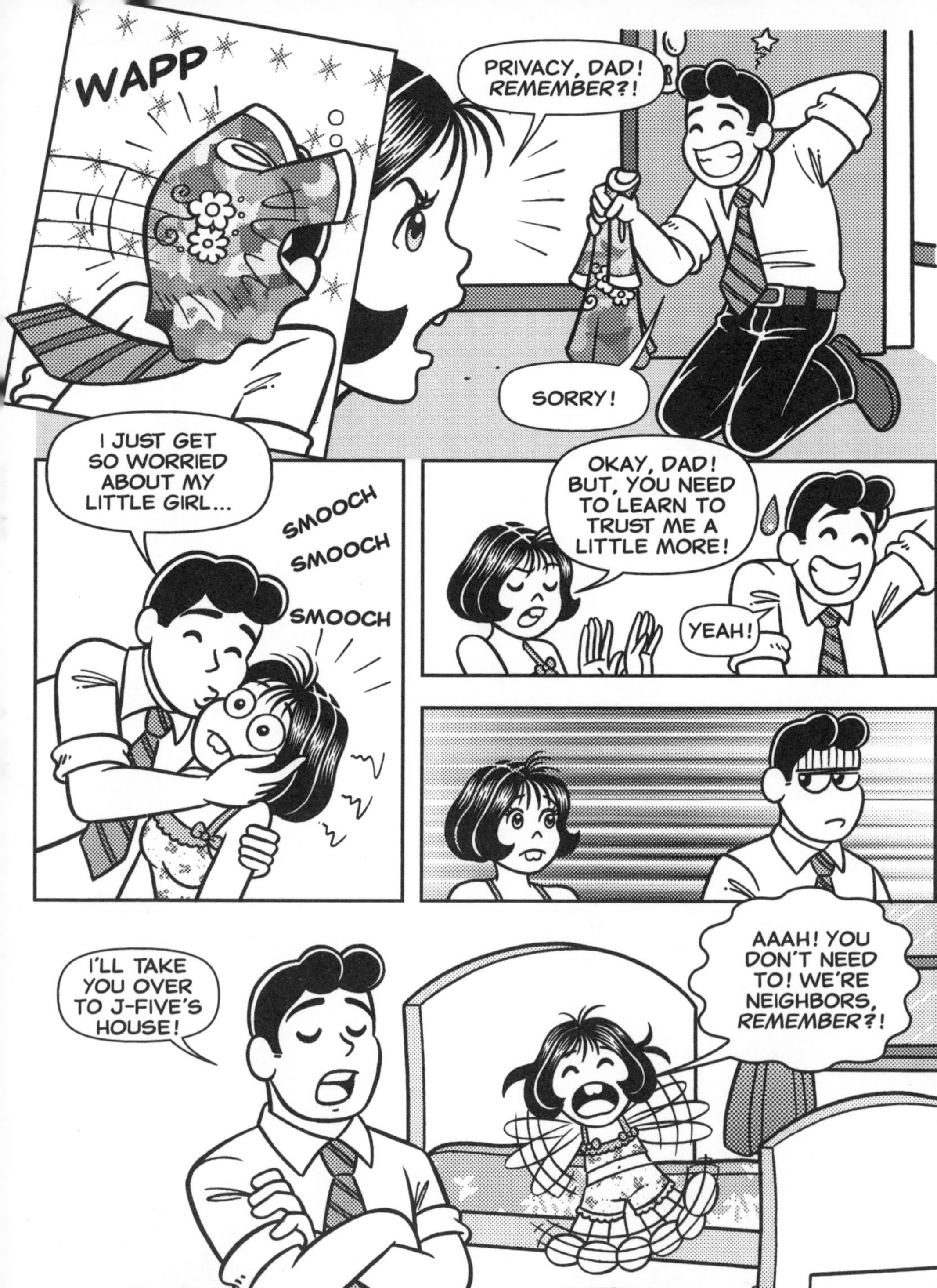
WAPP
PRIVACY, DAD! REMEMBER?!
SORRY!
I JUST GET SO WORRIED ABOUT MY LITTLE GIRL...
SMOOCH
SMOOCH
SMOOCH
OKAY, DAD! BUT, YOU NEED TO LEARN TO TRUST ME A LITTLE MORE!
YEAH!
I'LL TAKE YOU OVER TO J-FIVE'S HOUSE!
AAAH! YOU DON'T NEED TO! WE'RE NEIGHBORS, REMEMBER?!

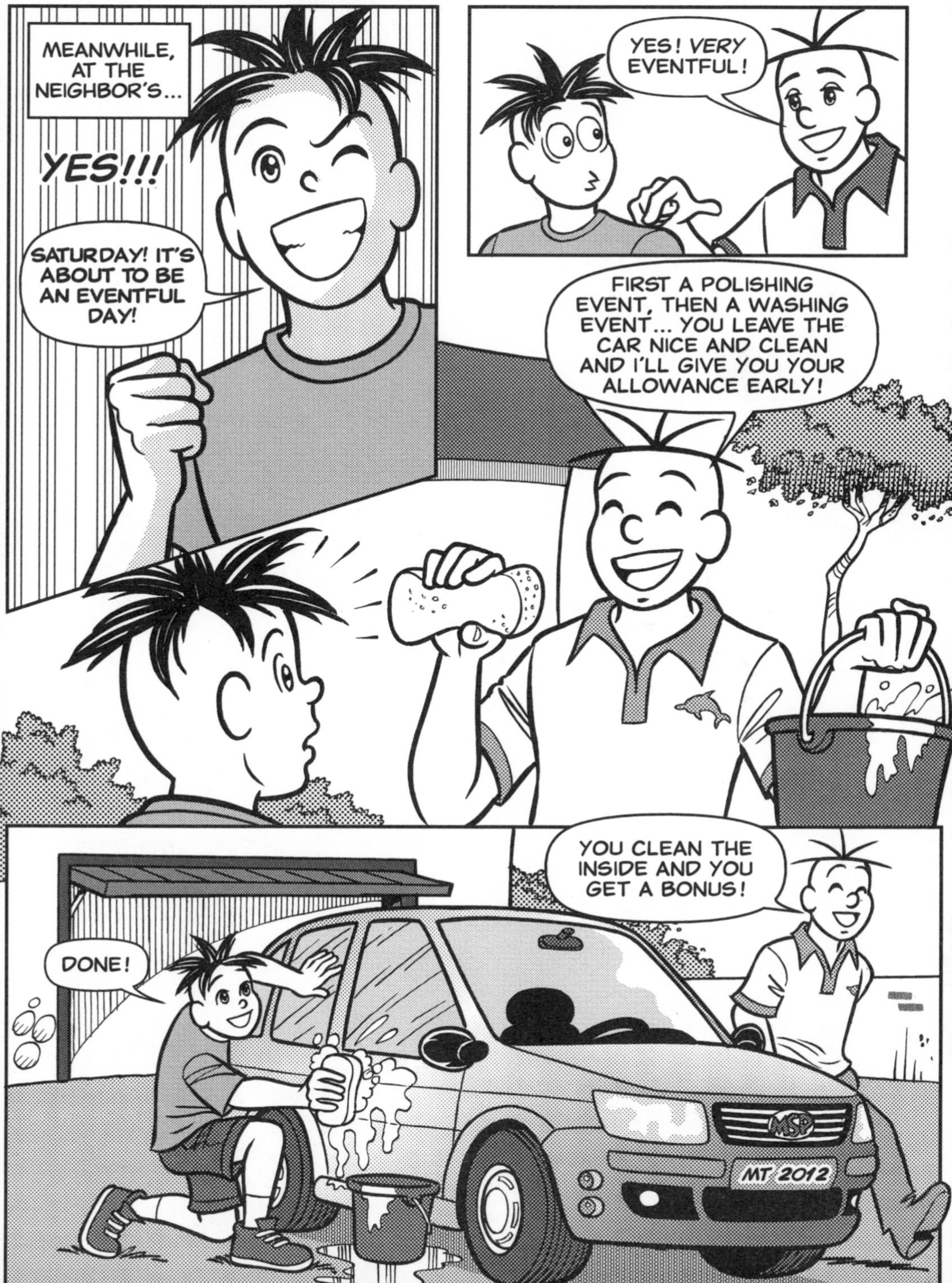
MEANWHILE, AT THE NEIGHBOR'S...
YES!!!
SATURDAY! IT'S ABOUT TO BE AN EVENTFUL DAY!
YES! VERY EVENTFUL!
FIRST A POLISHING EVENT, THEN A WASHING EVENT... YOU LEAVE THE CAR NICE AND CLEAN AND I'LL GIVE YOU YOUR ALLOWANCE EARLY!
DONE!
YOU CLEAN THE INSIDE AND YOU GET A BONUS!
MT 2012

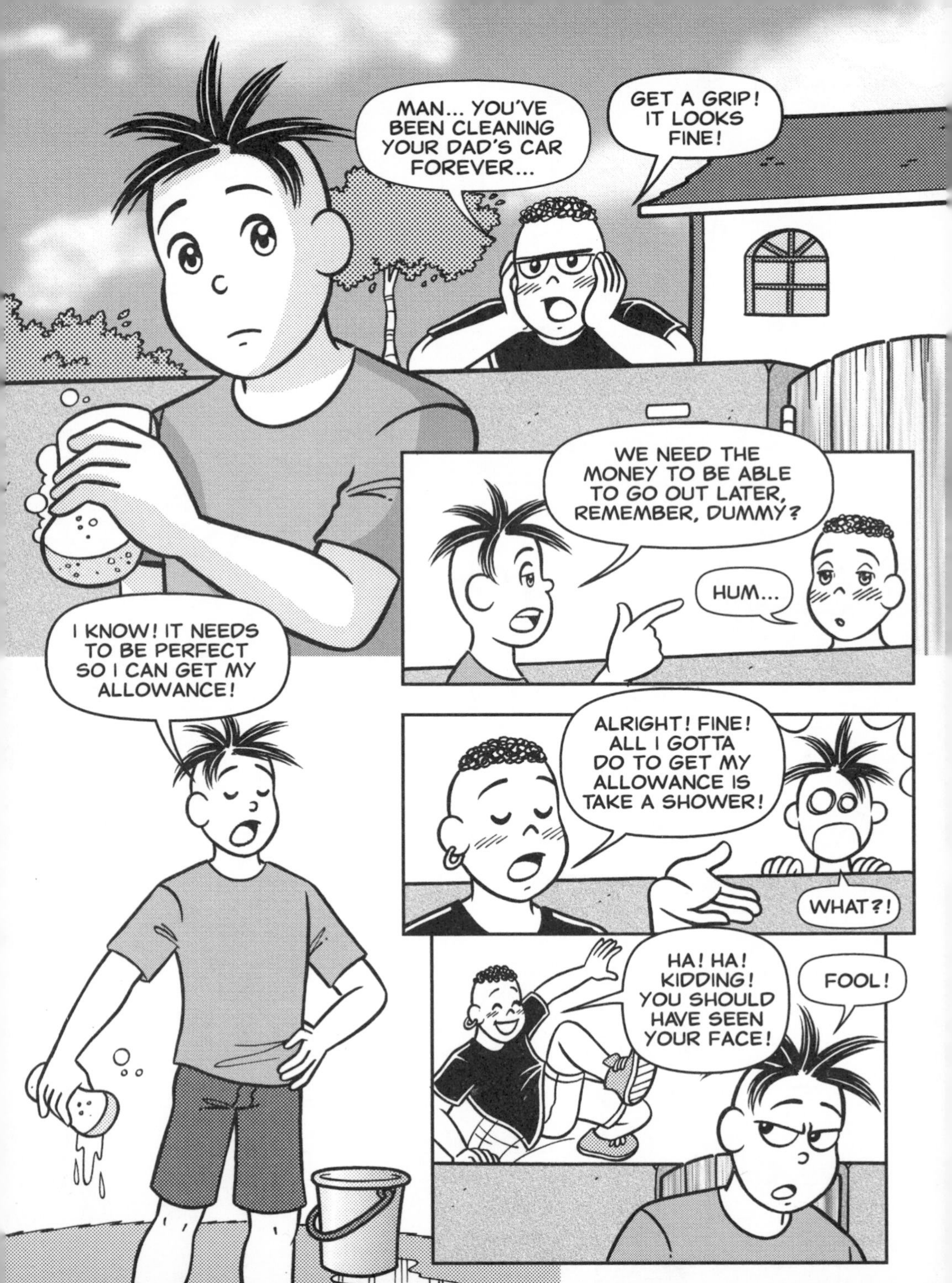
MAN... YOU'VE BEEN CLEANING YOUR DAD'S CAR FOREVER...
GET A GRIP! IT LOOKS FINE!
WE NEED THE MONEY TO BE ABLE TO GO OUT LATER, REMEMBER, DUMMY?
HUM...
I KNOW! IT NEEDS TO BE PERFECT SO I CAN GET MY ALLOWANCE!
ALRIGHT! FINE! ALL I GOTTA DO TO GET MY ALLOWANCE IS TAKE A SHOWER!
WHAT?!
HA! HA! KIDDING! YOU SHOULD HAVE SEEN YOUR FACE!
FOOL!

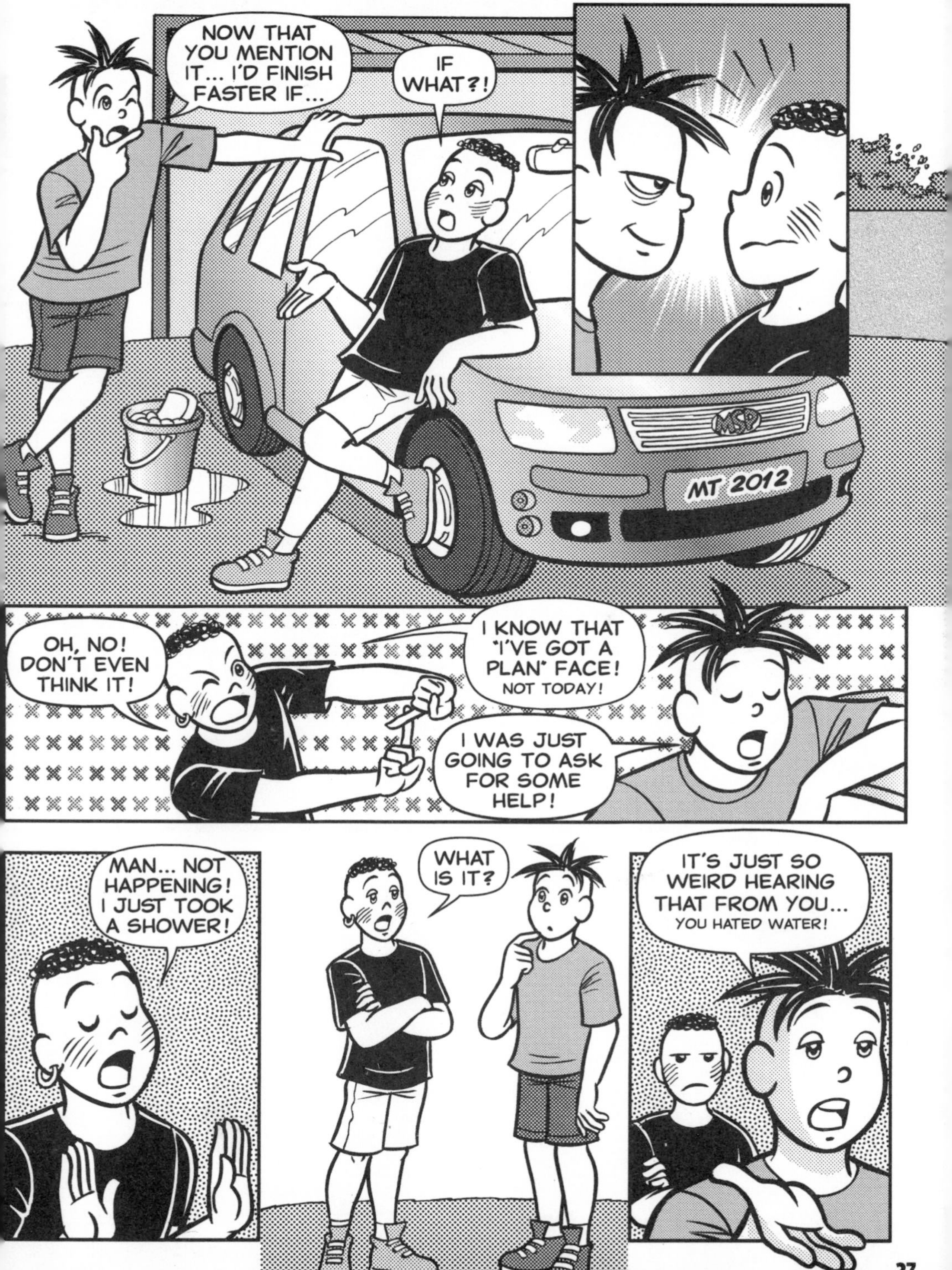
NOW THAT YOU MENTION IT... I'D FINISH FASTER IF...
IF WHAT?!
MT 2012
OH, NO! DON'T EVEN THINK IT!
I KNOW THAT "I'VE GOT A PLAN" FACE! NOT TODAY!
I WAS JUST GOING TO ASK FOR SOME HELP!
MAN... NOT HAPPENING! I JUST TOOK A SHOWER!
WHAT IS IT?
IT'S JUST SO WEIRD HEARING THAT FROM YOU... YOU HATED WATER!

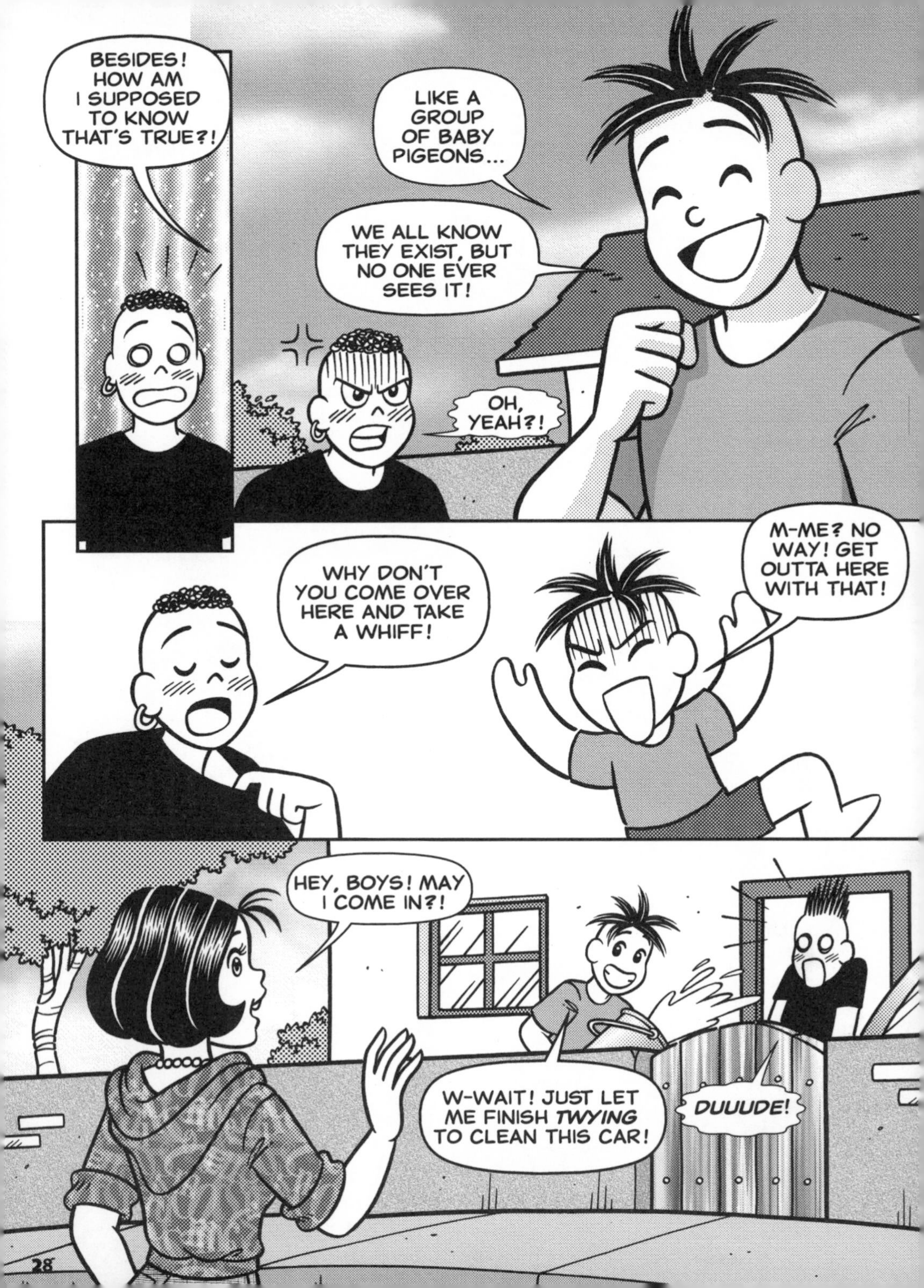

BESIDES! HOW AM I SUPPOSED TO KNOW THAT'S TRUE?!
LIKE A GROUP OF BABY PIGEONS...
WE ALL KNOW THEY EXIST, BUT NO ONE EVER SEES IT!
OH, YEAH?!
WHY DON'T YOU COME OVER HERE AND TAKE A WHIFF!
M-ME? NO WAY! GET OUTTA HERE WITH THAT!
HEY, BOYS! MAY I COME IN?!
W-WAIT! JUST LET ME FINISH *TWYING* TO CLEAN THIS CAR!
DUUUDE!

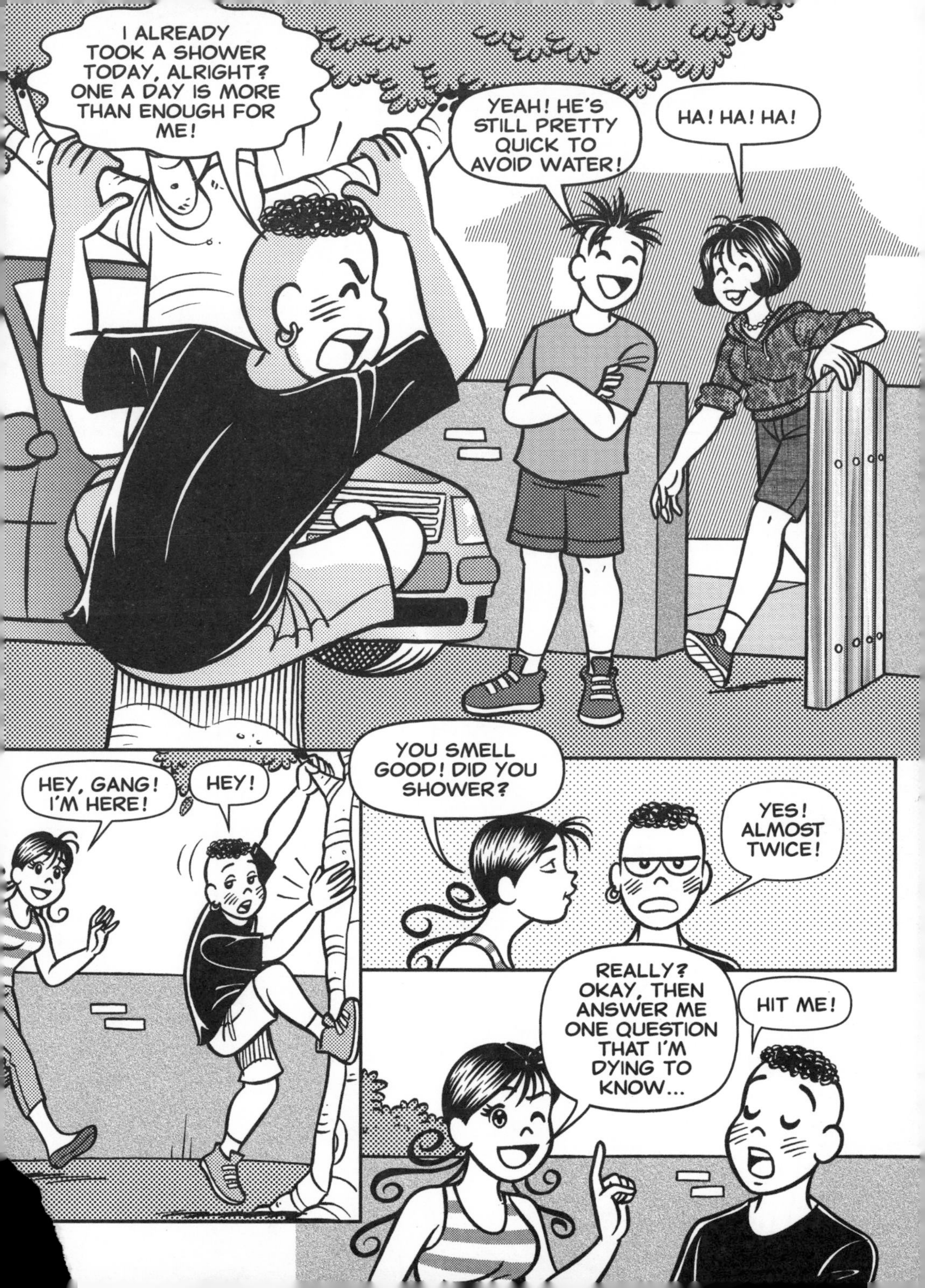
I ALREADY TOOK A SHOWER TODAY, ALRIGHT? ONE A DAY IS MORE THAN ENOUGH FOR ME!
YEAH! HE'S STILL PRETTY QUICK TO AVOID WATER!
HA! HA! HA!
HEY, GANG! I'M HERE!
HEY!
YOU SMELL GOOD! DID YOU SHOWER?
YES! ALMOST TWICE!
REALLY? OKAY, THEN ANSWER ME ONE QUESTION THAT I'M DYING TO KNOW...
HIT ME!

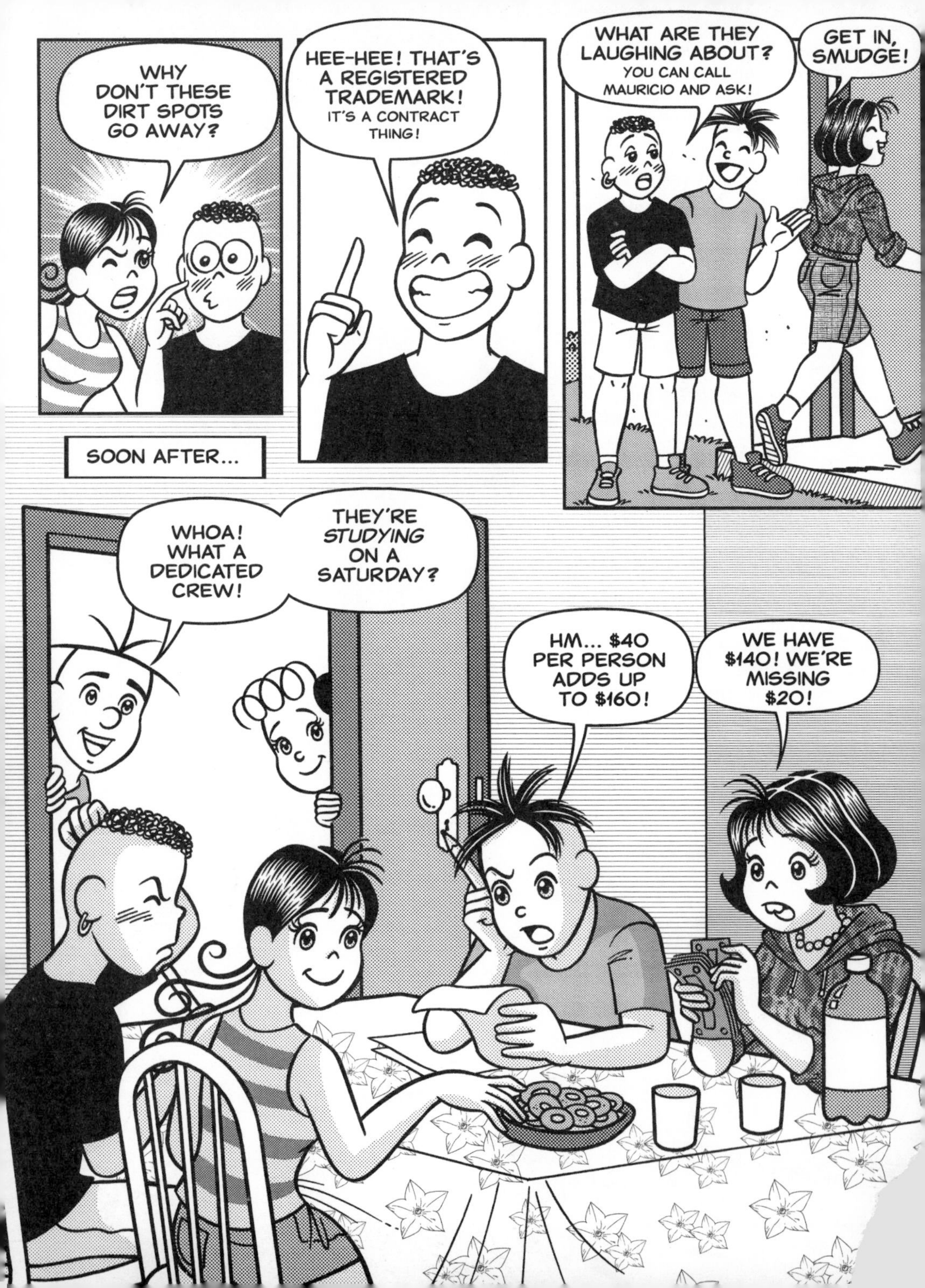
WHY DON'T THESE DIRT SPOTS GO AWAY?
HEE-HEE! THAT'S A REGISTERED TRADEMARK!
IT'S A CONTRACT THING!
SOON AFTER...
WHAT ARE THEY LAUGHING ABOUT?
YOU CAN CALL MAURICIO AND ASK!
GET IN, SMUDGE!
WHOA! WHAT A DEDICATED CREW!
THEY'RE *STUDYING* ON A SATURDAY?
HM... $40 PER PERSON ADDS UP TO $160!
WE HAVE $140! WE'RE MISSING $20!

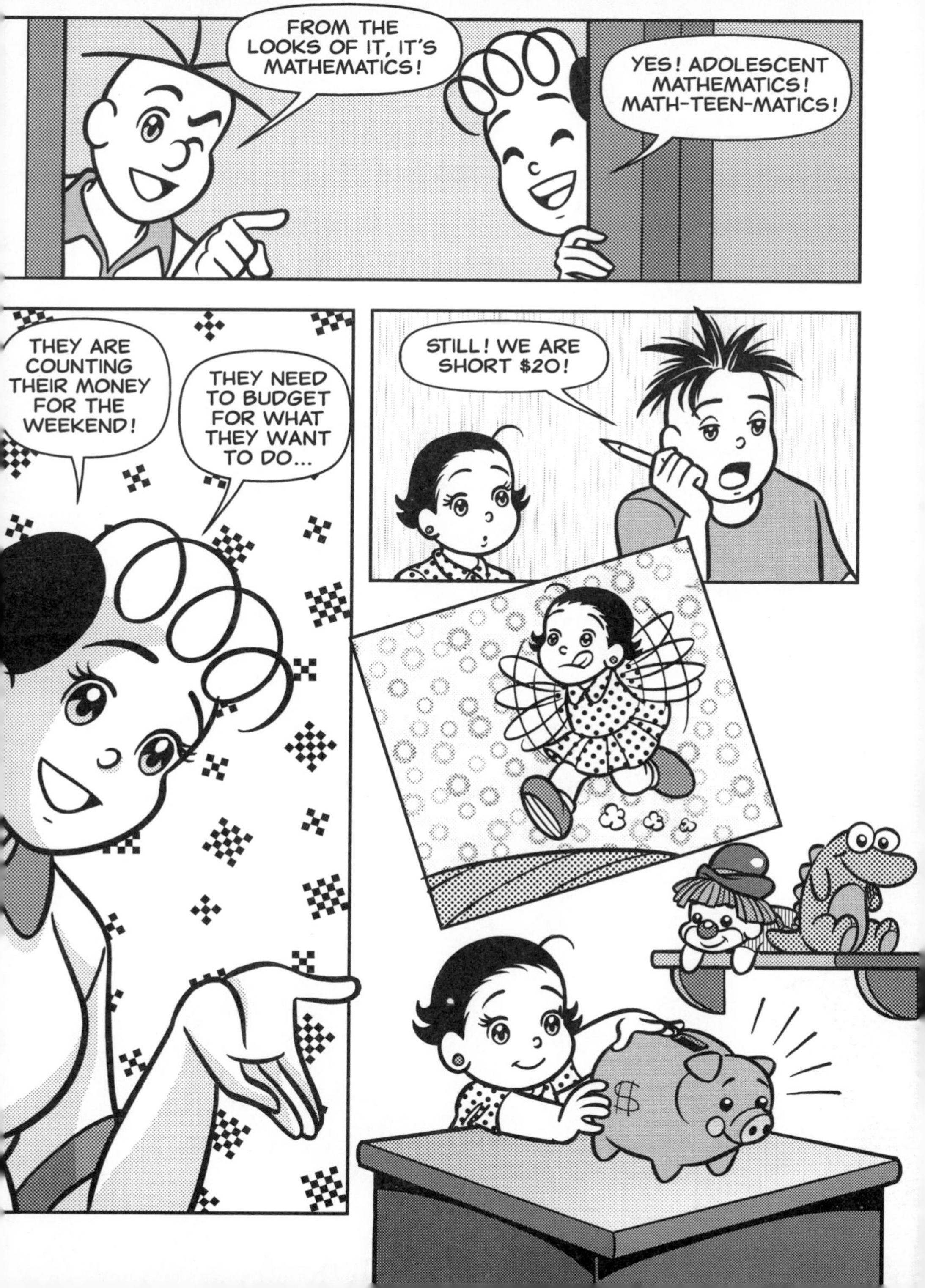
FROM THE LOOKS OF IT, IT'S MATHEMATICS!
YES! ADOLESCENT MATHEMATICS! MATH-TEEN-MATICS!
THEY ARE COUNTING THEIR MONEY FOR THE WEEKEND!
THEY NEED TO BUDGET FOR WHAT THEY WANT TO DO...
STILL! WE ARE SHORT $20!
$

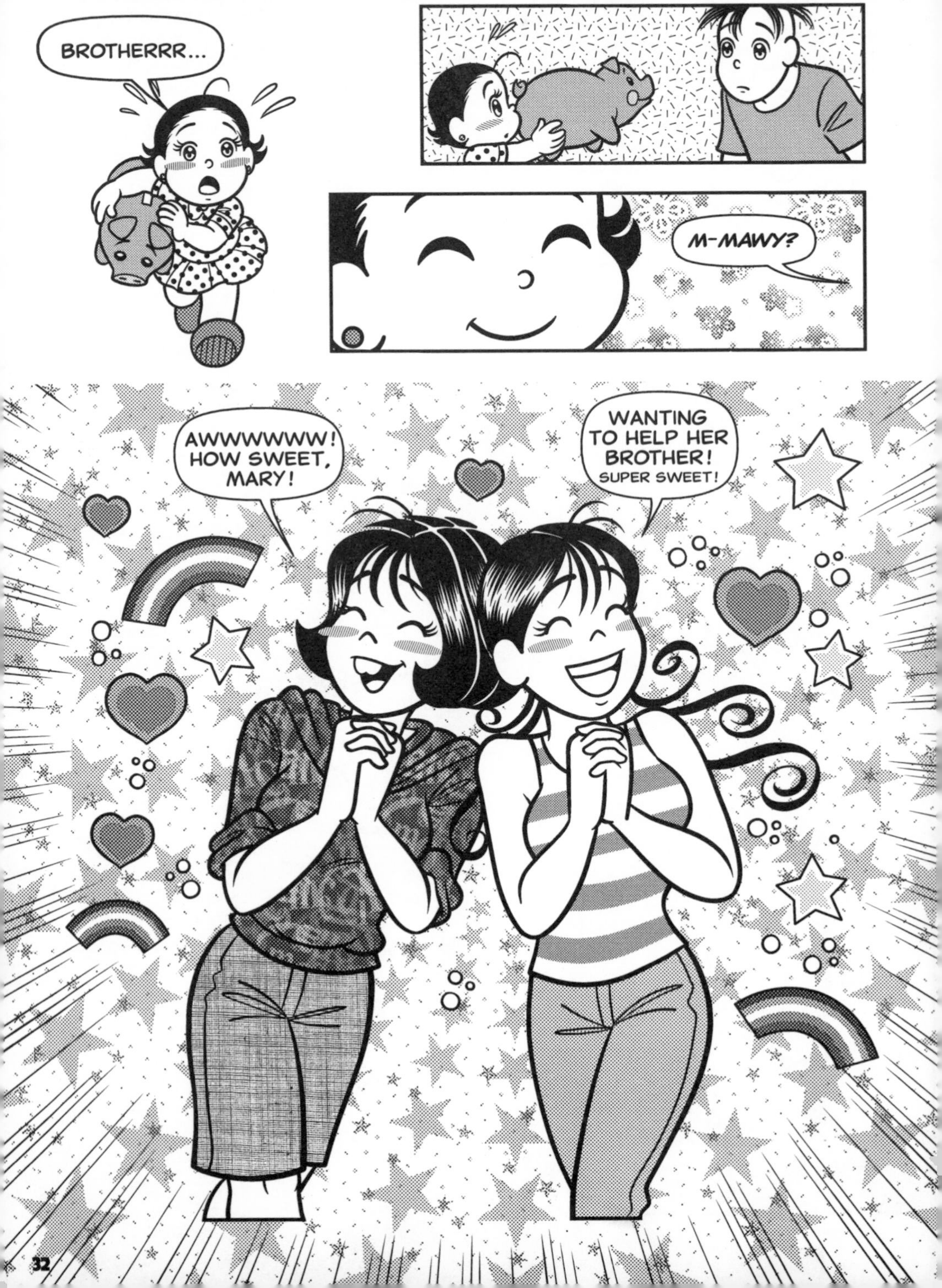
BROTHERRR...
M-MAWY?
AWWWWWW! HOW SWEET, MARY!
WANTING TO HELP HER BROTHER! SUPER SWEET!

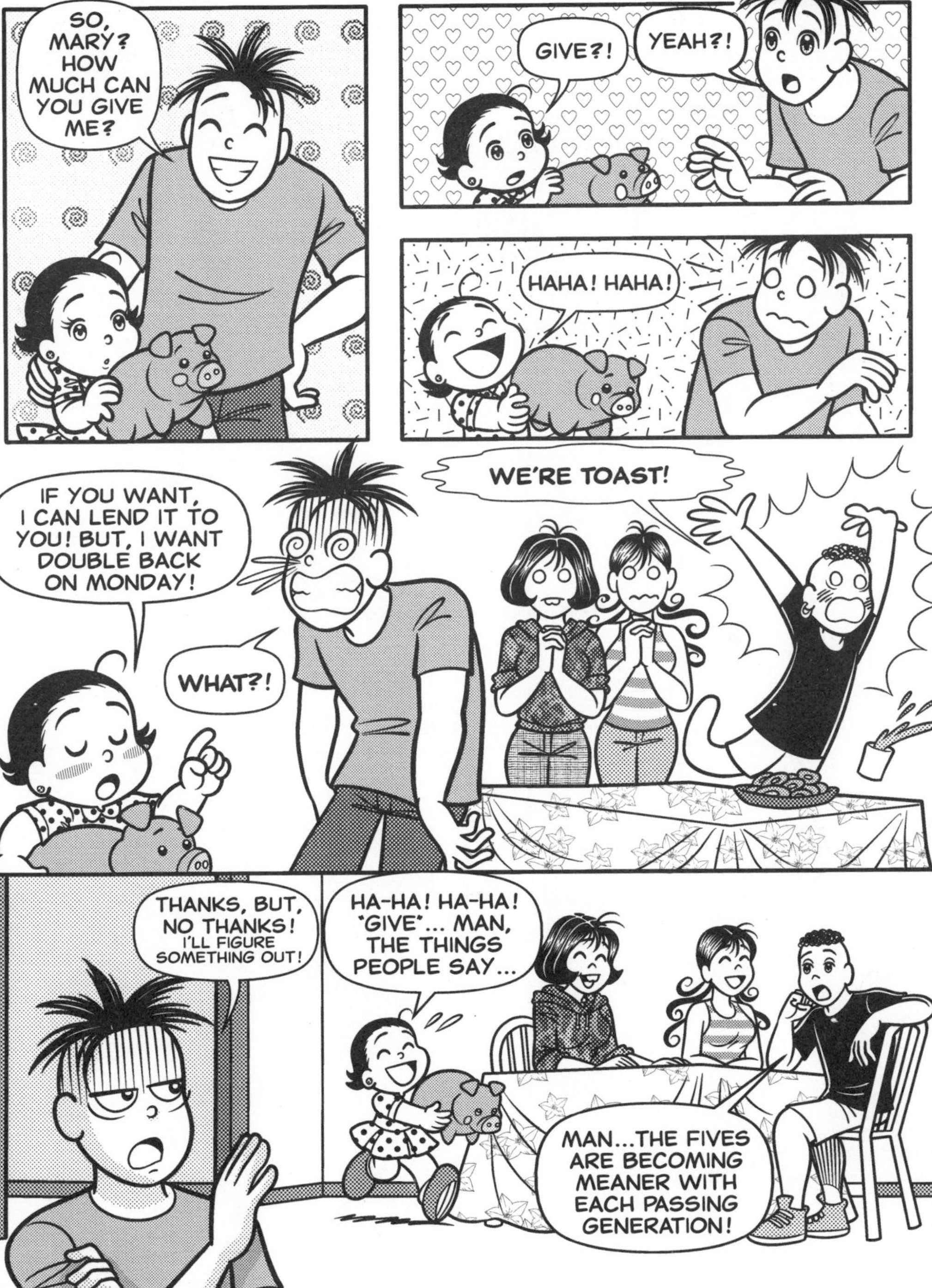
SO, MARY? HOW MUCH CAN YOU GIVE ME?
GIVE?!
YEAH?!
HAHA! HAHA!
IF YOU WANT, I CAN LEND IT TO YOU! BUT, I WANT DOUBLE BACK ON MONDAY!
WHAT?!
WE'RE TOAST!
THANKS, BUT, NO THANKS! I'LL FIGURE SOMETHING OUT!
HA-HA! HA-HA! "GIVE"... MAN, THE THINGS PEOPLE SAY...
MAN...THE FIVES ARE BECOMING MEANER WITH EACH PASSING GENERATION!

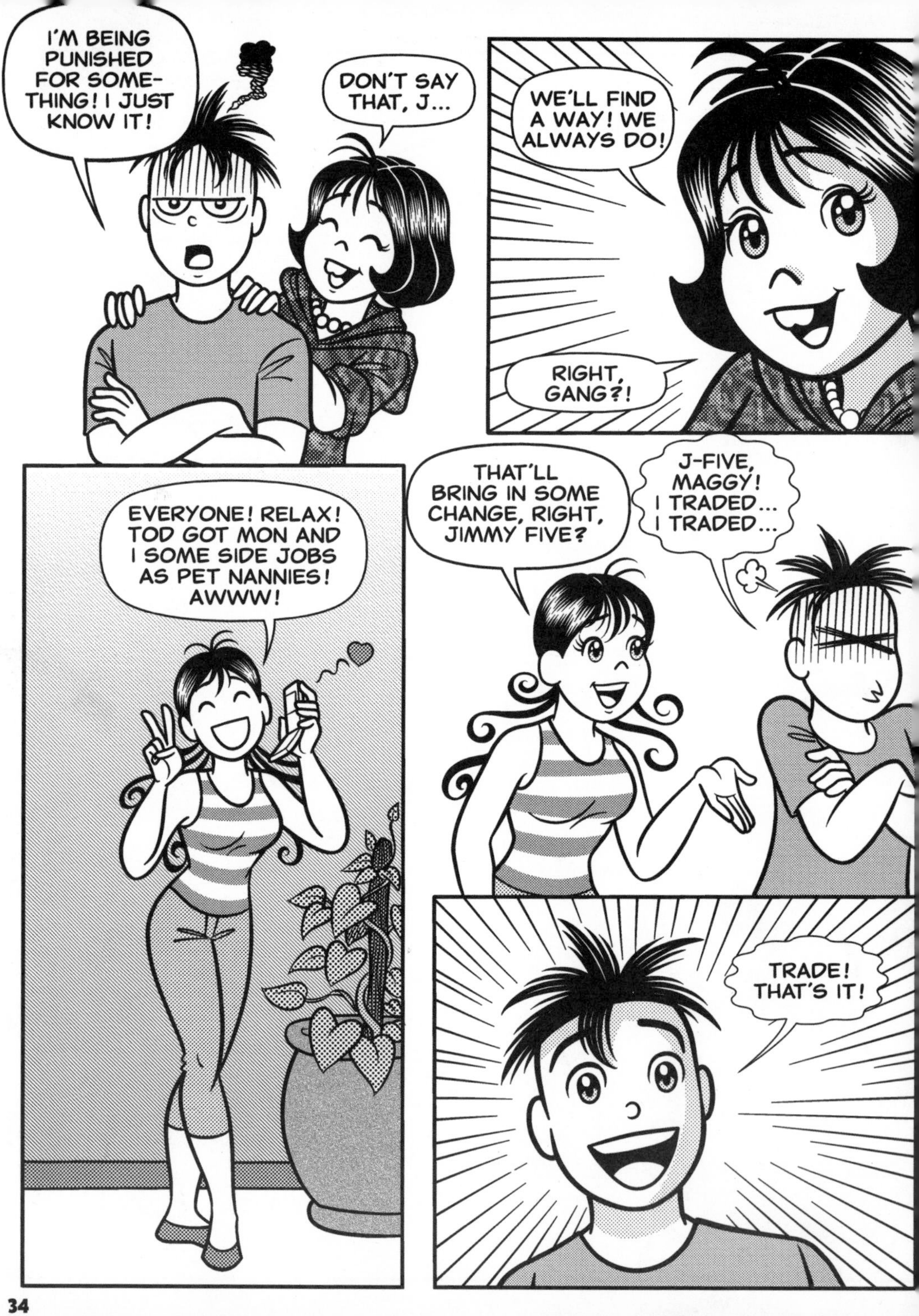
I'M BEING PUNISHED FOR SOME-THING! I JUST KNOW IT!
DON'T SAY THAT, J...
WE'LL FIND A WAY! WE ALWAYS DO!
RIGHT, GANG?!
EVERYONE! RELAX! TOD GOT MON AND I SOME SIDE JOBS AS PET NANNIES! AWWW!
THAT'LL BRING IN SOME CHANGE, RIGHT, JIMMY FIVE?
J-FIVE, MAGGY! I TRADED... I TRADED...
TRADE! THAT'S IT!

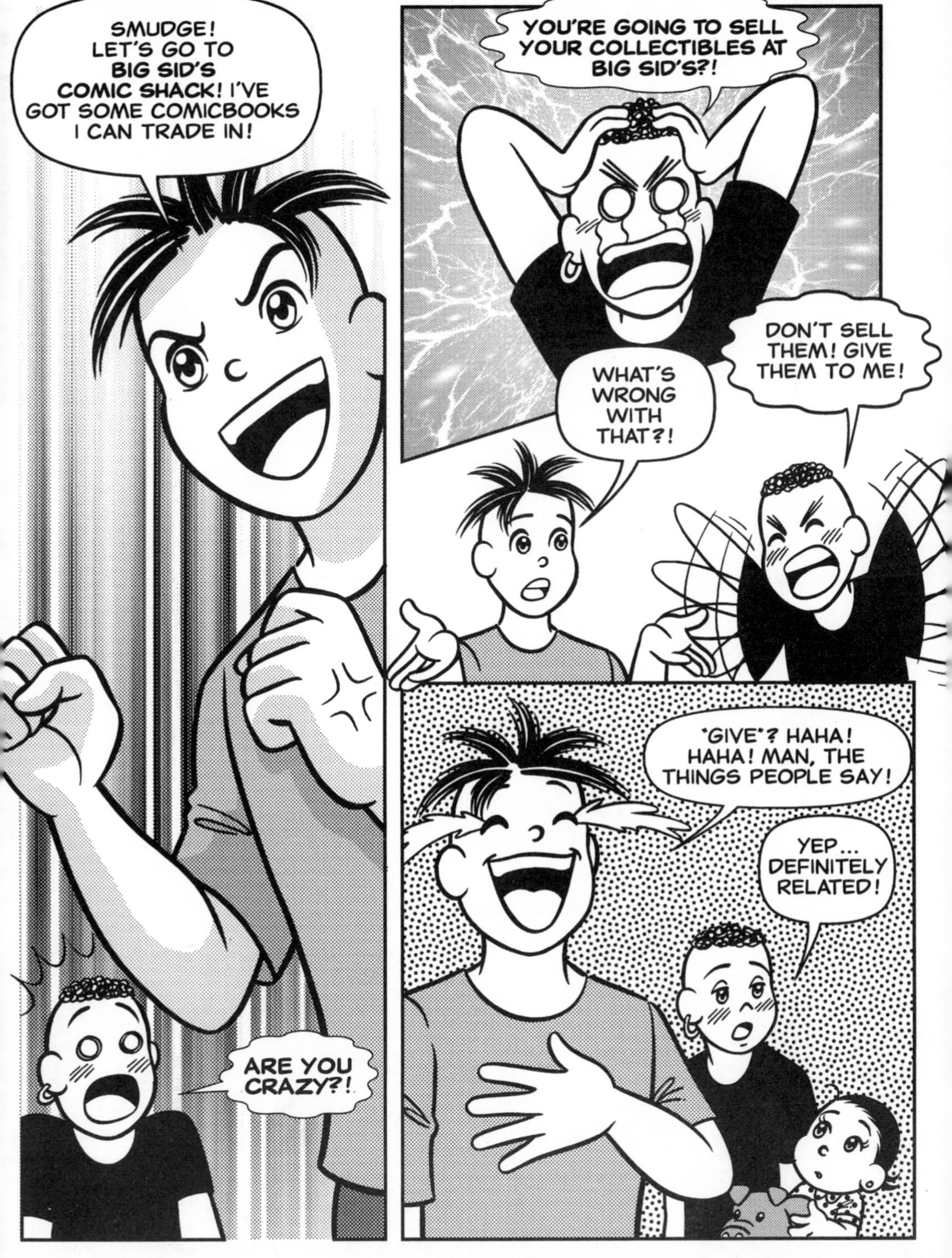
SMUDGE! LET'S GO TO BIG SID'S COMIC SHACK! I'VE GOT SOME COMICBOOKS I CAN TRADE IN!
ARE YOU CRAZY?!
YOU'RE GOING TO SELL YOUR COLLECTIBLES AT BIG SID'S?!
WHAT'S WRONG WITH THAT?!
DON'T SELL THEM! GIVE THEM TO ME!
"GIVE"? HAHA! HAHA! MAN, THE THINGS PEOPLE SAY!
YEP... DEFINITELY RELATED!

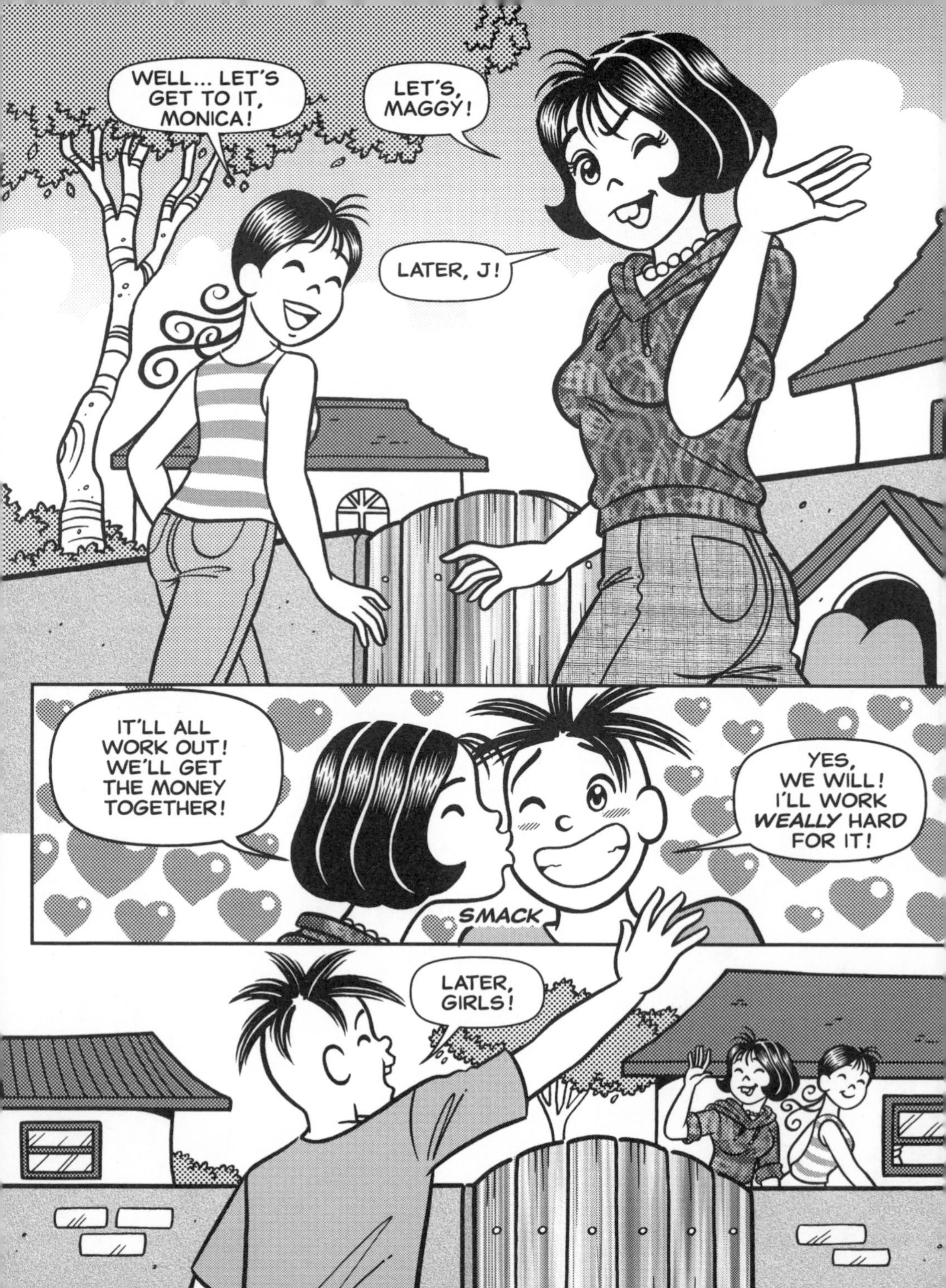
WELL... LET'S GET TO IT, MONICA!
LET'S, MAGGY!
LATER, J!
IT'LL ALL WORK OUT! WE'LL GET THE MONEY TOGETHER!
YES, WE WILL! I'LL WORK *WEALLY* HARD FOR IT!
SMACK
LATER, GIRLS!

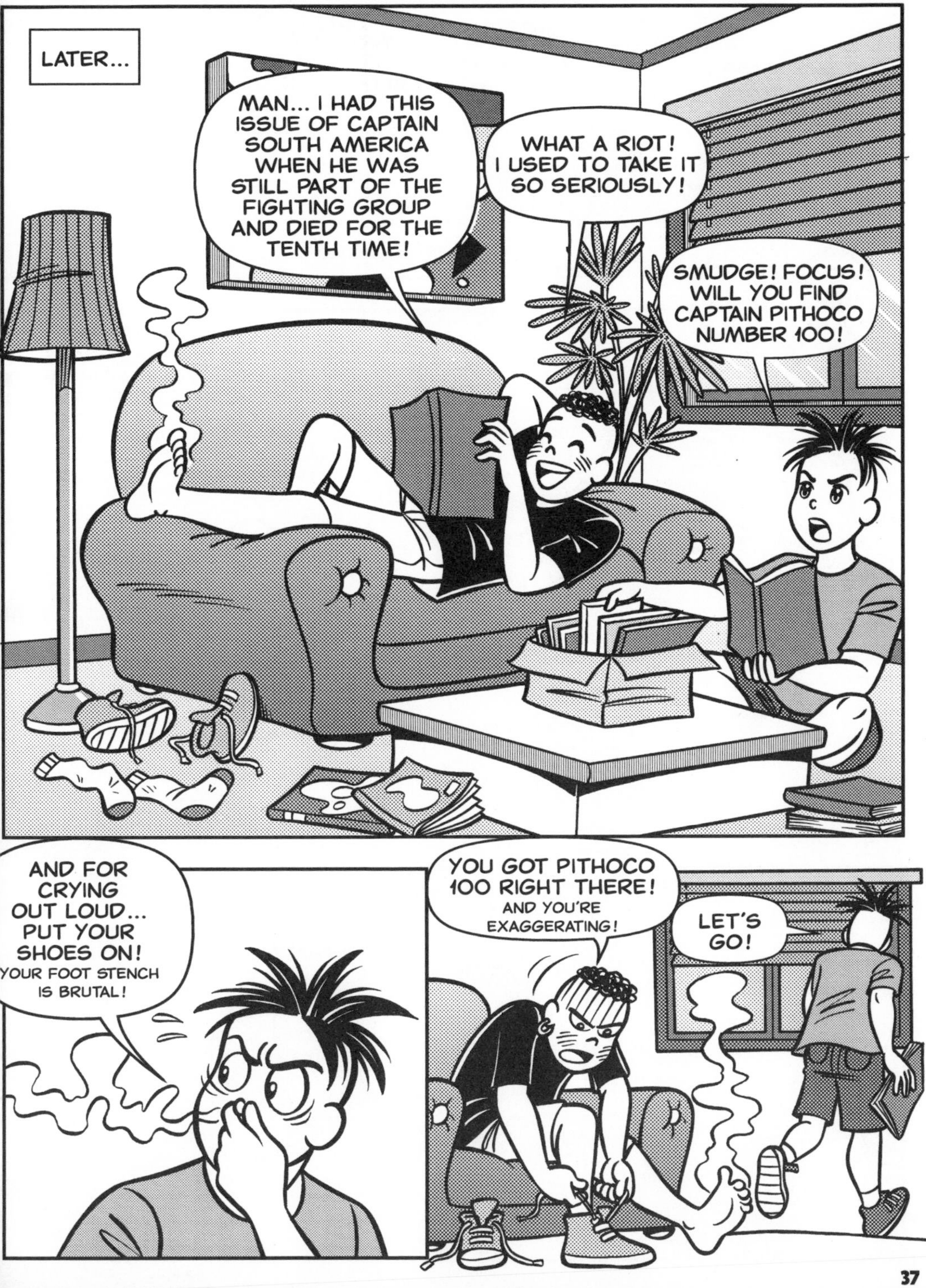

LATER...
MAN... I HAD THIS ISSUE OF CAPTAIN SOUTH AMERICA WHEN HE WAS STILL PART OF THE FIGHTING GROUP AND DIED FOR THE TENTH TIME!
WHAT A RIOT! I USED TO TAKE IT SO SERIOUSLY!
SMUDGE! FOCUS! WILL YOU FIND CAPTAIN PITHOCO NUMBER 100!
AND FOR CRYING OUT LOUD... PUT YOUR SHOES ON! YOUR FOOT STENCH IS BRUTAL!
YOU GOT PITHOCO 100 RIGHT THERE! AND YOU'RE EXAGGERATING!
LET'S GO!

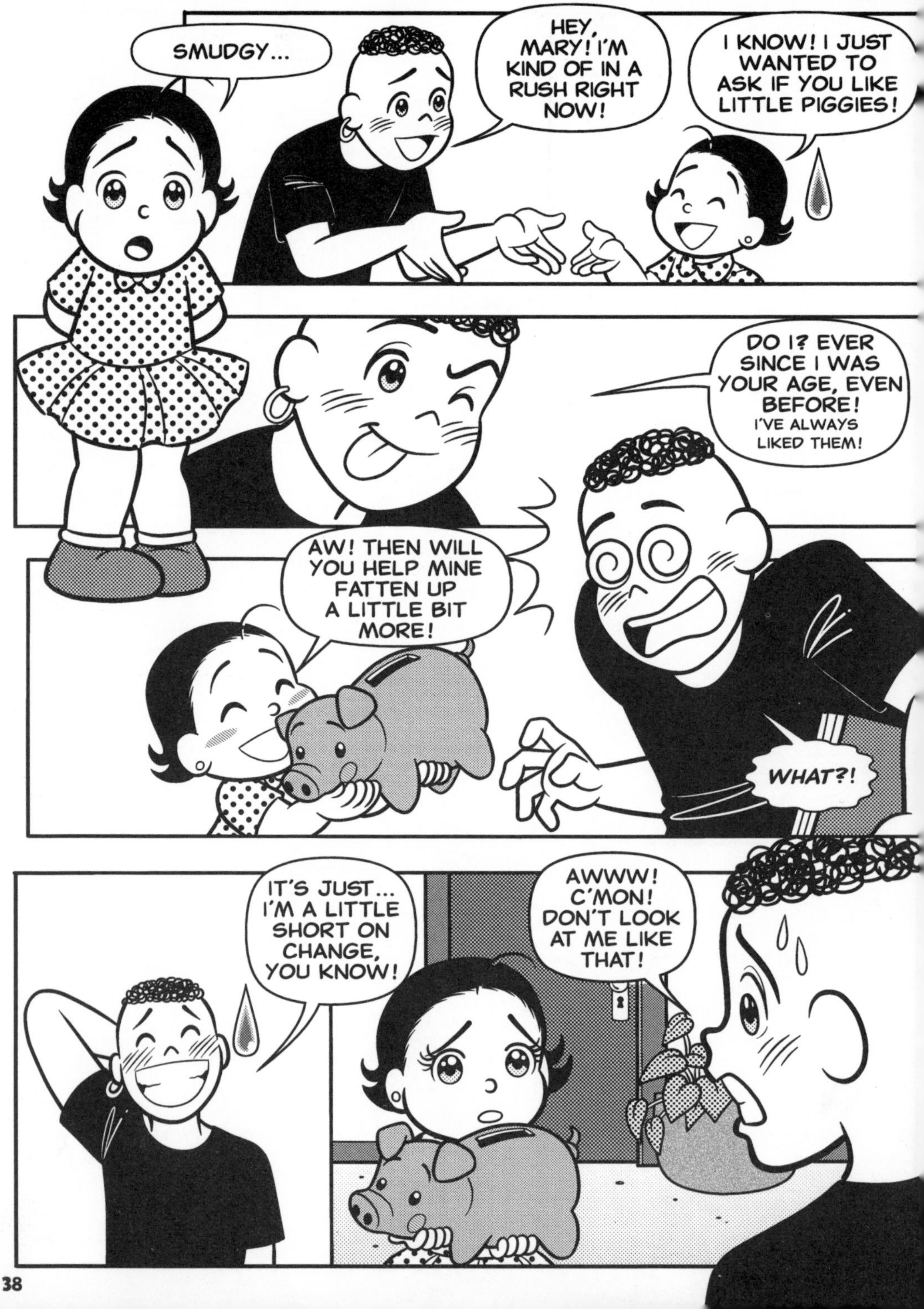

SMUDGY...
HEY, MARY! I'M KIND OF IN A RUSH RIGHT NOW!
I KNOW! I JUST WANTED TO ASK IF YOU LIKE LITTLE PIGGIES!
DO I? EVER SINCE I WAS YOUR AGE, EVEN BEFORE! I'VE ALWAYS LIKED THEM!
AW! THEN WILL YOU HELP MINE FATTEN UP A LITTLE BIT MORE!
WHAT?!
IT'S JUST... I'M A LITTLE SHORT ON CHANGE, YOU KNOW!
AWWW! C'MON! DON'T LOOK AT ME LIKE THAT!

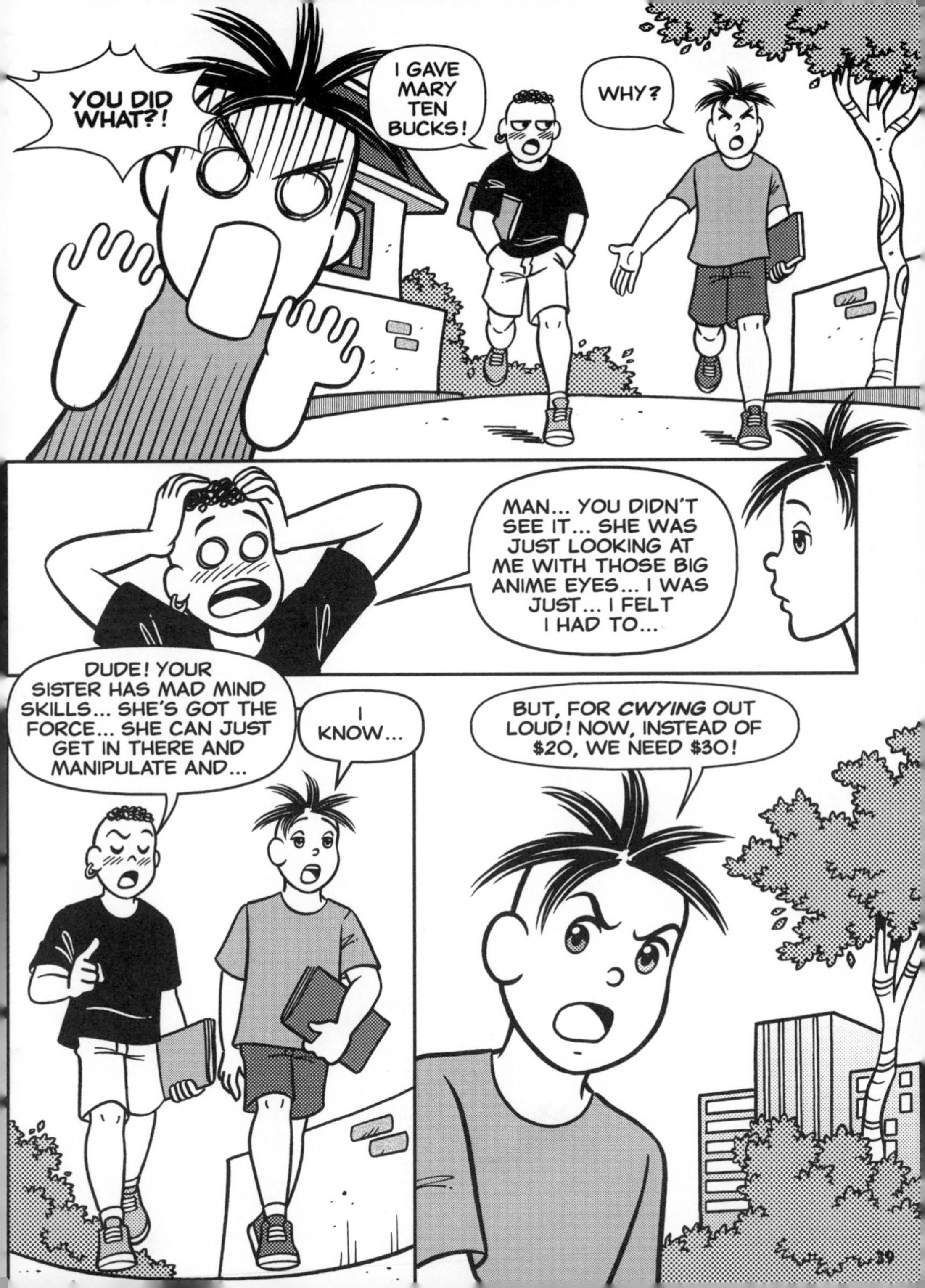
YOU DID WHAT?!
I GAVE MARY TEN BUCKS!
WHY?
MAN... YOU DIDN'T SEE IT... SHE WAS JUST LOOKING AT ME WITH THOSE BIG ANIME EYES... I WAS JUST... I FELT I HAD TO...
DUDE! YOUR SISTER HAS MAD MIND SKILLS... SHE'S GOT THE FORCE... SHE CAN JUST GET IN THERE AND MANIPULATE AND...
I KNOW...
BUT, FOR *CWYING* OUT LOUD! NOW, INSTEAD OF $20, WE NEED $30!

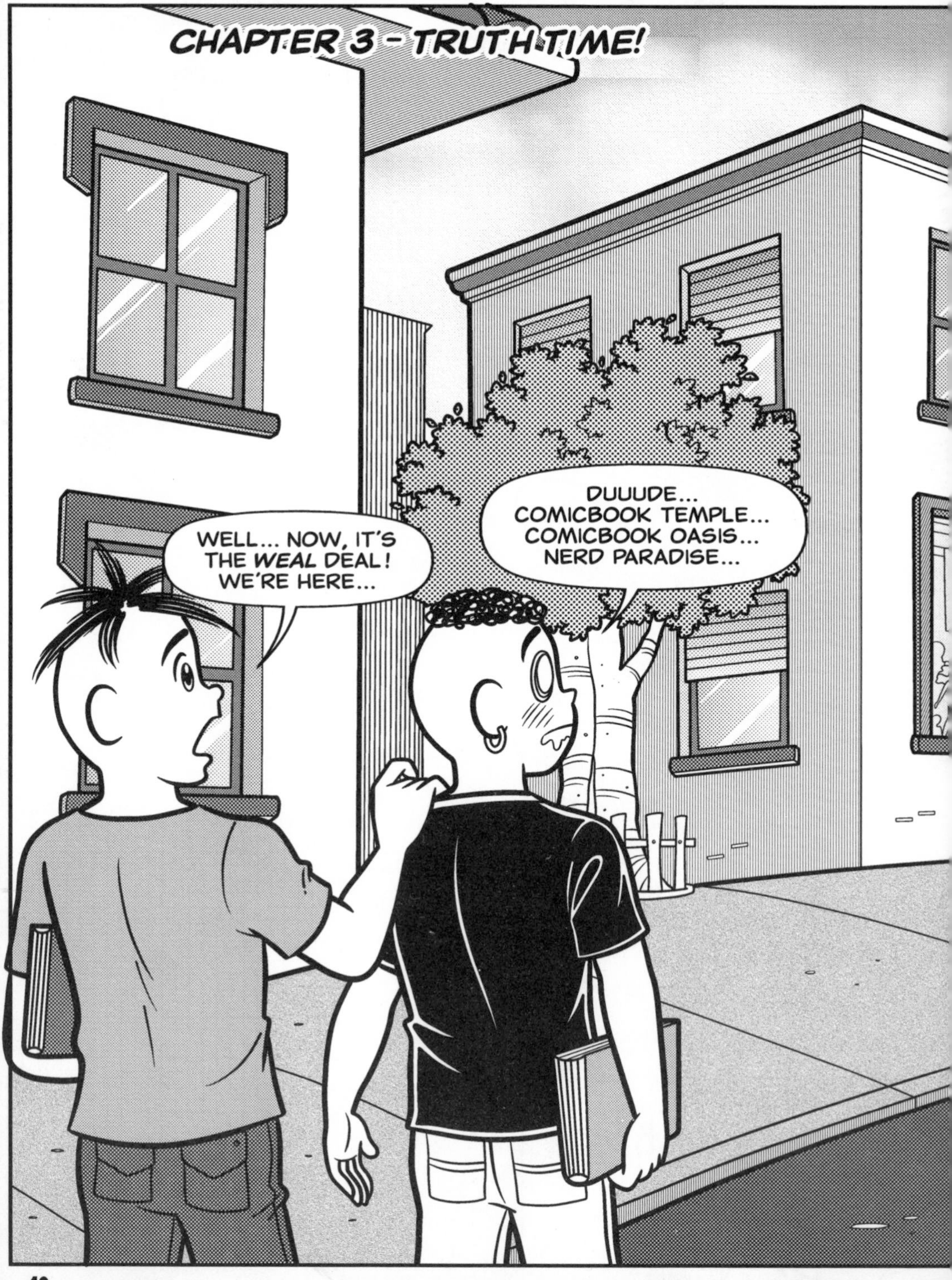
CHAPTER 3 – TRUTH TIME!
WELL... NOW, IT'S THE *WEAL* DEAL! WE'RE HERE...
DUUUDE... COMICBOOK TEMPLE... COMICBOOK OASIS... NERD PARADISE...

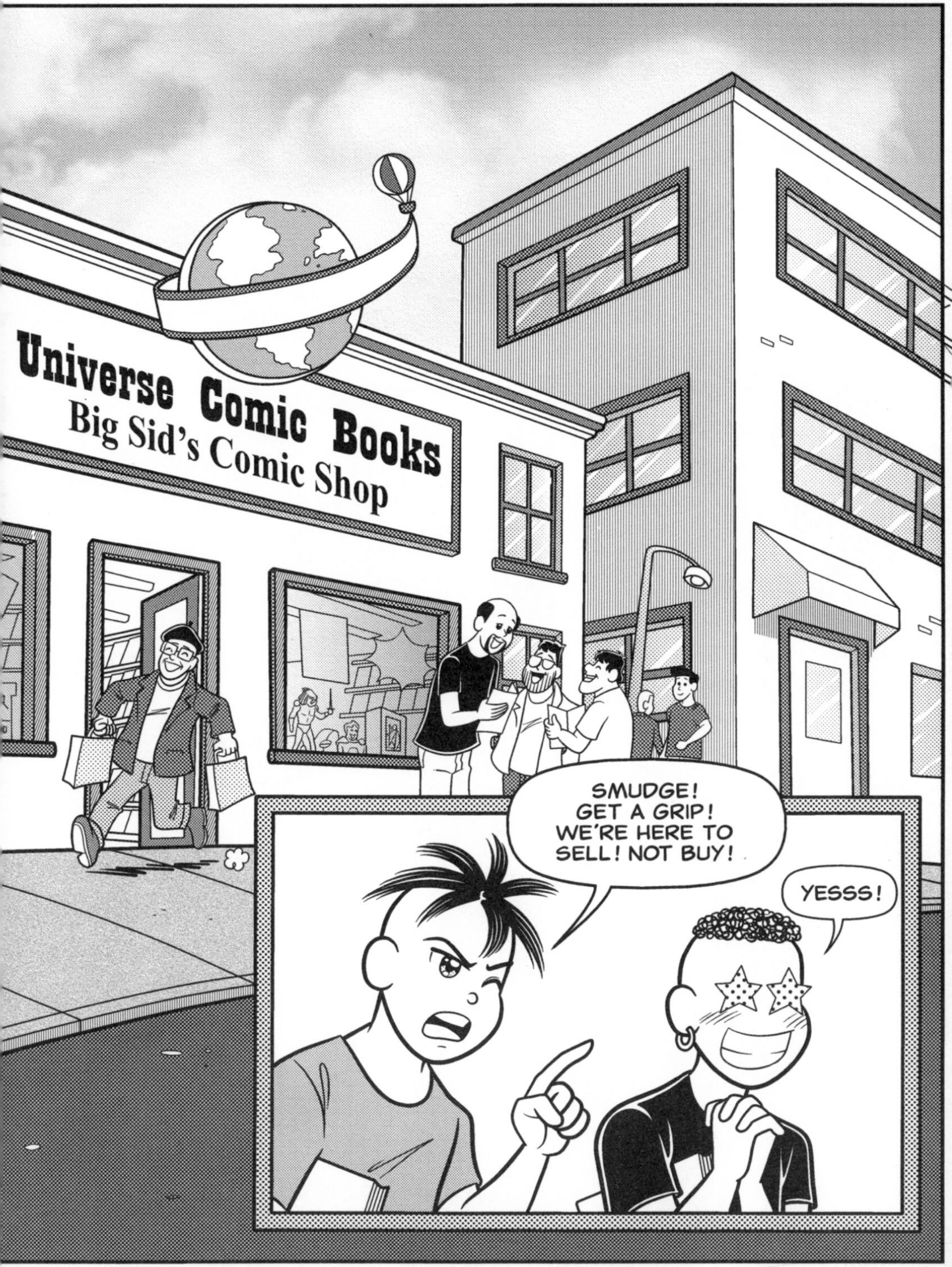
Universe Comic Books
Big Sid's Comic Shop
SMUDGE! GET A GRIP! WE'RE HERE TO SELL! NOT BUY!
YESSS!

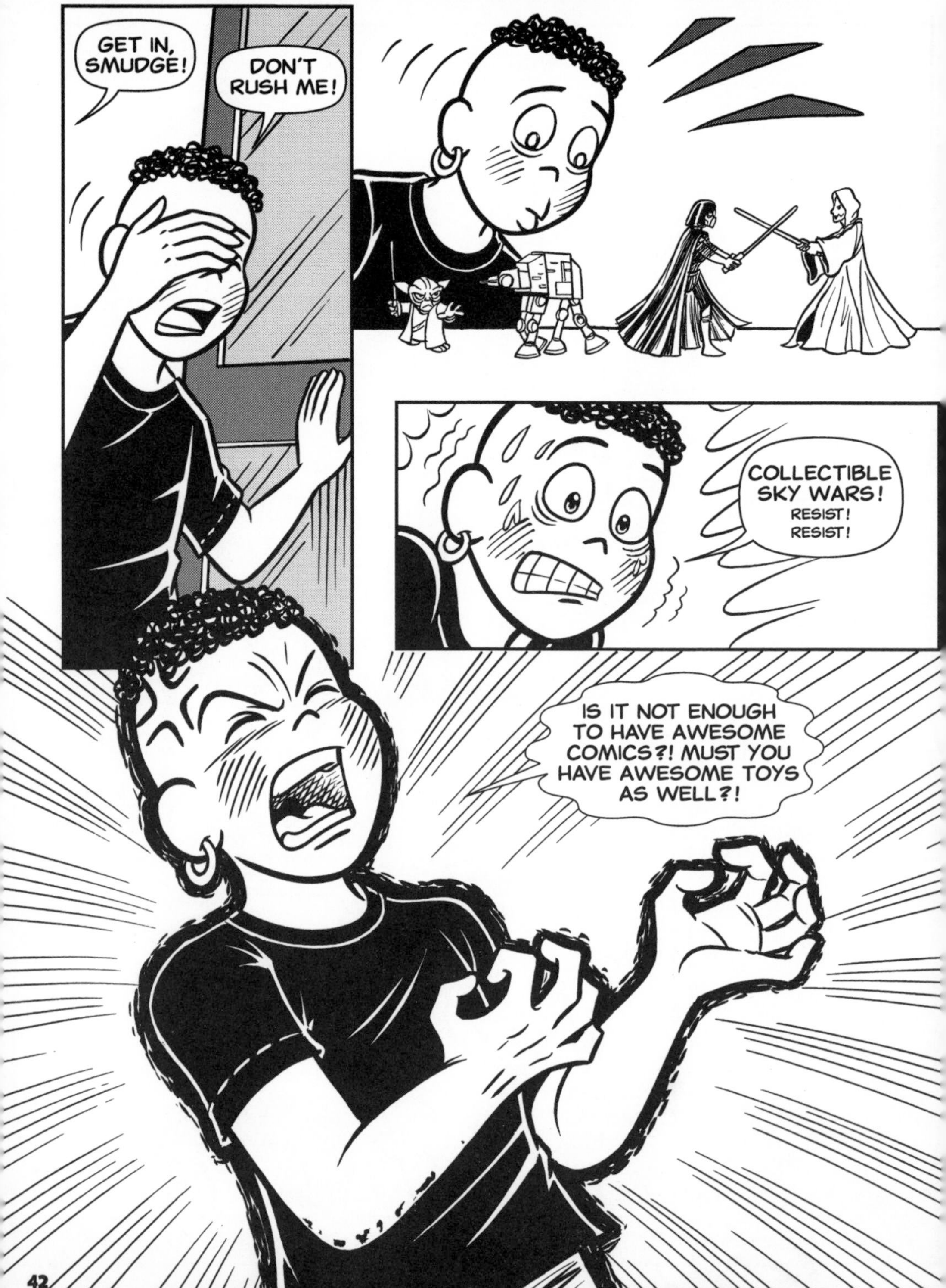
GET IN, SMUDGE!
DON'T RUSH ME!
COLLECTIBLE SKY WARS!
RESIST! RESIST!
IS IT NOT ENOUGH TO HAVE AWESOME COMICS?! MUST YOU HAVE AWESOME TOYS AS WELL?!

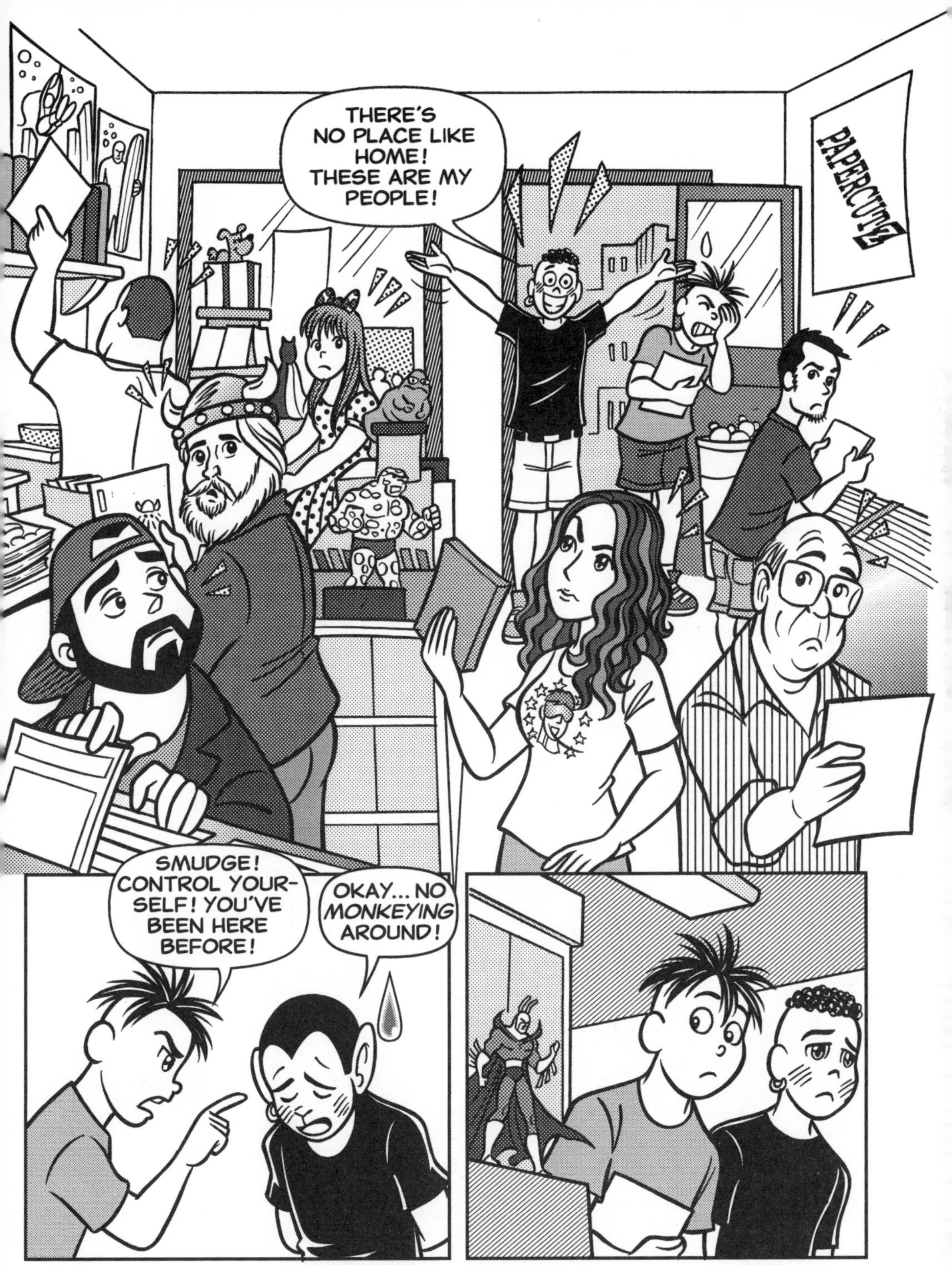
THERE'S NO PLACE LIKE HOME! THESE ARE MY PEOPLE!
PAPERCUTZ
SMUDGE! CONTROL YOURSELF! YOU'VE BEEN HERE BEFORE!
OKAY... NO MONKEYING AROUND!

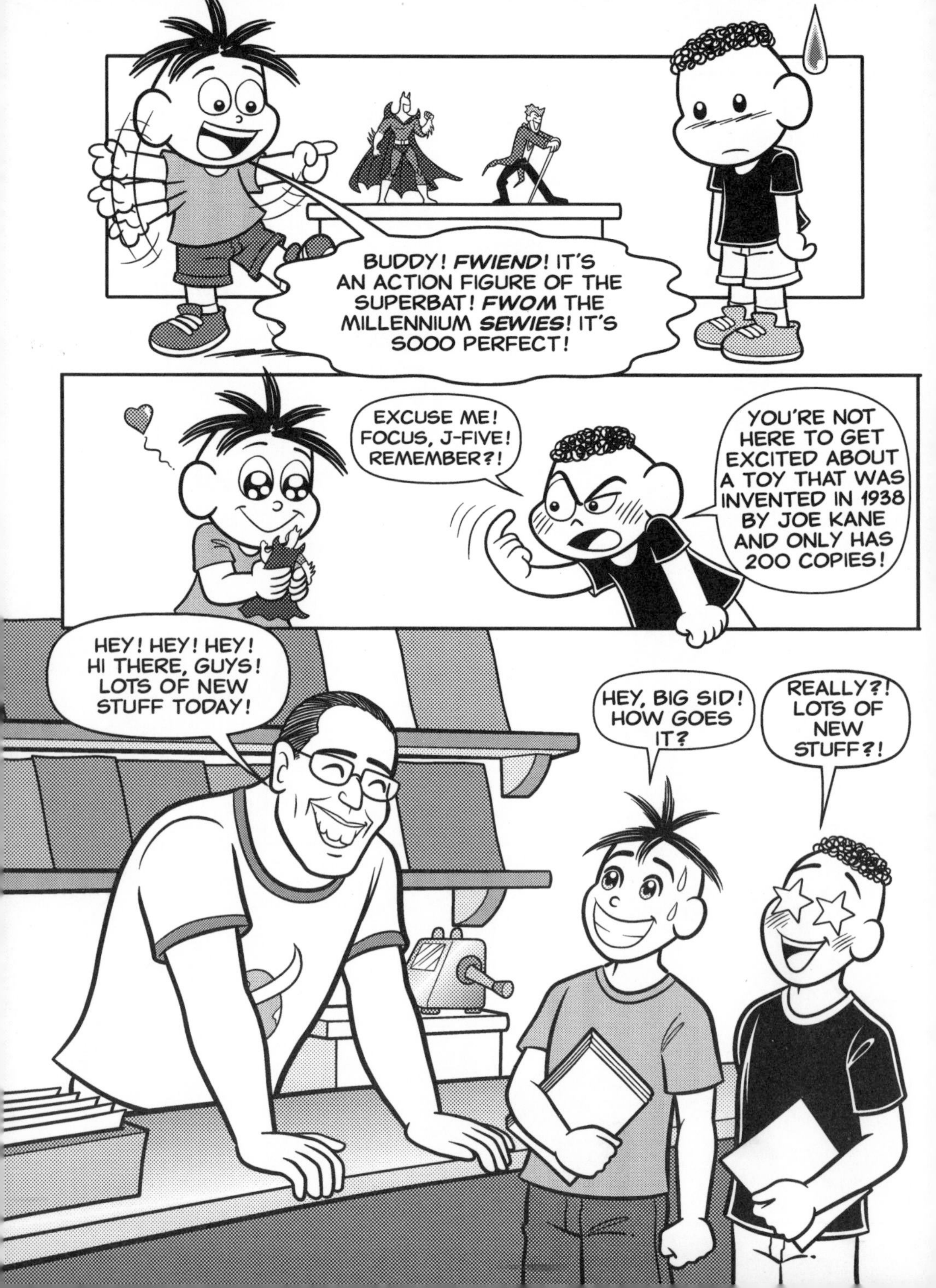
BUDDY! FWIEND! IT'S AN ACTION FIGURE OF THE SUPERBAT! FWOM THE MILLENNIUM SEWIES! IT'S SOOO PERFECT!
EXCUSE ME! FOCUS, J-FIVE! REMEMBER?!
YOU'RE NOT HERE TO GET EXCITED ABOUT A TOY THAT WAS INVENTED IN 1938 BY JOE KANE AND ONLY HAS 200 COPIES!
HEY! HEY! HEY! HI THERE, GUYS! LOTS OF NEW STUFF TODAY!
HEY, BIG SID! HOW GOES IT?
REALLY?! LOTS OF NEW STUFF?!

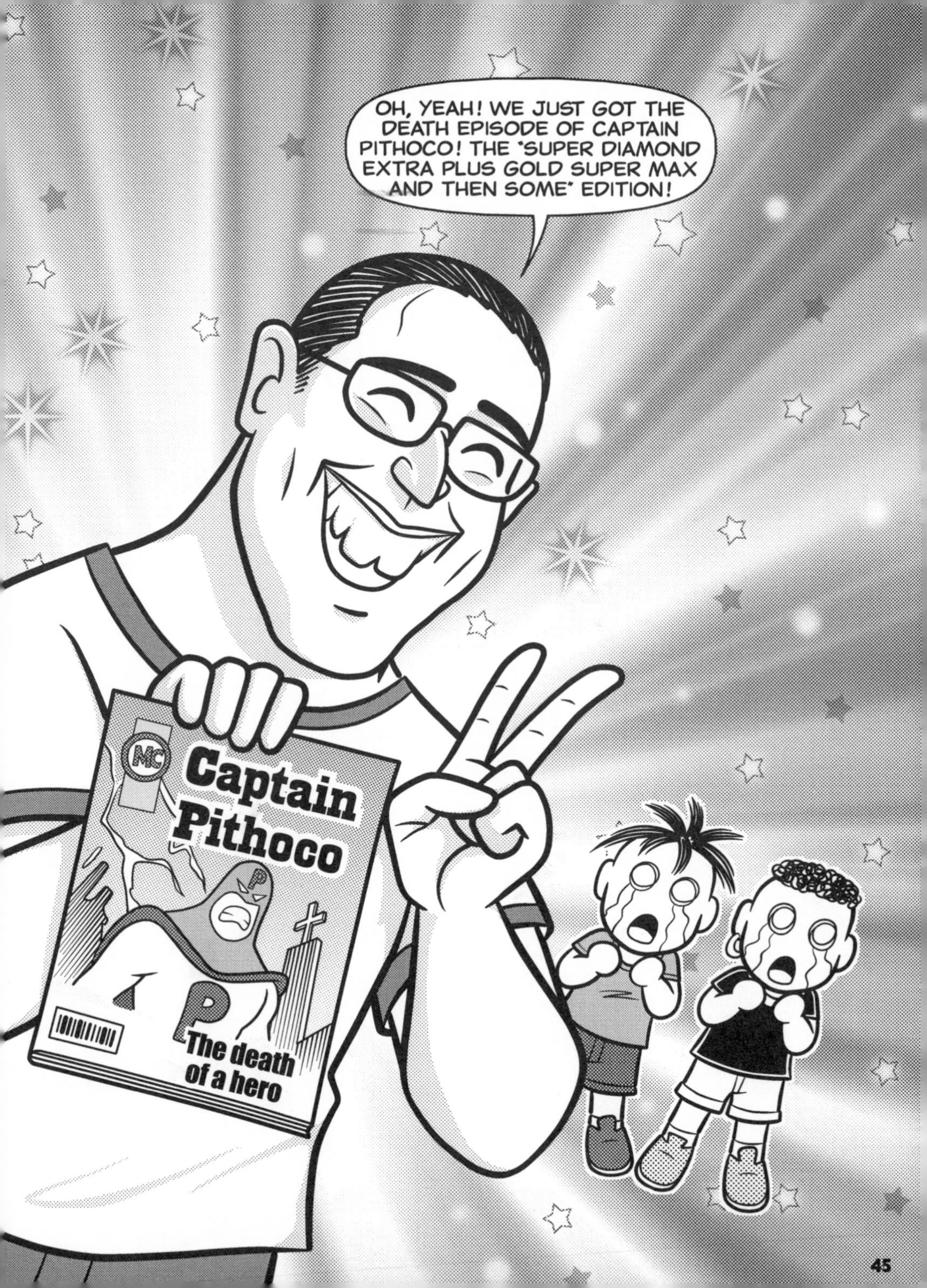
OH, YEAH! WE JUST GOT THE DEATH EPISODE OF CAPTAIN PITHOCO! THE "SUPER DIAMOND EXTRA PLUS GOLD SUPER MAX AND THEN SOME" EDITION!
MC
Captain Pithoco
The death of a hero

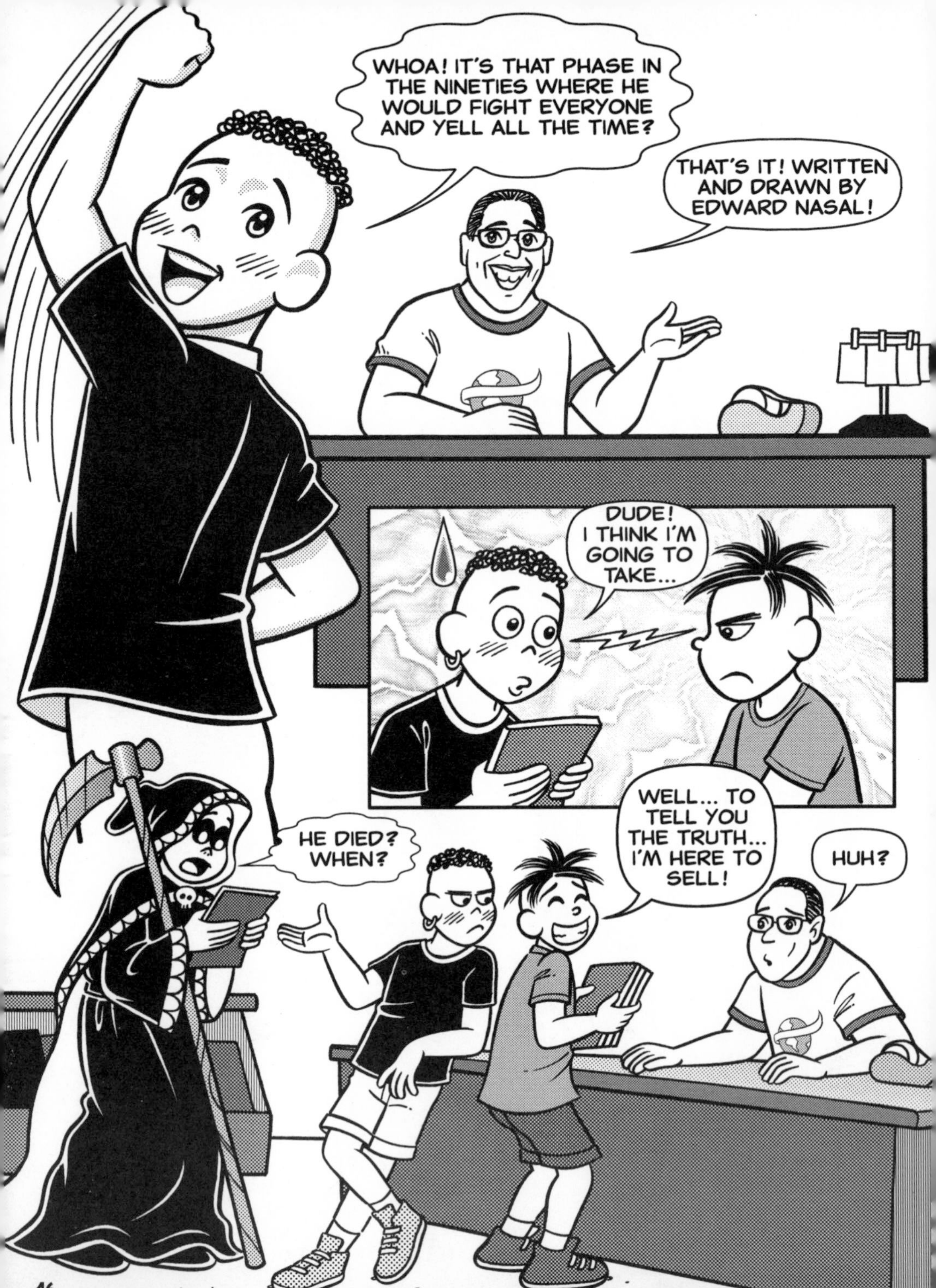
WHOA! IT'S THAT PHASE IN THE NINETIES WHERE HE WOULD FIGHT EVERYONE AND YELL ALL THE TIME?
THAT'S IT! WRITTEN AND DRAWN BY EDWARD NASAL!
DUDE! I THINK I'M GOING TO TAKE...
HE DIED? WHEN?
WELL... TO TELL YOU THE TRUTH... I'M HERE TO SELL!
HUH?

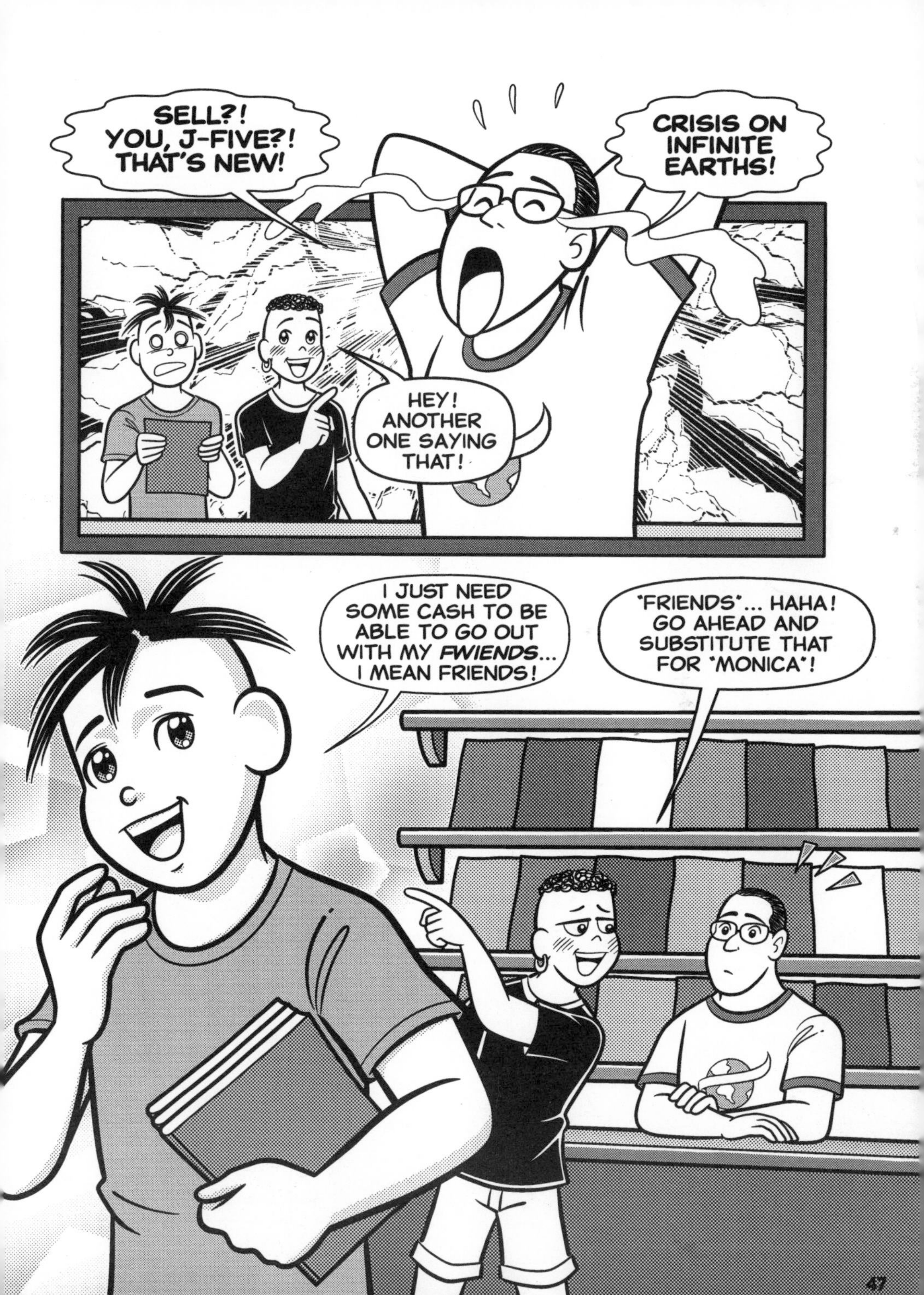
SELL?! YOU, J-FIVE?! THAT'S NEW!
CRISIS ON INFINITE EARTHS!
HEY! ANOTHER ONE SAYING THAT!
I JUST NEED SOME CASH TO BE ABLE TO GO OUT WITH MY *FWIENDS*... I MEAN FRIENDS!
"FRIENDS"... HAHA! GO AHEAD AND SUBSTITUTE THAT FOR "MONICA"!

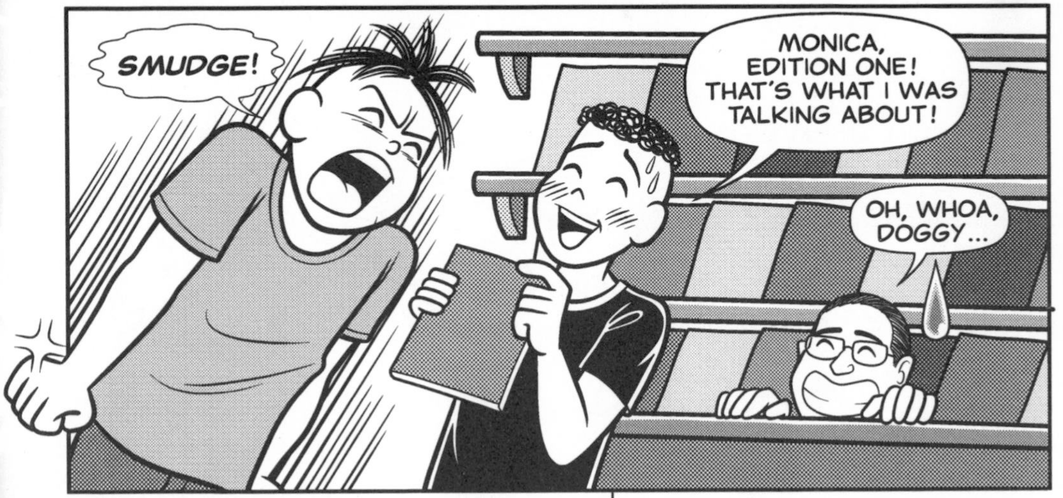
SMUDGE!
MONICA, EDITION ONE! THAT'S WHAT I WAS TALKING ABOUT!
OH, WHOA, DOGGY...
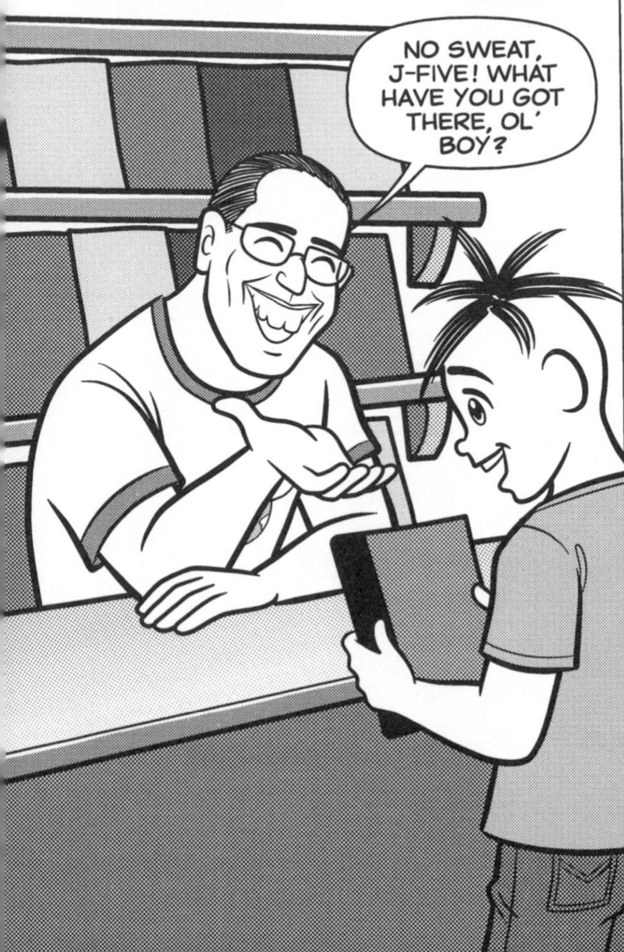
NO SWEAT, J-FIVE! WHAT HAVE YOU GOT THERE, OL' BOY?
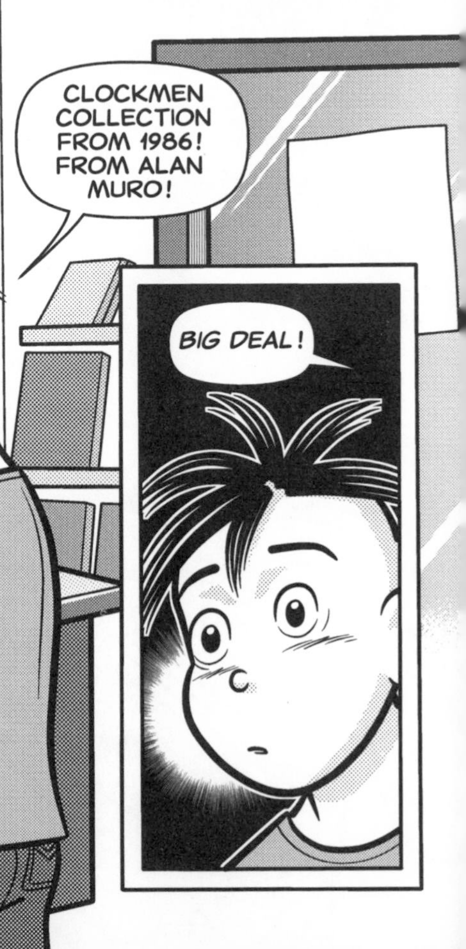
CLOCKMEN COLLECTION FROM 1986! FROM ALAN MURO!
BIG DEAL!

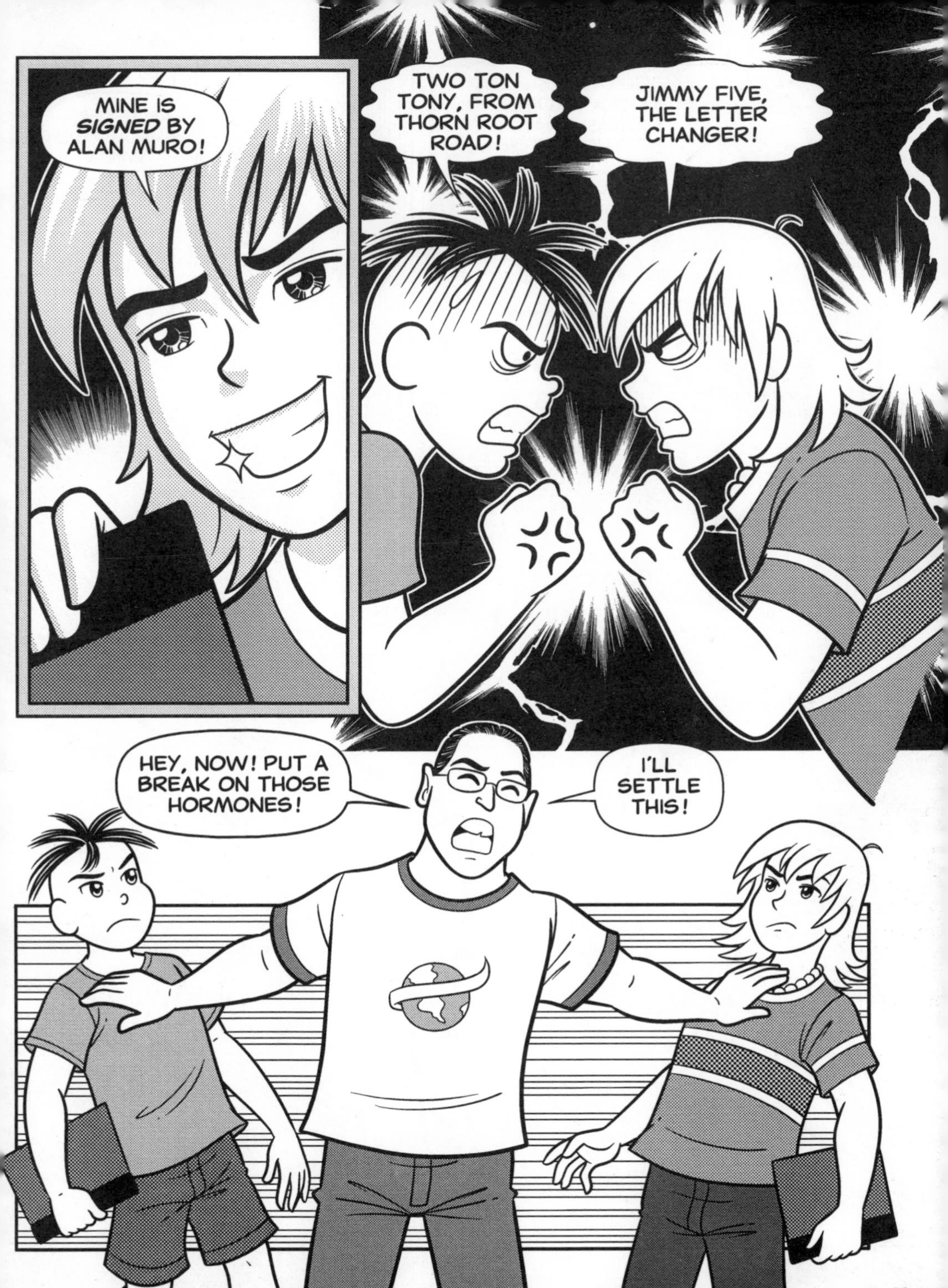
MINE IS *SIGNED* BY ALAN MURO!
TWO TON TONY, FROM THORN ROOT ROAD!
JIMMY FIVE, THE LETTER CHANGER!
HEY, NOW! PUT A BREAK ON THOSE HORMONES!
I'LL SETTLE THIS!

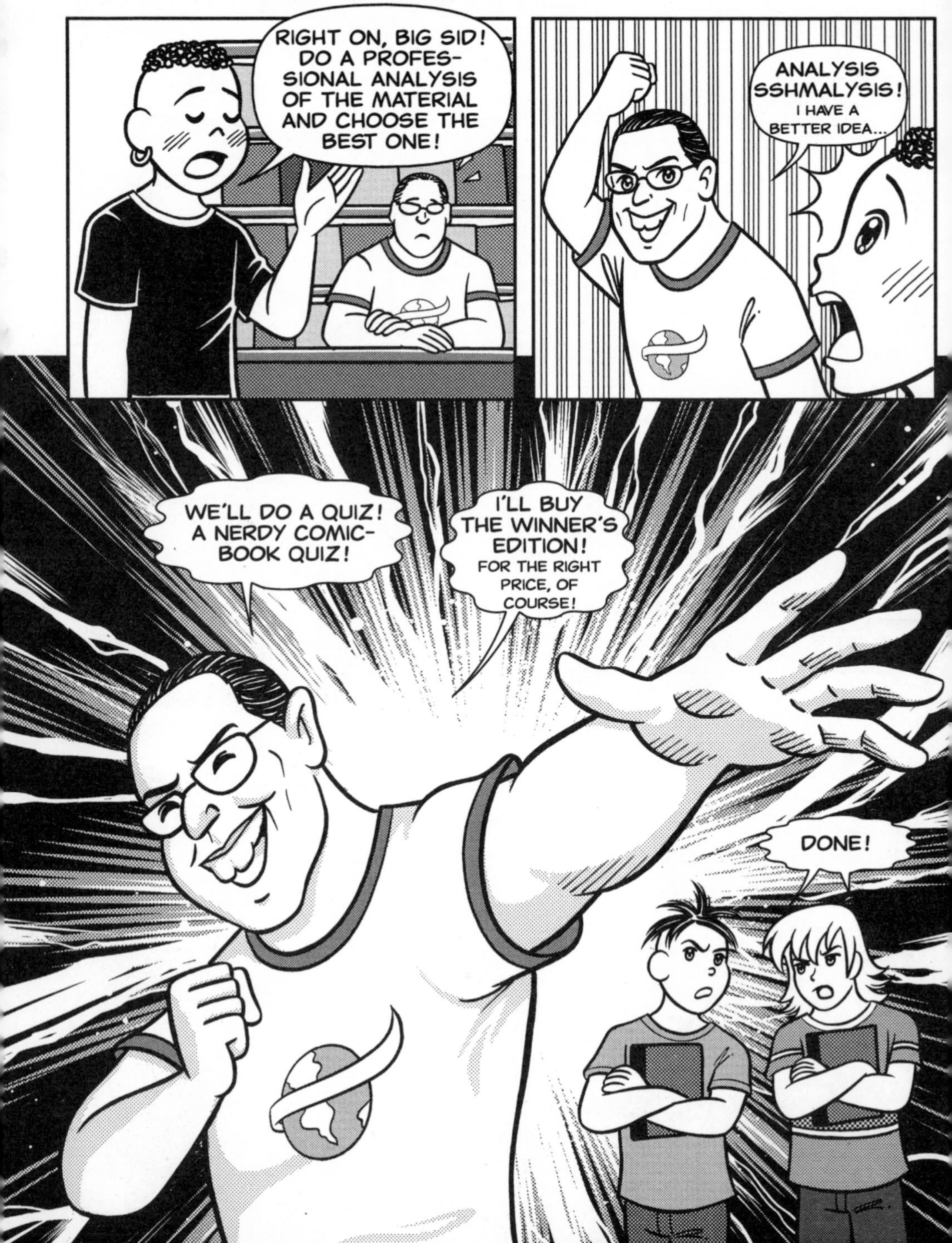
RIGHT ON, BIG SID! DO A PROFES- SIONAL ANALYSIS OF THE MATERIAL AND CHOOSE THE BEST ONE!
ANALYSIS SSHMALYSIS! I HAVE A BETTER IDEA...
WE'LL DO A QUIZ! A NERDY COMIC-BOOK QUIZ!
I'LL BUY THE WINNER'S EDITION! FOR THE RIGHT PRICE, OF COURSE!
DONE!

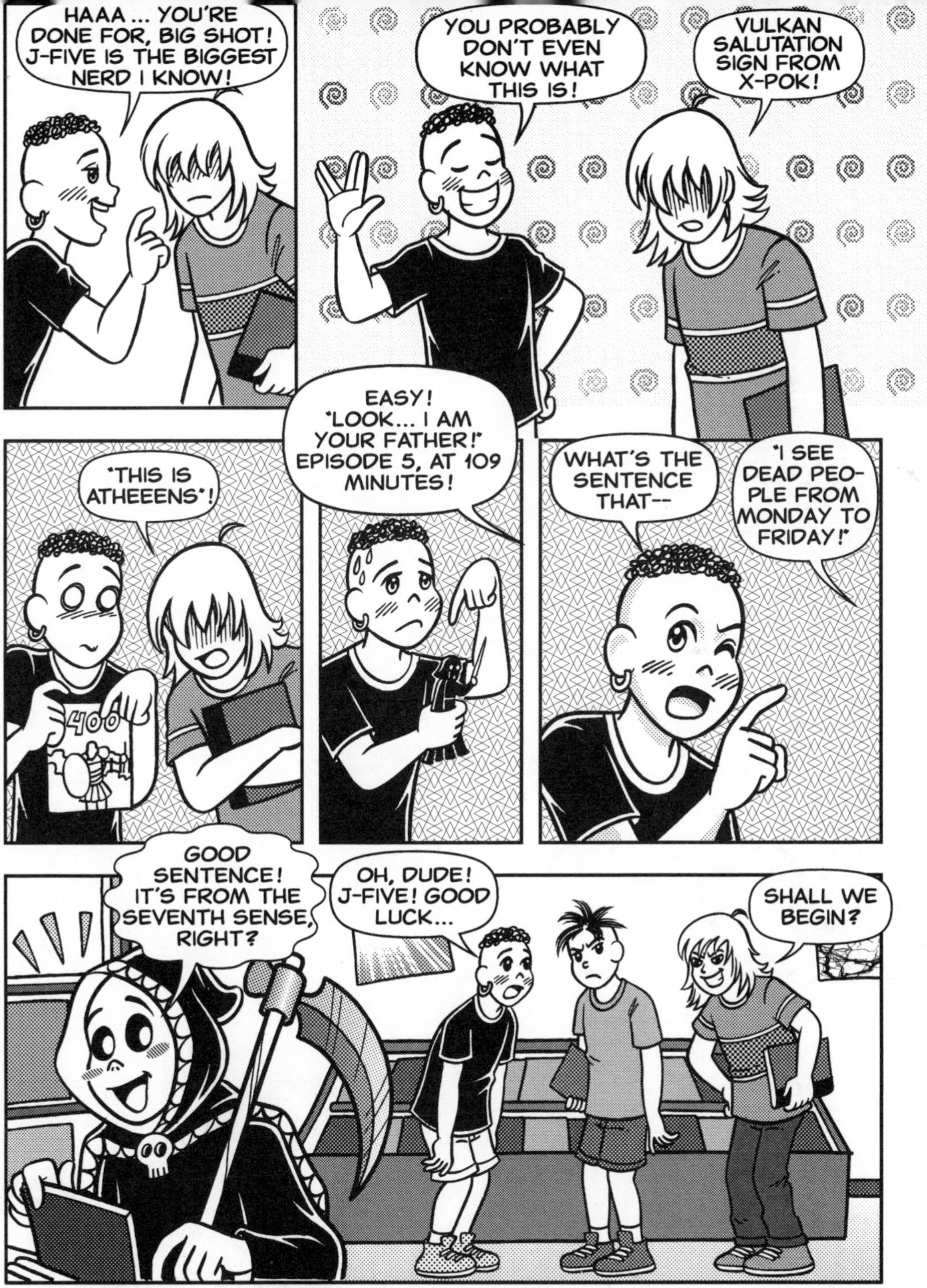
HAAA... YOU'RE DONE FOR, BIG SHOT! J-FIVE IS THE BIGGEST NERD I KNOW!
YOU PROBABLY DON'T EVEN KNOW WHAT THIS IS!
VULKAN SALUTATION SIGN FROM X-POK!
"THIS IS ATHEEENS"!
400
EASY! "LOOK... I AM YOUR FATHER!" EPISODE 5, AT 109 MINUTES!
WHAT'S THE SENTENCE THAT--
"I SEE DEAD PEO-PLE FROM MONDAY TO FRIDAY!"
GOOD SENTENCE! IT'S FROM THE SEVENTH SENSE, RIGHT?
OH, DUDE! J-FIVE! GOOD LUCK...
SHALL WE BEGIN?

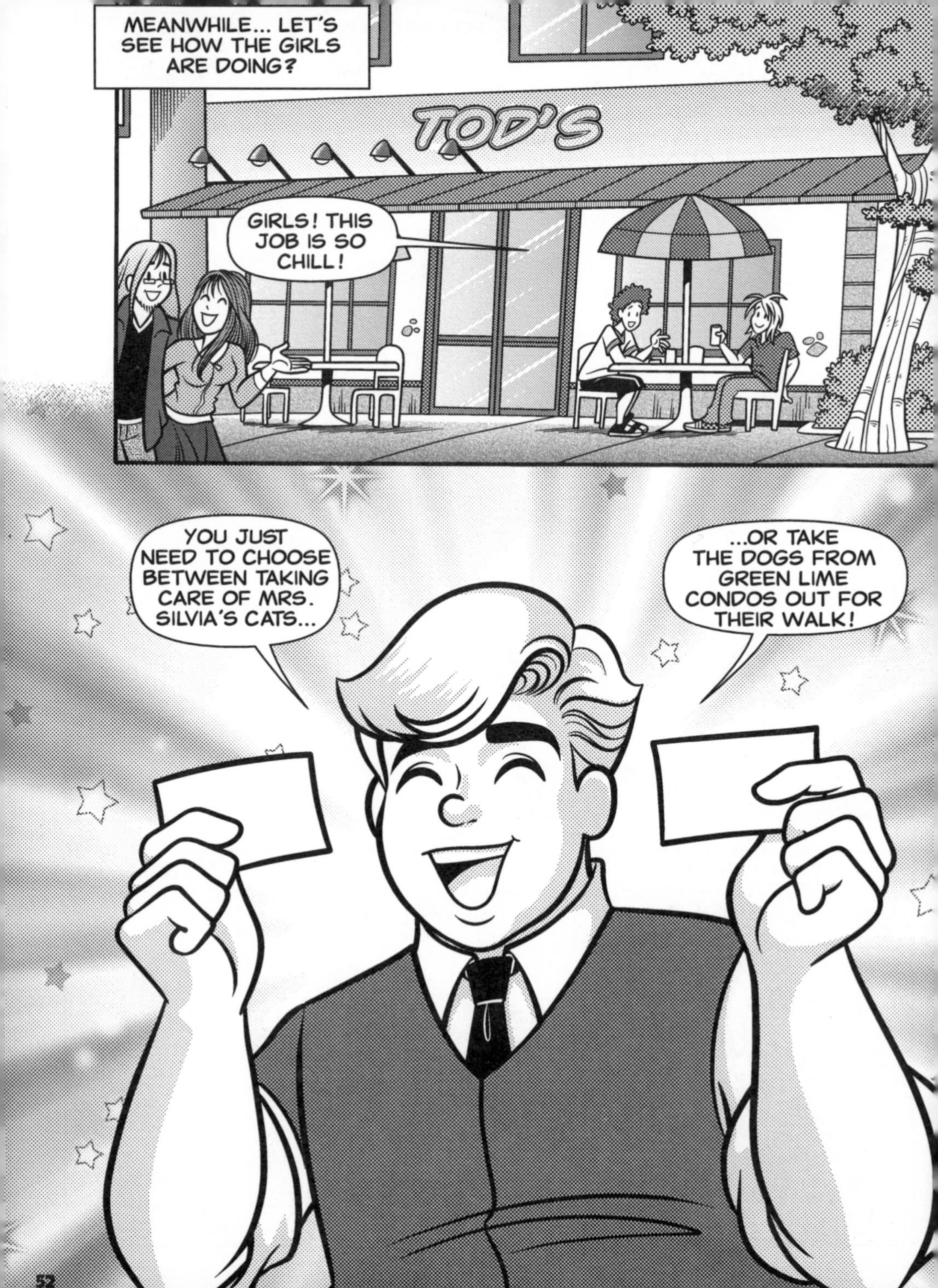

MEANWHILE... LET'S SEE HOW THE GIRLS ARE DOING?
TOD'S
GIRLS! THIS JOB IS SO CHILL!
YOU JUST NEED TO CHOOSE BETWEEN TAKING CARE OF MRS. SILVIA'S CATS...
...OR TAKE THE DOGS FROM GREEN LIME CONDOS OUT FOR THEIR WALK!

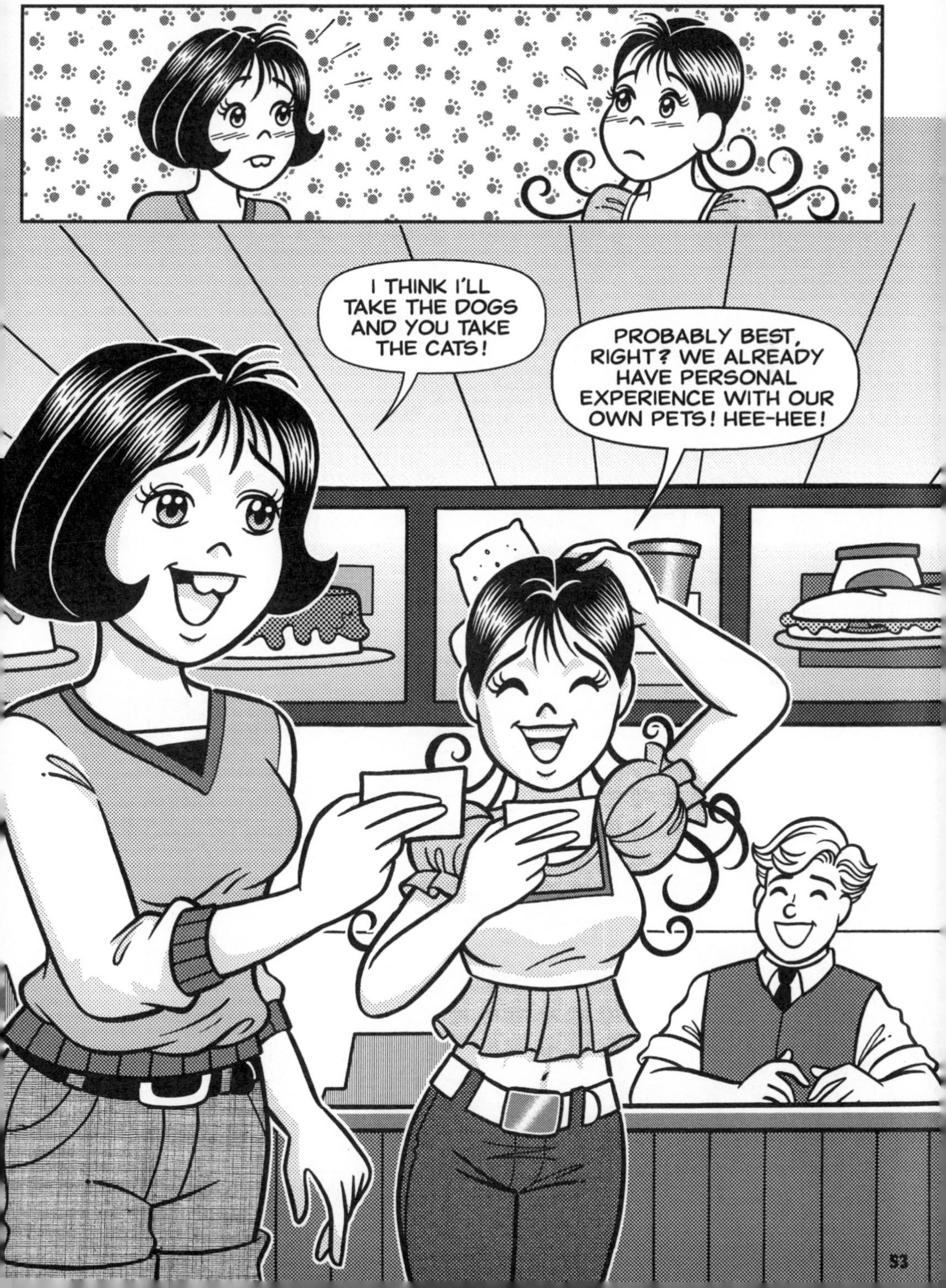
I THINK I'LL TAKE THE DOGS AND YOU TAKE THE CATS!
PROBABLY BEST, RIGHT? WE ALREADY HAVE PERSONAL EXPERIENCE WITH OUR OWN PETS! HEE-HEE!

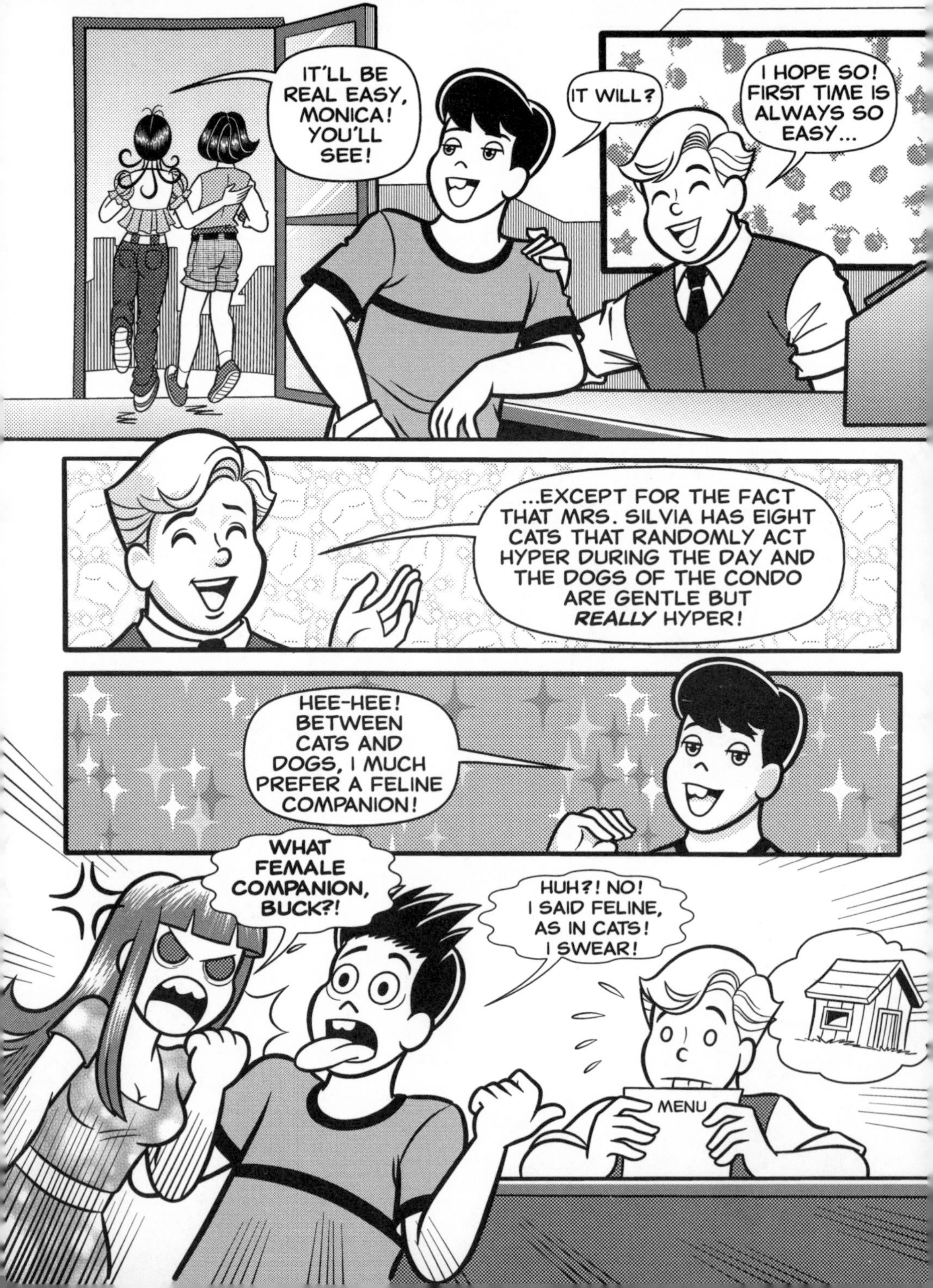
IT'LL BE REAL EASY, MONICA! YOU'LL SEE!
IT WILL?
I HOPE SO! FIRST TIME IS ALWAYS SO EASY...
...EXCEPT FOR THE FACT THAT MRS. SILVIA HAS EIGHT CATS THAT RANDOMLY ACT HYPER DURING THE DAY AND THE DOGS OF THE CONDO ARE GENTLE BUT *REALLY* HYPER!
HEE-HEE! BETWEEN CATS AND DOGS, I MUCH PREFER A FELINE COMPANION!
WHAT FEMALE COMPANION, BUCK?!
HUH?! NO! I SAID FELINE, AS IN CATS! I SWEAR!
MENU

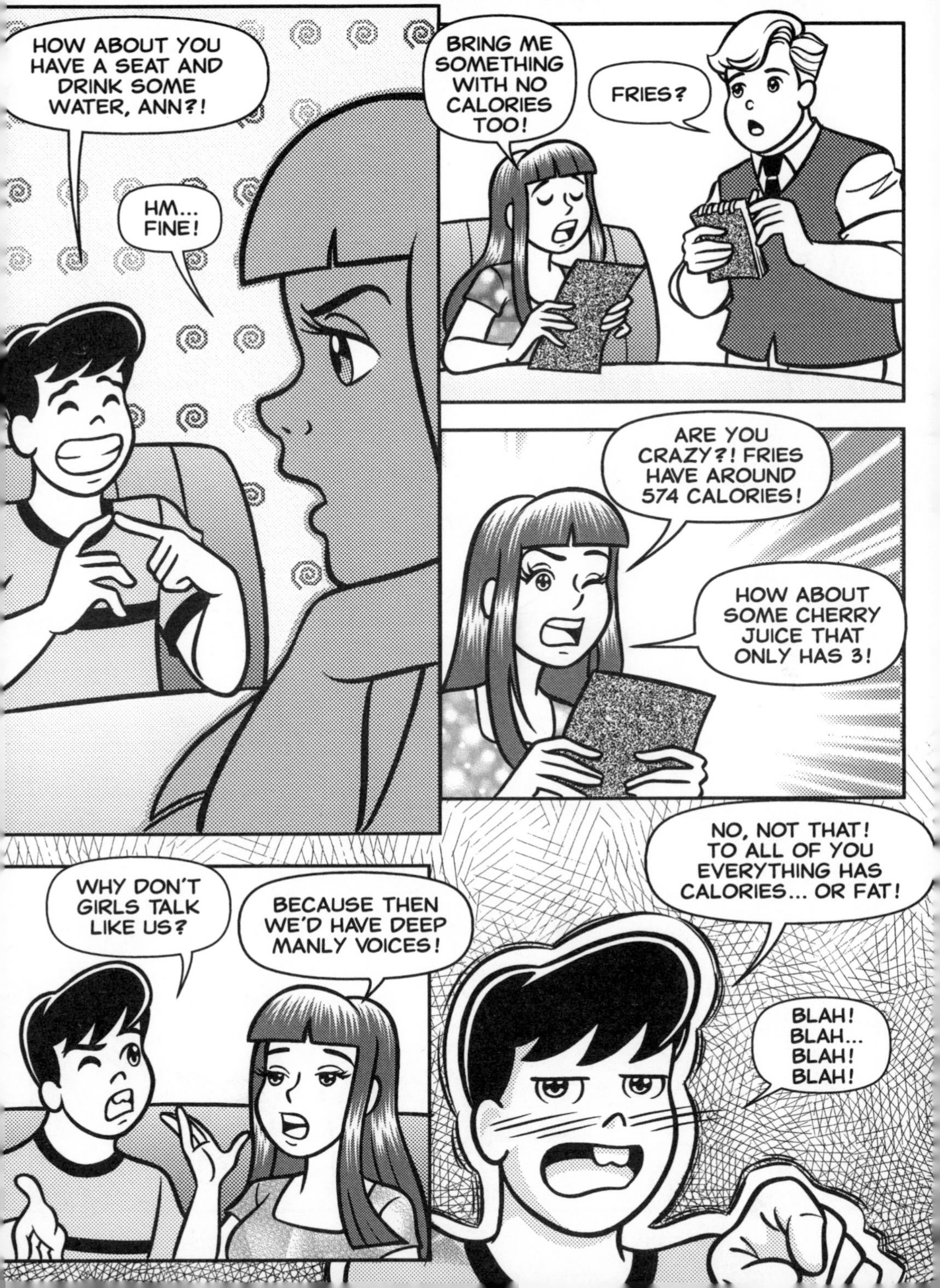
HOW ABOUT YOU HAVE A SEAT AND DRINK SOME WATER, ANN?!
HM... FINE!
BRING ME SOMETHING WITH NO CALORIES TOO!
FRIES?
ARE YOU CRAZY?! FRIES HAVE AROUND 574 CALORIES!
HOW ABOUT SOME CHERRY JUICE THAT ONLY HAS 3!
WHY DON'T GIRLS TALK LIKE US?
BECAUSE THEN WE'D HAVE DEEP MANLY VOICES!
NO, NOT THAT! TO ALL OF YOU EVERYTHING HAS CALORIES... OR FAT!
BLAH! BLAH... BLAH! BLAH!

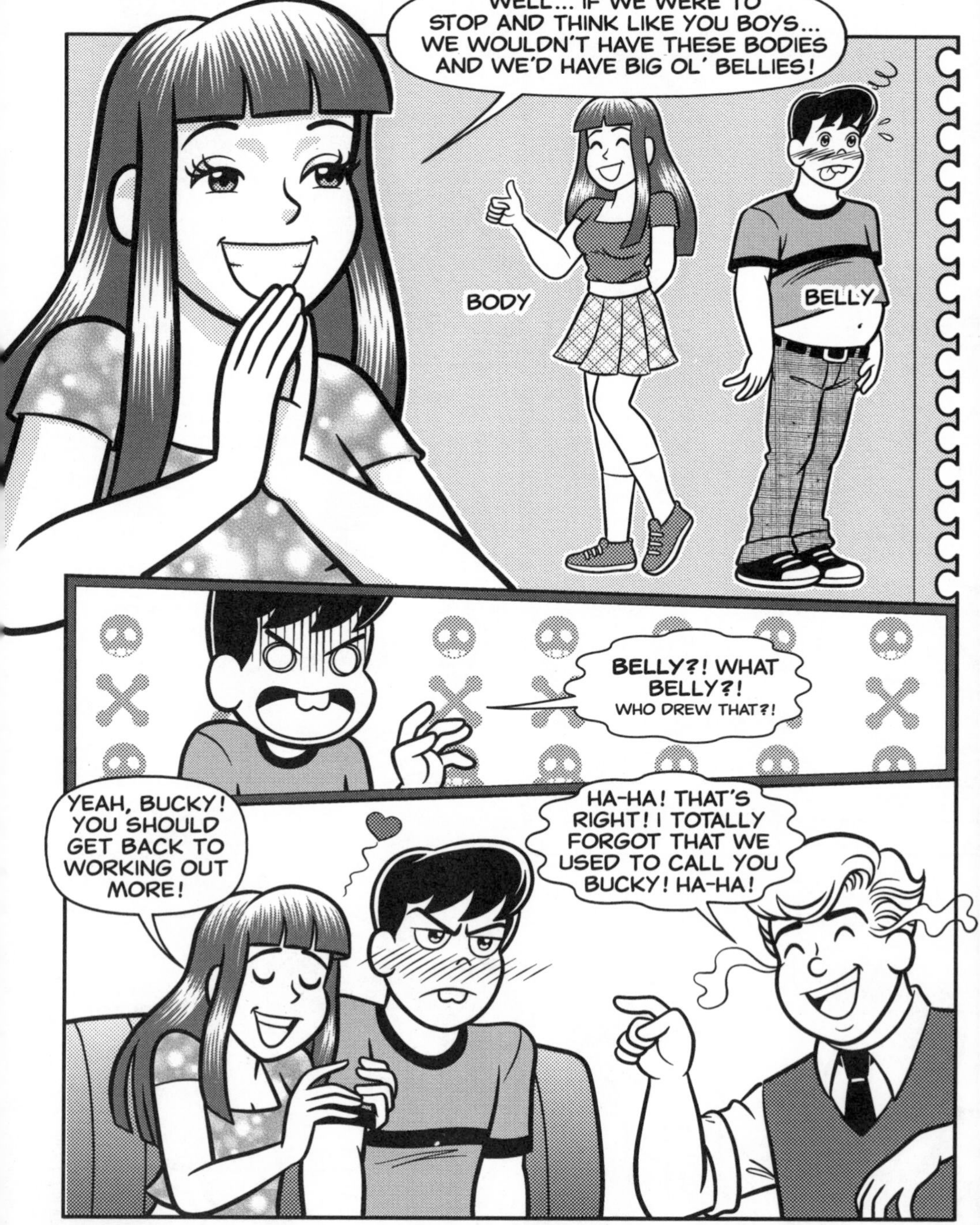
WELL... IF WE WERE TO STOP AND THINK LIKE YOU BOYS... WE WOULDN'T HAVE THESE BODIES AND WE'D HAVE BIG OL' BELLIES!
BODY
BELLY
BELLY?! WHAT BELLY?! WHO DREW THAT?!
YEAH, BUCKY! YOU SHOULD GET BACK TO WORKING OUT MORE!
HA-HA! THAT'S RIGHT! I TOTALLY FORGOT THAT WE USED TO CALL YOU BUCKY! HA-HA!

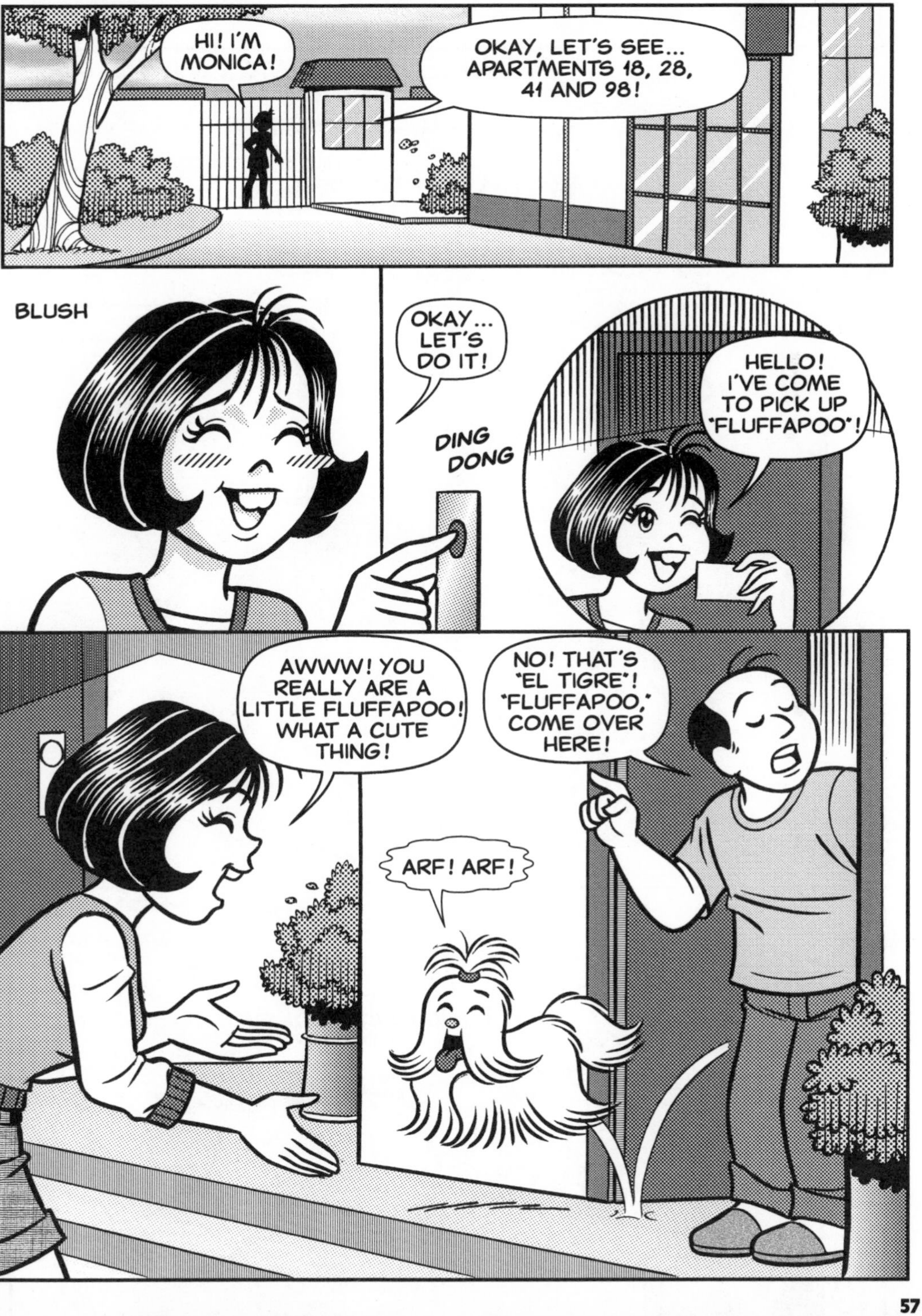
HI! I'M MONICA!
OKAY, LET'S SEE... APARTMENTS 18, 28, 41 AND 98!
BLUSH
OKAY... LET'S DO IT!
DING DONG
HELLO! I'VE COME TO PICK UP "FLUFFAPOO"!
AWWW! YOU REALLY ARE A LITTLE FLUFFAPOO! WHAT A CUTE THING!
NO! THAT'S "EL TIGRE"! "FLUFFAPOO," COME OVER HERE!
ARF! ARF!

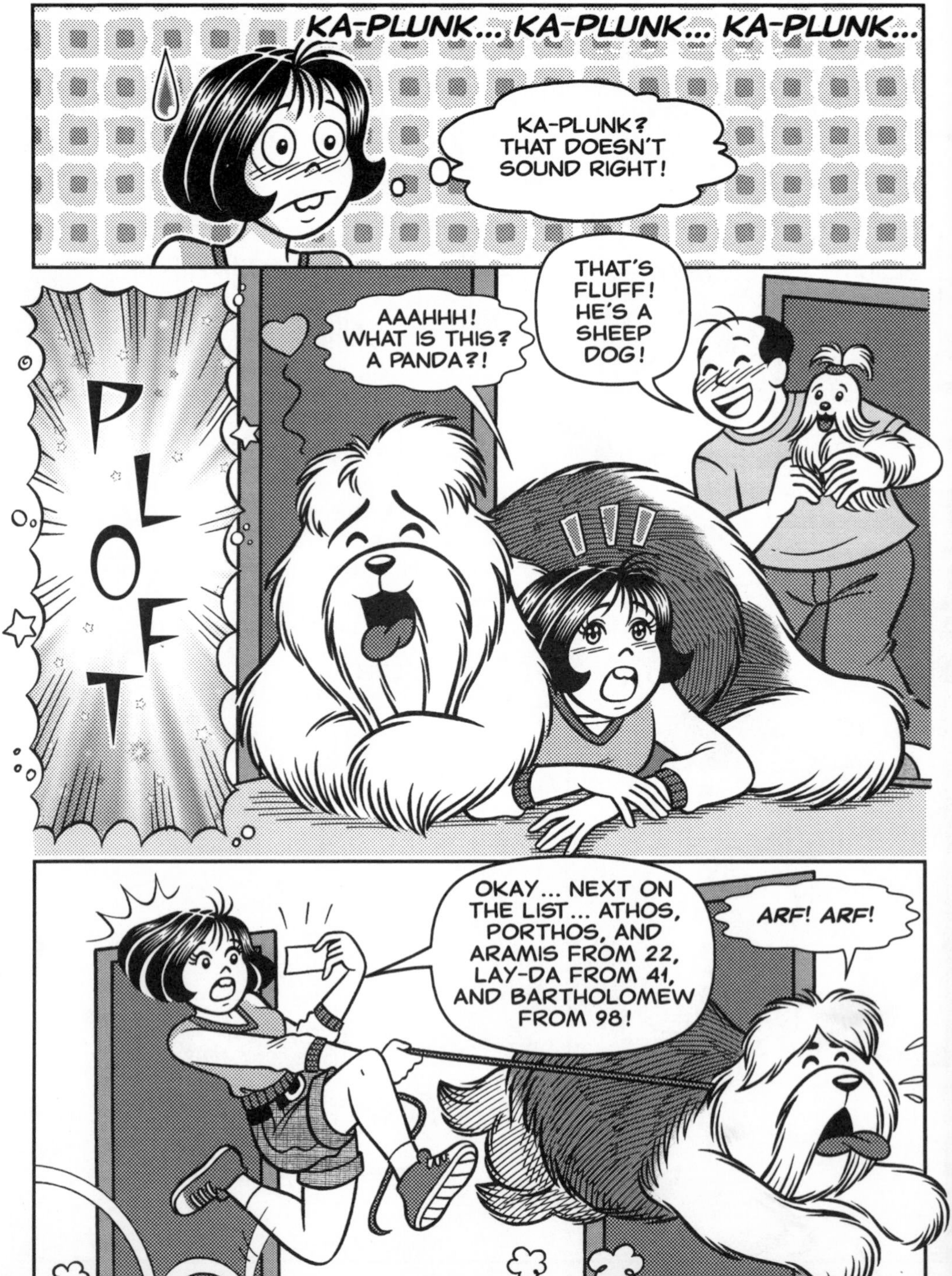
KA-PLUNK... KA-PLUNK... KA-PLUNK...
KA-PLUNK? THAT DOESN'T SOUND RIGHT!
PLOFT
AAAHHH! WHAT IS THIS? A PANDA?!
THAT'S FLUFF! HE'S A SHEEP DOG!
OKAY... NEXT ON THE LIST... ATHOS, PORTHOS, AND ARAMIS FROM 22, LAY-DA FROM 41, AND BARTHOLOMEW FROM 98!
ARF! ARF!

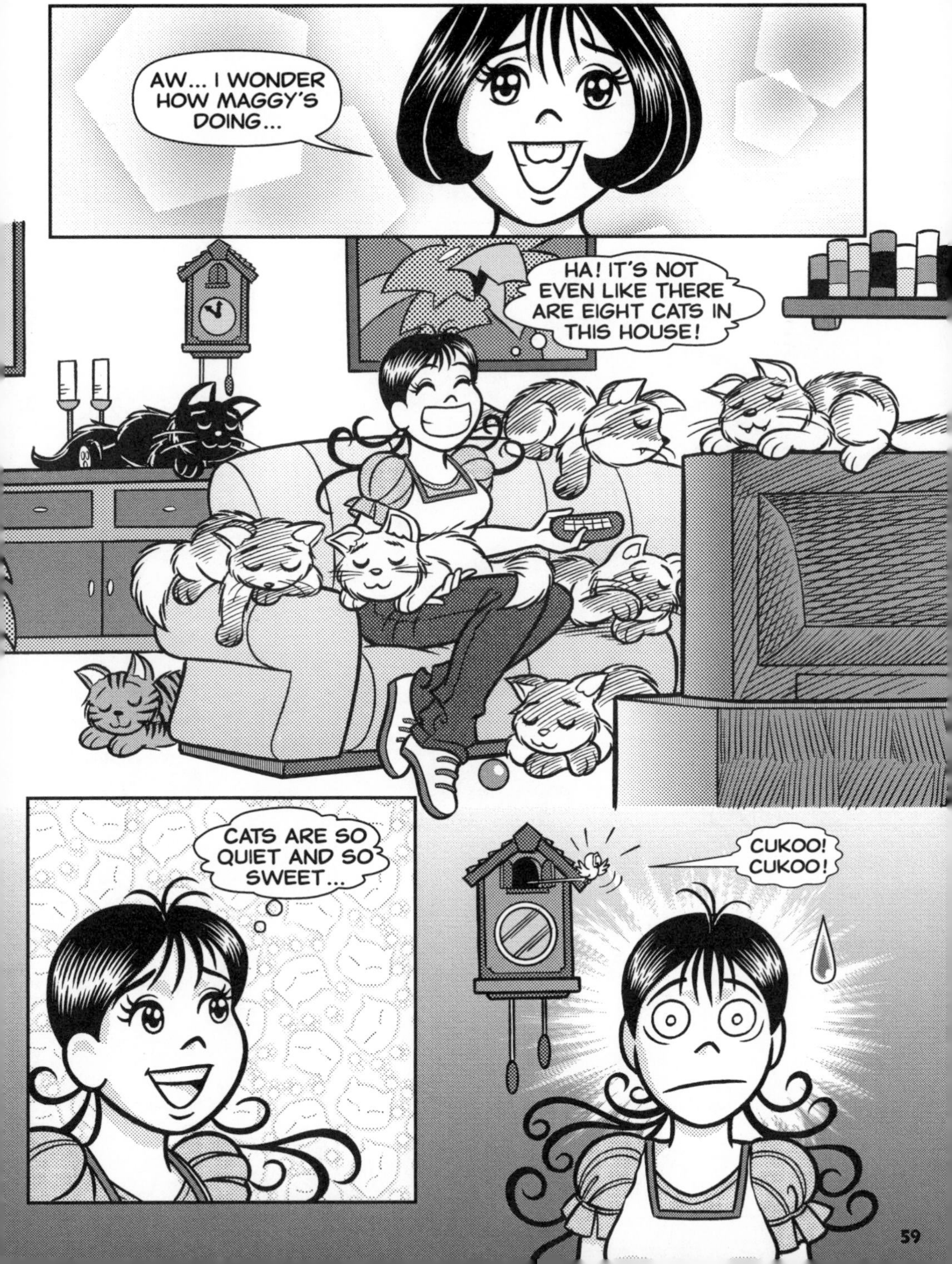
AW... I WONDER HOW MAGGY'S DOING...
HA! IT'S NOT EVEN LIKE THERE ARE EIGHT CATS IN THIS HOUSE!
CATS ARE SO QUIET AND SO SWEET...
CUKOO! CUKOO!

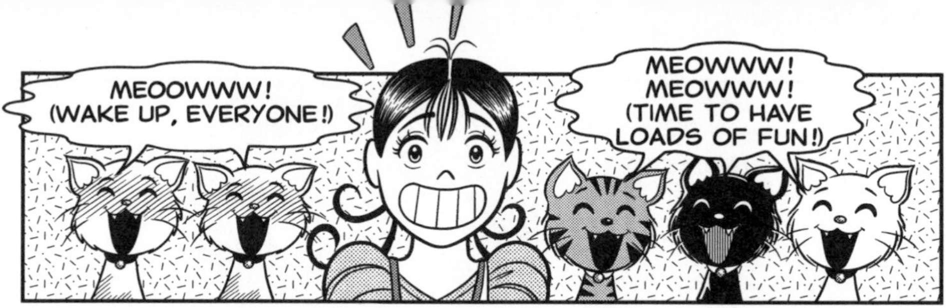
MEOOWWW! (WAKE UP, EVERYONE!)
MEOWWW! MEOWWW! (TIME TO HAVE LOADS OF FUN!)

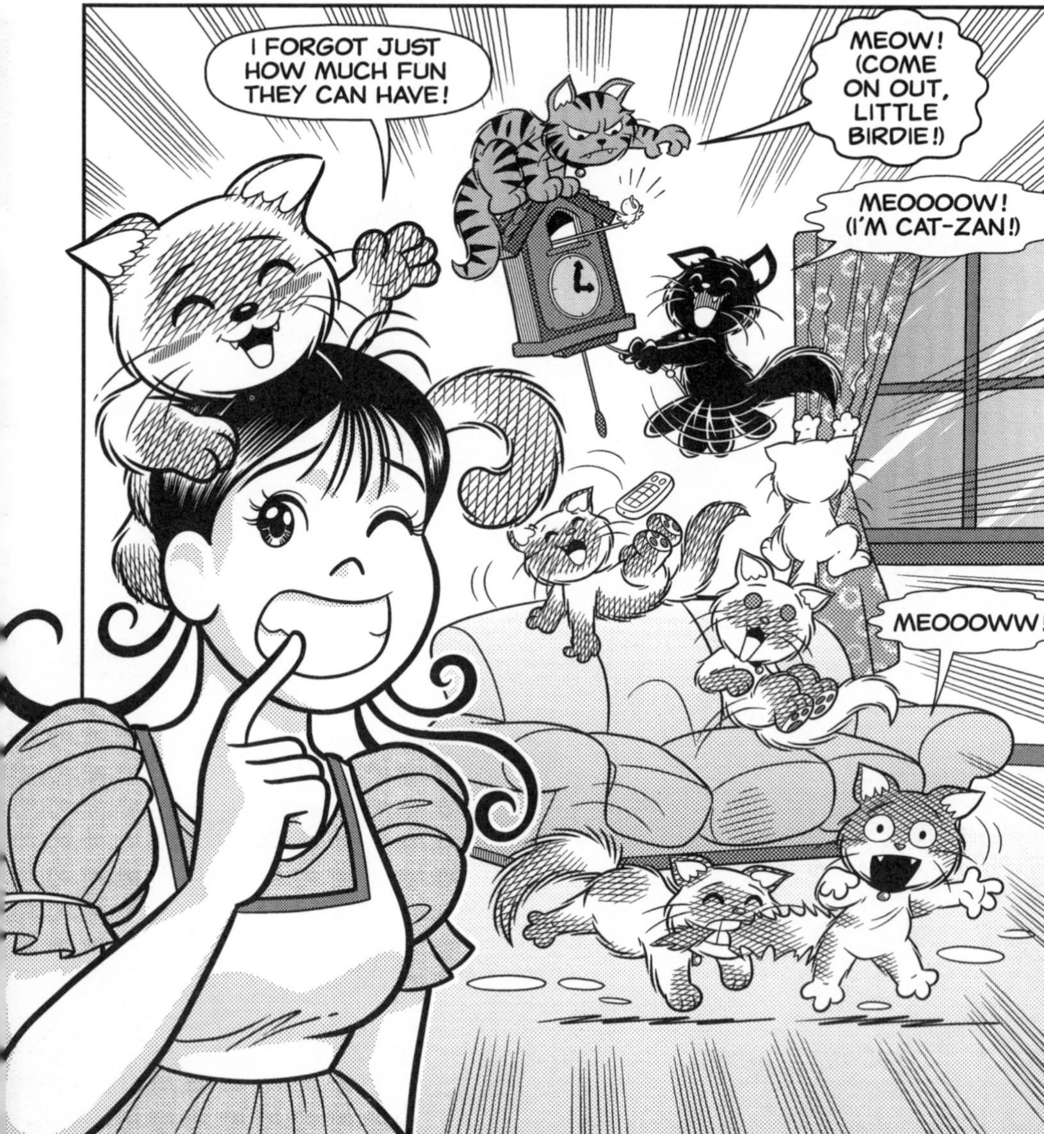
I FORGOT JUST HOW MUCH FUN THEY CAN HAVE!
MEOW! (COME ON OUT, LITTLE BIRDIE!)
MEOOOOW! (I'M CAT-ZAN!)
MEOOOWW!

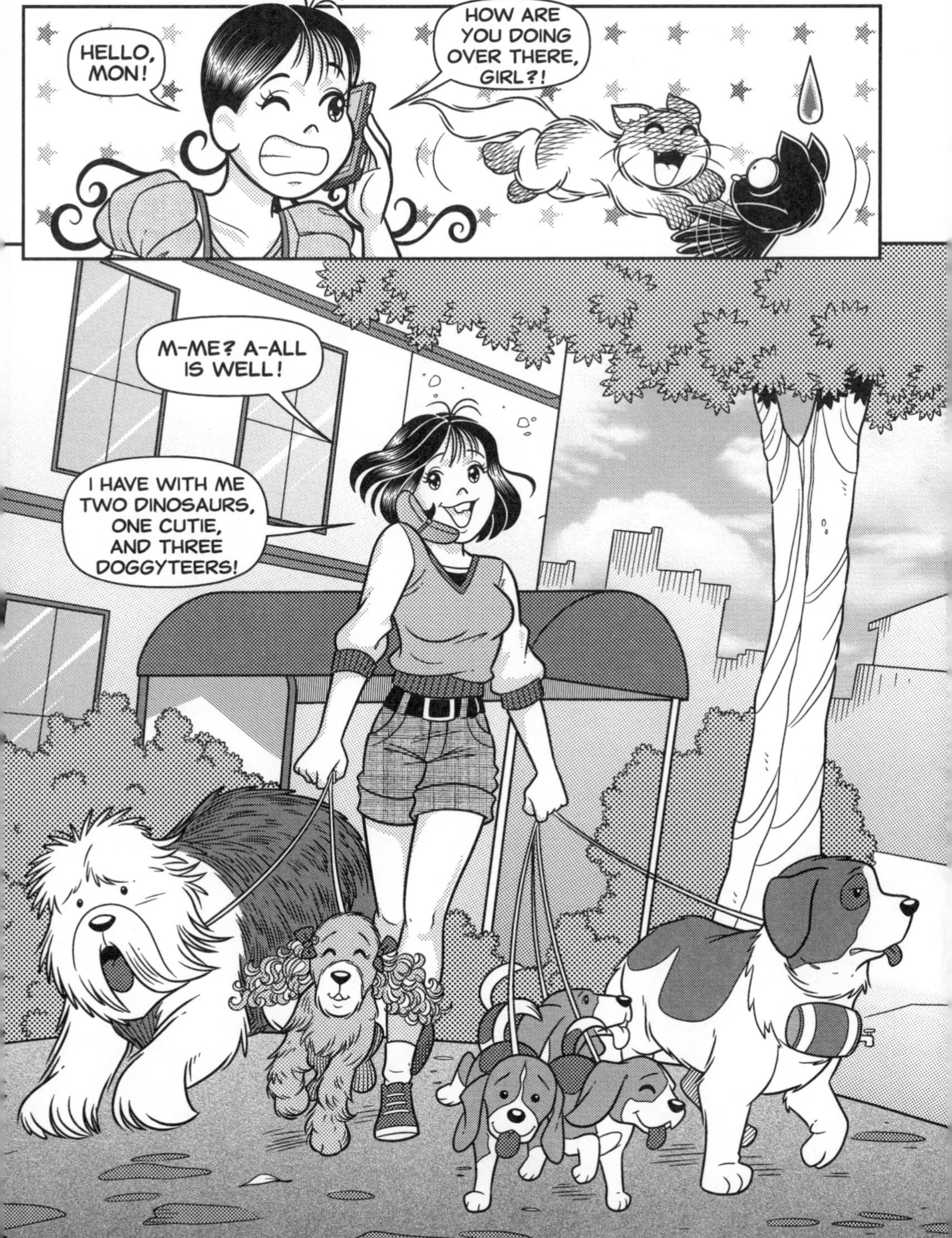
HELLO, MON!
HOW ARE YOU DOING OVER THERE, GIRL?!
M-ME? A-ALL IS WELL!
I HAVE WITH ME TWO DINOSAURS, ONE CUTIE, AND THREE DOGGYTEERS!

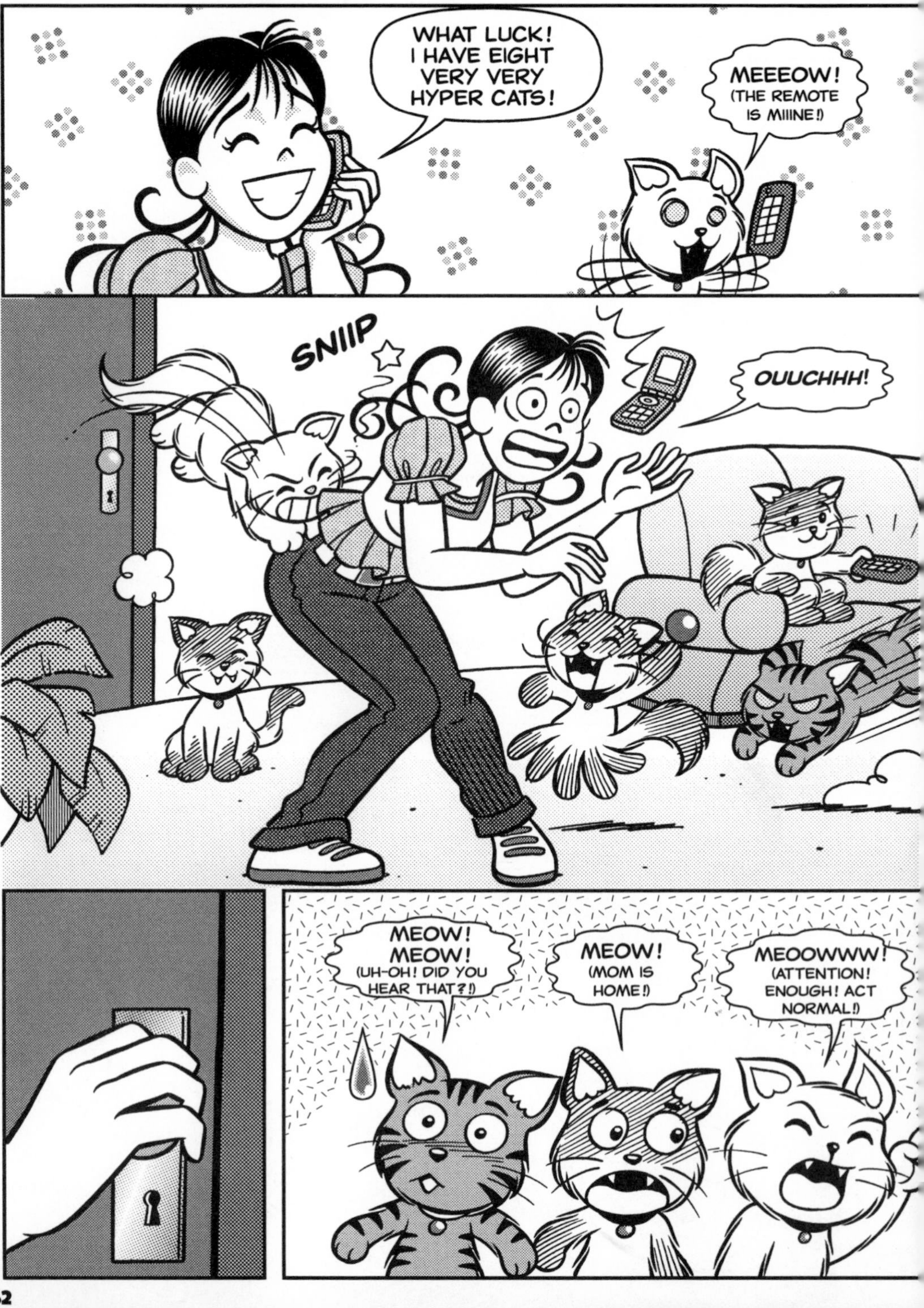
WHAT LUCK! I HAVE EIGHT VERY VERY HYPER CATS!
MEEEOW! (THE REMOTE IS MIIINE!)
SNIIP
OUUCHHH!
MEOW! MEOW! (UH-OH! DID YOU HEAR THAT?!)
MEOW! (MOM IS HOME!)
MEOOWWW! (ATTENTION! ENOUGH! ACT NORMAL!)

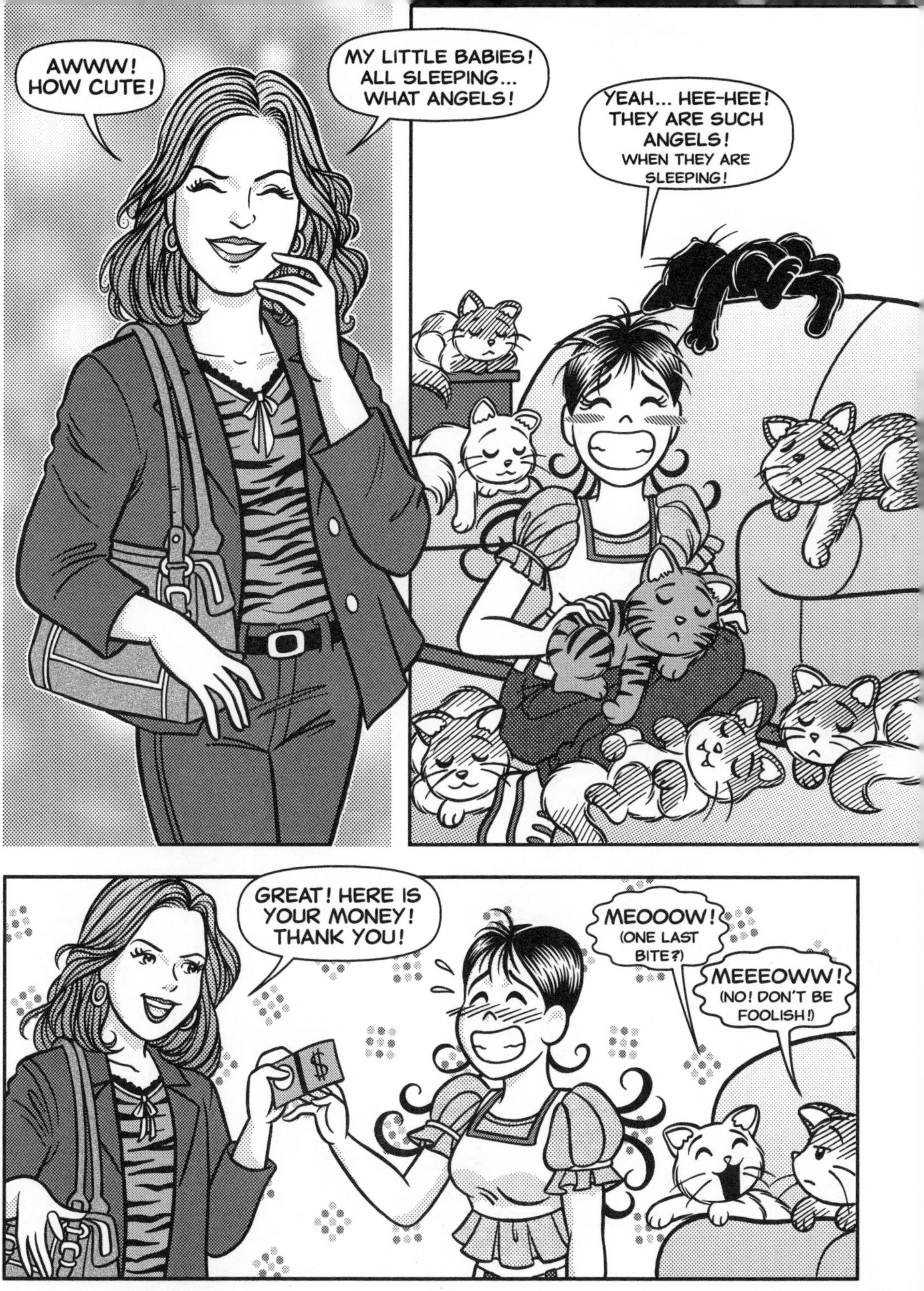
AWWW! HOW CUTE!
MY LITTLE BABIES! ALL SLEEPING... WHAT ANGELS!
YEAH... HEE-HEE! THEY ARE SUCH ANGELS! WHEN THEY ARE SLEEPING!
GREAT! HERE IS YOUR MONEY! THANK YOU!
MEOOOW! (ONE LAST BITE?)
MEEEOWW! (NO! DON'T BE FOOLISH!)

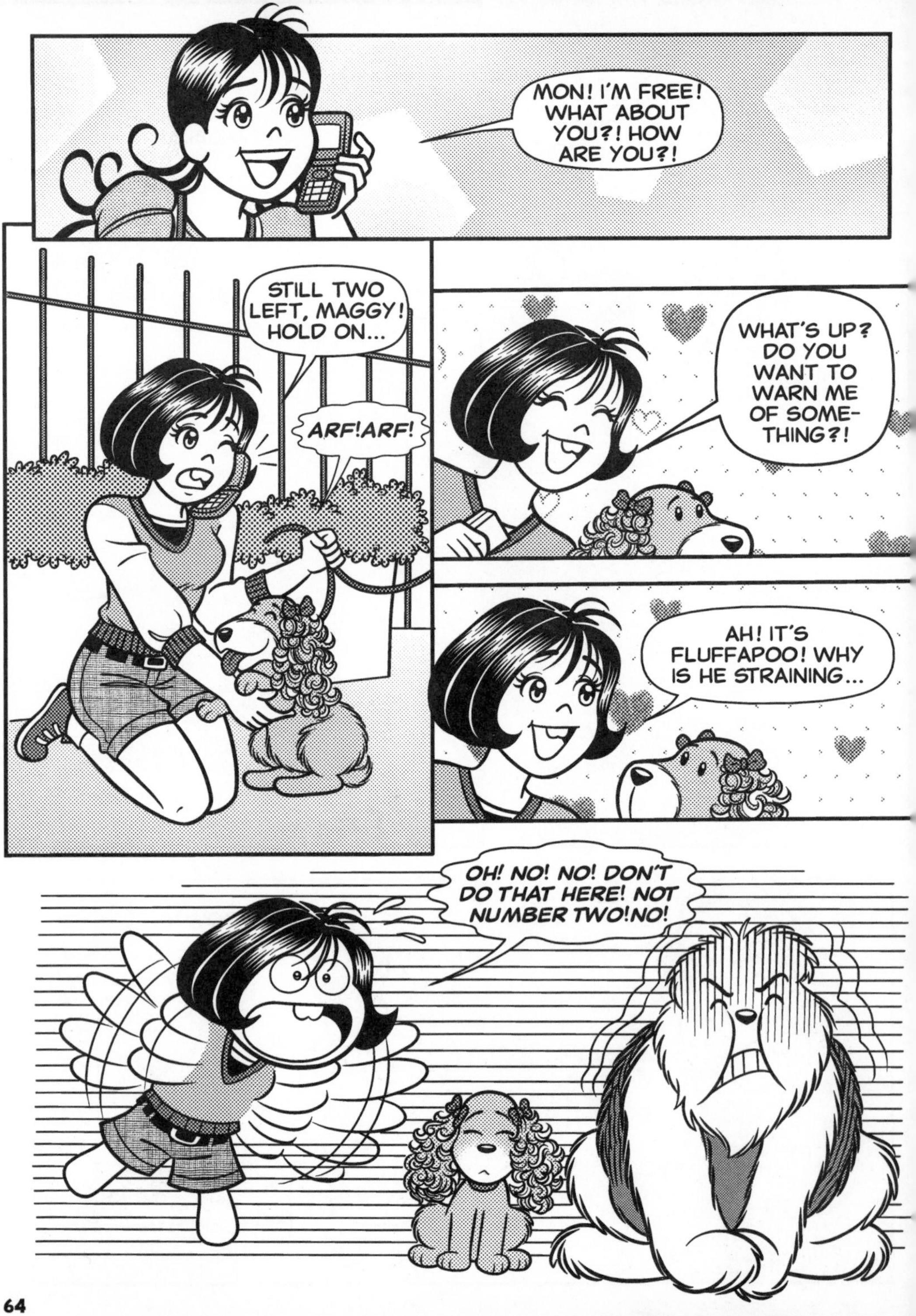
MON! I'M FREE! WHAT ABOUT YOU?! HOW ARE YOU?!
STILL TWO LEFT, MAGGY! HOLD ON...
ARF!ARF!
WHAT'S UP? DO YOU WANT TO WARN ME OF SOME-THING?!
AH! IT'S FLUFFAPOO! WHY IS HE STRAINING...
OH! NO! NO! DON'T DO THAT HERE! NOT NUMBER TWO!NO!

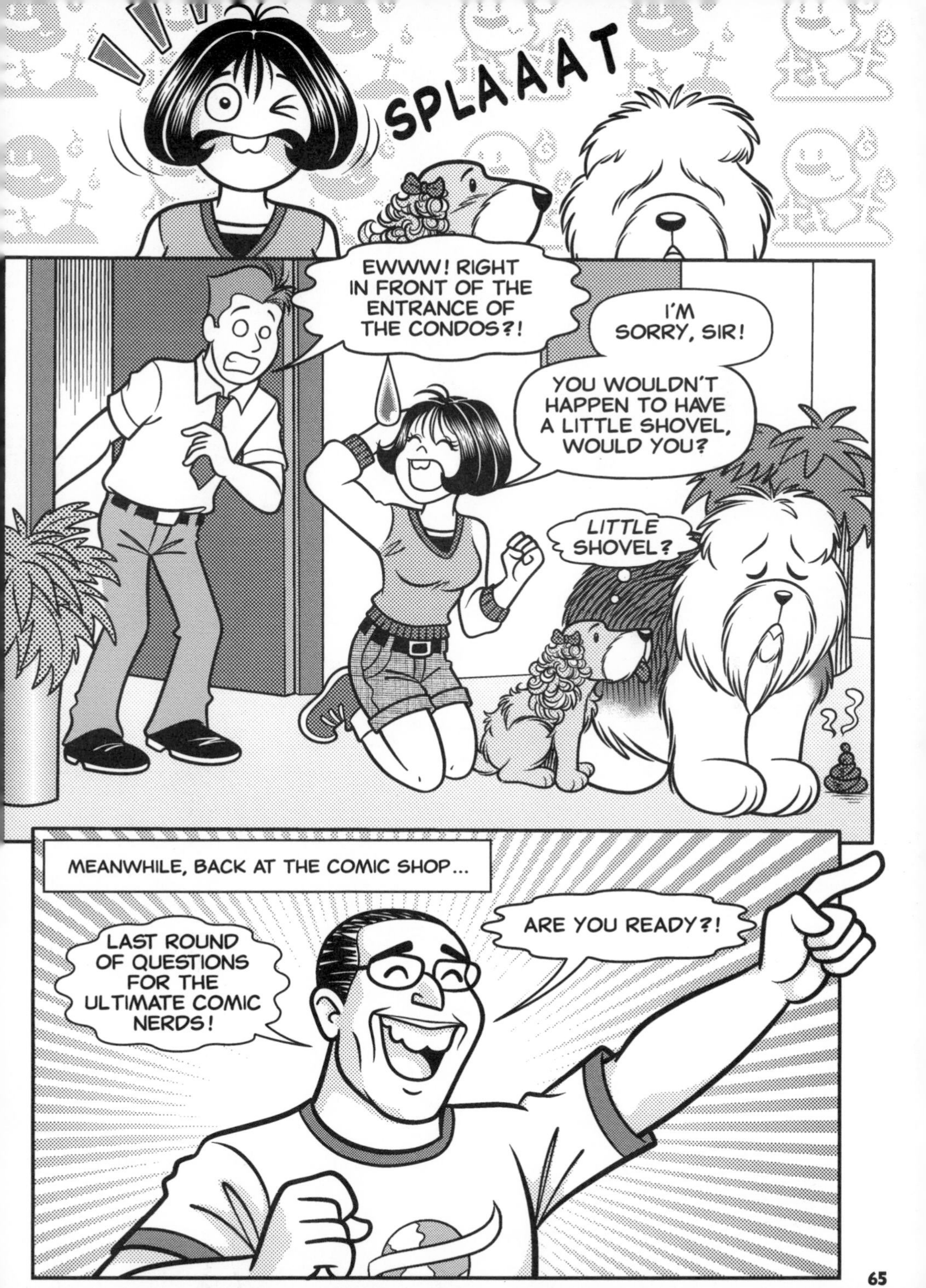
SPLAAAT
EWWW! RIGHT IN FRONT OF THE ENTRANCE OF THE CONDOS?!
I'M SORRY, SIR!
YOU WOULDN'T HAPPEN TO HAVE A LITTLE SHOVEL, WOULD YOU?
LITTLE SHOVEL?
MEANWHILE, BACK AT THE COMIC SHOP...
LAST ROUND OF QUESTIONS FOR THE ULTIMATE COMIC NERDS!
ARE YOU READY?!

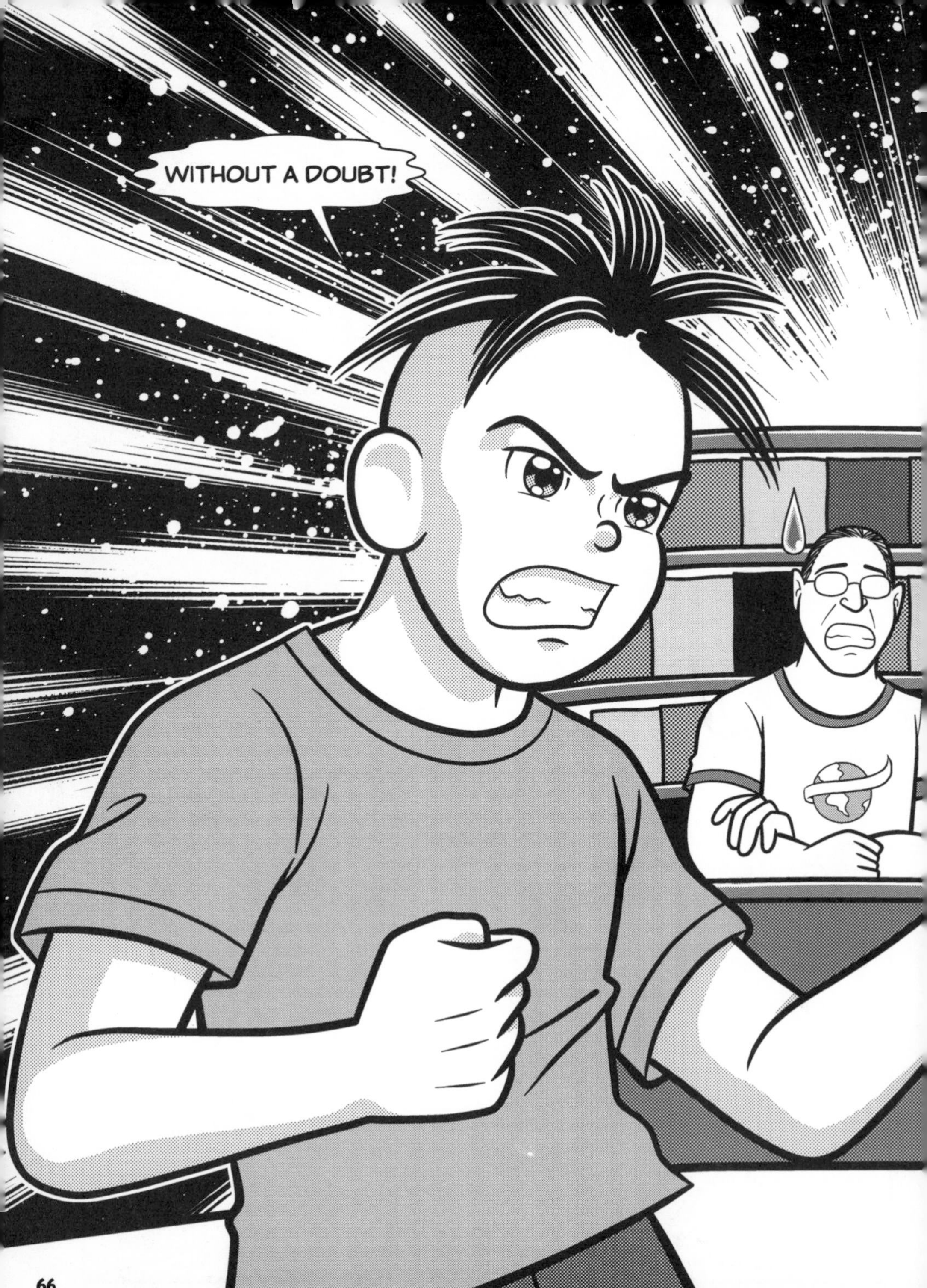
WITHOUT A DOUBT!

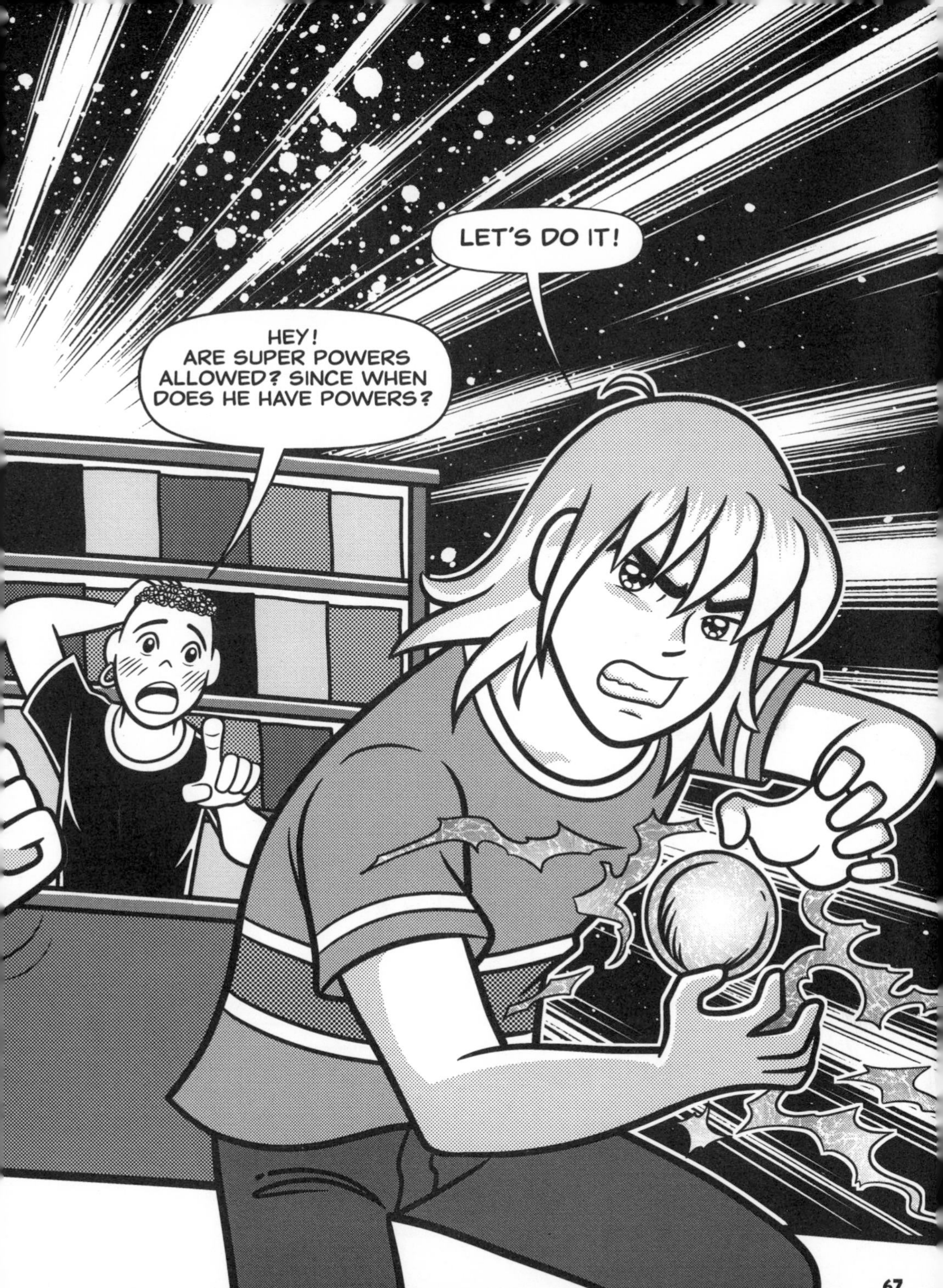
LET'S DO IT!
HEY! ARE SUPER POWERS ALLOWED? SINCE WHEN DOES HE HAVE POWERS?

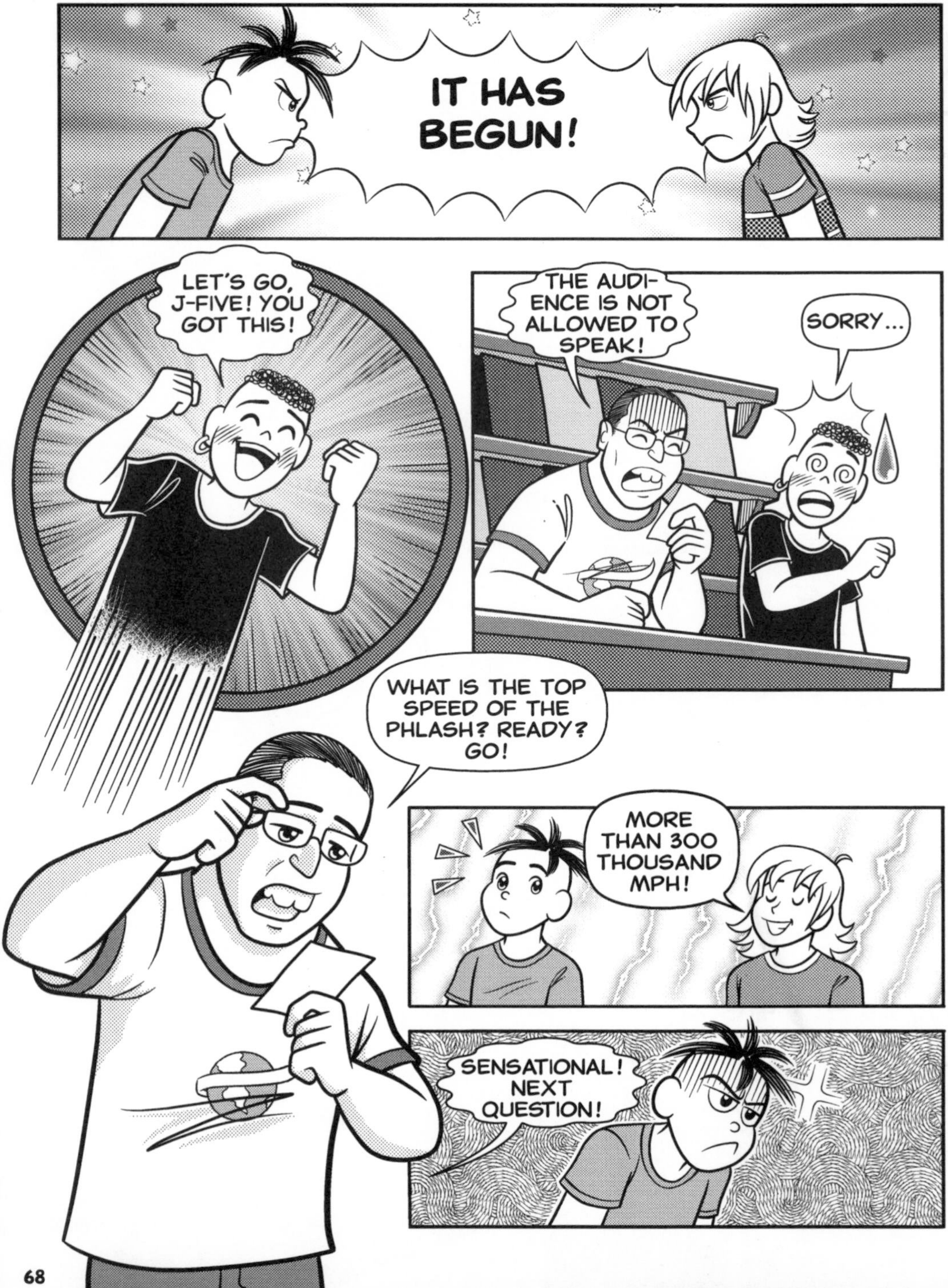
IT HAS BEGUN!
LET'S GO, J-FIVE! YOU GOT THIS!
THE AUDI-ENCE IS NOT ALLOWED TO SPEAK!
SORRY...
WHAT IS THE TOP SPEED OF THE PHLASH? READY? GO!
MORE THAN 300 THOUSAND MPH!
SENSATIONAL! NEXT QUESTION!

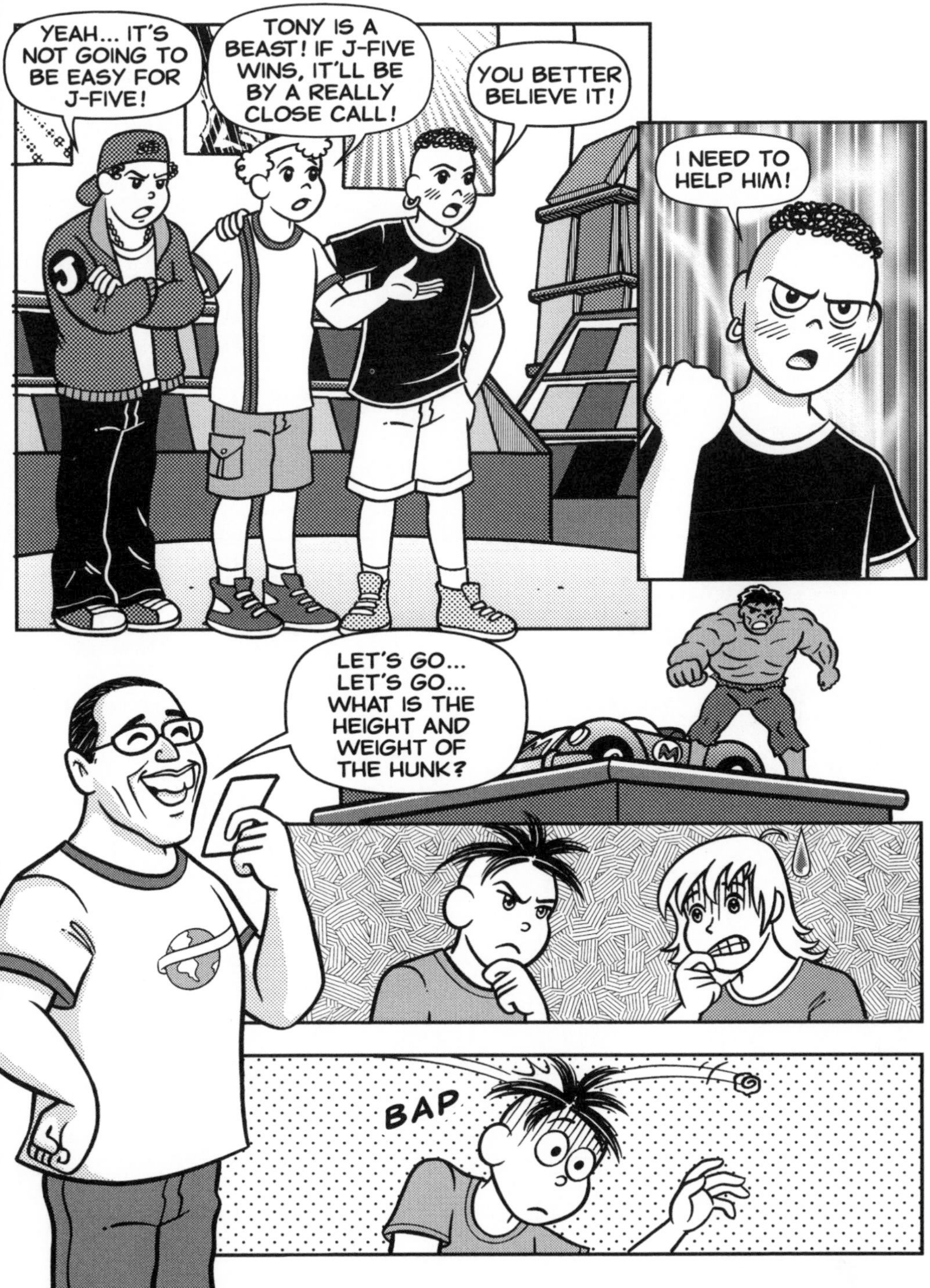
YEAH... IT'S NOT GOING TO BE EASY FOR J-FIVE!
TONY IS A BEAST! IF J-FIVE WINS, IT'LL BE BY A REALLY CLOSE CALL!
YOU BETTER BELIEVE IT!
I NEED TO HELP HIM!
LET'S GO... LET'S GO... WHAT IS THE HEIGHT AND WEIGHT OF THE HUNK?
BAP

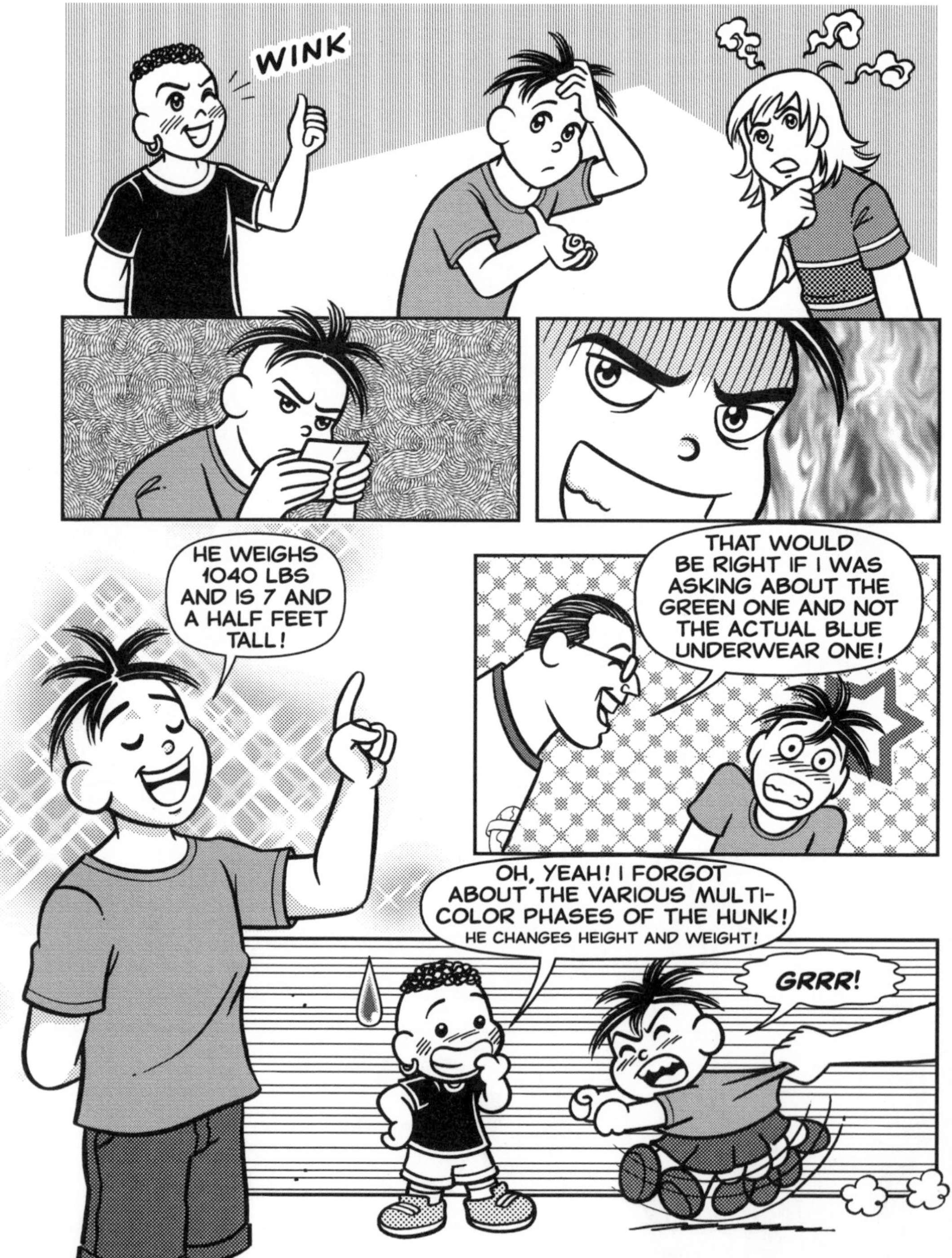
WINK
HE WEIGHS 1040 LBS AND IS 7 AND A HALF FEET TALL!
THAT WOULD BE RIGHT IF I WAS ASKING ABOUT THE GREEN ONE AND NOT THE ACTUAL BLUE UNDERWEAR ONE!
OH, YEAH! I FORGOT ABOUT THE VARIOUS MULTI-COLOR PHASES OF THE HUNK! HE CHANGES HEIGHT AND WEIGHT!
GRRR!

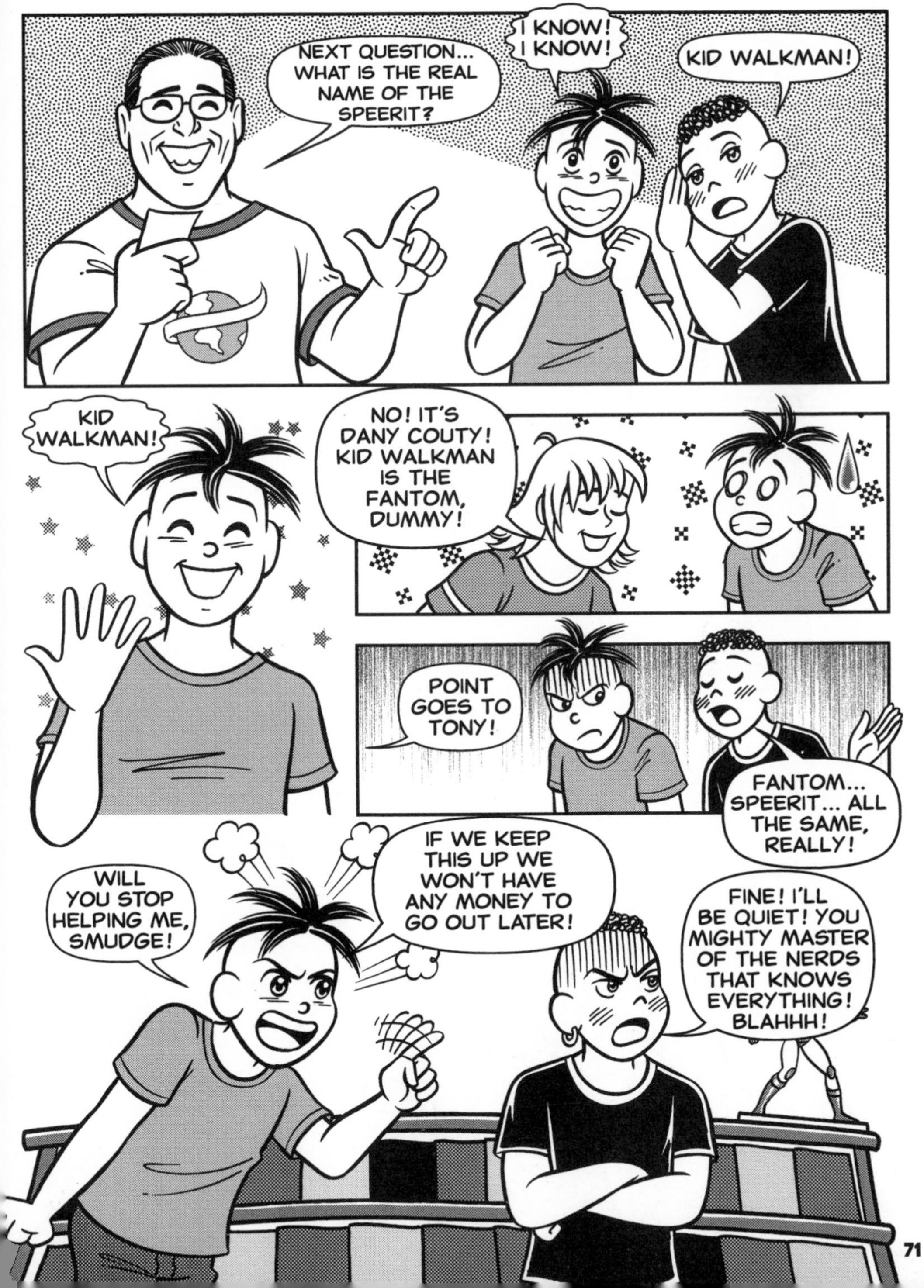
NEXT QUESTION... WHAT IS THE REAL NAME OF THE SPEERIT?
I KNOW! I KNOW!
KID WALKMAN!
KID WALKMAN!
NO! IT'S DANY COUTY! KID WALKMAN IS THE FANTOM, DUMMY!
POINT GOES TO TONY!
FANTOM... SPEERIT... ALL THE SAME, REALLY!
WILL YOU STOP HELPING ME, SMUDGE!
IF WE KEEP THIS UP WE WON'T HAVE ANY MONEY TO GO OUT LATER!
FINE! I'LL BE QUIET! YOU MIGHTY MASTER OF THE NERDS THAT KNOWS EVERYTHING! BLAHHH!

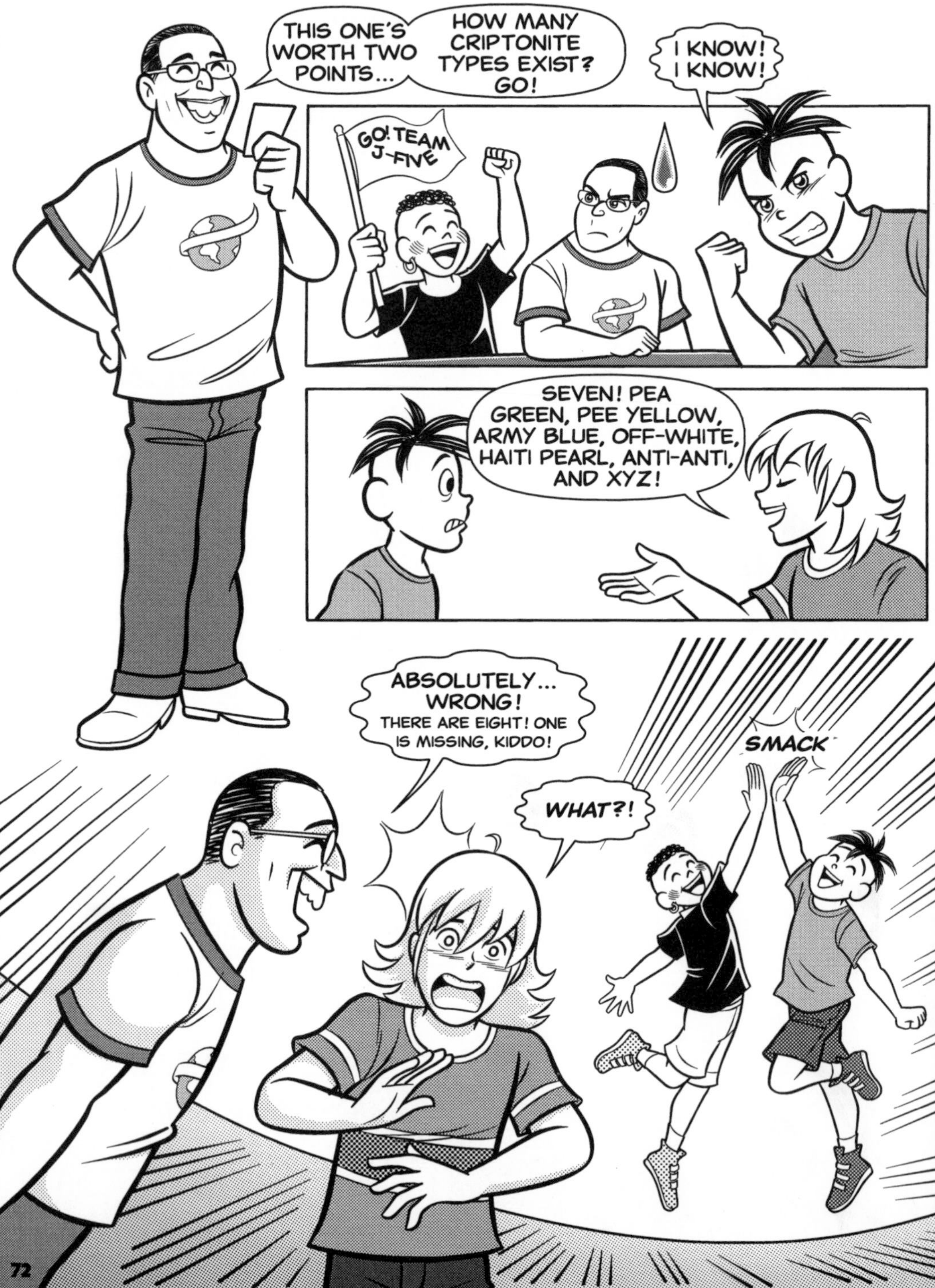
THIS ONE'S WORTH TWO POINTS...
HOW MANY CRIPTONITE TYPES EXIST? GO!
GO! TEAM J-FIVE
I KNOW! I KNOW!
SEVEN! PEA GREEN, PEE YELLOW, ARMY BLUE, OFF-WHITE, HAITI PEARL, ANTI-ANTI, AND XYZ!
ABSOLUTELY... WRONG! THERE ARE EIGHT! ONE IS MISSING, KIDDO!
WHAT?!
SMACK

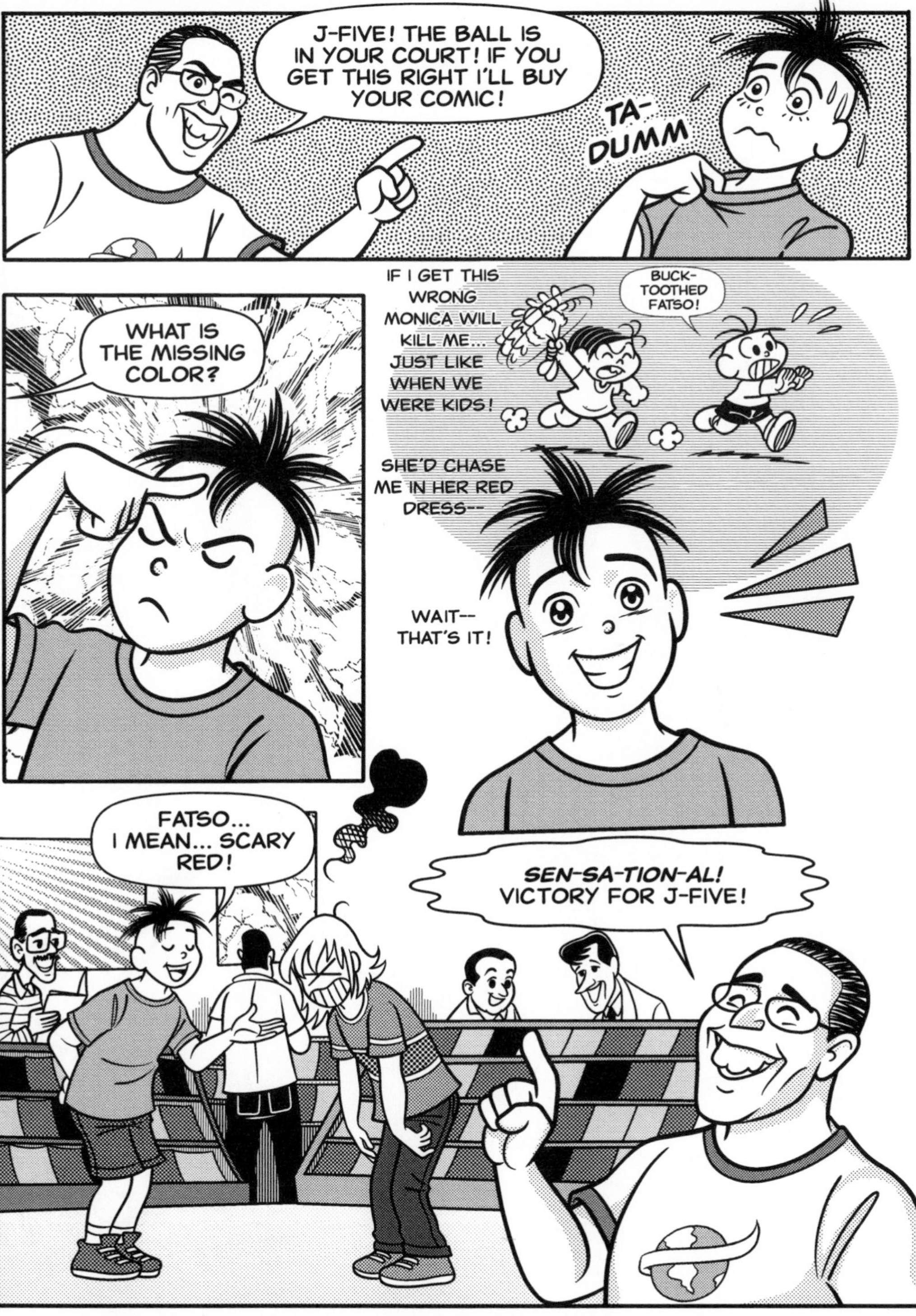
J-FIVE! THE BALL IS IN YOUR COURT! IF YOU GET THIS RIGHT I'LL BUY YOUR COMIC!
TA-DUMM
WHAT IS THE MISSING COLOR?
IF I GET THIS WRONG MONICA WILL KILL ME... JUST LIKE WHEN WE WERE KIDS!
BUCK-TOOTHED FATSO!
SHE'D CHASE ME IN HER RED DRESS--
WAIT-- THAT'S IT!
FATSO... I MEAN... SCARY RED!
SEN-SA-TION-AL! VICTORY FOR J-FIVE!

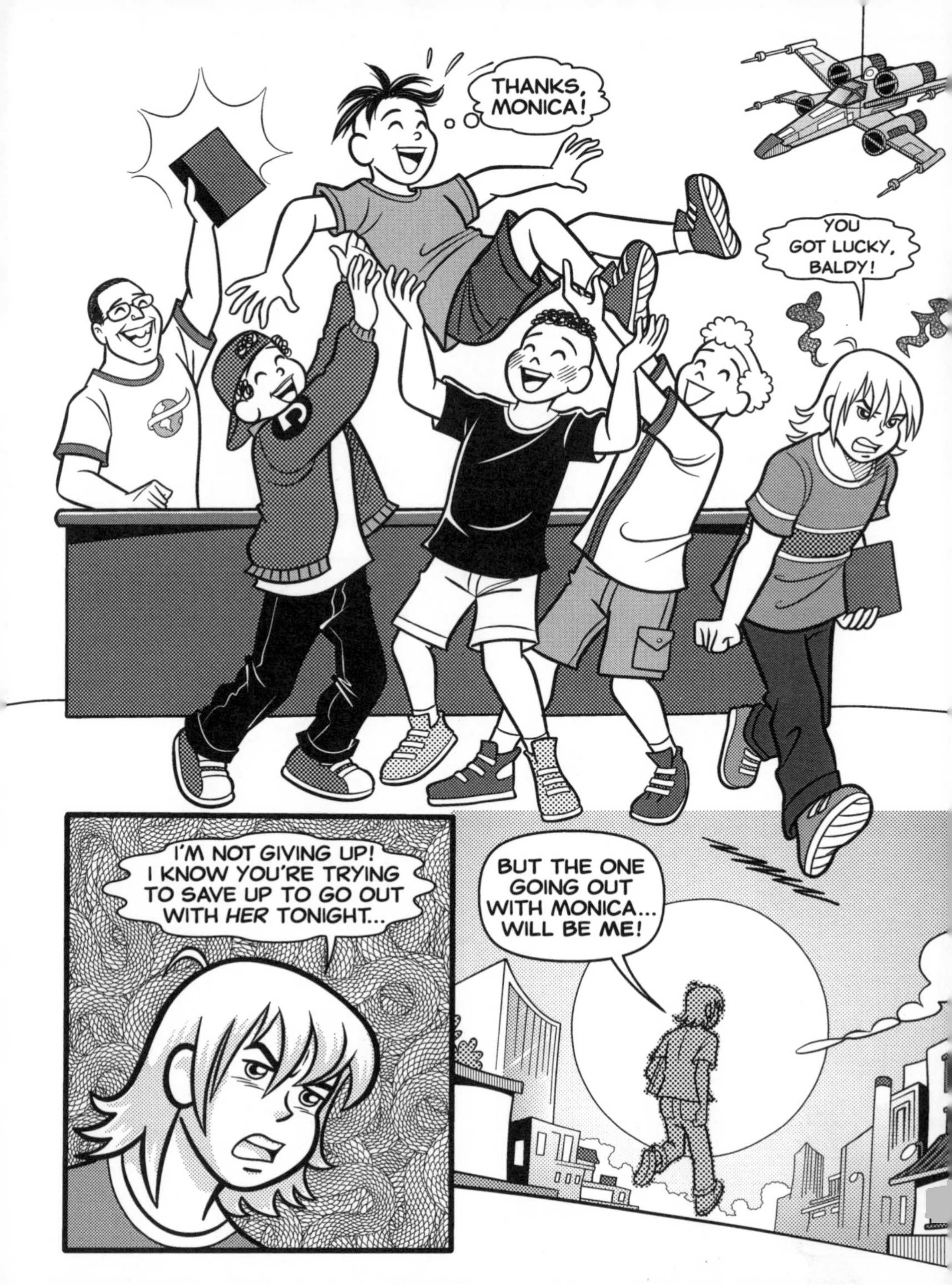
THANKS, MONICA!
YOU GOT LUCKY, BALDY!
I'M NOT GIVING UP! I KNOW YOU'RE TRYING TO SAVE UP TO GO OUT WITH *HER* TONIGHT...
BUT THE ONE GOING OUT WITH MONICA... WILL BE ME!

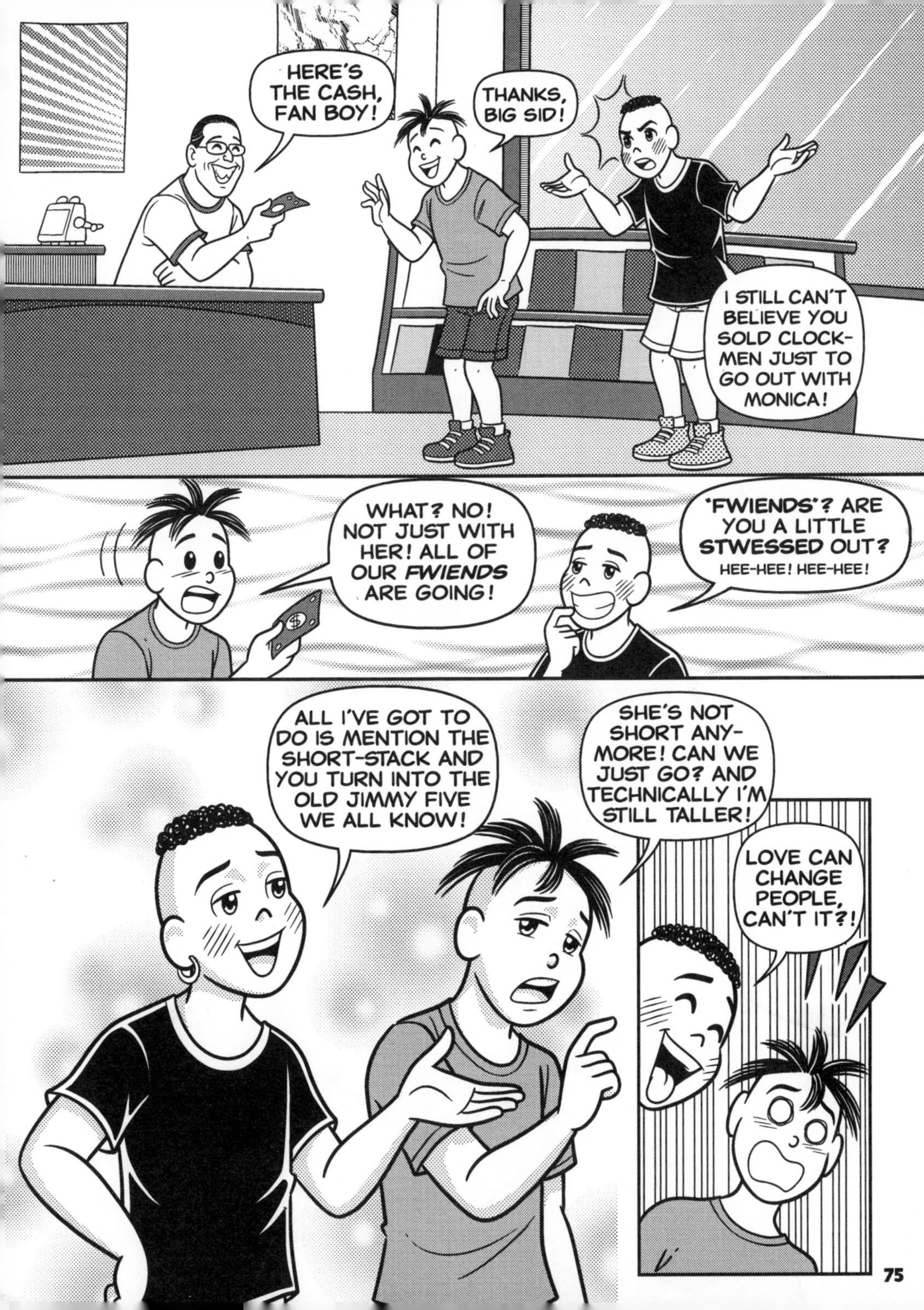
HERE'S THE CASH, FAN BOY!
THANKS, BIG SID!
I STILL CAN'T BELIEVE YOU SOLD CLOCK-MEN JUST TO GO OUT WITH MONICA!
WHAT? NO! NOT JUST WITH HER! ALL OF OUR FWIENDS ARE GOING!
'FWIENDS'? ARE YOU A LITTLE STWESSED OUT?
HEE-HEE! HEE-HEE!
ALL I'VE GOT TO DO IS MENTION THE SHORT-STACK AND YOU TURN INTO THE OLD JIMMY FIVE WE ALL KNOW!
SHE'S NOT SHORT ANY-MORE! CAN WE JUST GO? AND TECHNICALLY I'M STILL TALLER!
LOVE CAN CHANGE PEOPLE, CAN'T IT?!

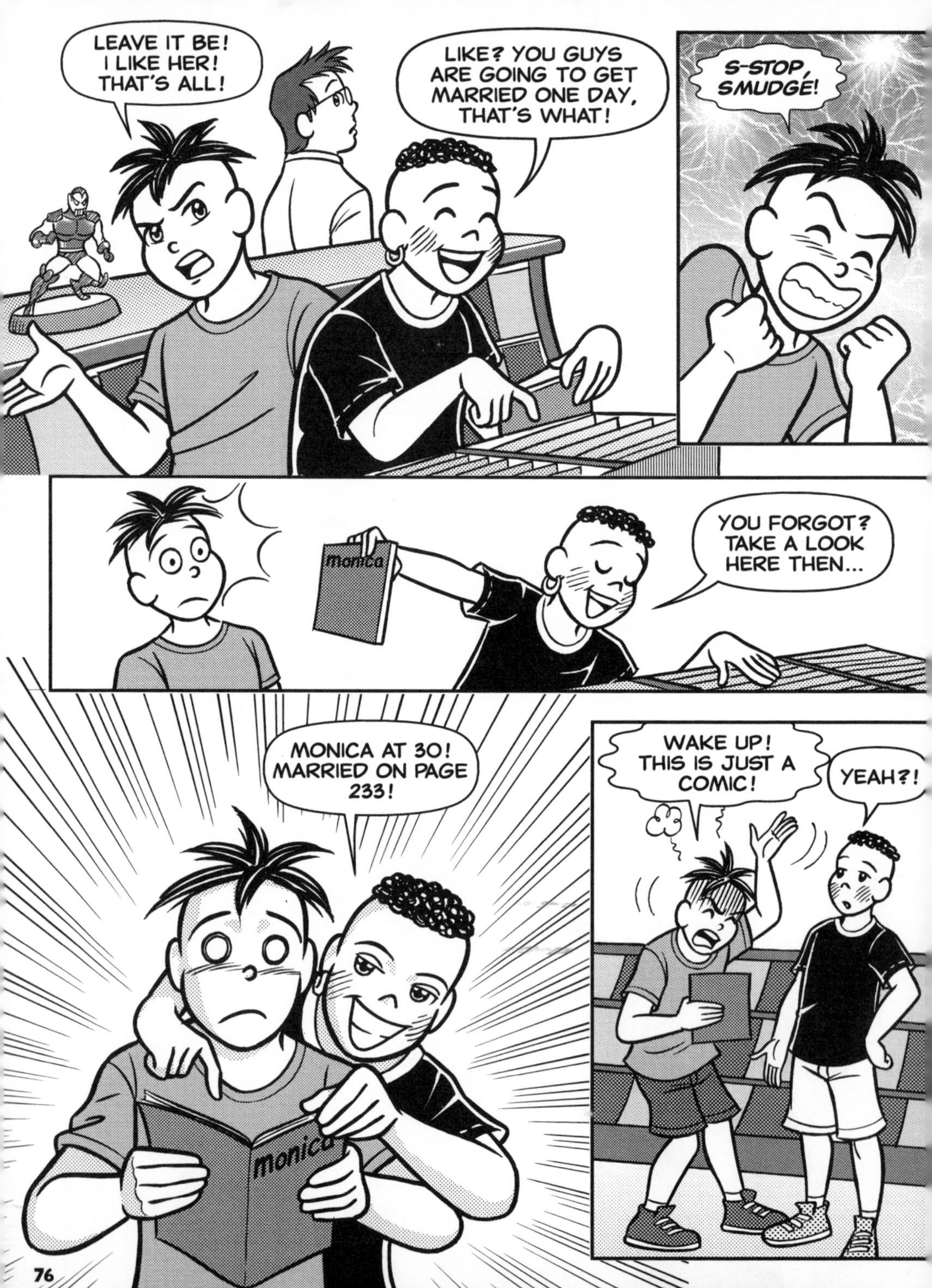
LEAVE IT BE! I LIKE HER! THAT'S ALL!
LIKE? YOU GUYS ARE GOING TO GET MARRIED ONE DAY, THAT'S WHAT!
S-STOP, SMUDGE!
monica
YOU FORGOT? TAKE A LOOK HERE THEN...
MONICA AT 30! MARRIED ON PAGE 233!
monica
WAKE UP! THIS IS JUST A COMIC!
YEAH?!

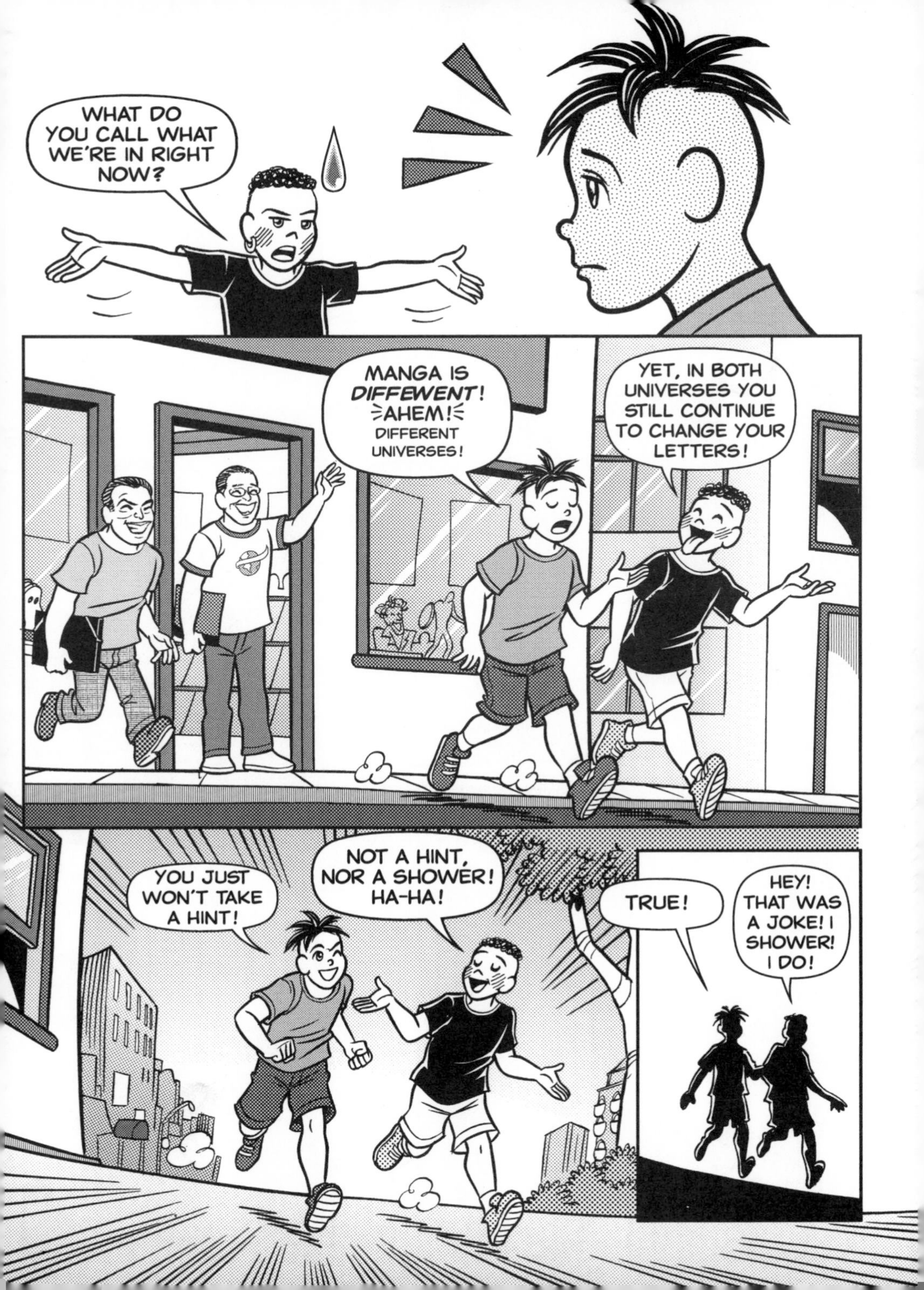
WHAT DO YOU CALL WHAT WE'RE IN RIGHT NOW?
MANGA IS DIFFEWENT! AHEM! DIFFERENT UNIVERSES!
YET, IN BOTH UNIVERSES YOU STILL CONTINUE TO CHANGE YOUR LETTERS!
YOU JUST WON'T TAKE A HINT!
NOT A HINT, NOR A SHOWER! HA-HA!
TRUE!
HEY! THAT WAS A JOKE! I SHOWER! I DO!

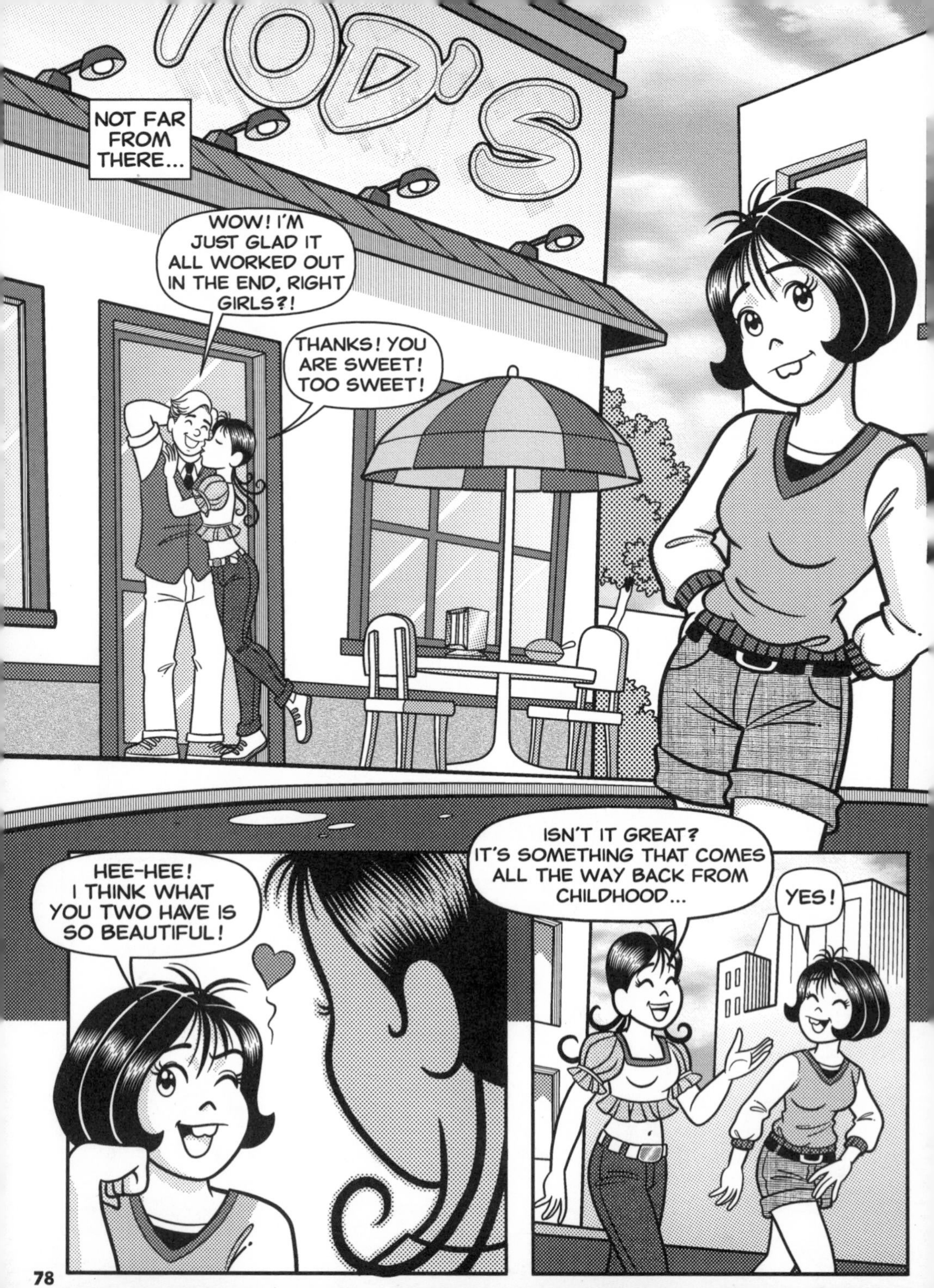
NOT FAR FROM THERE...
WOW! I'M JUST GLAD IT ALL WORKED OUT IN THE END, RIGHT GIRLS?!
THANKS! YOU ARE SWEET! TOO SWEET!
HEE-HEE! I THINK WHAT YOU TWO HAVE IS SO BEAUTIFUL!
ISN'T IT GREAT? IT'S SOMETHING THAT COMES ALL THE WAY BACK FROM CHILDHOOD...
YES!

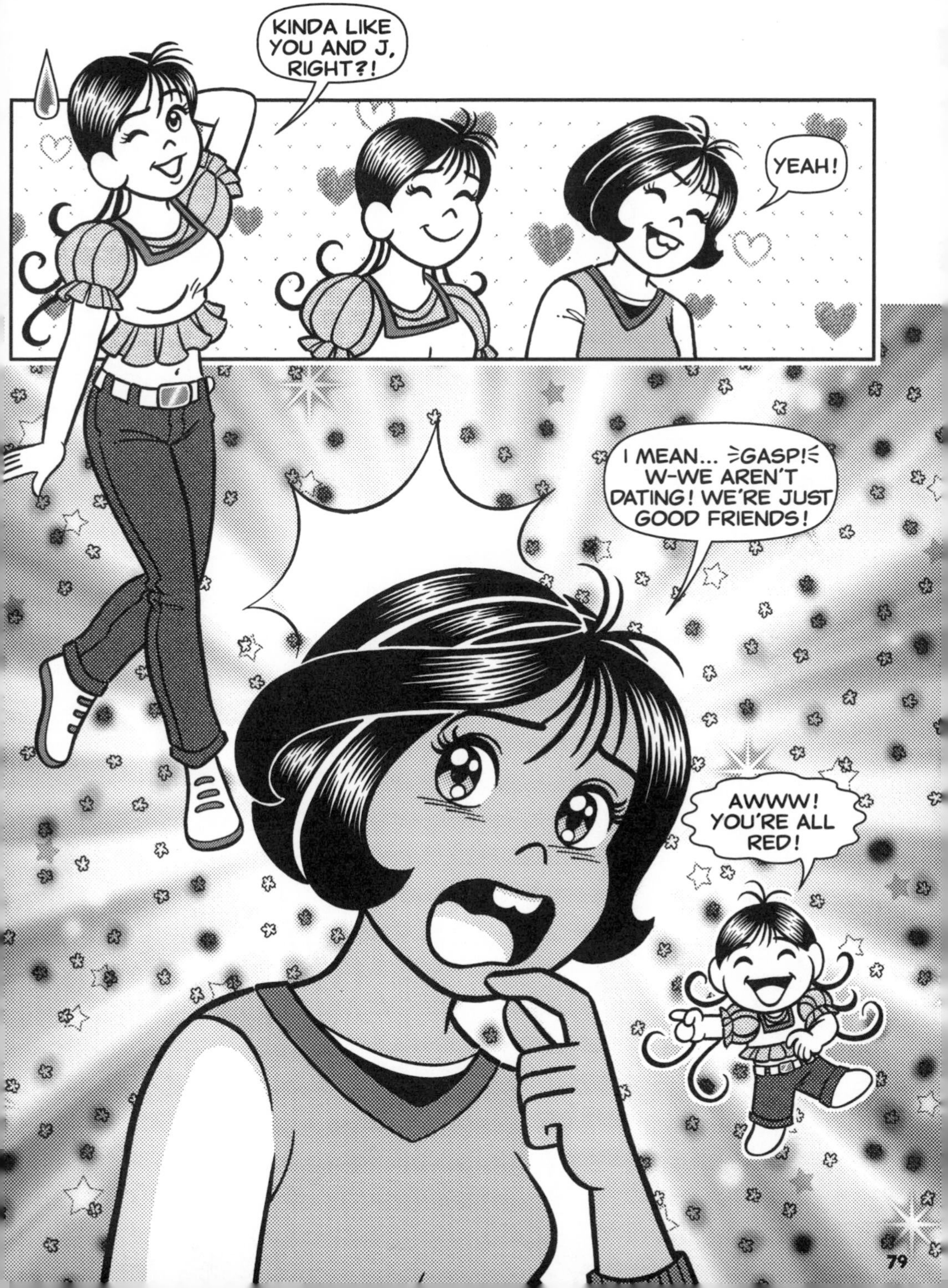
KINDA LIKE YOU AND J, RIGHT?!
YEAH!
I MEAN... GASP! W-WE AREN'T DATING! WE'RE JUST GOOD FRIENDS!
AWWW! YOU'RE ALL RED!

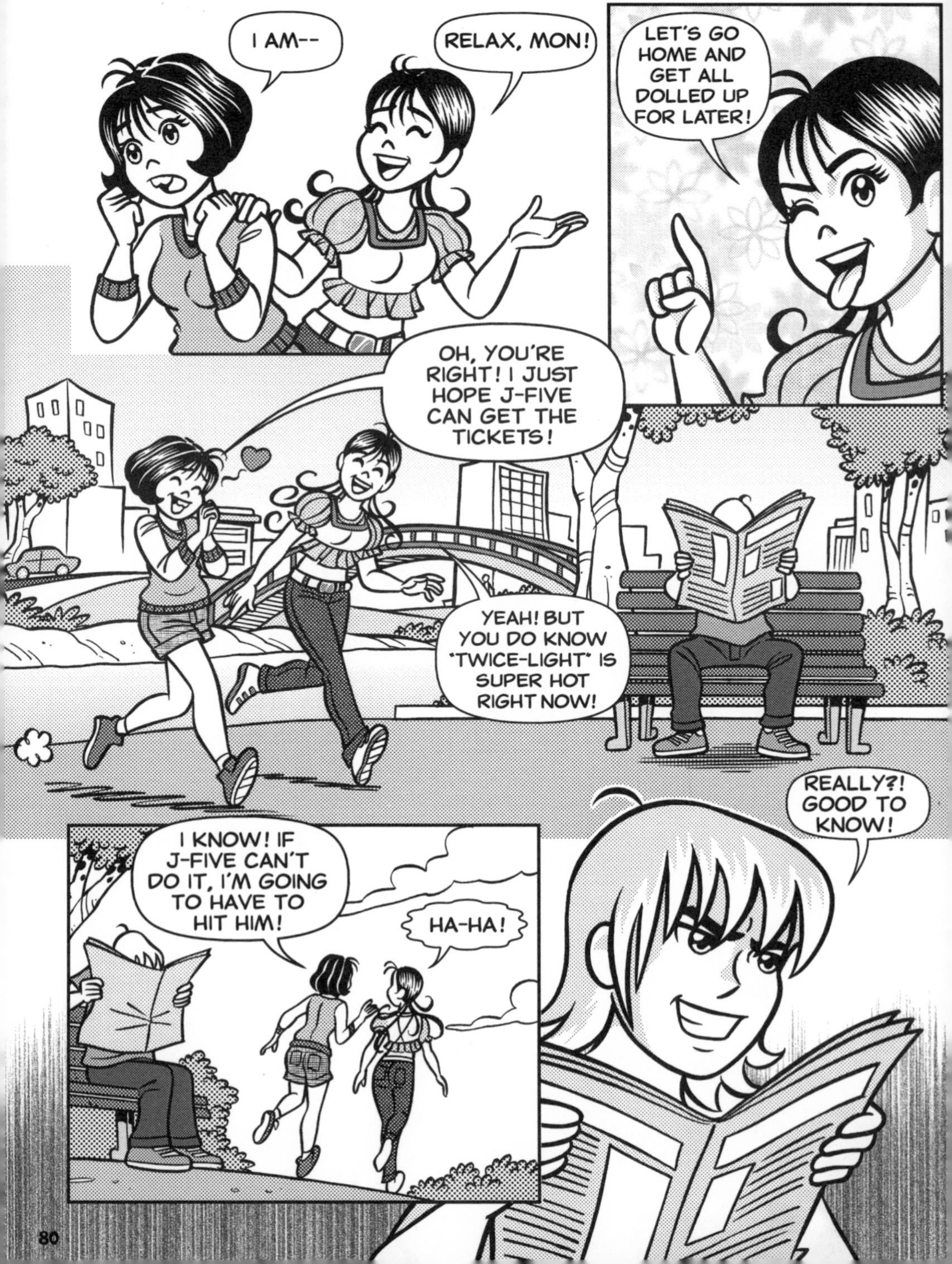
I AM--
RELAX, MON!
LET'S GO HOME AND GET ALL DOLLED UP FOR LATER!
OH, YOU'RE RIGHT! I JUST HOPE J-FIVE CAN GET THE TICKETS!
YEAH! BUT YOU DO KNOW "TWICE-LIGHT" IS SUPER HOT RIGHT NOW!
I KNOW! IF J-FIVE CAN'T DO IT, I'M GOING TO HAVE TO HIT HIM!
HA-HA!
REALLY?! GOOD TO KNOW!

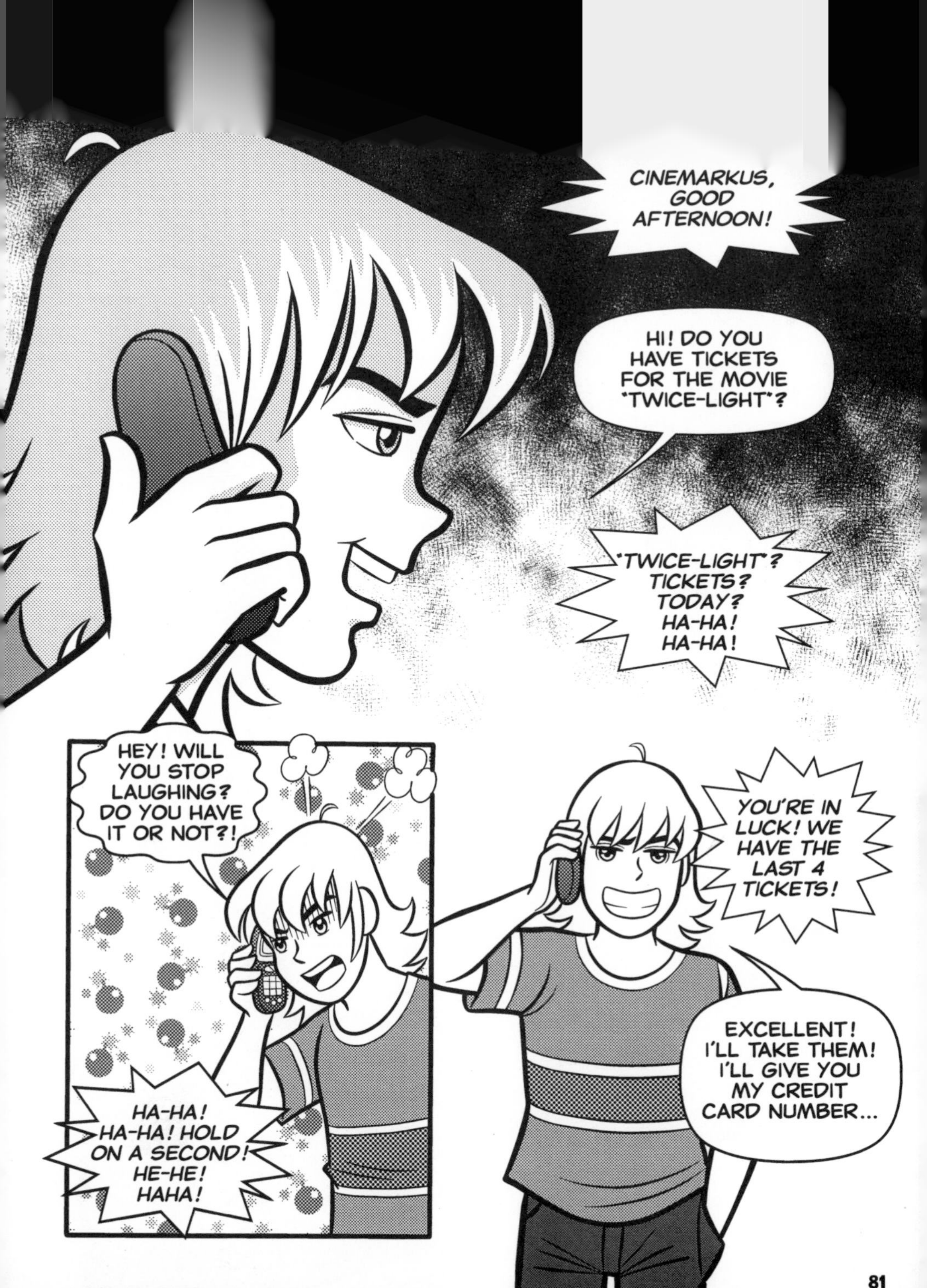
CINEMARKUS, GOOD AFTERNOON!
HI! DO YOU HAVE TICKETS FOR THE MOVIE "TWICE-LIGHT"?
"TWICE-LIGHT"? TICKETS? TODAY? HA-HA! HA-HA!
HEY! WILL YOU STOP LAUGHING? DO YOU HAVE IT OR NOT?!
YOU'RE IN LUCK! WE HAVE THE LAST 4 TICKETS!
EXCELLENT! I'LL TAKE THEM! I'LL GIVE YOU MY CREDIT CARD NUMBER...
HA-HA! HA-HA! HOLD ON A SECOND! HE-HE! HAHA!

CHAPTER 4 - ON THE WAY TO THE MALL

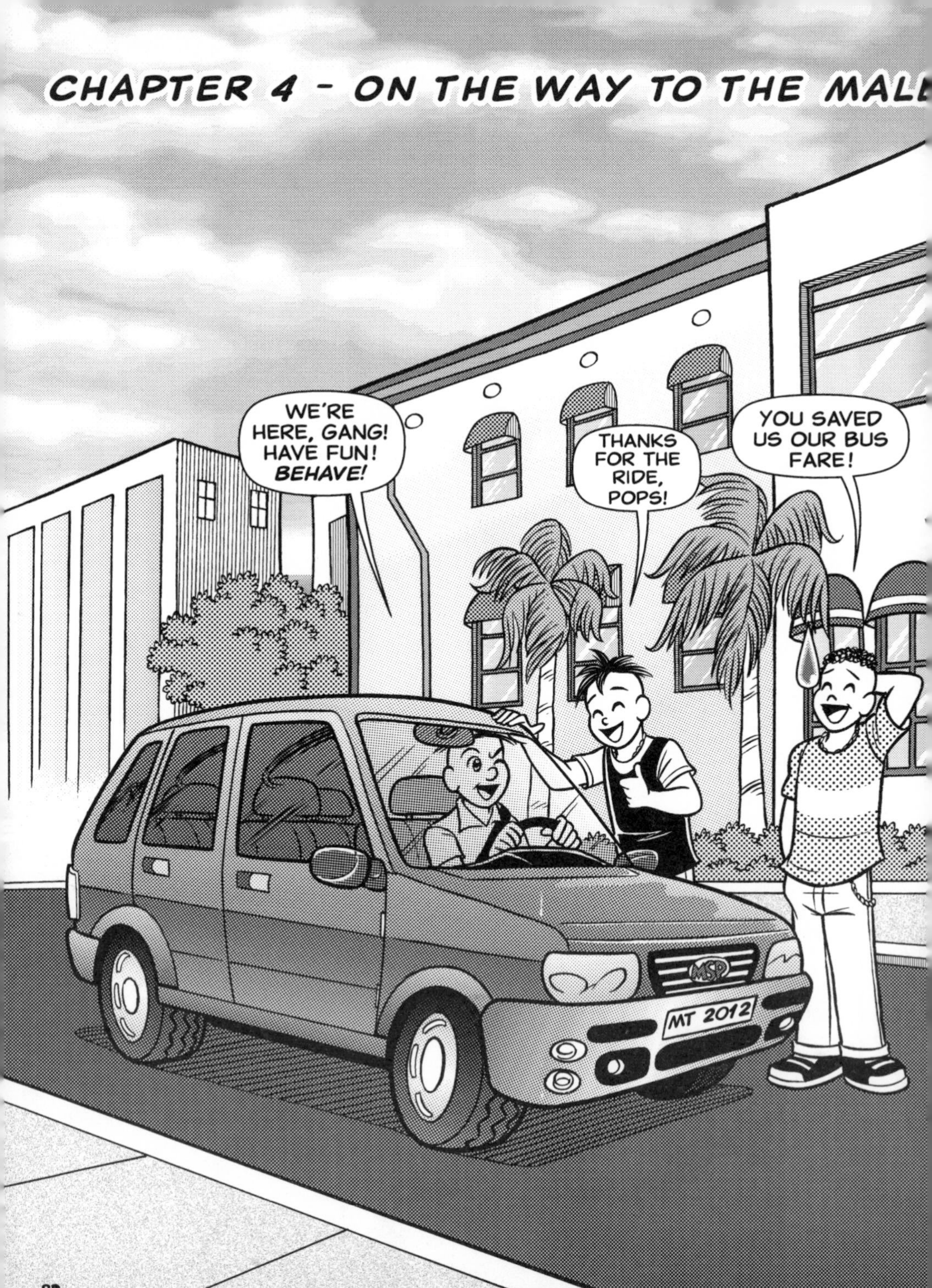
WE'RE HERE, GANG! HAVE FUN! *BEHAVE!*
THANKS FOR THE RIDE, POPS!
YOU SAVED US OUR BUS FARE!
MT 2012
MSP

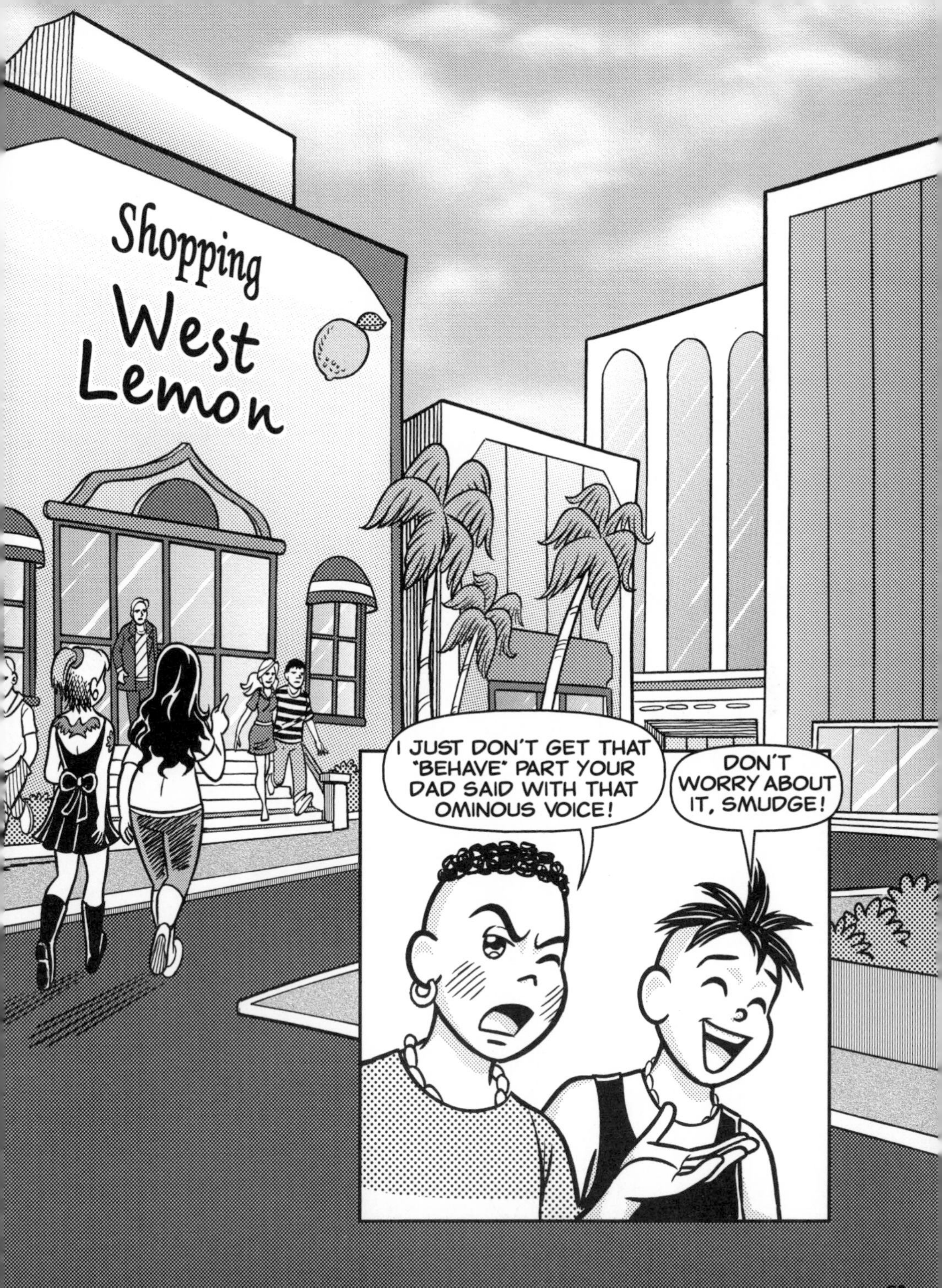
Shopping West Lemon
I JUST DON'T GET THAT "BEHAVE" PART YOUR DAD SAID WITH THAT OMINOUS VOICE!
DON'T WORRY ABOUT IT, SMUDGE!

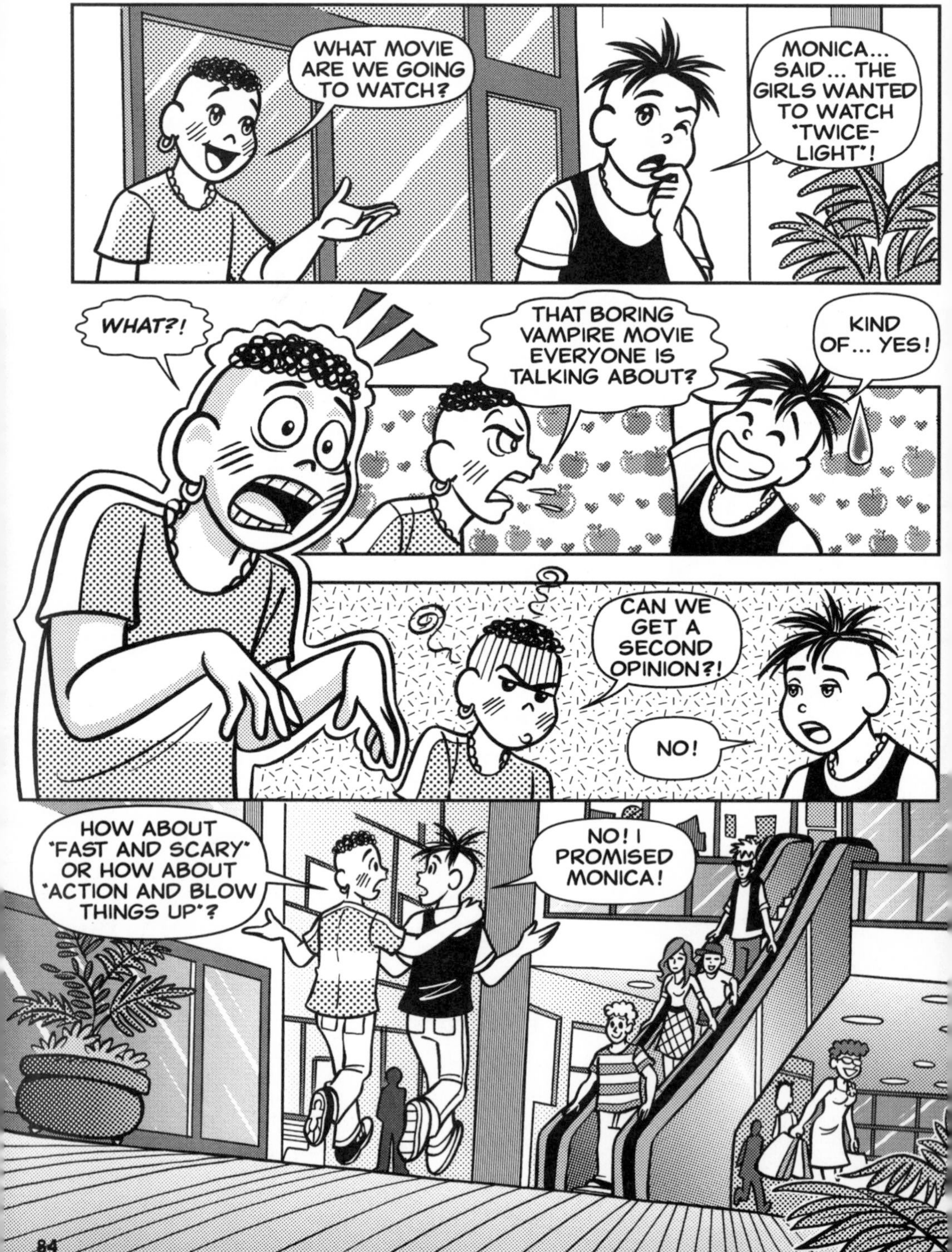
WHAT MOVIE ARE WE GOING TO WATCH?
MONICA... SAID... THE GIRLS WANTED TO WATCH "TWICE-LIGHT"!
WHAT?!
THAT BORING VAMPIRE MOVIE EVERYONE IS TALKING ABOUT?
KIND OF... YES!
CAN WE GET A SECOND OPINION?!
NO!
HOW ABOUT "FAST AND SCARY" OR HOW ABOUT "ACTION AND BLOW THINGS UP"?
NO! I PROMISED MONICA!

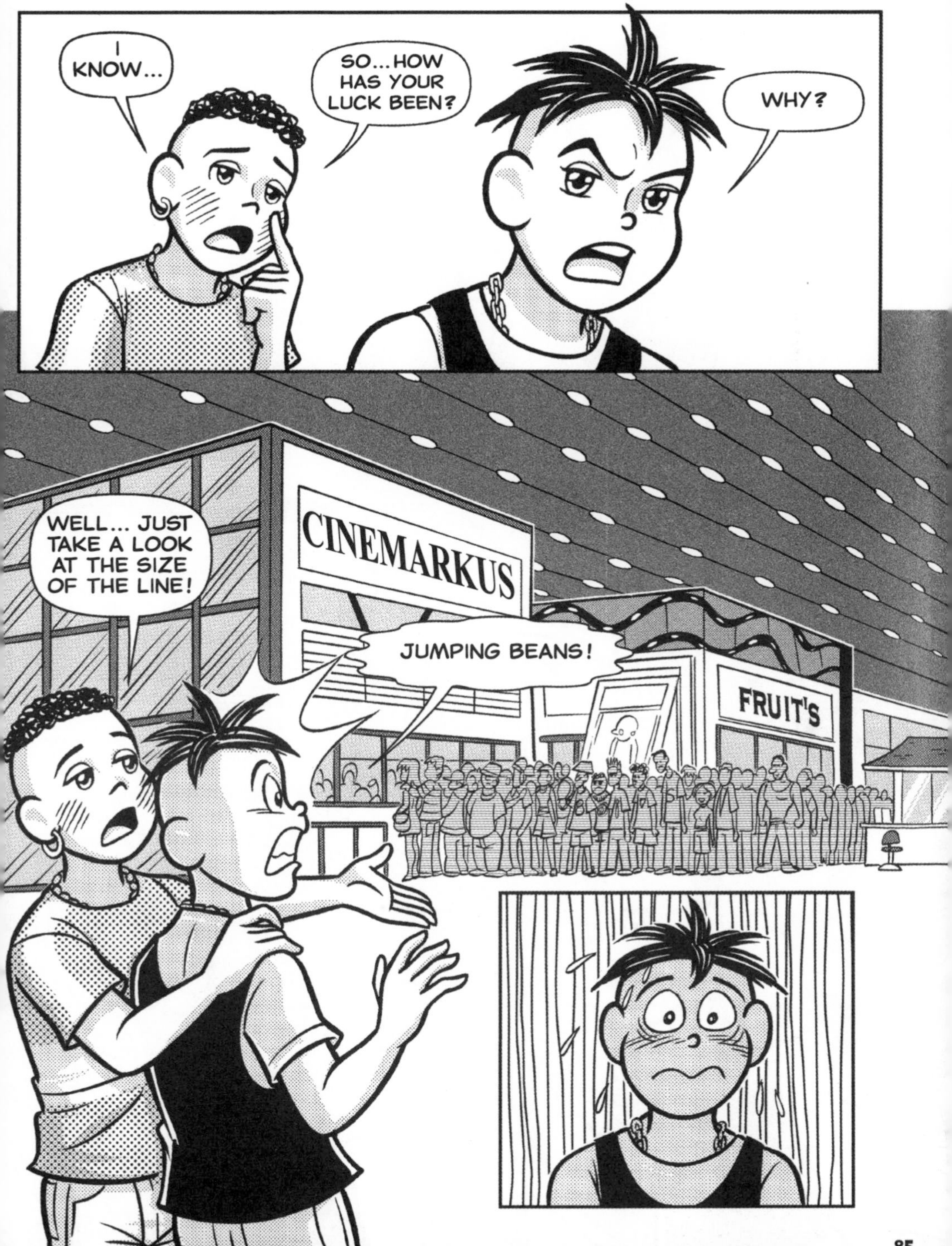
I KNOW...
SO...HOW HAS YOUR LUCK BEEN?
WHY?
CINEMARKUS
WELL... JUST TAKE A LOOK AT THE SIZE OF THE LINE!
JUMPING BEANS!
FRUIT'S

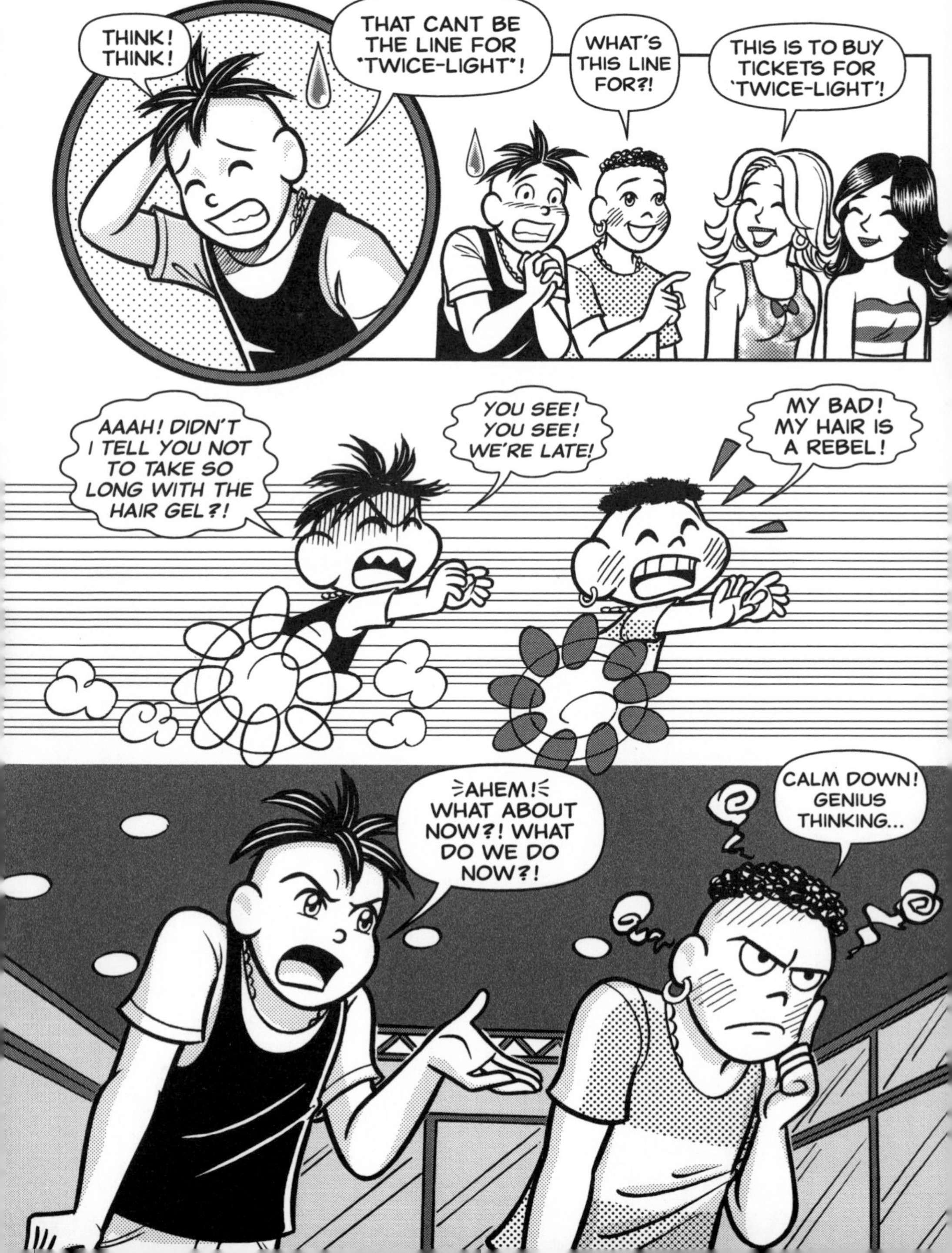
THINK! THINK!
THAT CANT BE THE LINE FOR "TWICE-LIGHT"!
WHAT'S THIS LINE FOR?!
THIS IS TO BUY TICKETS FOR 'TWICE-LIGHT'!
AAAH! DIDN'T I TELL YOU NOT TO TAKE SO LONG WITH THE HAIR GEL?!
YOU SEE! YOU SEE! WE'RE LATE!
MY BAD! MY HAIR IS A REBEL!
AHEM! WHAT ABOUT NOW?! WHAT DO WE DO NOW?!
CALM DOWN! GENIUS THINKING...

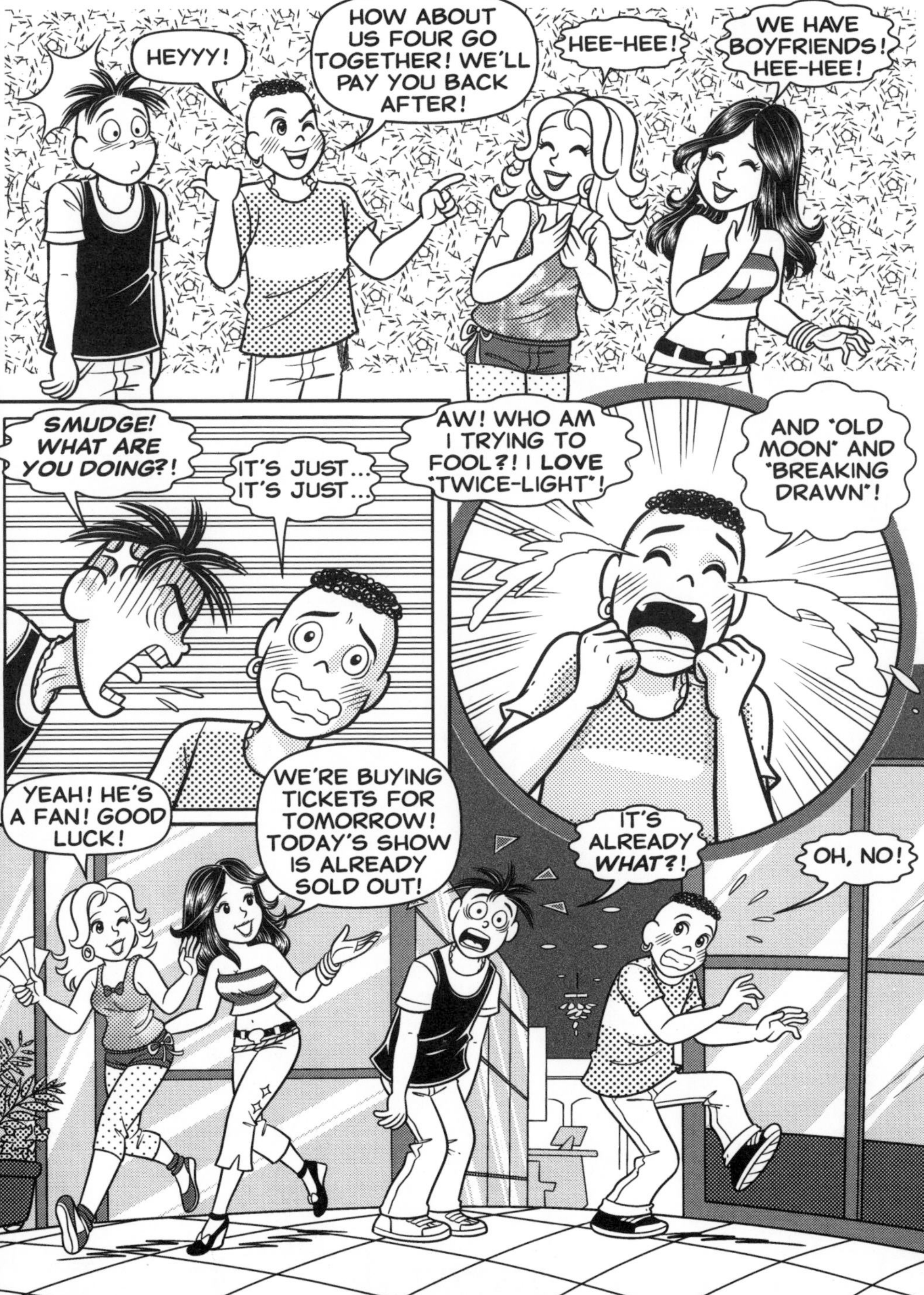
HEYYY!
HOW ABOUT US FOUR GO TOGETHER! WE'LL PAY YOU BACK AFTER!
HEE-HEE!
WE HAVE BOYFRIENDS! HEE-HEE!
SMUDGE! WHAT ARE YOU DOING?!
IT'S JUST... IT'S JUST...
AW! WHO AM I TRYING TO FOOL?! I LOVE "TWICE-LIGHT"!
AND "OLD MOON" AND "BREAKING DRAWN"!
YEAH! HE'S A FAN! GOOD LUCK!
WE'RE BUYING TICKETS FOR TOMORROW! TODAY'S SHOW IS ALREADY SOLD OUT!
IT'S ALREADY WHAT?!
OH, NO!

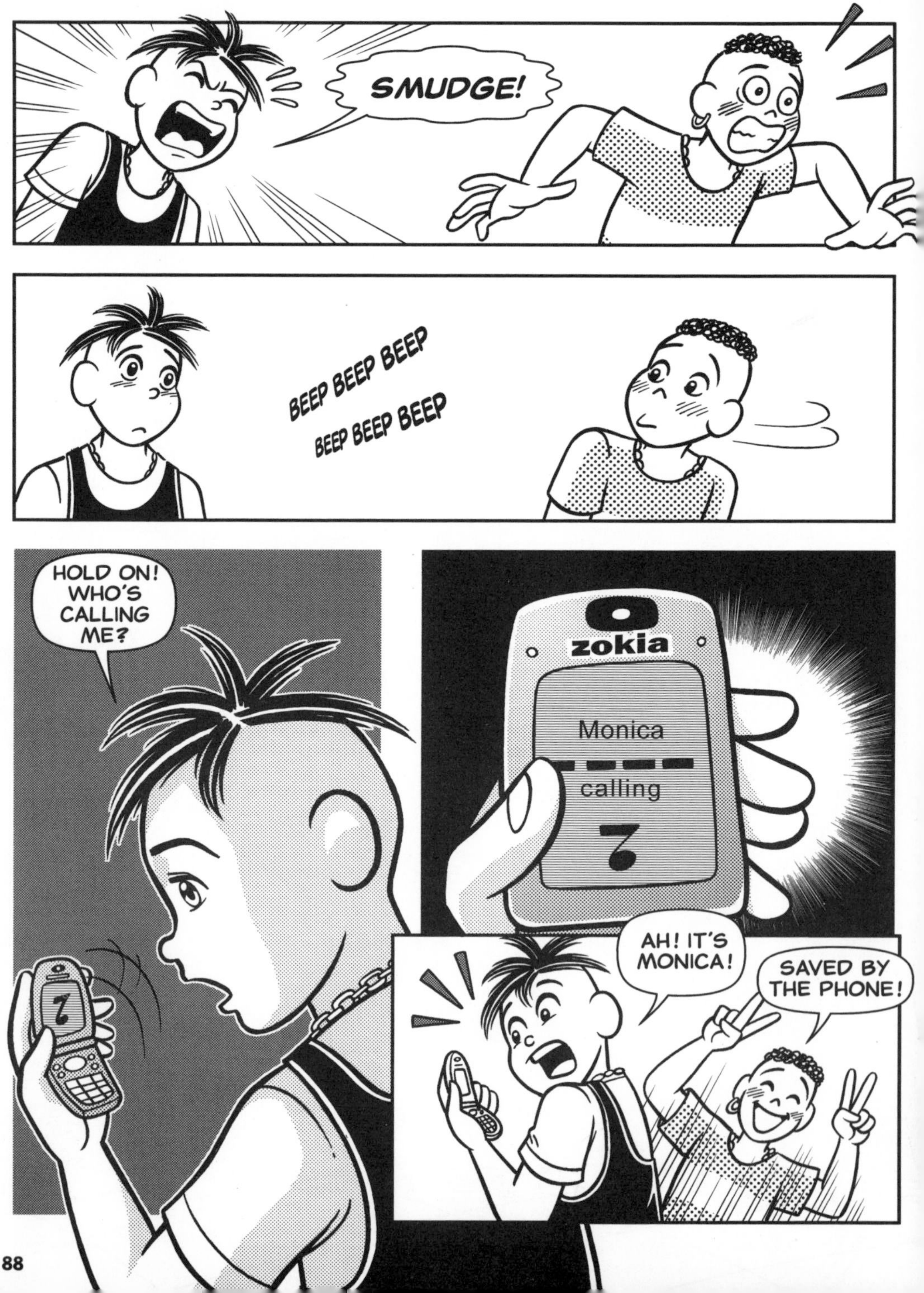
SMUDGE!
BEEP BEEP BEEP
BEEP BEEP BEEP
HOLD ON! WHO'S CALLING ME?
zokia
Monica
calling
AH! IT'S MONICA!
SAVED BY THE PHONE!

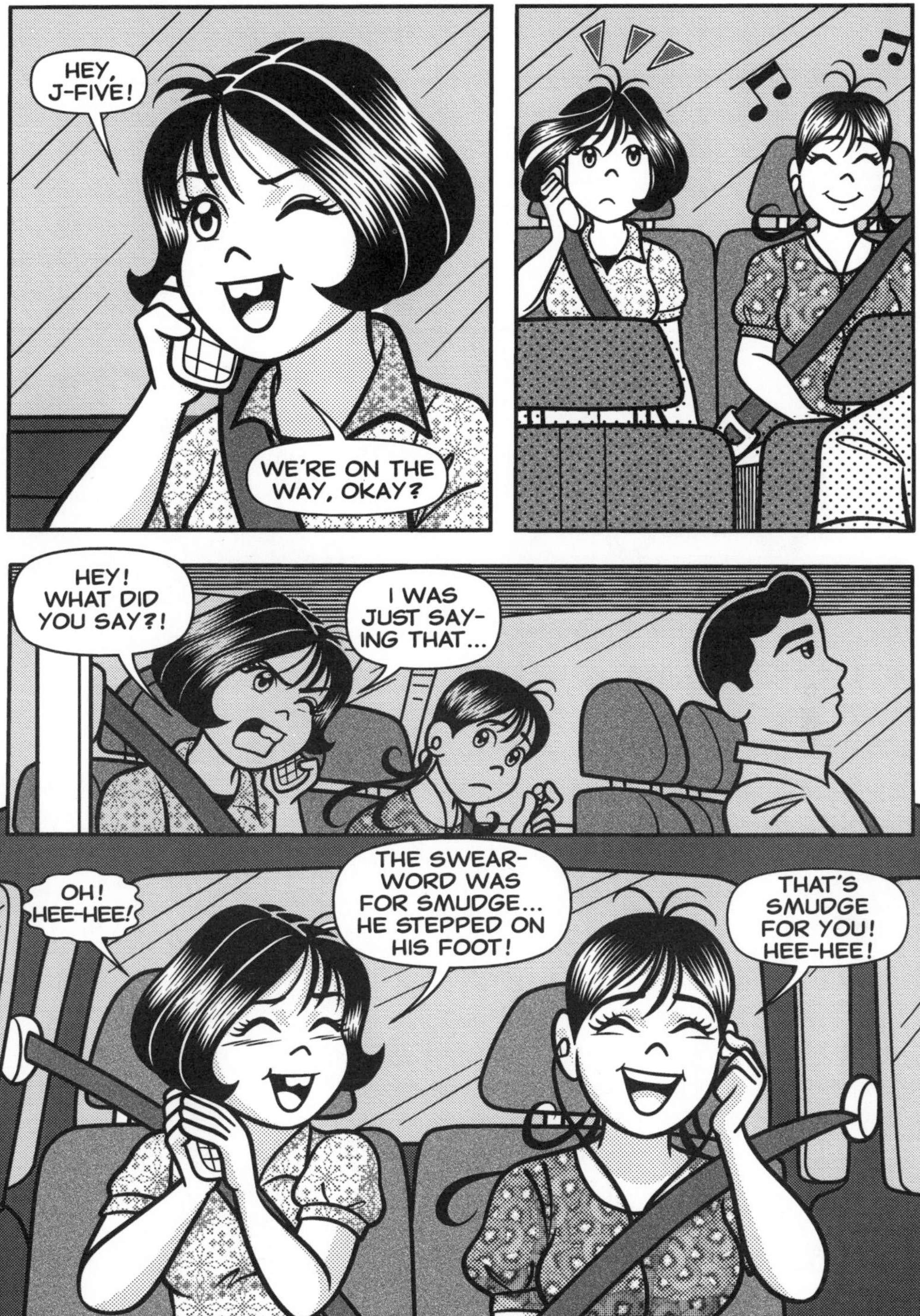
HEY, J-FIVE!
WE'RE ON THE WAY, OKAY?
HEY! WHAT DID YOU SAY?!
I WAS JUST SAY-ING THAT...
OH! HEE-HEE!
THE SWEAR-WORD WAS FOR SMUDGE... HE STEPPED ON HIS FOOT!
THAT'S SMUDGE FOR YOU! HEE-HEE!

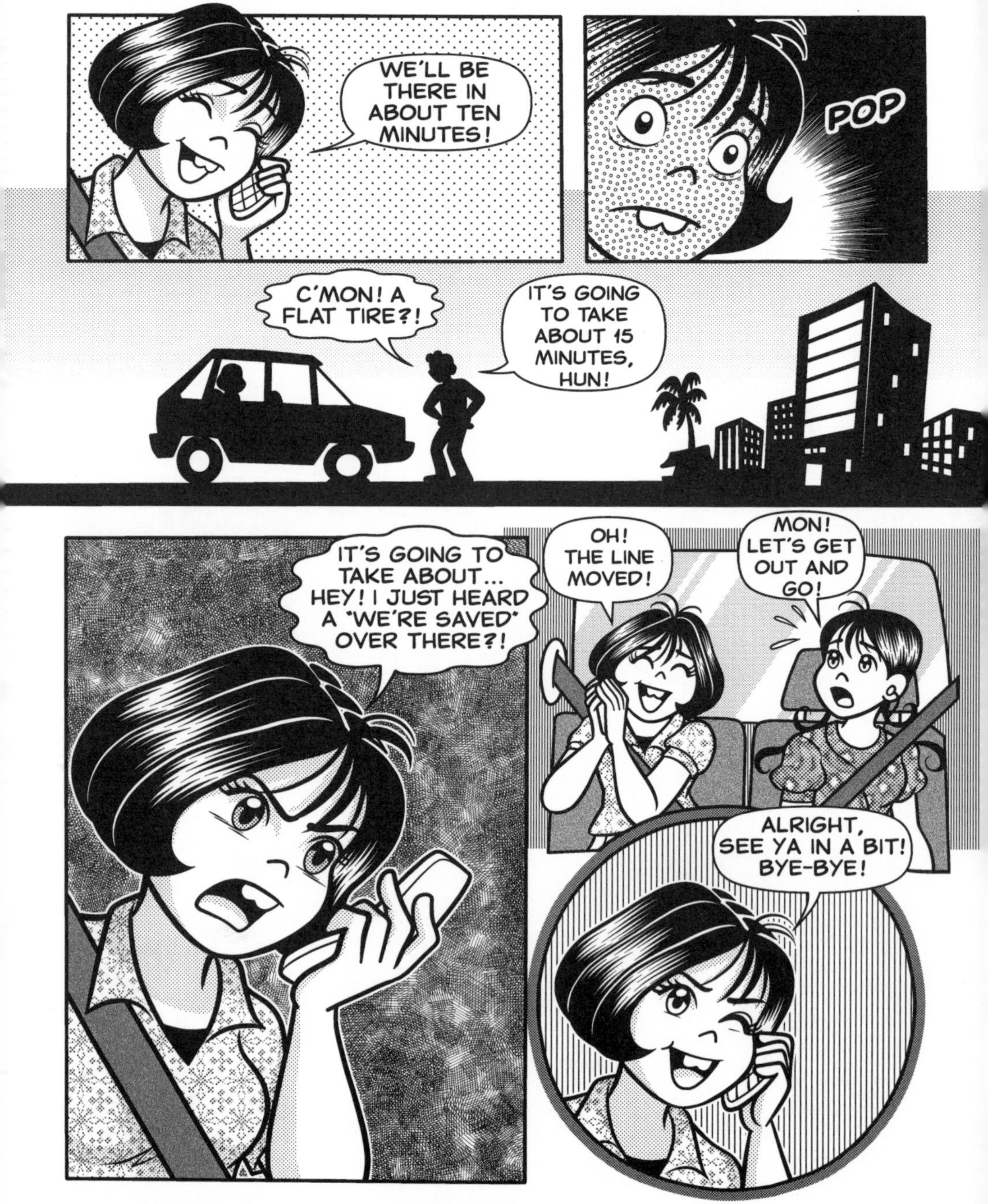
WE'LL BE THERE IN ABOUT TEN MINUTES!
POP
C'MON! A FLAT TIRE?!
IT'S GOING TO TAKE ABOUT 15 MINUTES, HUN!
IT'S GOING TO TAKE ABOUT... HEY! I JUST HEARD A "WE'RE SAVED" OVER THERE?!
OH! THE LINE MOVED!
MON! LET'S GET OUT AND GO!
ALRIGHT, SEE YA IN A BIT! BYE-BYE!

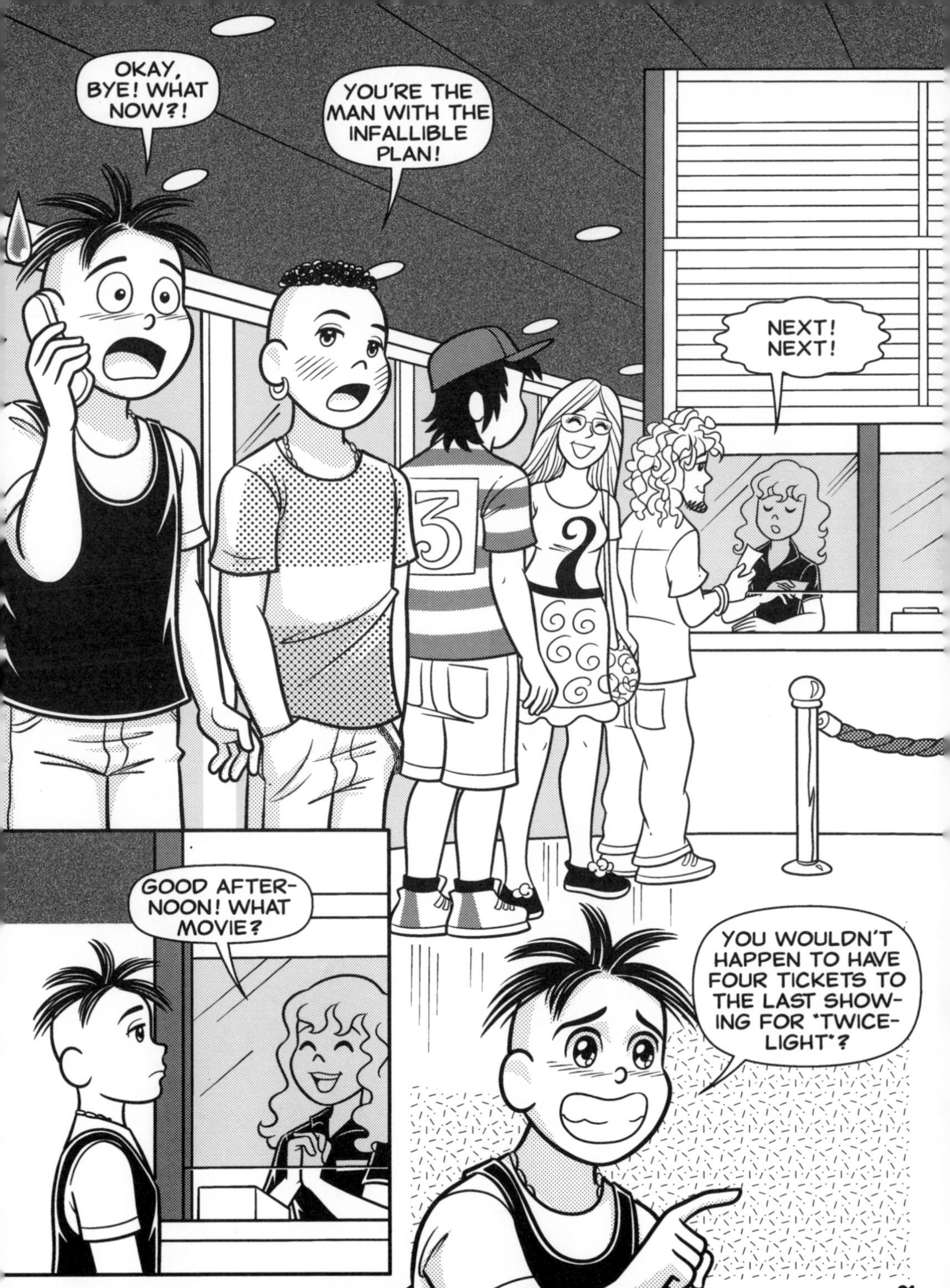
OKAY, BYE! WHAT NOW?!
YOU'RE THE MAN WITH THE INFALLIBLE PLAN!
NEXT! NEXT!
GOOD AFTER-NOON! WHAT MOVIE?
YOU WOULDN'T HAPPEN TO HAVE FOUR TICKETS TO THE LAST SHOW-ING FOR "TWICE-LIGHT"?

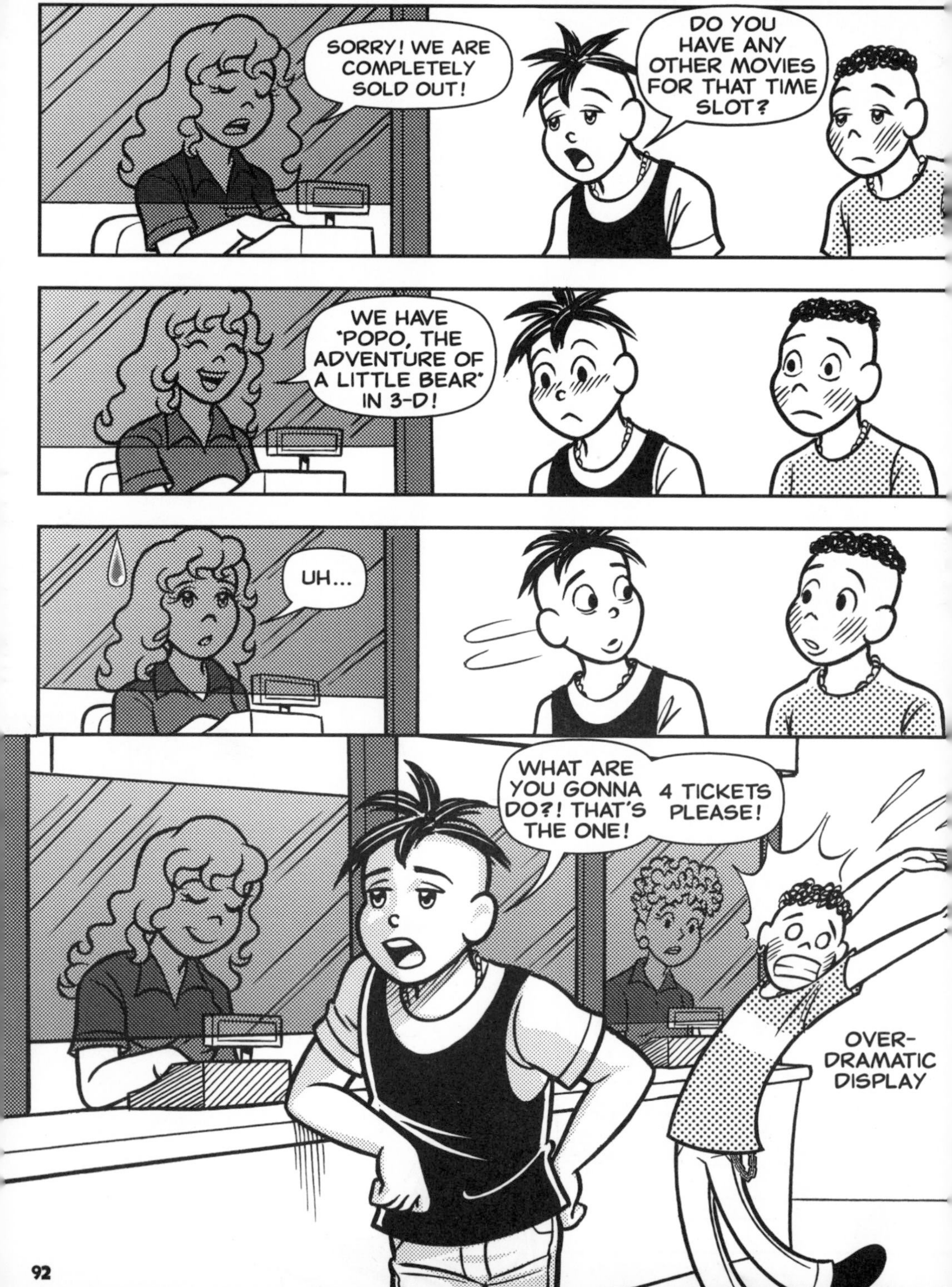
SORRY! WE ARE COMPLETELY SOLD OUT!
DO YOU HAVE ANY OTHER MOVIES FOR THAT TIME SLOT?
WE HAVE "POPO, THE ADVENTURE OF A LITTLE BEAR" IN 3-D!
UH...
WHAT ARE YOU GONNA DO?! THAT'S THE ONE!
4 TICKETS PLEASE!
OVER-DRAMATIC DISPLAY

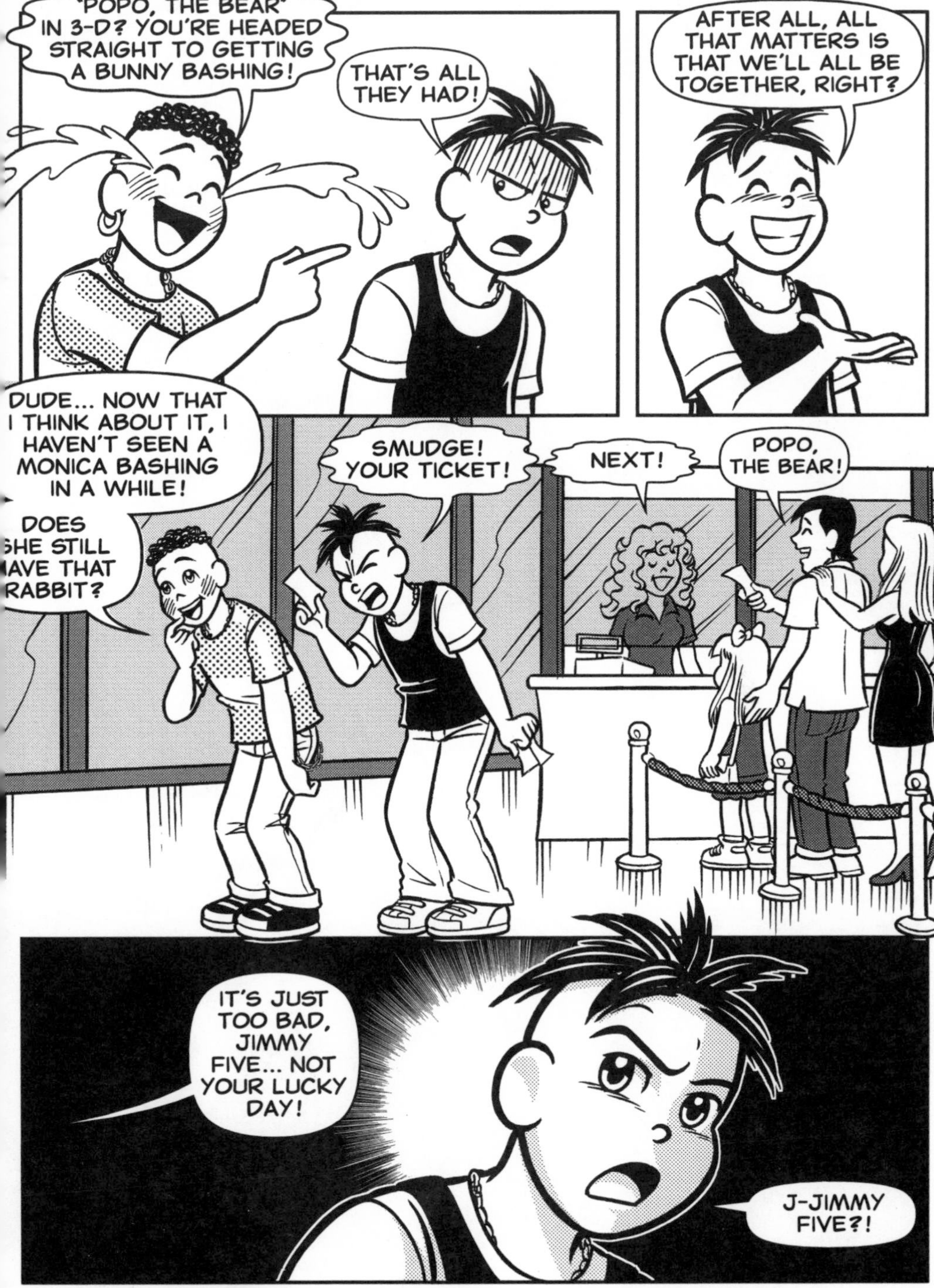
"POPO, THE BEAR" IN 3-D? YOU'RE HEADED STRAIGHT TO GETTING A BUNNY BASHING!
THAT'S ALL THEY HAD!
AFTER ALL, ALL THAT MATTERS IS THAT WE'LL ALL BE TOGETHER, RIGHT?
DUDE... NOW THAT I THINK ABOUT IT, I HAVEN'T SEEN A MONICA BASHING IN A WHILE!
DOES SHE STILL HAVE THAT RABBIT?
SMUDGE! YOUR TICKET!
NEXT!
POPO, THE BEAR!
IT'S JUST TOO BAD, JIMMY FIVE... NOT YOUR LUCKY DAY!
J-JIMMY FIVE?!

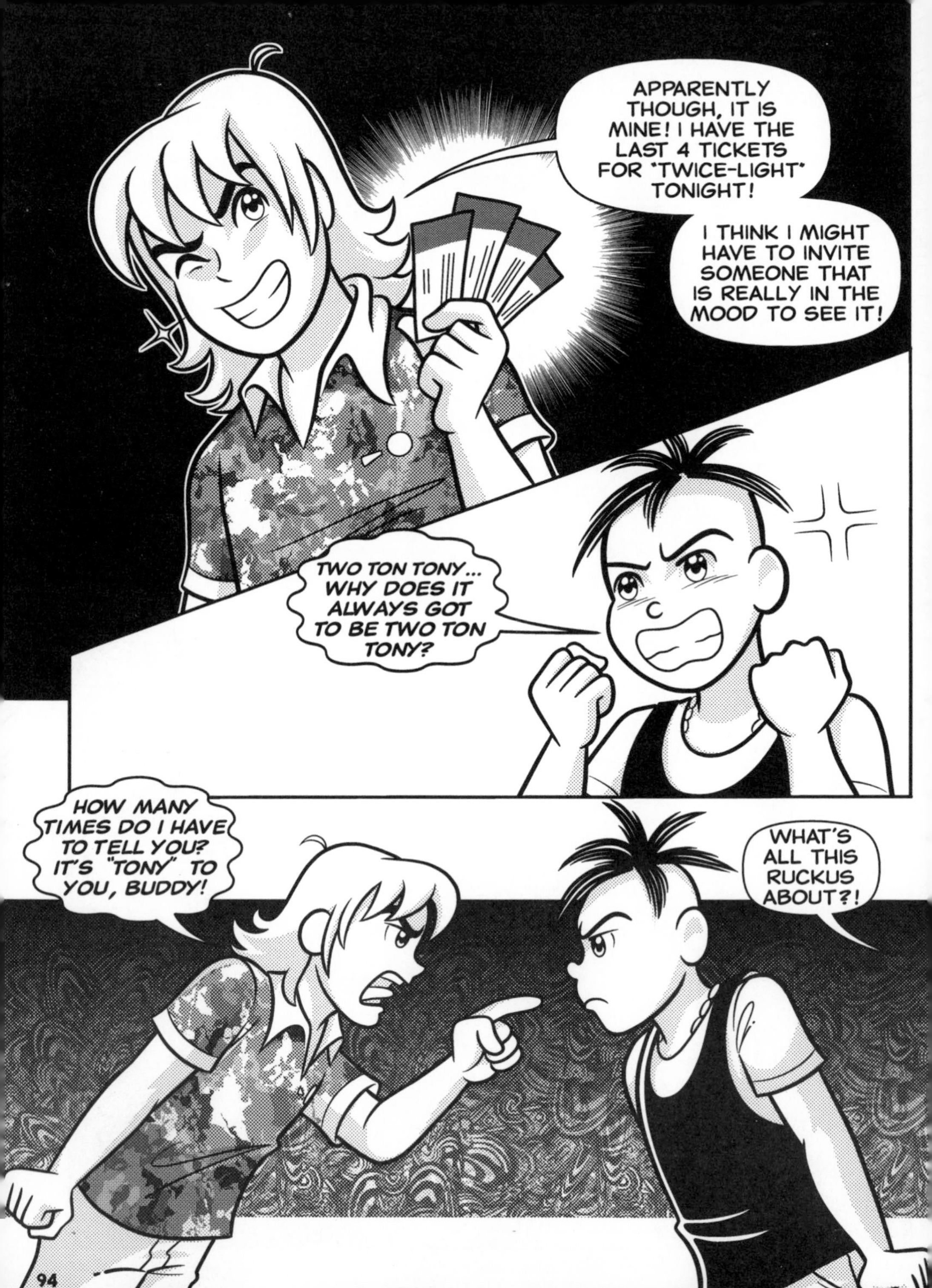
APPARENTLY THOUGH, IT IS MINE! I HAVE THE LAST 4 TICKETS FOR "TWICE-LIGHT" TONIGHT!
I THINK I MIGHT HAVE TO INVITE SOMEONE THAT IS REALLY IN THE MOOD TO SEE IT!
TWO TON TONY... WHY DOES IT ALWAYS GOT TO BE TWO TON TONY?
HOW MANY TIMES DO I HAVE TO TELL YOU? IT'S "TONY" TO YOU, BUDDY!
WHAT'S ALL THIS RUCKUS ABOUT?!

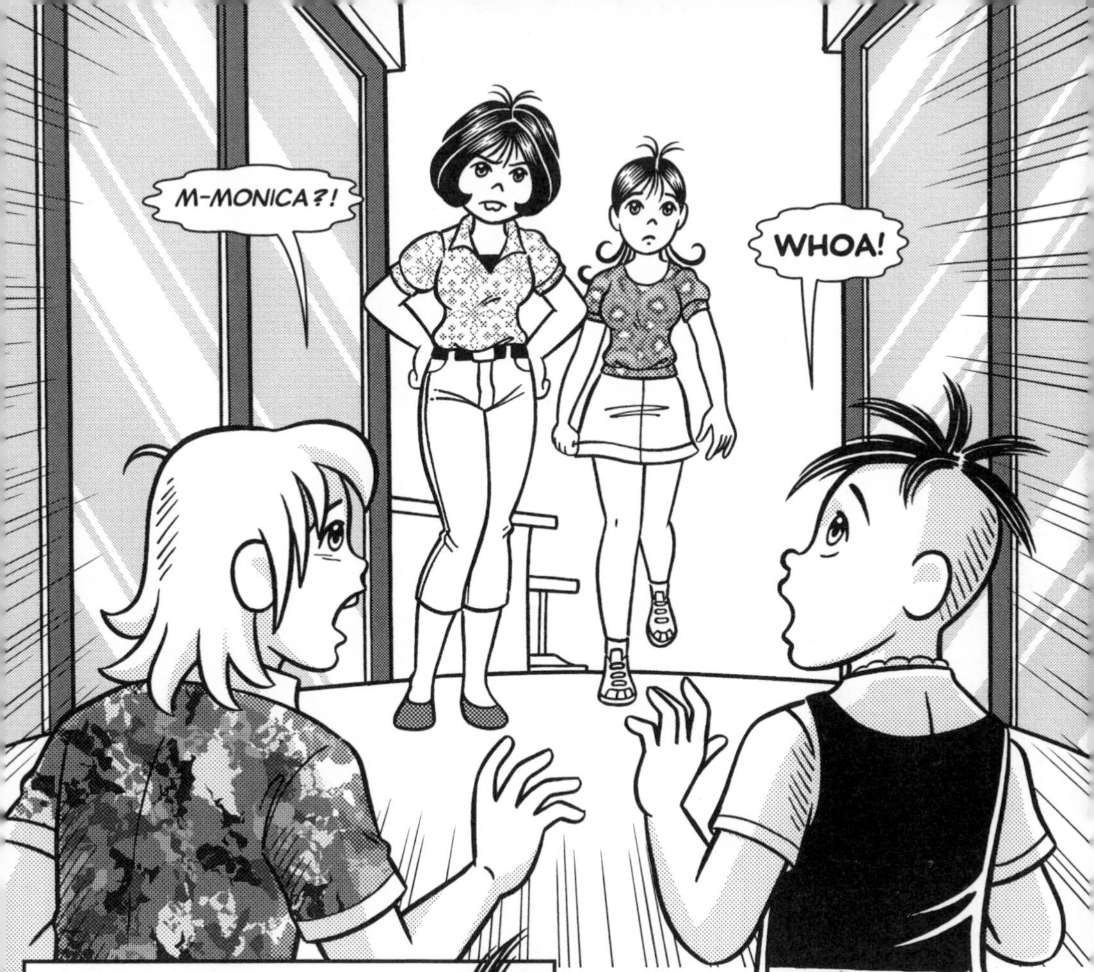
M-MONICA?!
WHOA!
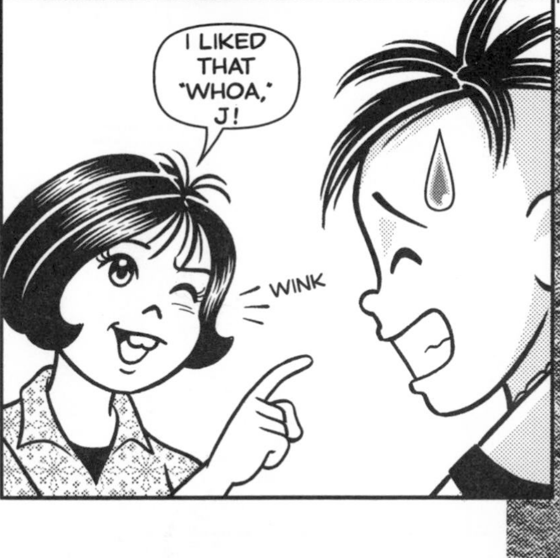
I LIKED THAT "WHOA," J!
WINK
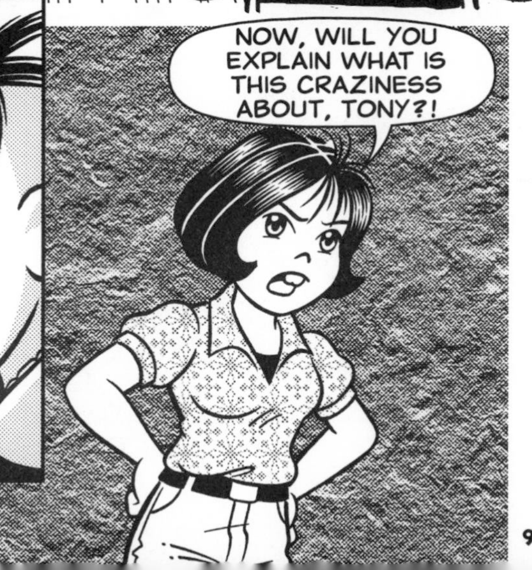
NOW, WILL YOU EXPLAIN WHAT IS THIS CRAZINESS ABOUT, TONY?!

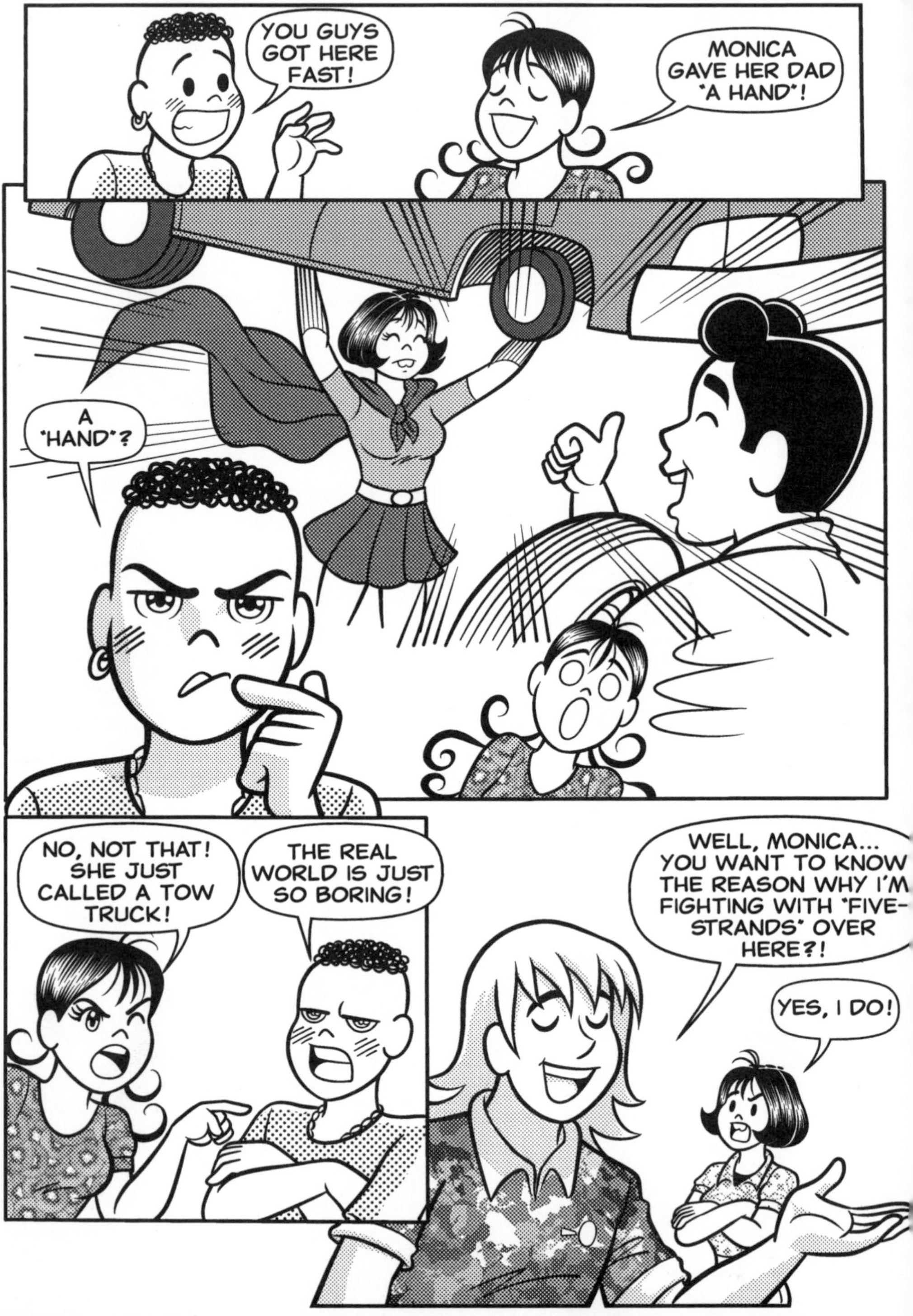
YOU GUYS GOT HERE FAST!
MONICA GAVE HER DAD "A HAND"!
A "HAND"?
NO, NOT THAT! SHE JUST CALLED A TOW TRUCK!
THE REAL WORLD IS JUST SO BORING!
WELL, MONICA... YOU WANT TO KNOW THE REASON WHY I'M FIGHTING WITH "FIVE-STRANDS" OVER HERE?!
YES, I DO!

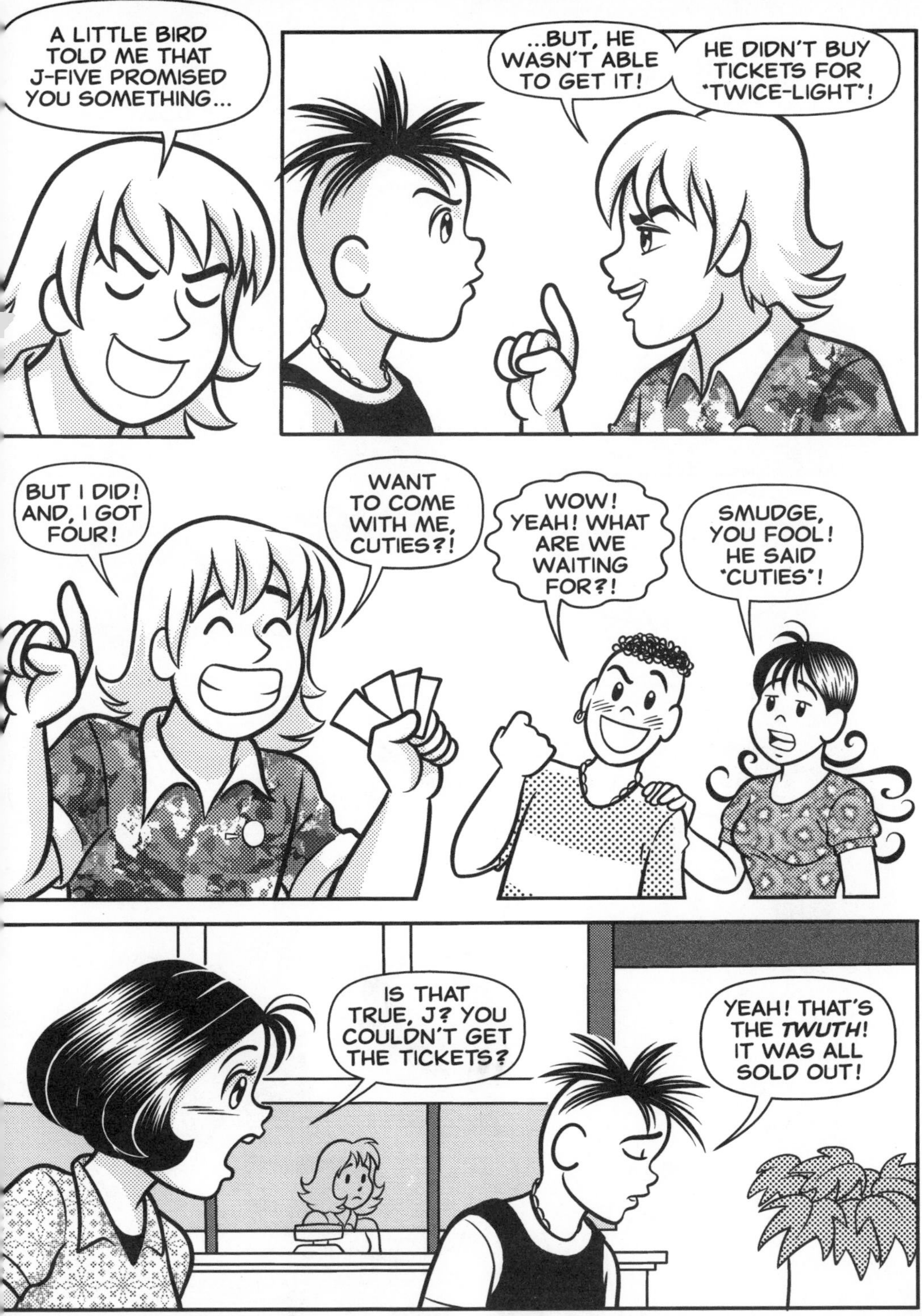

A LITTLE BIRD TOLD ME THAT J-FIVE PROMISED YOU SOMETHING...
...BUT, HE WASN'T ABLE TO GET IT!
HE DIDN'T BUY TICKETS FOR "TWICE-LIGHT"!
BUT I DID! AND, I GOT FOUR!
WANT TO COME WITH ME, CUTIES?!
WOW! YEAH! WHAT ARE WE WAITING FOR?!
SMUDGE, YOU FOOL! HE SAID "CUTIES"!
IS THAT TRUE, J? YOU COULDN'T GET THE TICKETS?
YEAH! THAT'S THE *TWUTH*! IT WAS ALL SOLD OUT!

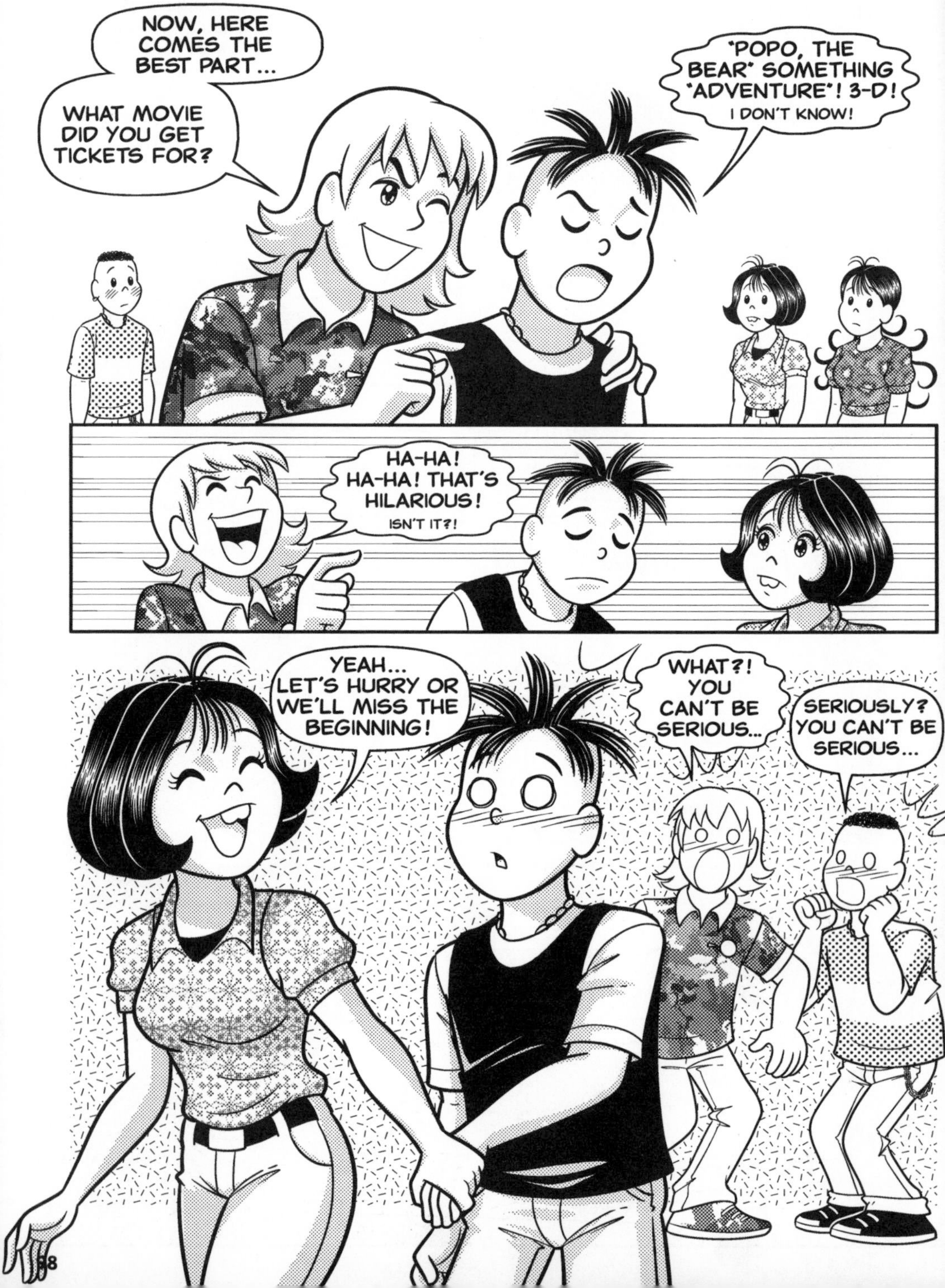
NOW, HERE COMES THE BEST PART...
WHAT MOVIE DID YOU GET TICKETS FOR?
"POPO, THE BEAR" SOMETHING "ADVENTURE"! 3-D! I DON'T KNOW!
HA-HA! HA-HA! THAT'S HILARIOUS! ISN'T IT?!
YEAH... LET'S HURRY OR WE'LL MISS THE BEGINNING!
WHAT?! YOU CAN'T BE SERIOUS...
SERIOUSLY? YOU CAN'T BE SERIOUS...

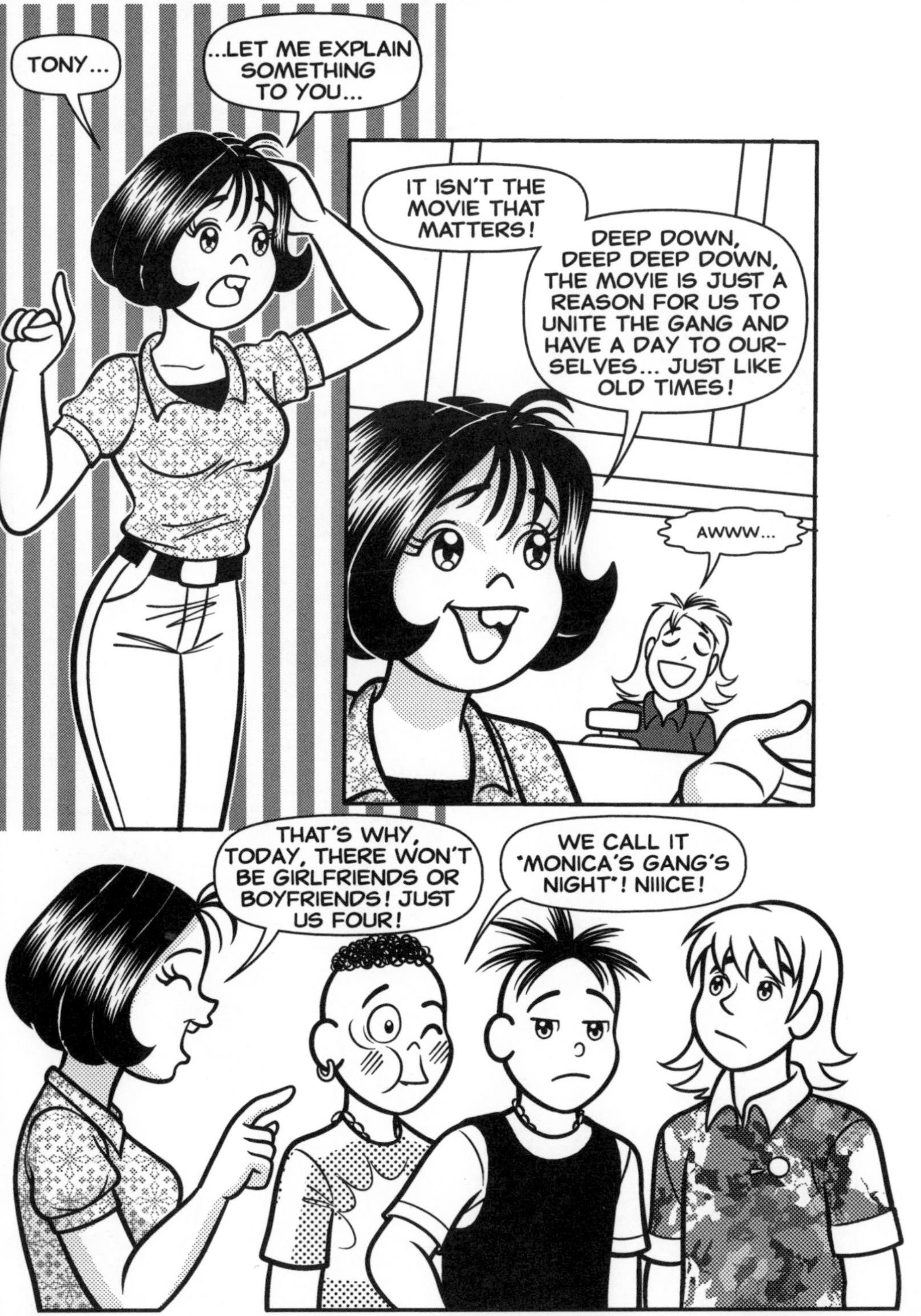
TONY...
...LET ME EXPLAIN SOMETHING TO YOU...
IT ISN'T THE MOVIE THAT MATTERS!
DEEP DOWN, DEEP DEEP DOWN, THE MOVIE IS JUST A REASON FOR US TO UNITE THE GANG AND HAVE A DAY TO OUR-SELVES... JUST LIKE OLD TIMES!
AWWW...
THAT'S WHY, TODAY, THERE WON'T BE GIRLFRIENDS OR BOYFRIENDS! JUST US FOUR!
WE CALL IT "MONICA'S GANG'S NIGHT"! NIIICE!

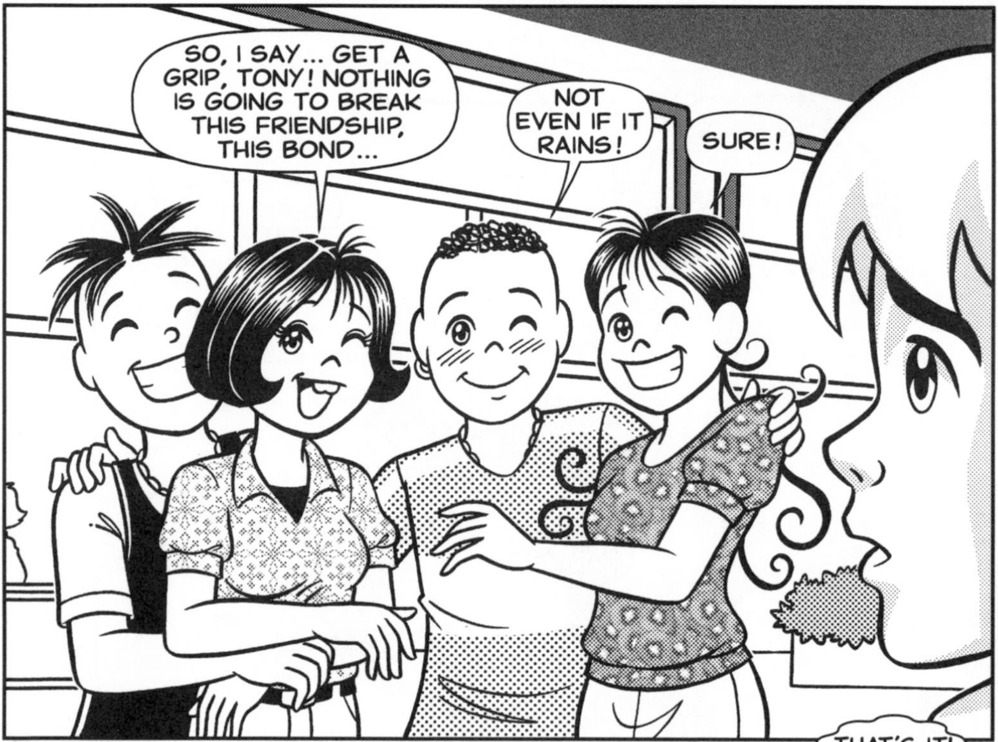
SO, I SAY... GET A GRIP, TONY! NOTHING IS GOING TO BREAK THIS FRIENDSHIP, THIS BOND...
NOT EVEN IF IT RAINS!
SURE!
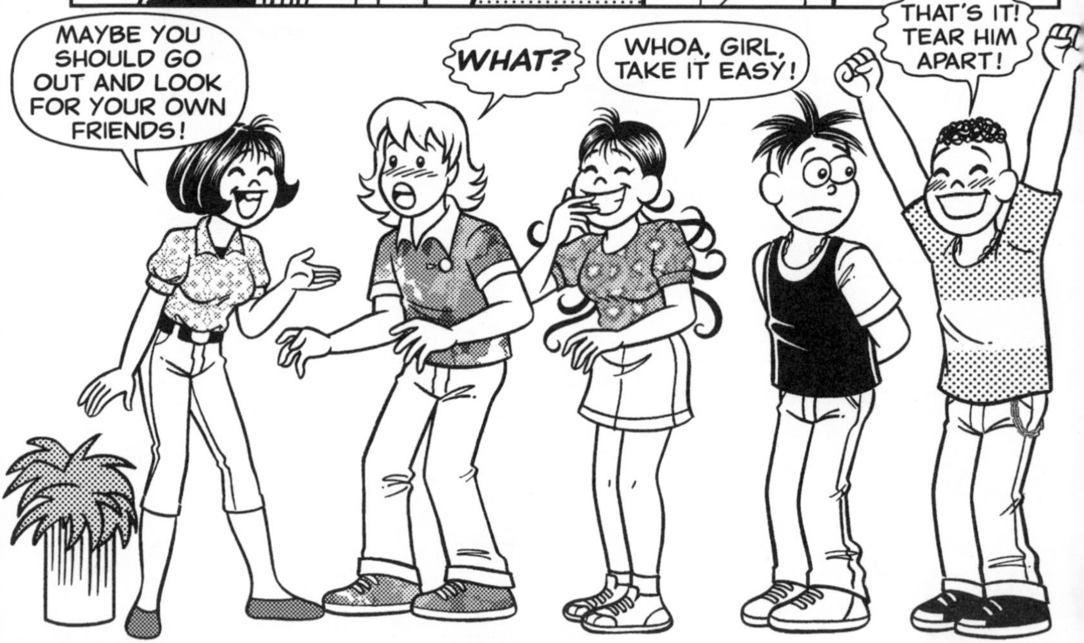
MAYBE YOU SHOULD GO OUT AND LOOK FOR YOUR OWN FRIENDS!
WHAT?
WHOA, GIRL, TAKE IT EASY!
THAT'S IT! TEAR HIM APART!

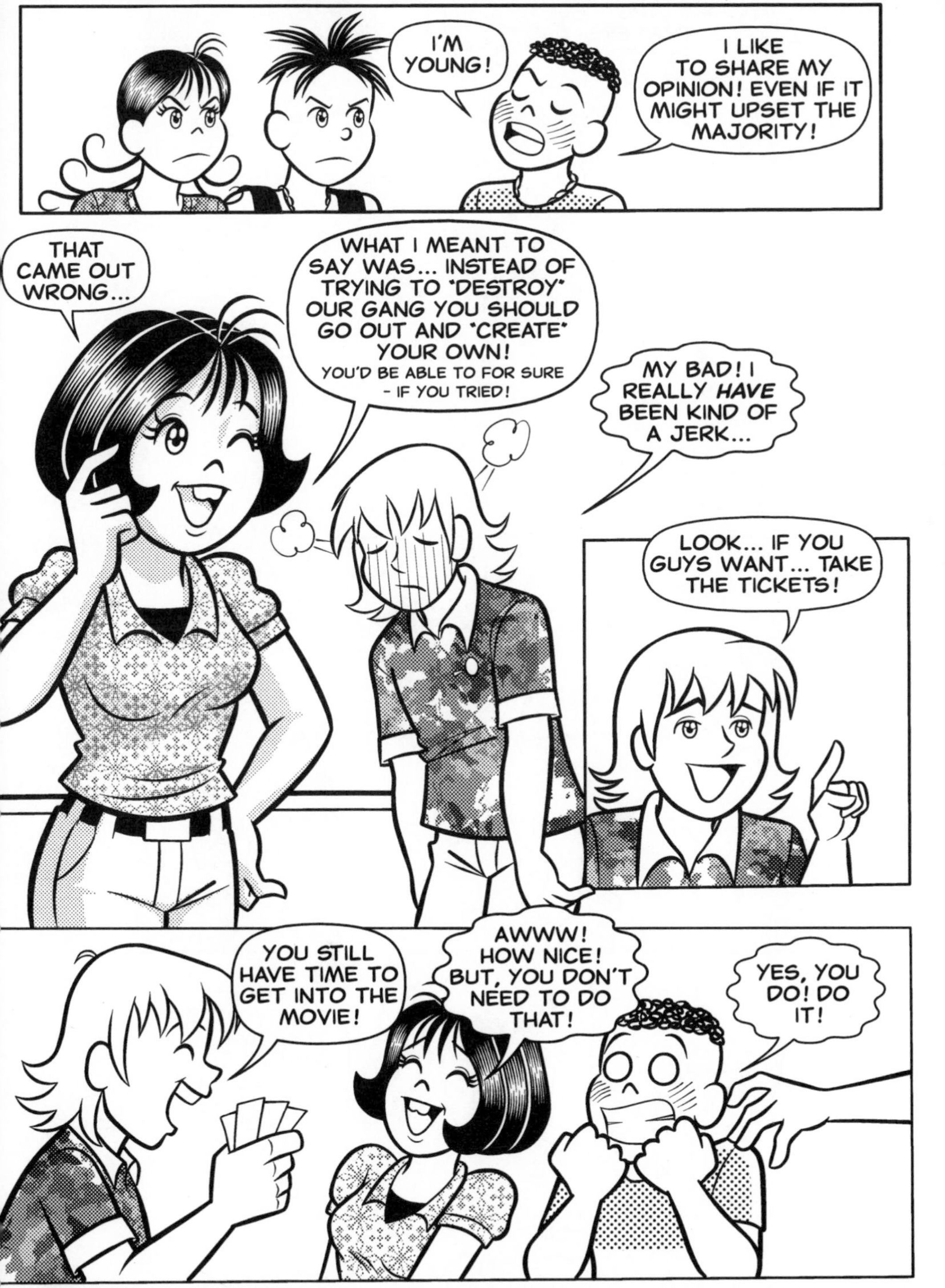

I'M YOUNG!
I LIKE TO SHARE MY OPINION! EVEN IF IT MIGHT UPSET THE MAJORITY!
THAT CAME OUT WRONG...
WHAT I MEANT TO SAY WAS... INSTEAD OF TRYING TO "DESTROY" OUR GANG YOU SHOULD GO OUT AND "CREATE" YOUR OWN! YOU'D BE ABLE TO FOR SURE - IF YOU TRIED!
MY BAD! I REALLY *HAVE* BEEN KIND OF A JERK...
LOOK... IF YOU GUYS WANT... TAKE THE TICKETS!
YOU STILL HAVE TIME TO GET INTO THE MOVIE!
AWWW! HOW NICE! BUT, YOU DON'T NEED TO DO THAT!
YES, YOU DO! DO IT!

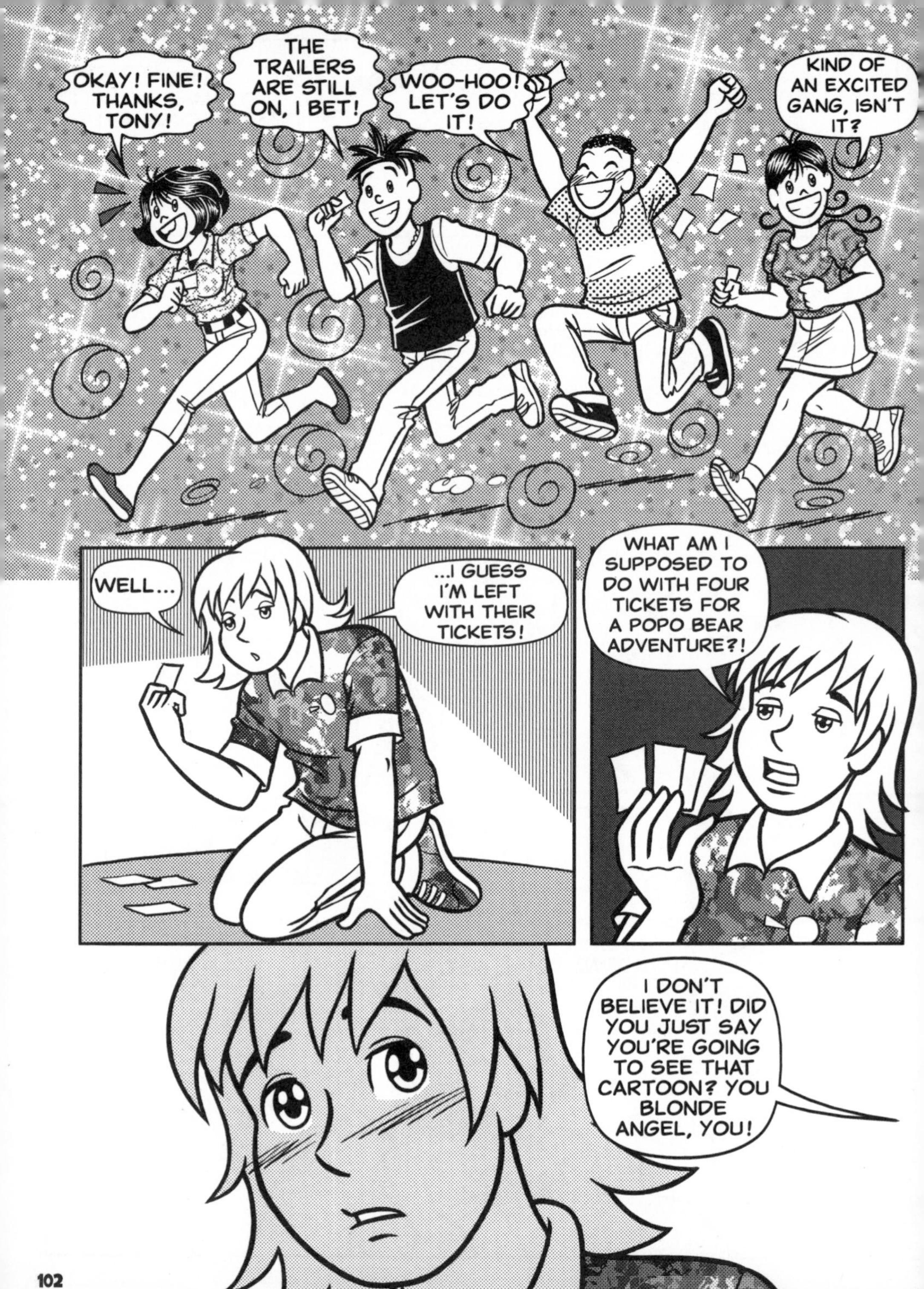
OKAY! FINE! THANKS, TONY!
THE TRAILERS ARE STILL ON, I BET!
WOO-HOO! LET'S DO IT!
KIND OF AN EXCITED GANG, ISN'T IT?
WELL...
...I GUESS I'M LEFT WITH THEIR TICKETS!
WHAT AM I SUPPOSED TO DO WITH FOUR TICKETS FOR A POPO BEAR ADVENTURE?!
I DON'T BELIEVE IT! DID YOU JUST SAY YOU'RE GOING TO SEE THAT CARTOON? YOU BLONDE ANGEL, YOU!

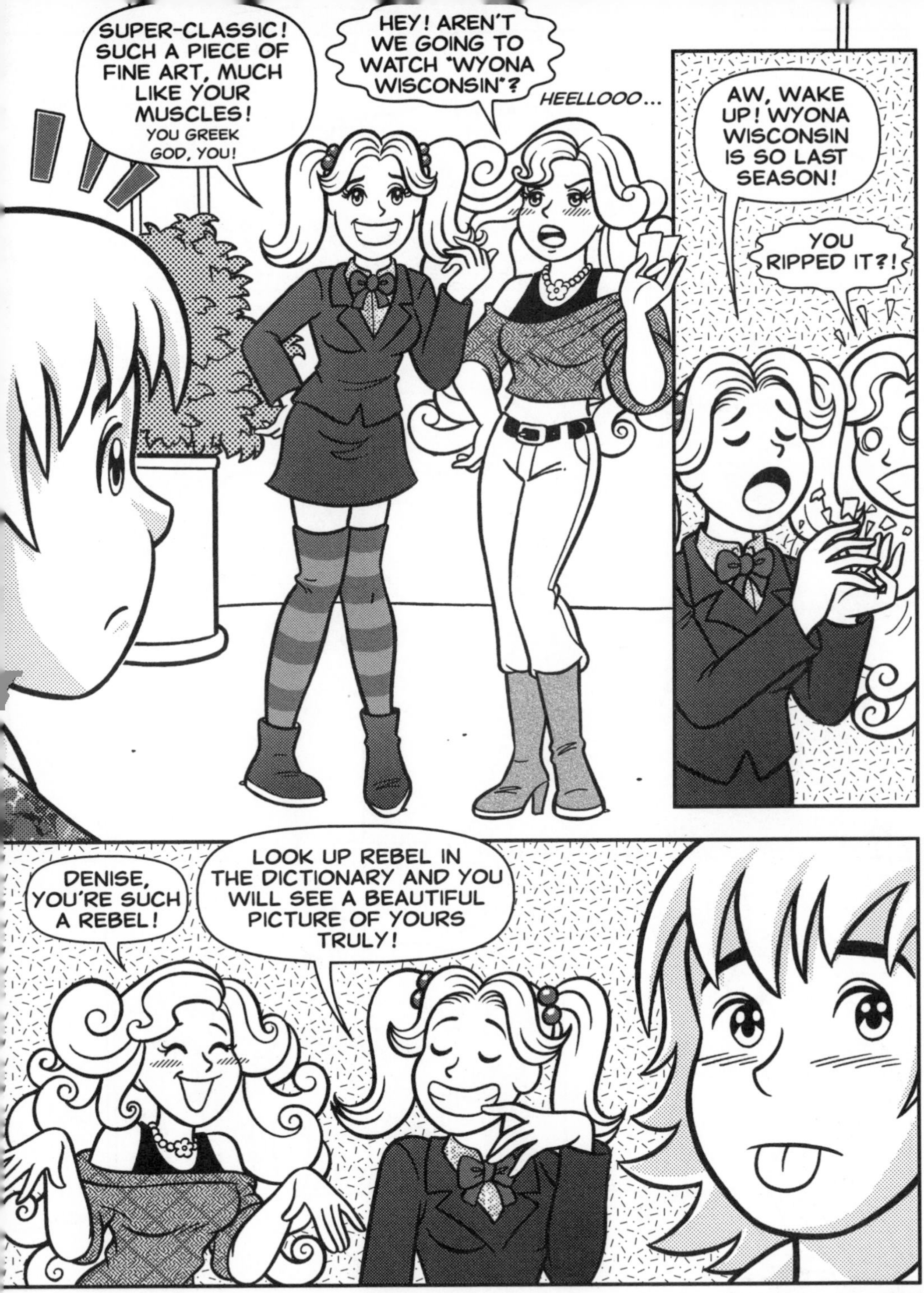

SUPER-CLASSIC! SUCH A PIECE OF FINE ART, MUCH LIKE YOUR MUSCLES! YOU GREEK GOD, YOU!
HEY! AREN'T WE GOING TO WATCH "WYONA WISCONSIN"?
HEELLOOO...
AW, WAKE UP! WYONA WISCONSIN IS SO LAST SEASON!
YOU RIPPED IT?!
DENISE, YOU'RE SUCH A REBEL!
LOOK UP REBEL IN THE DICTIONARY AND YOU WILL SEE A BEAUTIFUL PICTURE OF YOURS TRULY!

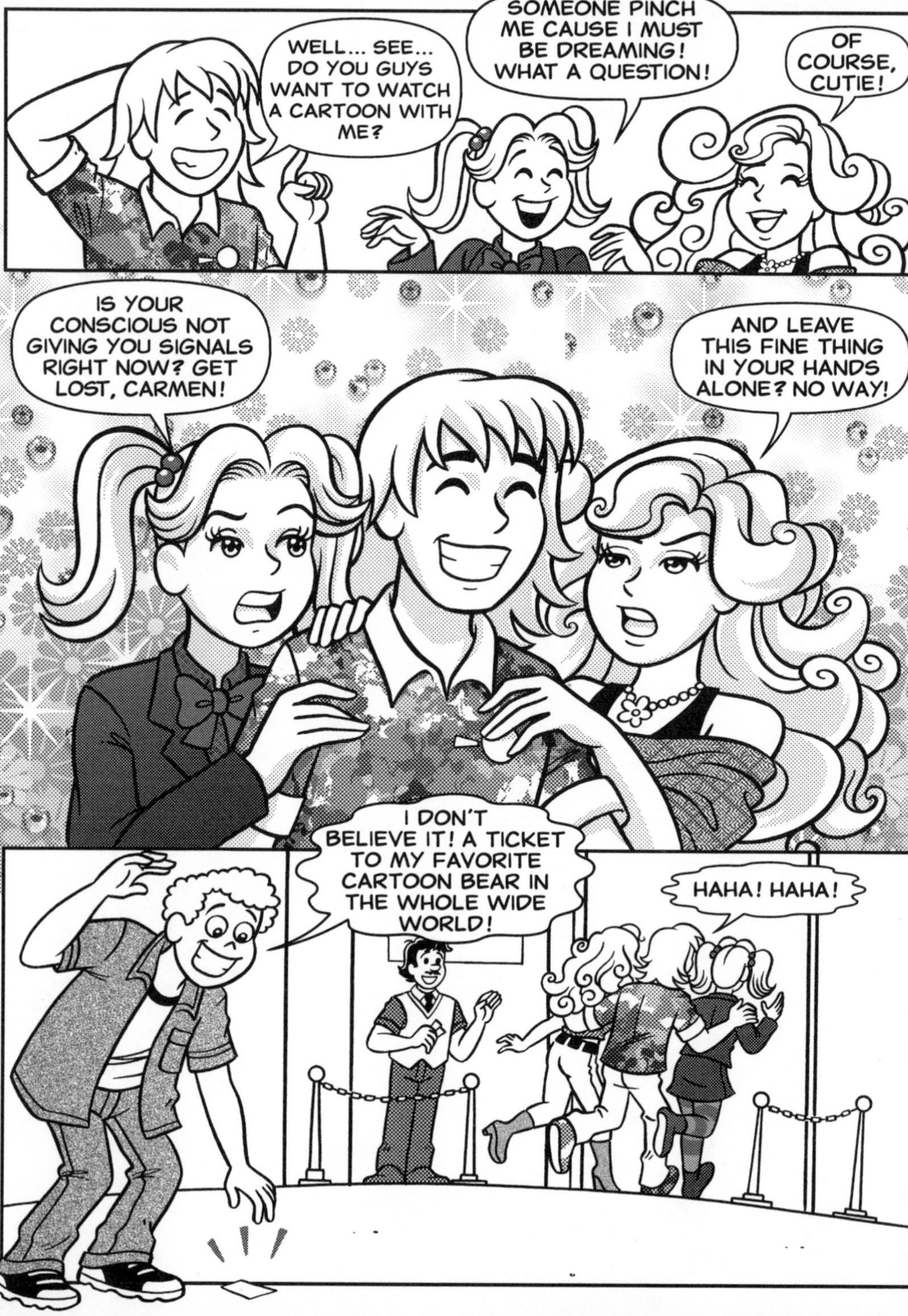
WELL... SEE... DO YOU GUYS WANT TO WATCH A CARTOON WITH ME?
SOMEONE PINCH ME CAUSE I MUST BE DREAMING! WHAT A QUESTION!
OF COURSE, CUTIE!
IS YOUR CONSCIOUS NOT GIVING YOU SIGNALS RIGHT NOW? GET LOST, CARMEN!
AND LEAVE THIS FINE THING IN YOUR HANDS ALONE? NO WAY!
I DON'T BELIEVE IT! A TICKET TO MY FAVORITE CARTOON BEAR IN THE WHOLE WIDE WORLD!
HAHA! HAHA!

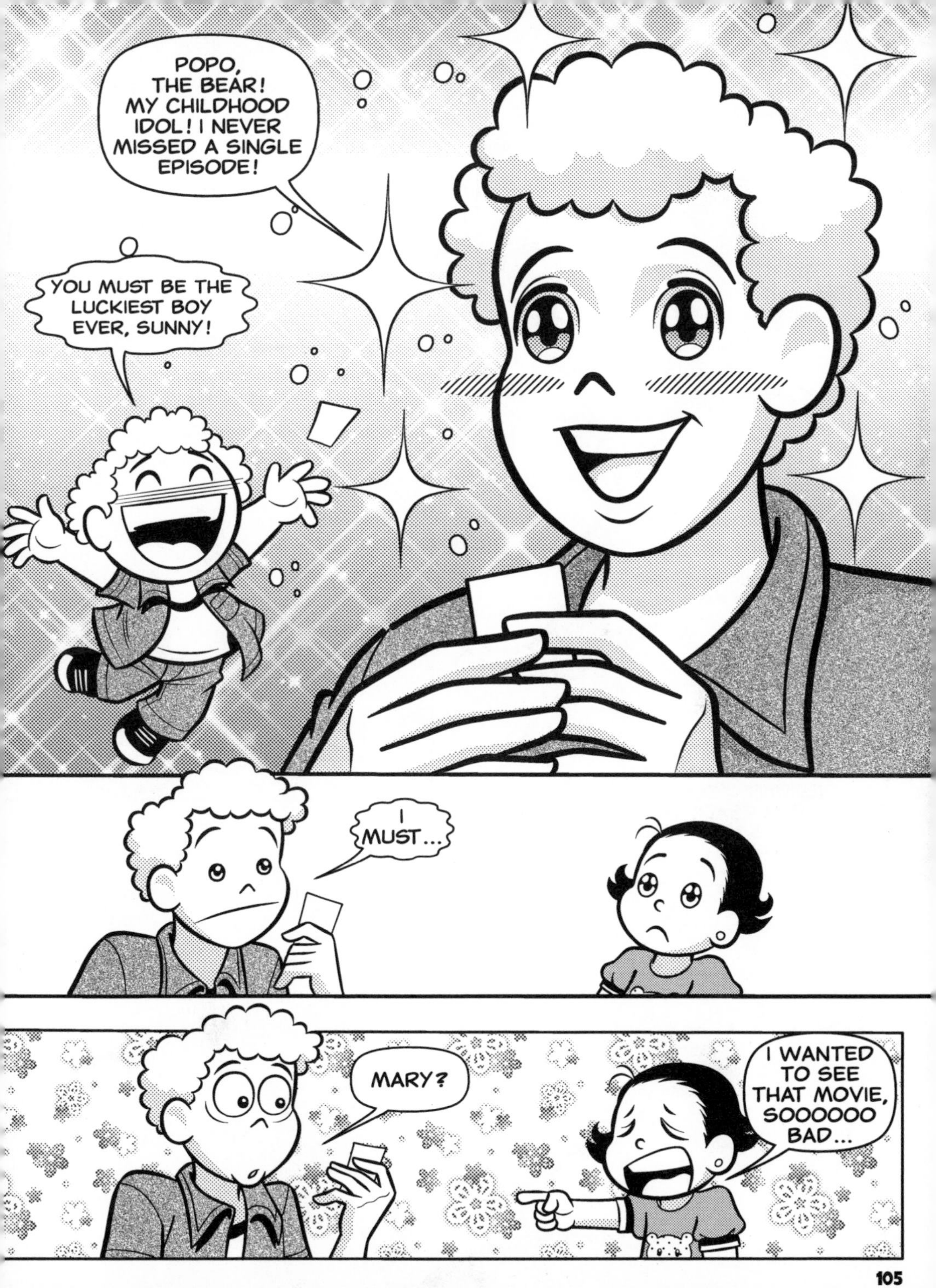
POPO, THE BEAR! MY CHILDHOOD IDOL! I NEVER MISSED A SINGLE EPISODE!
YOU MUST BE THE LUCKIEST BOY EVER, SUNNY!
I MUST...
MARY?
I WANTED TO SEE THAT MOVIE, SOOOOOO BAD...

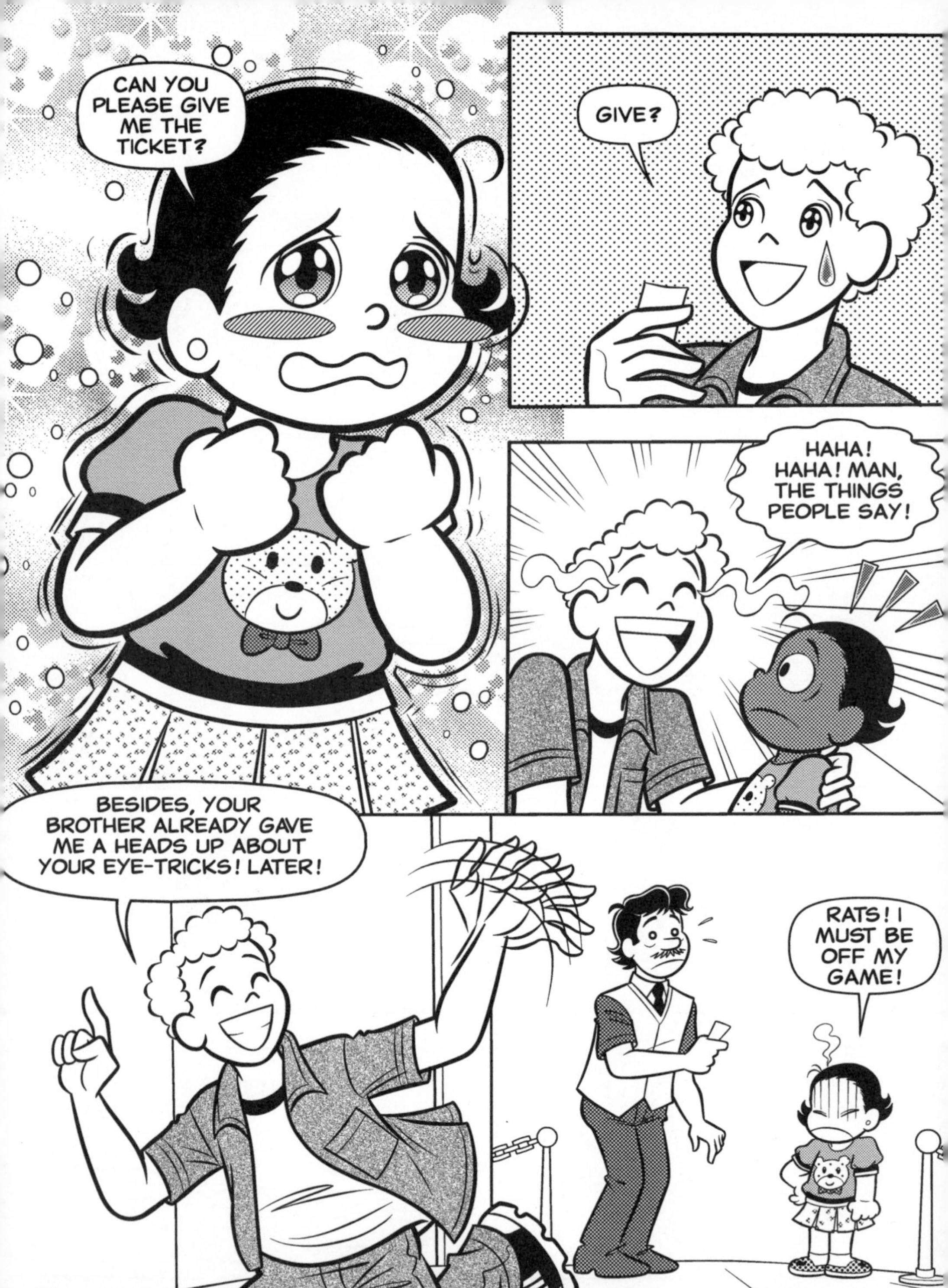
CAN YOU PLEASE GIVE ME THE TICKET?
GIVE?
HAHA! HAHA! MAN, THE THINGS PEOPLE SAY!
BESIDES, YOUR BROTHER ALREADY GAVE ME A HEADS UP ABOUT YOUR EYE-TRICKS! LATER!
RATS! I MUST BE OFF MY GAME!

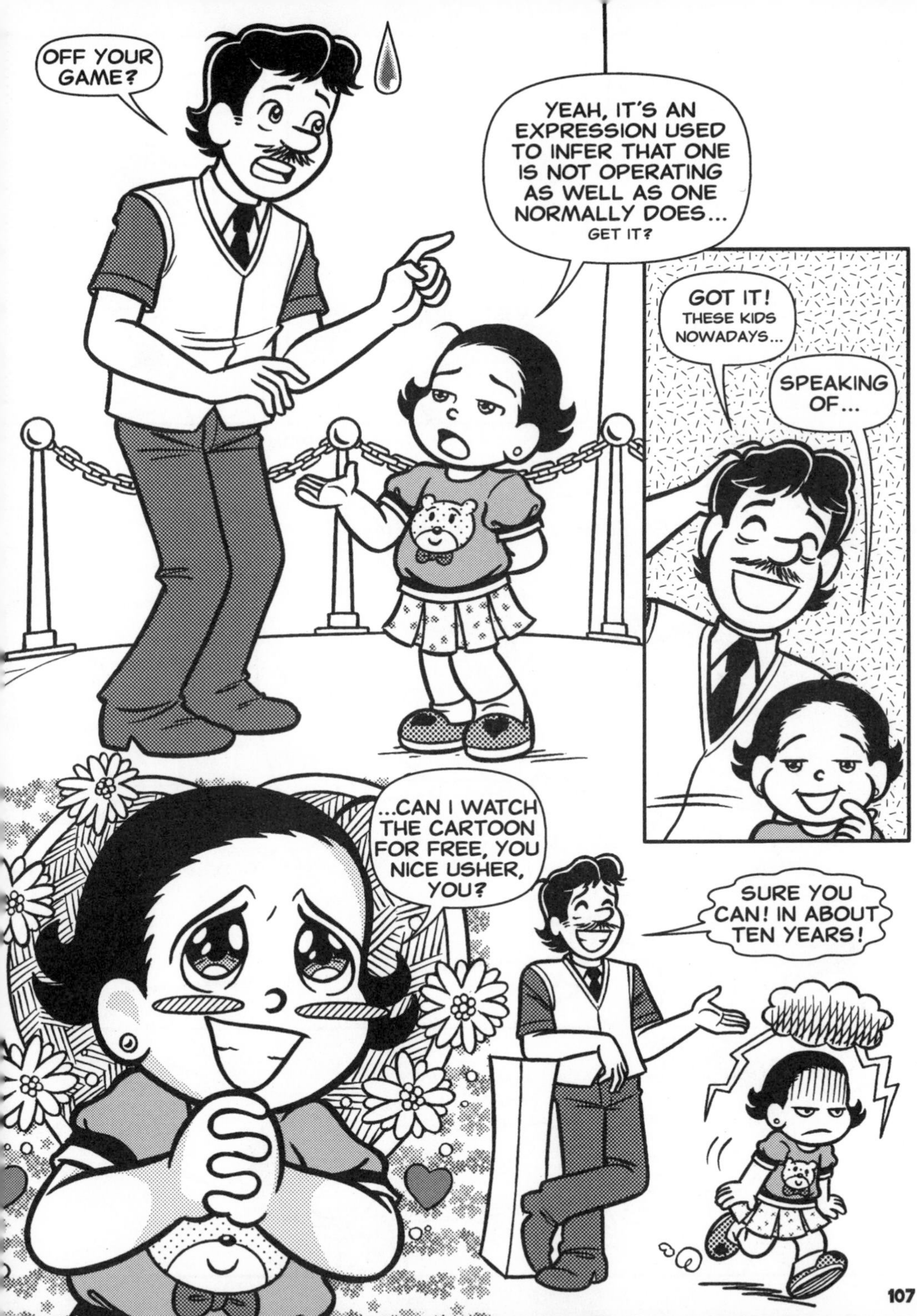
OFF YOUR GAME?
YEAH, IT'S AN EXPRESSION USED TO INFER THAT ONE IS NOT OPERATING AS WELL AS ONE NORMALLY DOES... GET IT?
GOT IT! THESE KIDS NOWADAYS...
SPEAKING OF...
...CAN I WATCH THE CARTOON FOR FREE, YOU NICE USHER, YOU?
SURE YOU CAN! IN ABOUT TEN YEARS!

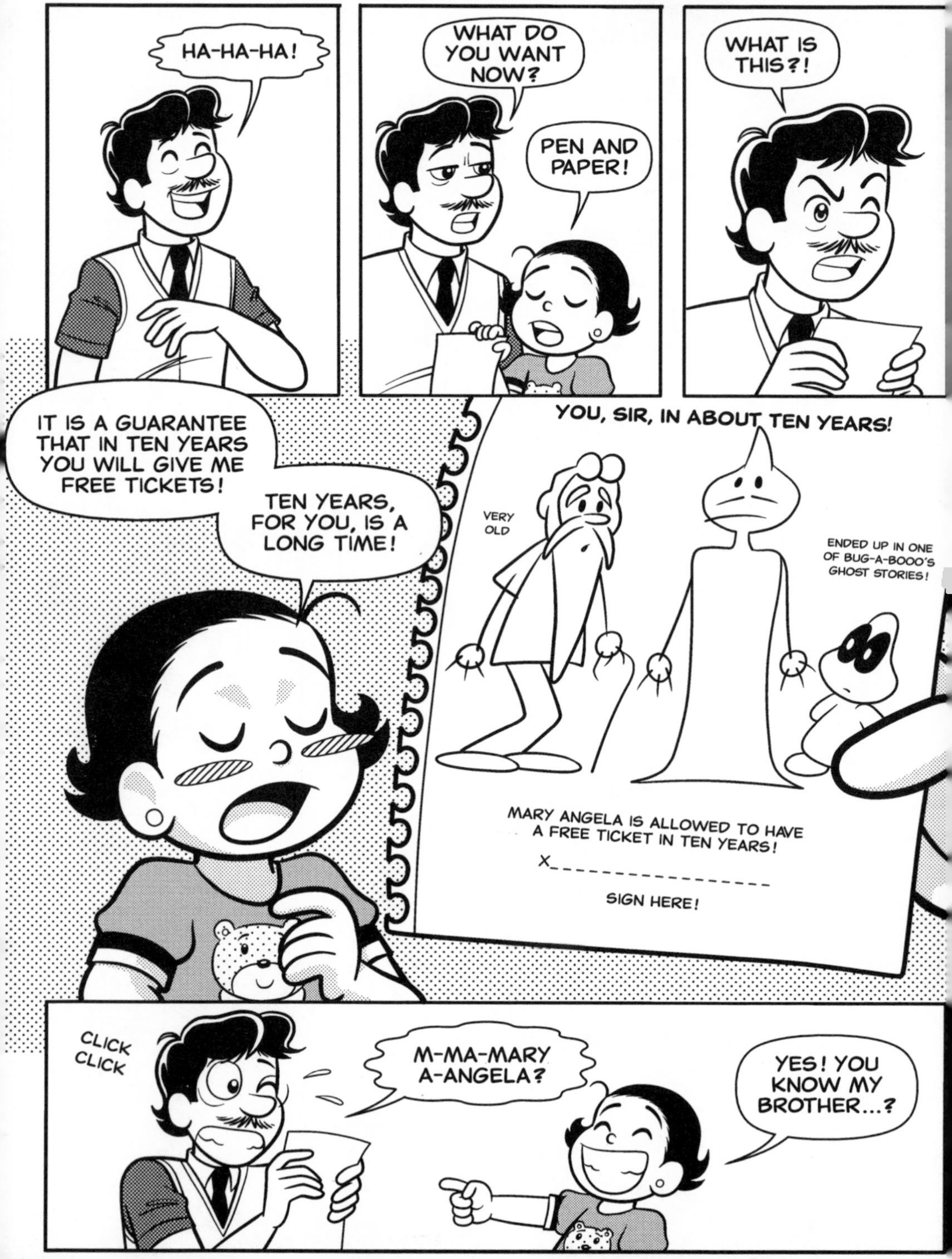
HA-HA-HA!
WHAT DO YOU WANT NOW?
PEN AND PAPER!
WHAT IS THIS?!
IT IS A GUARANTEE THAT IN TEN YEARS YOU WILL GIVE ME FREE TICKETS!
TEN YEARS, FOR YOU, IS A LONG TIME!
YOU, SIR, IN ABOUT TEN YEARS!
VERY OLD
ENDED UP IN ONE OF BUG-A-BOOO'S GHOST STORIES!
MARY ANGELA IS ALLOWED TO HAVE A FREE TICKET IN TEN YEARS!
X________________
SIGN HERE!
CLICK CLICK
M-MA-MARY A-ANGELA?
YES! YOU KNOW MY BROTHER...?

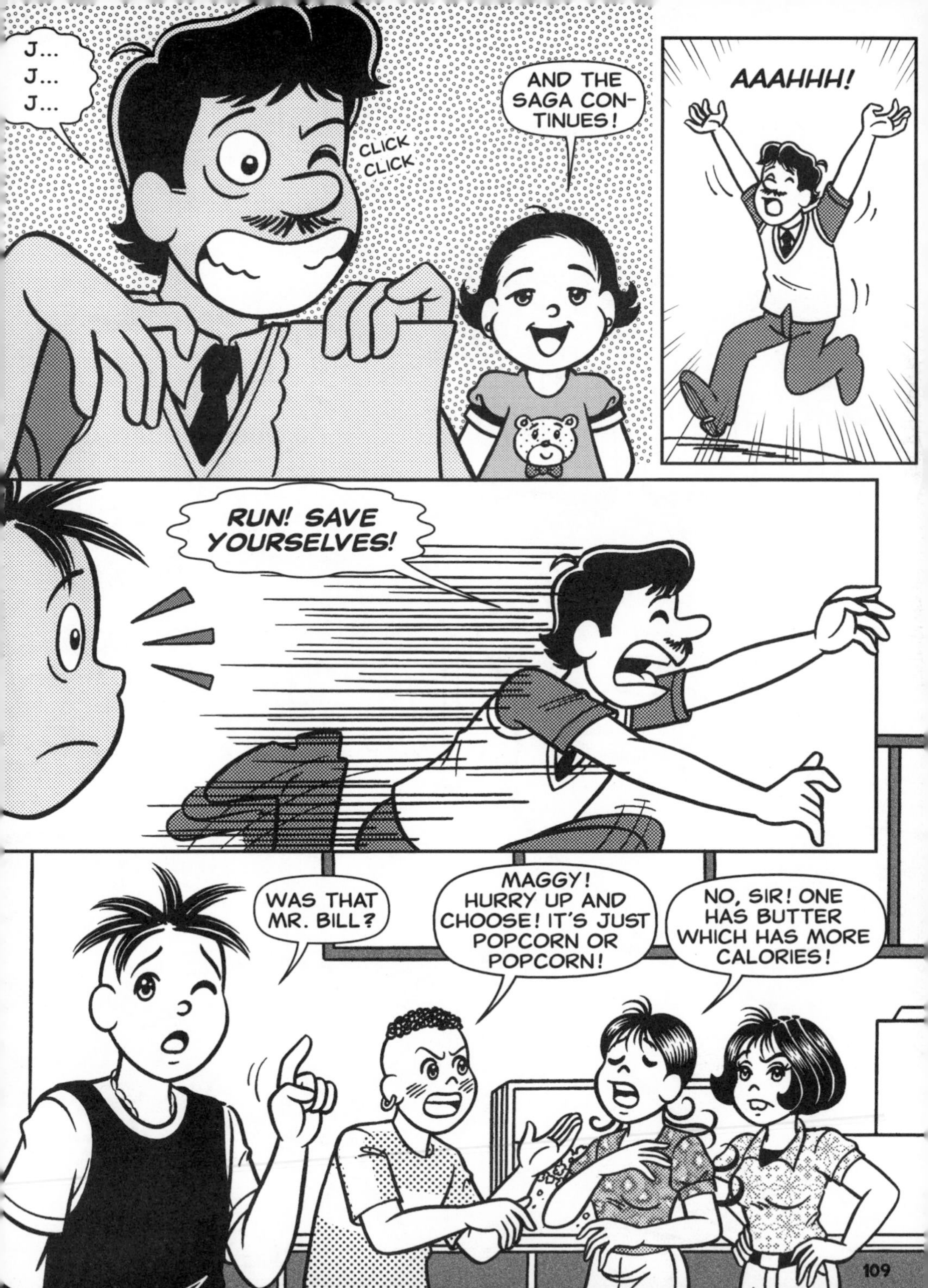
J...
J...
J...
CLICK
CLICK
AND THE SAGA CONTINUES!
AAAHHH!
RUN! SAVE YOURSELVES!
WAS THAT MR. BILL?
MAGGY! HURRY UP AND CHOOSE! IT'S JUST POPCORN OR POPCORN!
NO, SIR! ONE HAS BUTTER WHICH HAS MORE CALORIES!

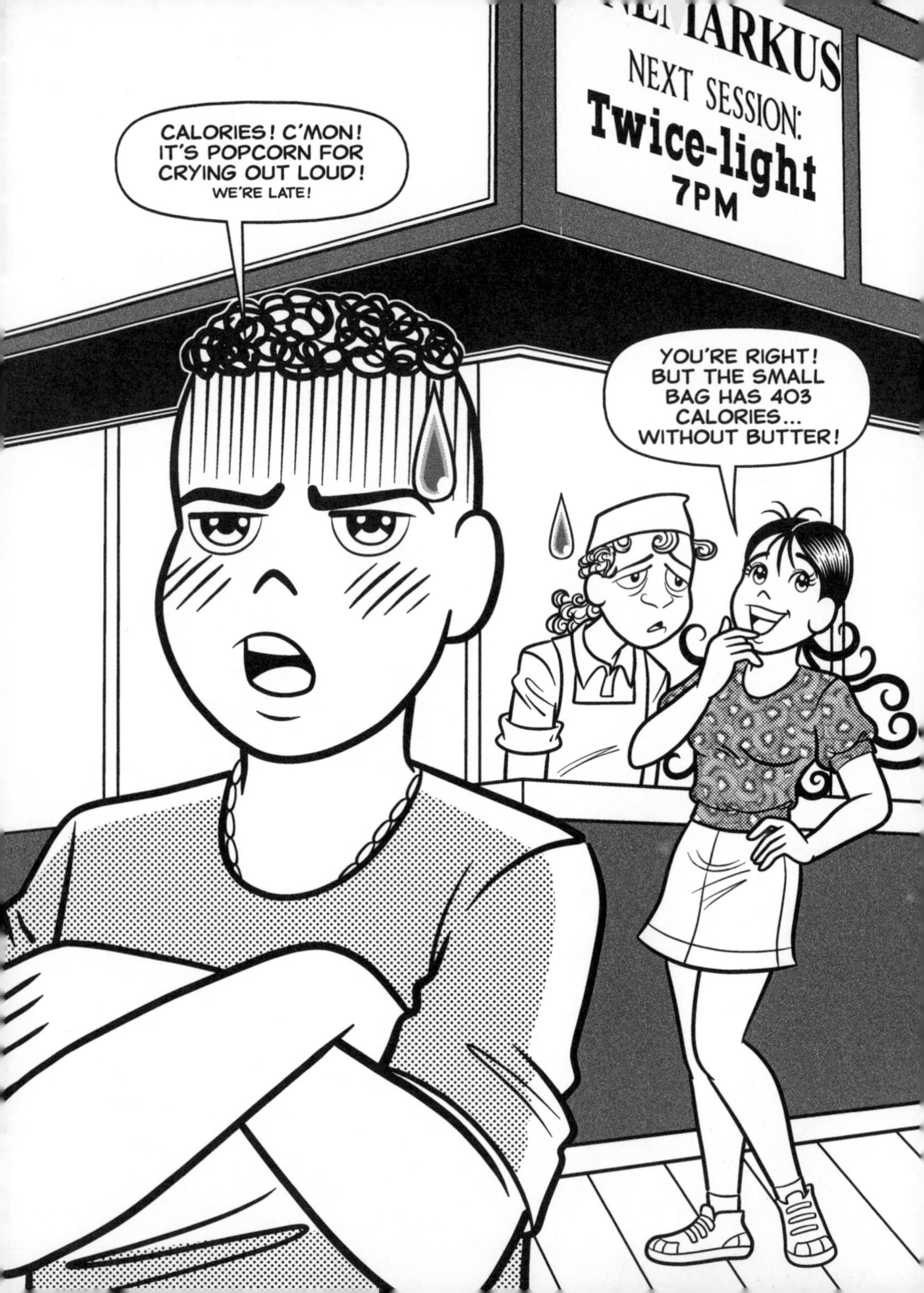
CALORIES! C'MON! IT'S POPCORN FOR CRYING OUT LOUD! WE'RE LATE!
NEXT SESSION:
Twice-light
7PM
YOU'RE RIGHT! BUT THE SMALL BAG HAS 403 CALORIES... WITHOUT BUTTER!

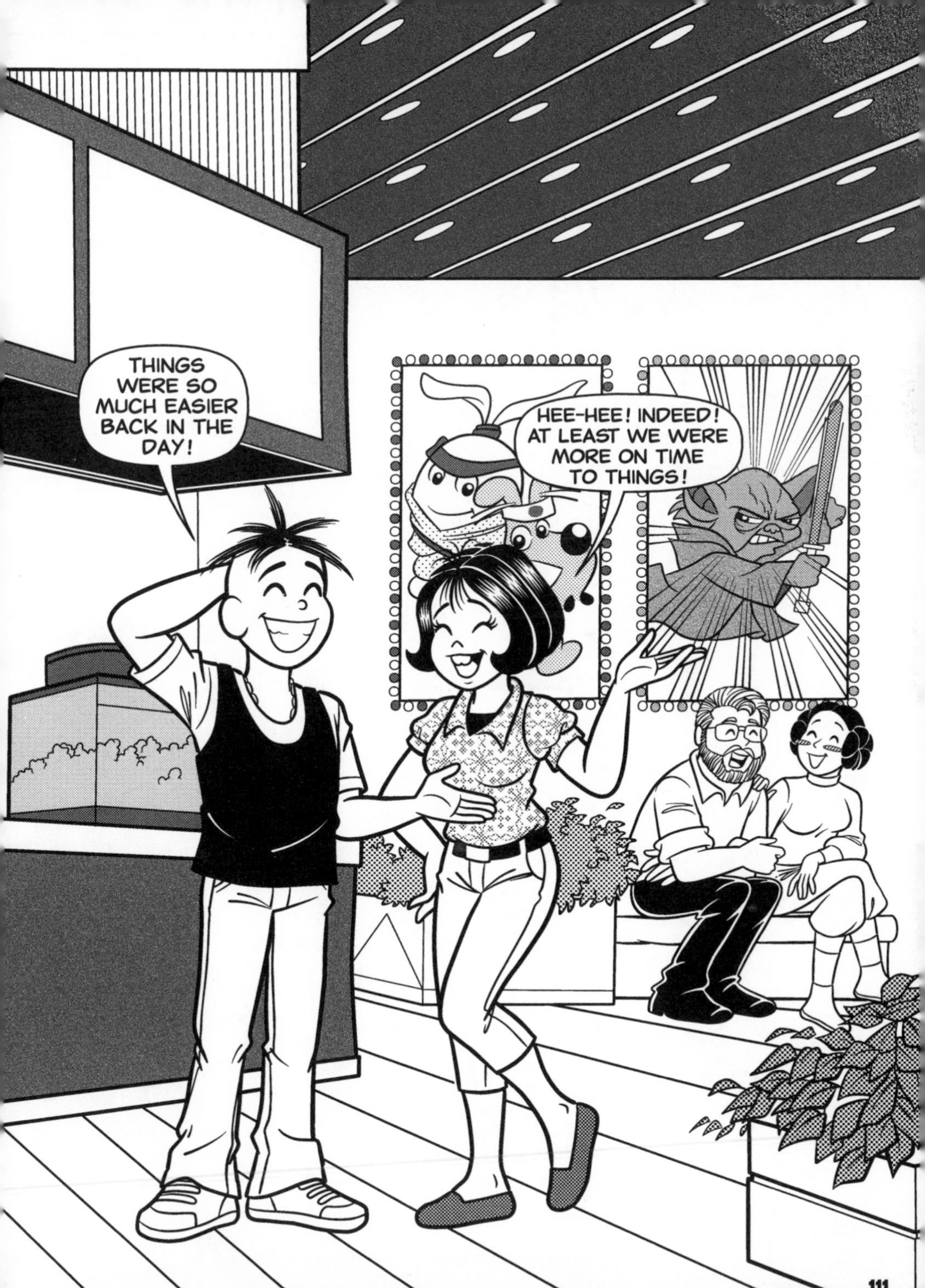
THINGS WERE SO MUCH EASIER BACK IN THE DAY!
HEE-HEE! INDEED! AT LEAST WE WERE MORE ON TIME TO THINGS!

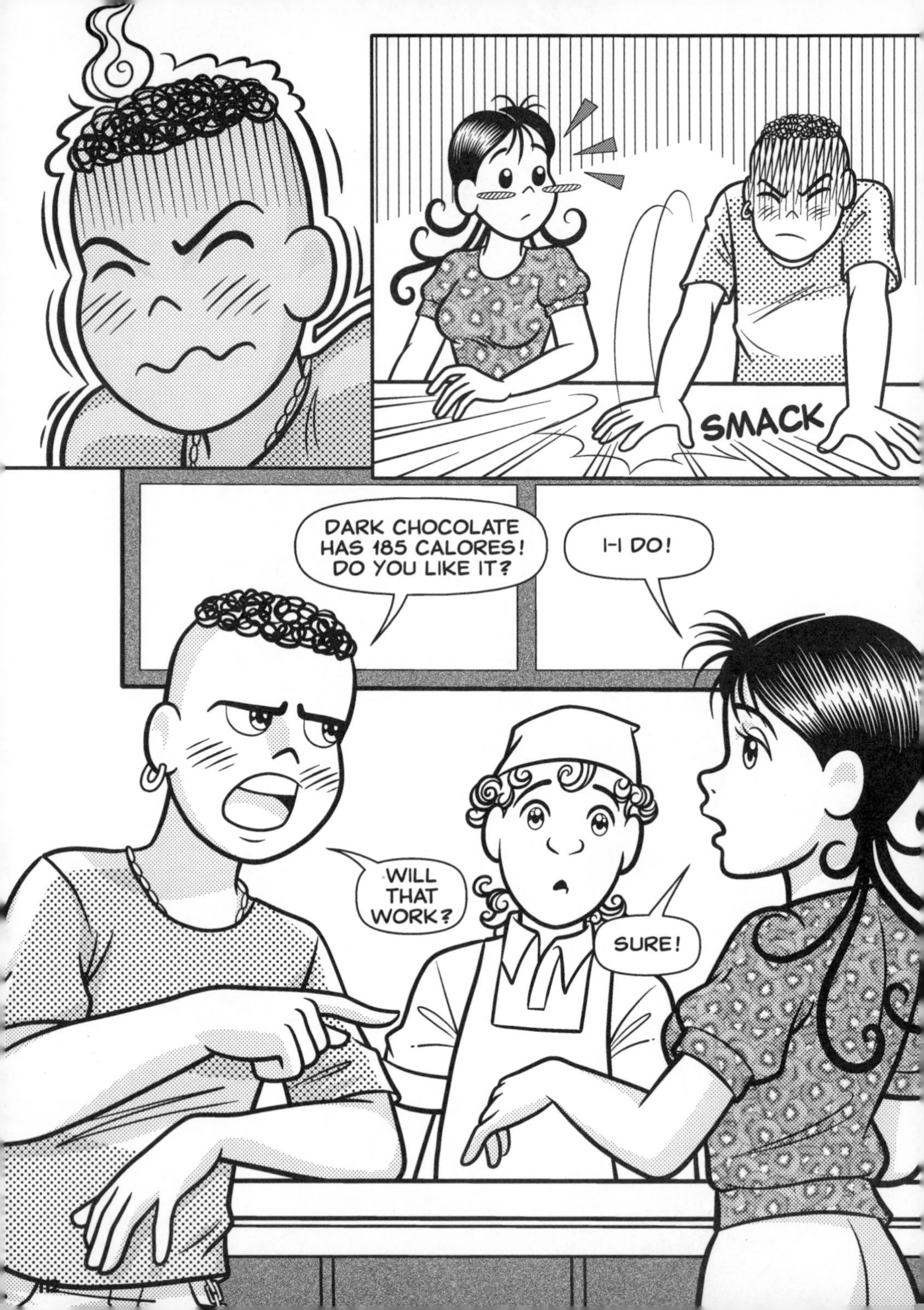
SMACK
DARK CHOCOLATE HAS 185 CALORES! DO YOU LIKE IT?
I-I DO!
WILL THAT WORK?
SURE!

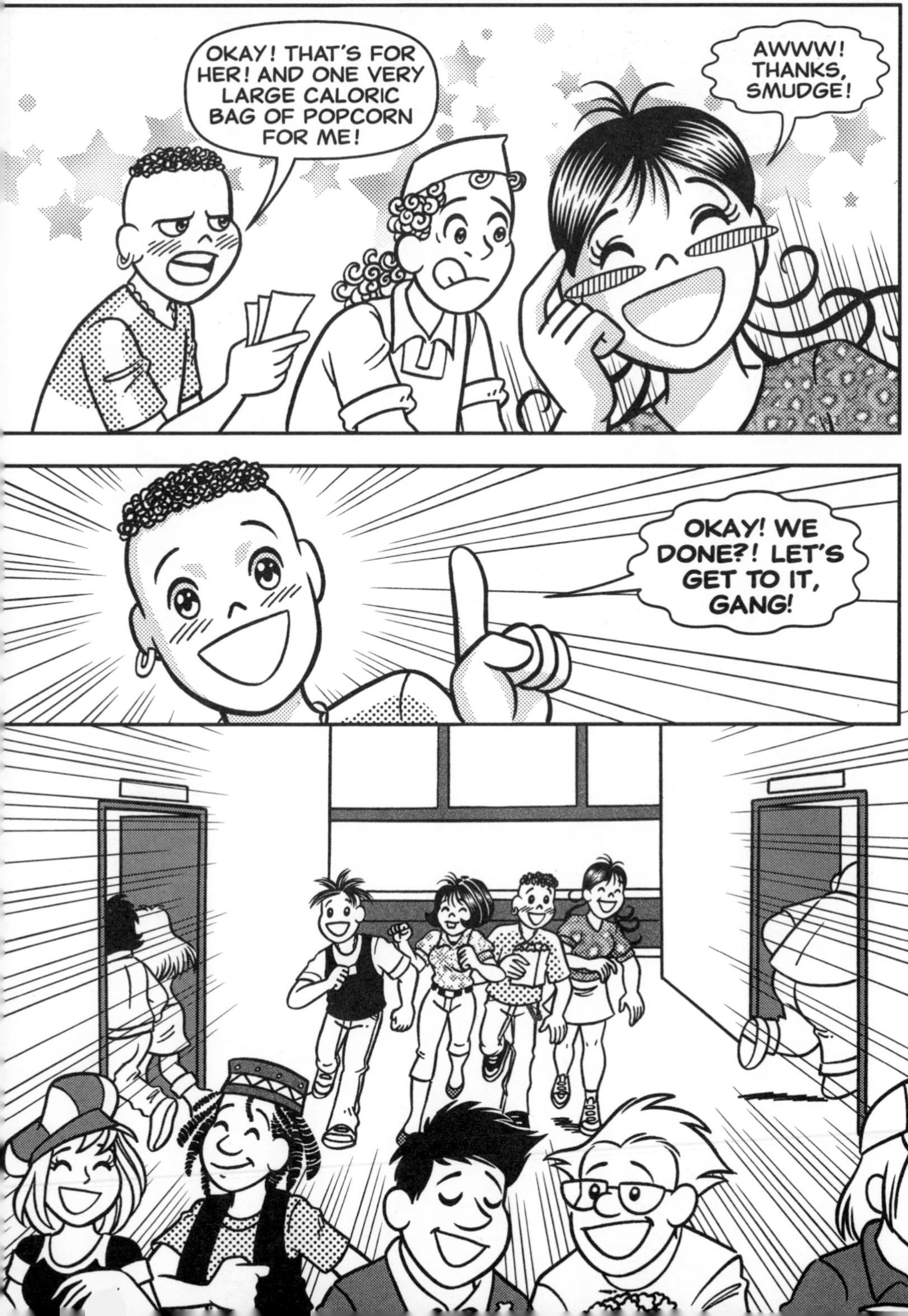
OKAY! THAT'S FOR HER! AND ONE VERY LARGE CALORIC BAG OF POPCORN FOR ME!
AWWW! THANKS, SMUDGE!
OKAY! WE DONE?! LET'S GET TO IT, GANG!

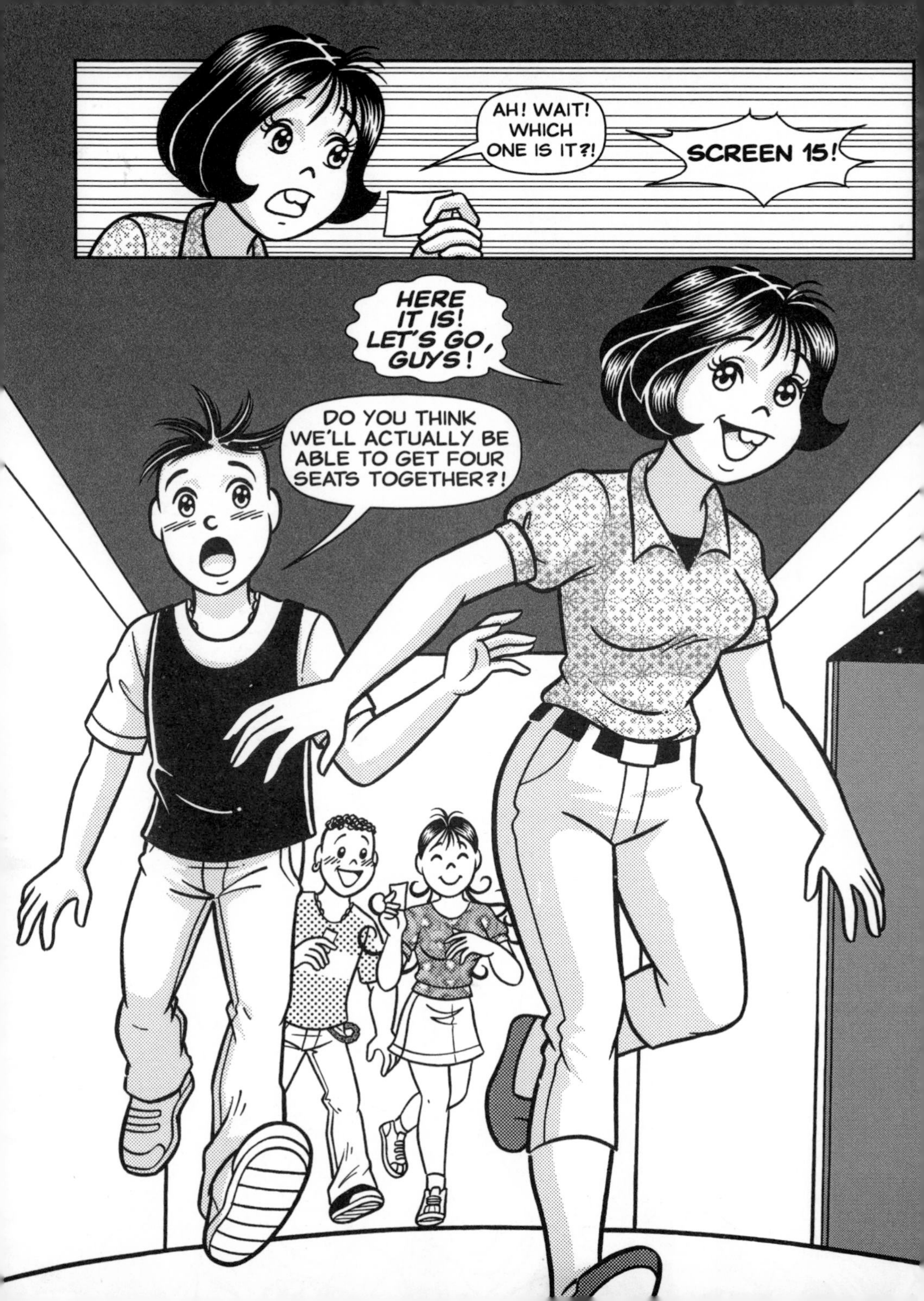
AH! WAIT! WHICH ONE IS IT?!
SCREEN 15!
HERE IT IS! LET'S GO, GUYS!
DO YOU THINK WE'LL ACTUALLY BE ABLE TO GET FOUR SEATS TOGETHER?!

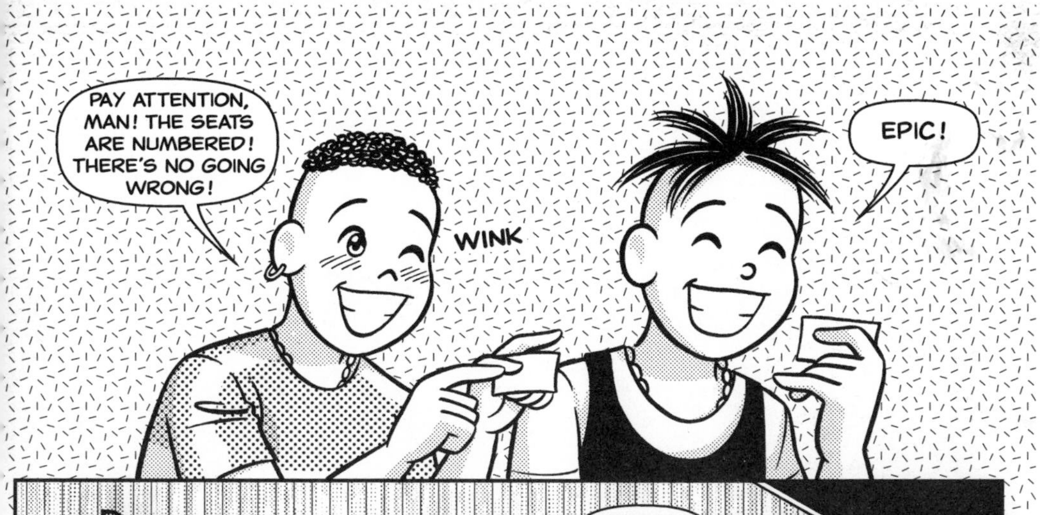
PAY ATTENTION, MAN! THE SEATS ARE NUMBERED! THERE'S NO GOING WRONG!
WINK
EPIC!

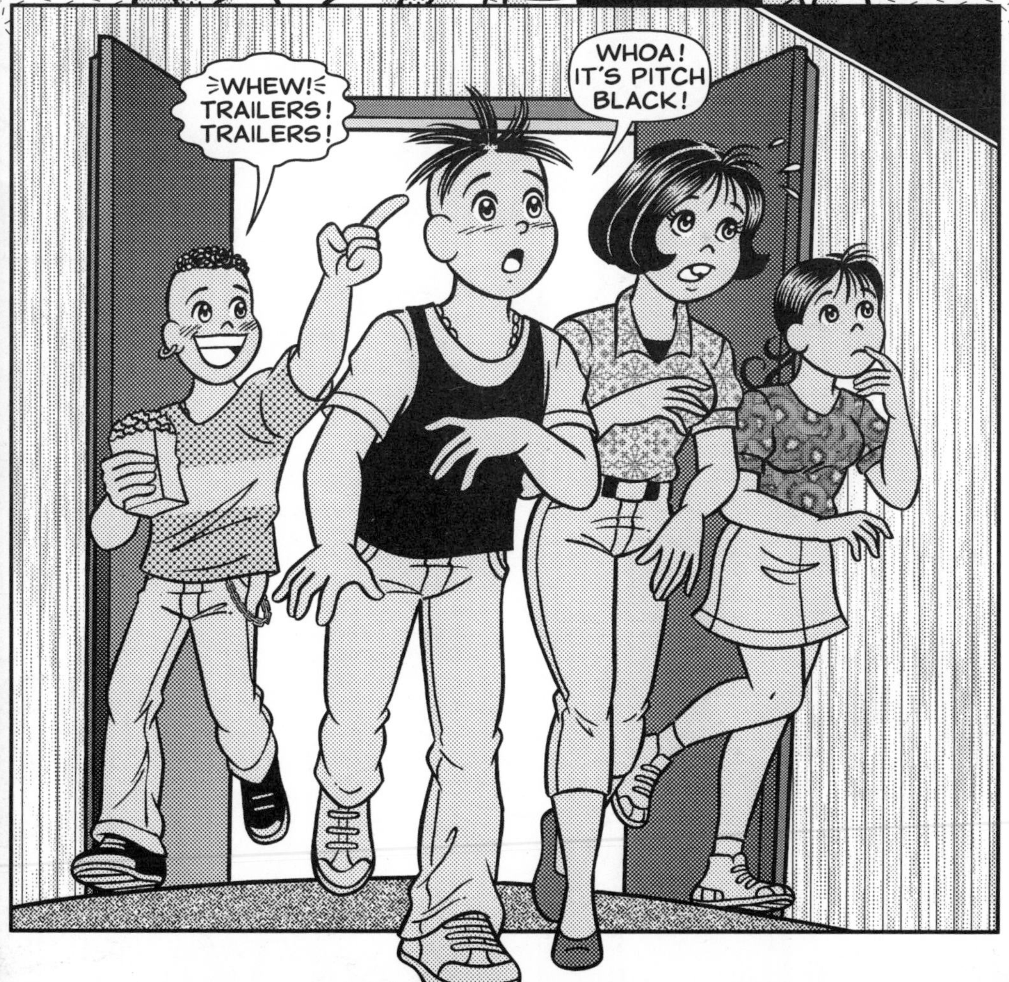
WHEW! TRAILERS! TRAILERS!
WHOA! IT'S PITCH BLACK!

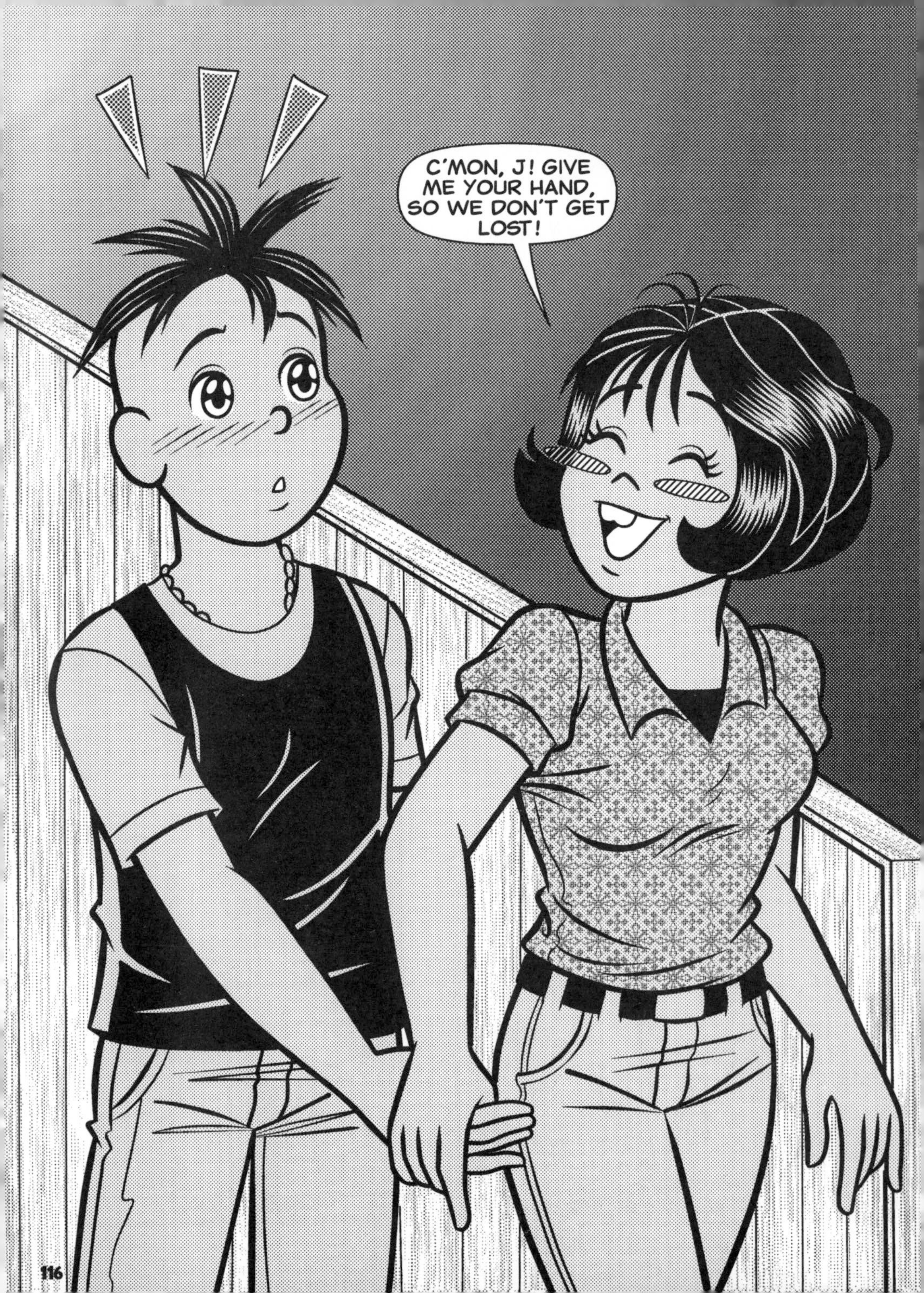
C'MON, J! GIVE ME YOUR HAND, SO WE DON'T GET LOST!

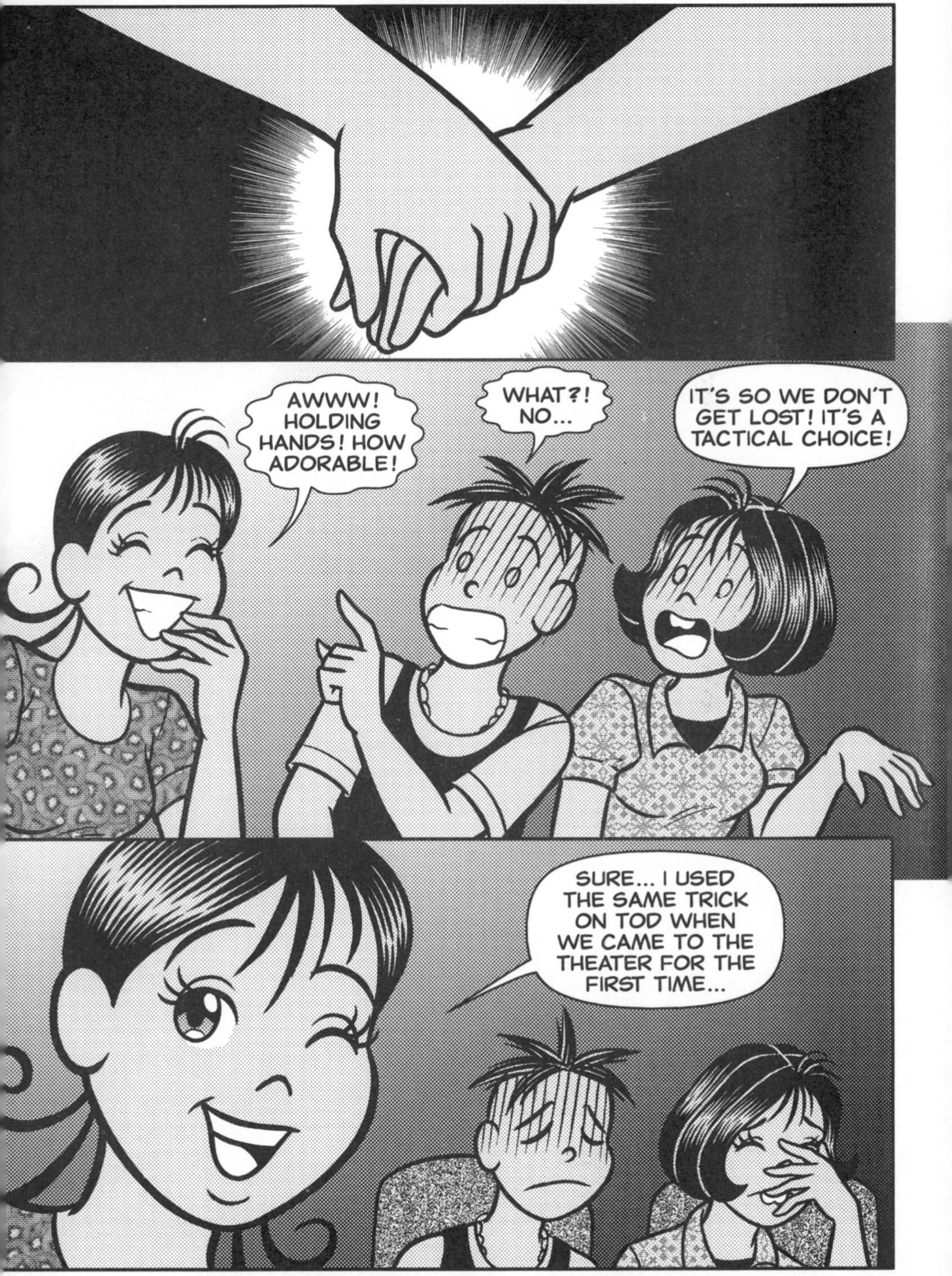
AWWW! HOLDING HANDS! HOW ADORABLE!
WHAT?! NO...
IT'S SO WE DON'T GET LOST! IT'S A TACTICAL CHOICE!
SURE... I USED THE SAME TRICK ON TOD WHEN WE CAME TO THE THEATER FOR THE FIRST TIME...

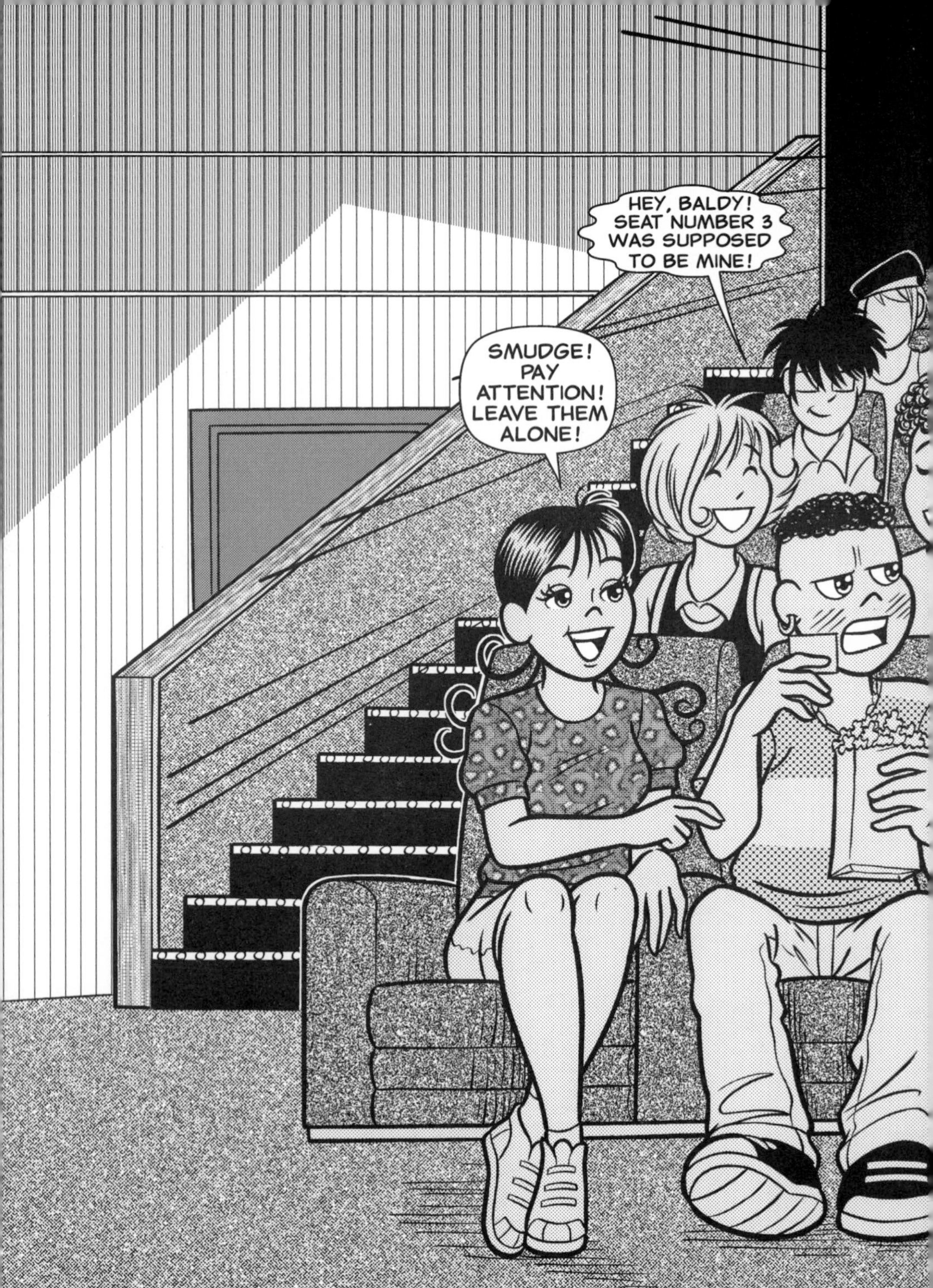
HEY, BALDY! SEAT NUMBER 3 WAS SUPPOSED TO BE MINE!
SMUDGE! PAY ATTENTION! LEAVE THEM ALONE!

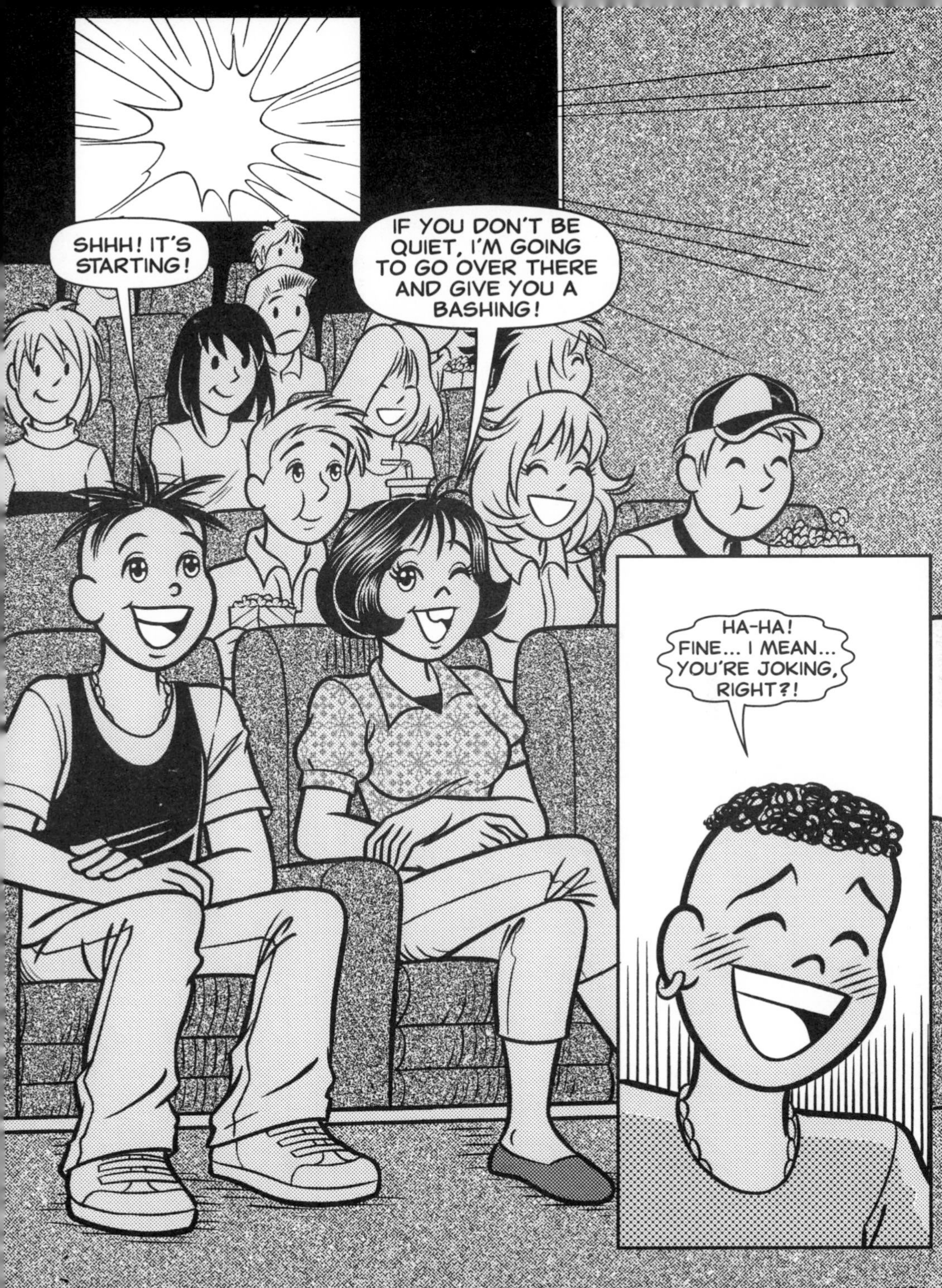
SHHH! IT'S STARTING!
IF YOU DON'T BE QUIET, I'M GOING TO GO OVER THERE AND GIVE YOU A BASHING!
HA-HA! FINE... I MEAN... YOU'RE JOKING, RIGHT?!

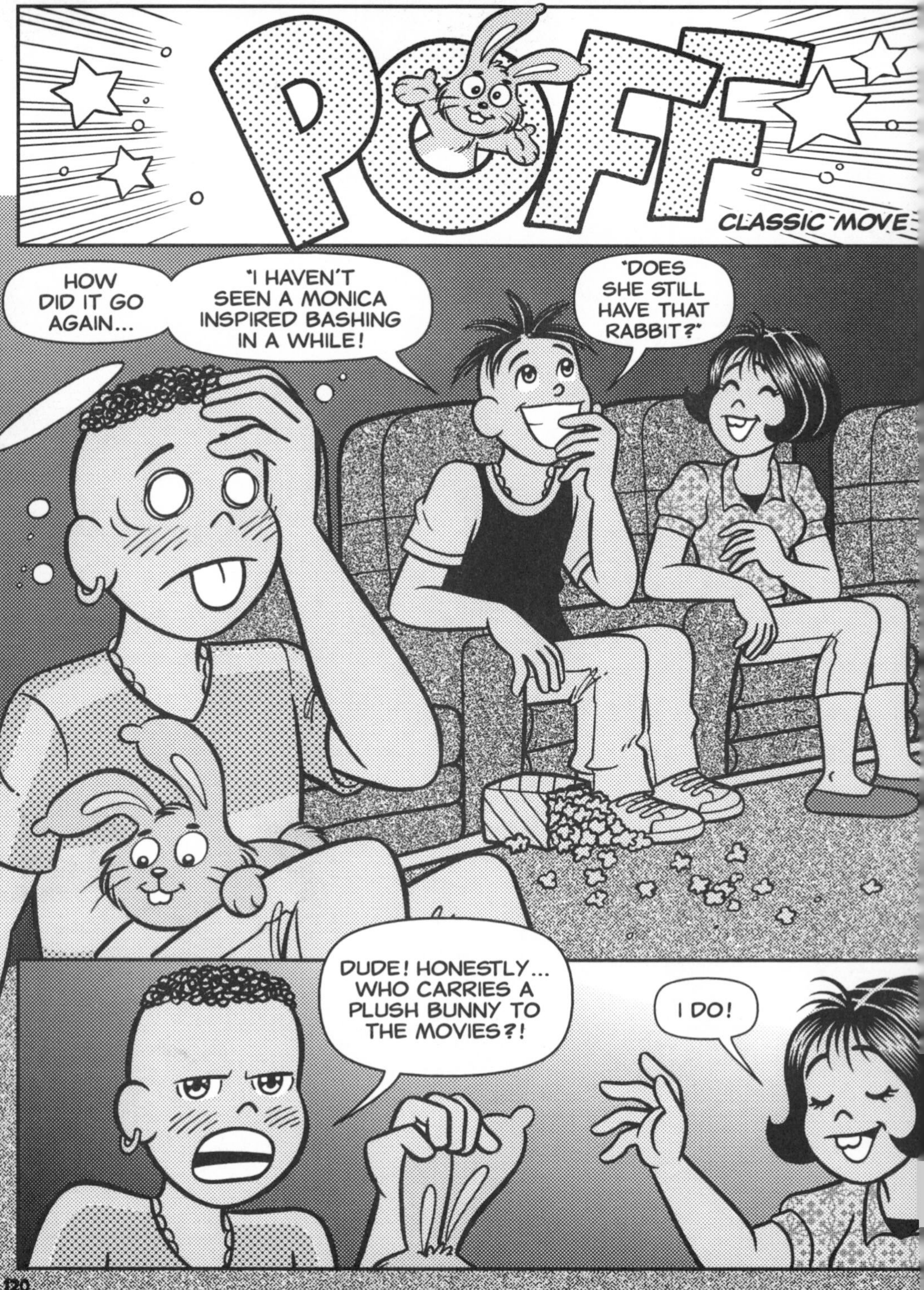
POFF
CLASSIC MOVE
HOW DID IT GO AGAIN...
"I HAVEN'T SEEN A MONICA INSPIRED BASHING IN A WHILE!
"DOES SHE STILL HAVE THAT RABBIT?"
DUDE! HONESTLY... WHO CARRIES A PLUSH BUNNY TO THE MOVIES?!
I DO!

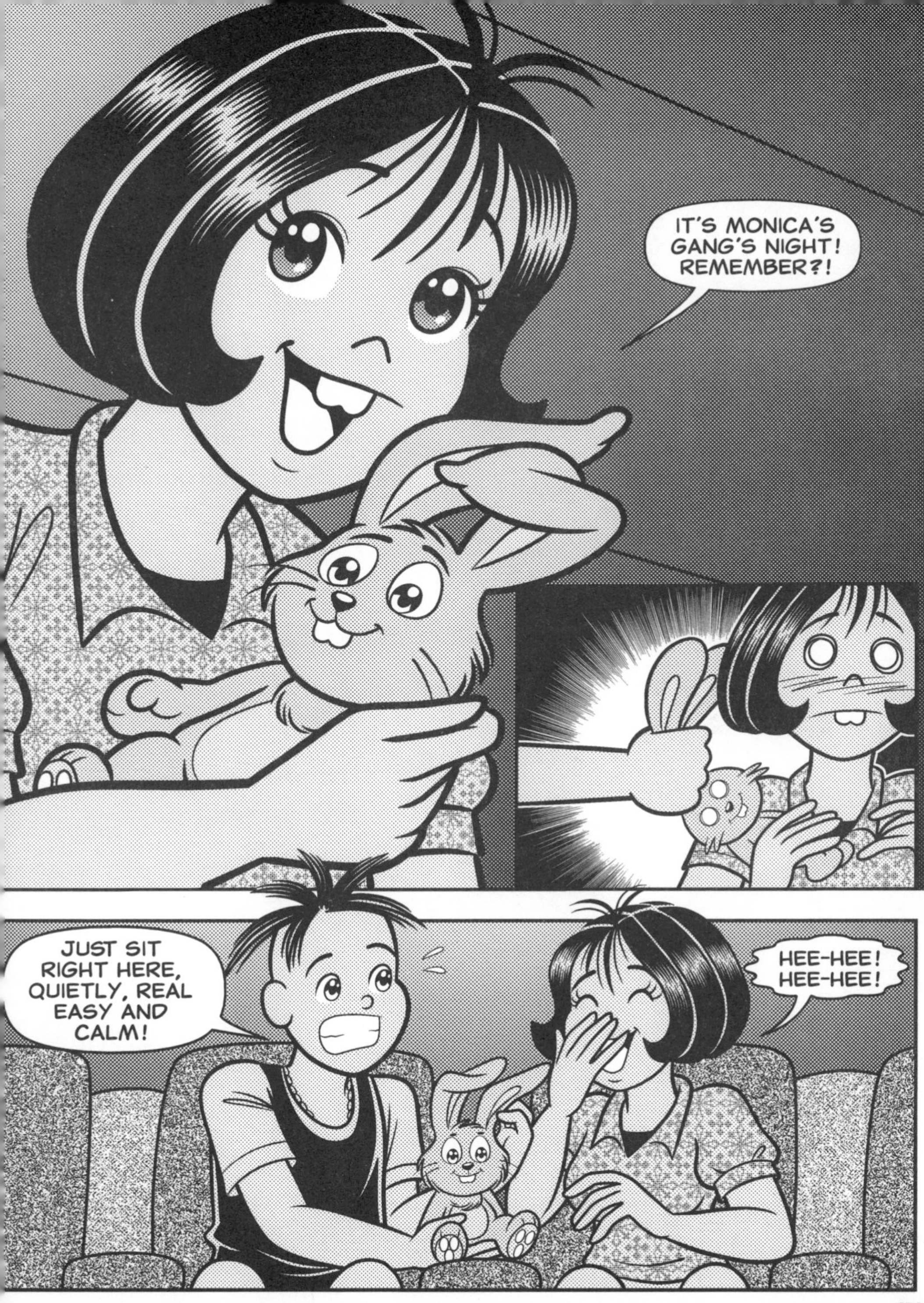
IT'S MONICA'S GANG'S NIGHT! REMEMBER?!
JUST SIT RIGHT HERE, QUIETLY, REAL EASY AND CALM!
HEE-HEE! HEE-HEE!

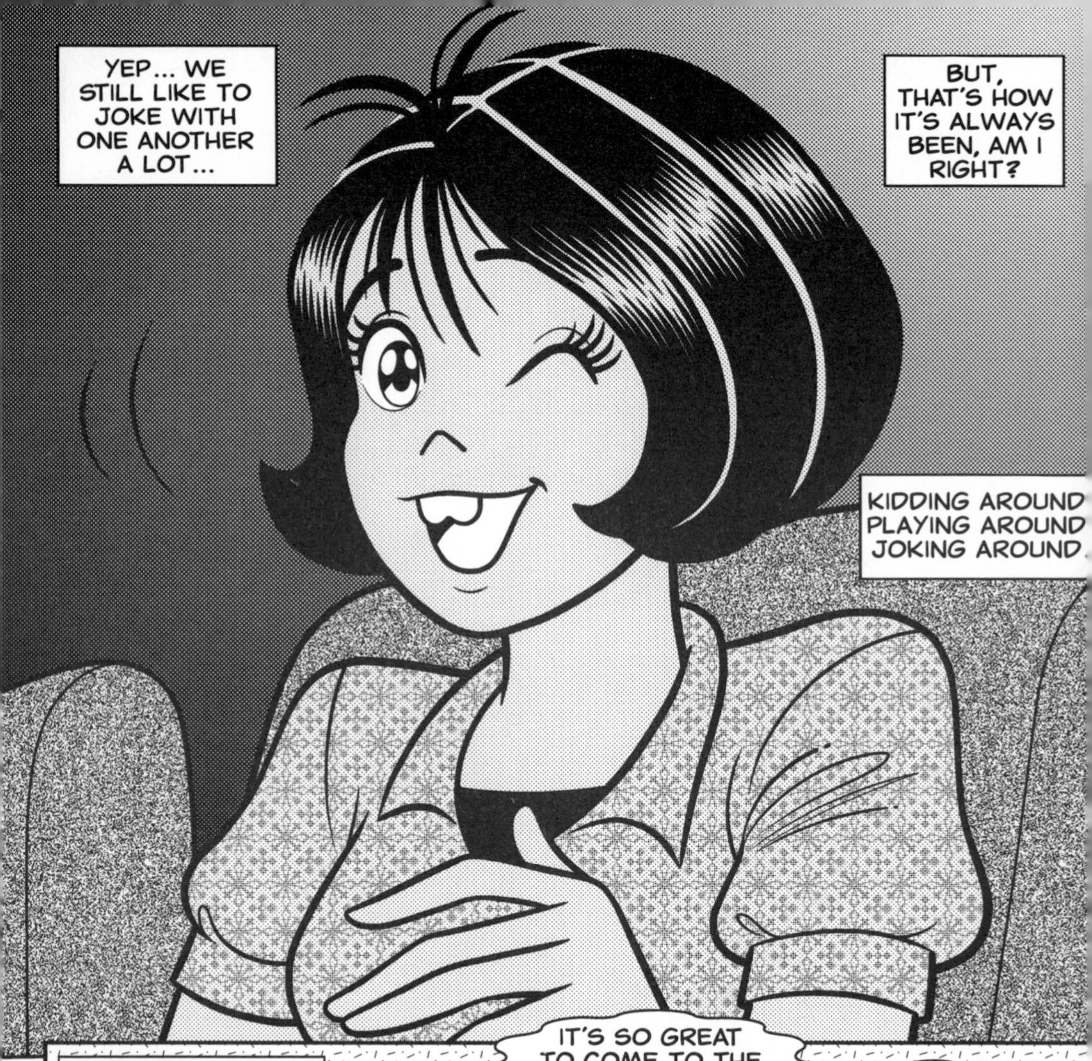
YEP... WE STILL LIKE TO JOKE WITH ONE ANOTHER A LOT...
BUT, THAT'S HOW IT'S ALWAYS BEEN, AM I RIGHT?
KIDDING AROUND
PLAYING AROUND
JOKING AROUND

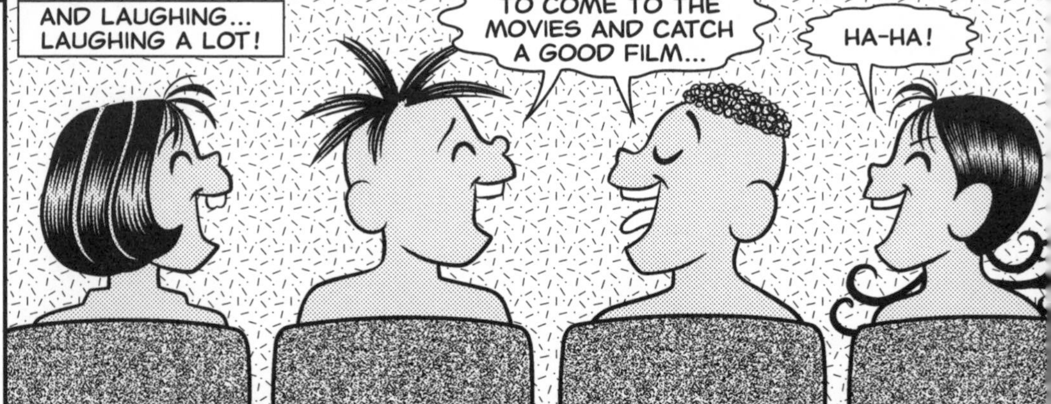
AND LAUGHING... LAUGHING A LOT!
IT'S SO GREAT TO COME TO THE MOVIES AND CATCH A GOOD FILM...
HA-HA!

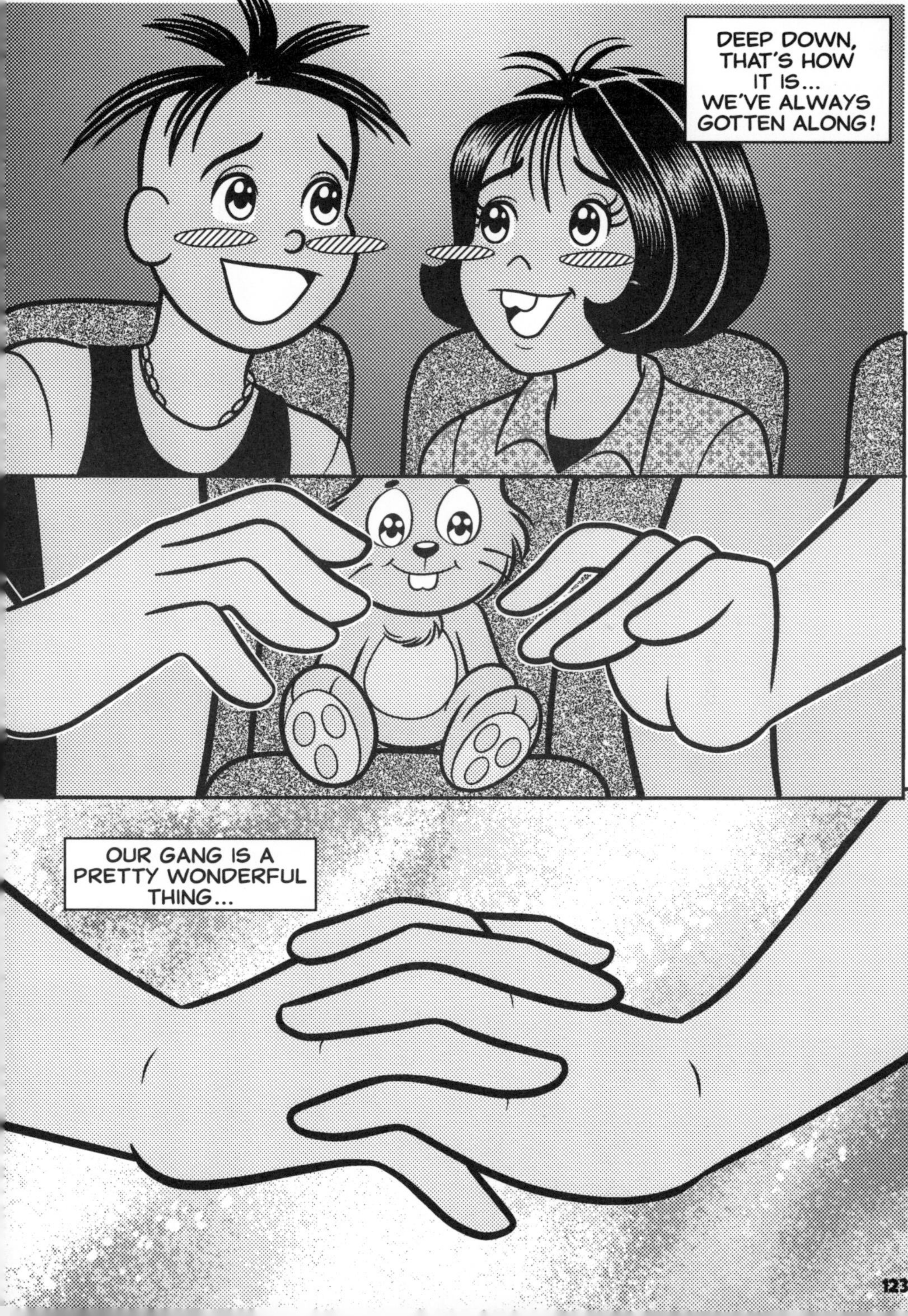
DEEP DOWN, THAT'S HOW IT IS... WE'VE ALWAYS GOTTEN ALONG!
OUR GANG IS A PRETTY WONDERFUL THING...

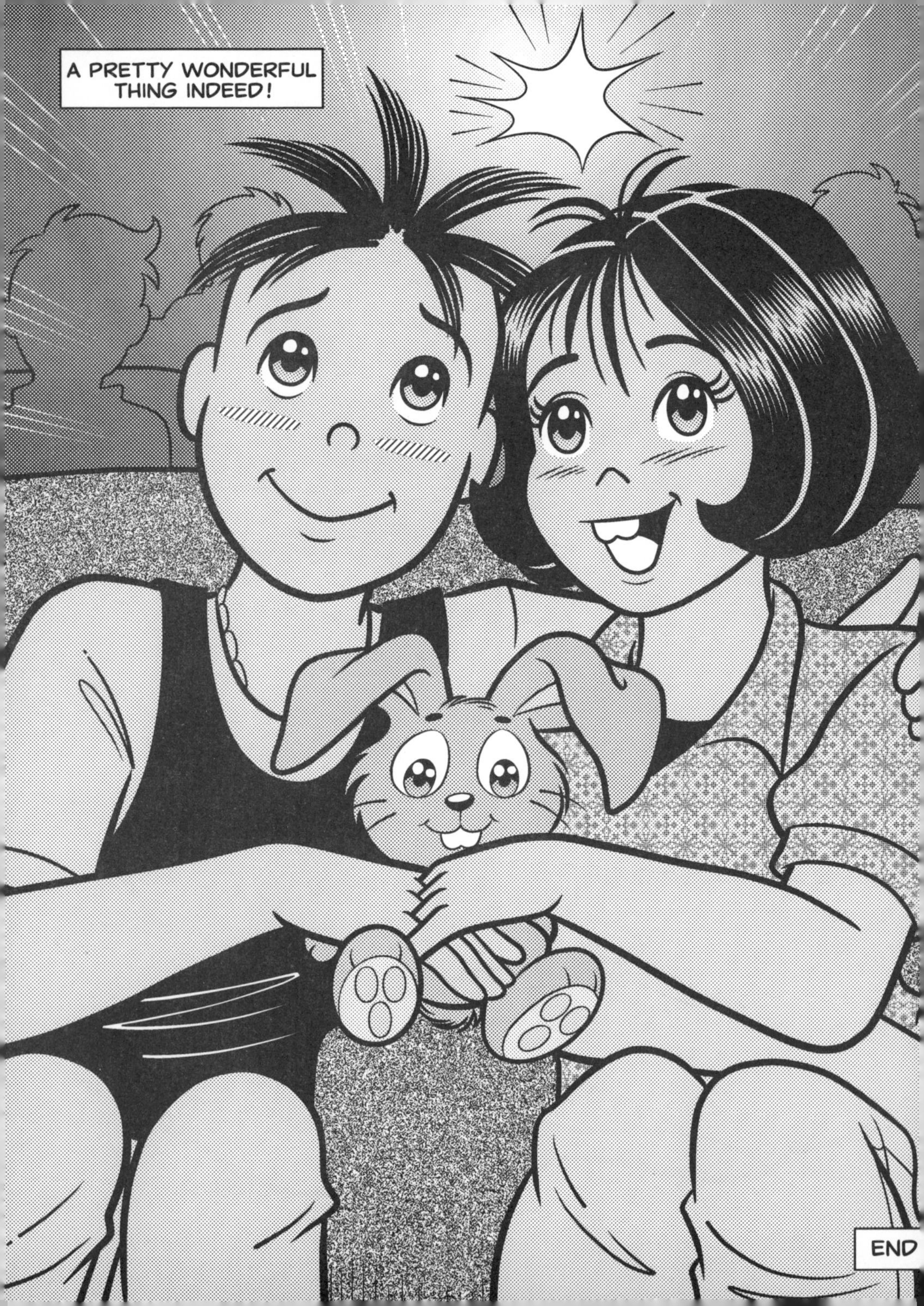
A PRETTY WONDERFUL THING INDEED!
END

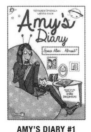

Charmz chat

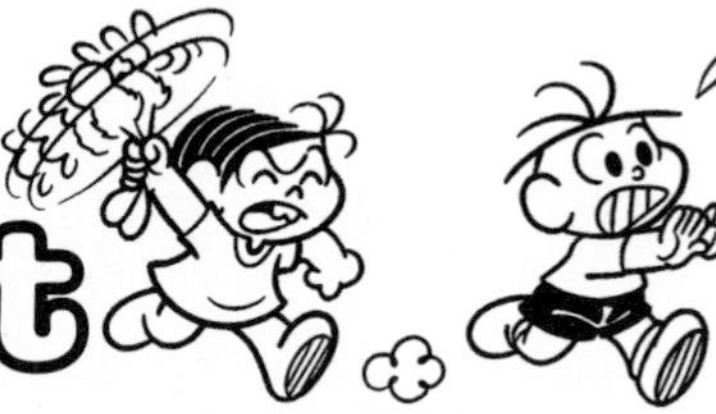

Welcome to the exciting Charmz debut of MONICA ADVENTURES, brought to you by the Papercutz imprint devoted to romantic and fun graphic novels. We're incredibly excited to bring MONICA to you and to a whole new generation of North American fans. MONICA is created by the legendary cartoonist Mauricio de Sousa, a beloved comics maker with millions of fans worldwide.

MONICA originates from Brazil, where Monica, J-Five, Maggy, Smudge and Two To—Tony, (just Tony now) are all comicbook superstars. Known almost everywhere else in the world, Monica (and the gang) has been translated into many languages, has been celebrated in the international comics community and has won the coveted Yellow Kid award. MONICA is also credited with fostering friendship and understanding and for teaching generations of Brazilians how to read. Monica has starred in countless films, animated series, video games, shorts, books, stage shows, and countless adaptations. she is the Queen of Brazilian comics and even the cultural ambassador of Brazil for UNICEF.

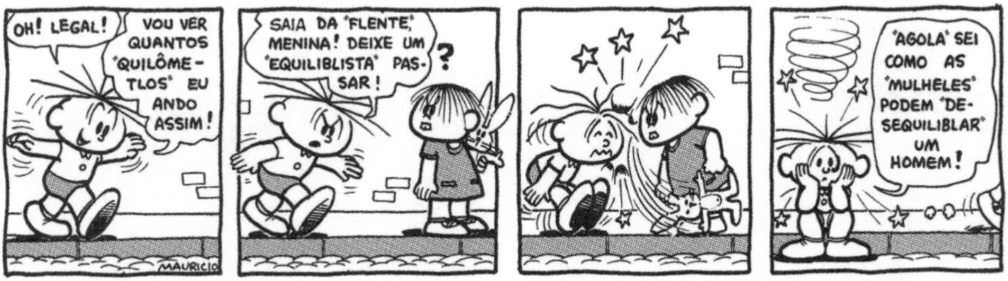
OH! LEGAL!
VOU VER QUANTOS 'QUILÔME-TLOS' EU ANDO ASSIM!
MAURICIO
SAIA DA 'FLENTE', MENINA! DEIXE UM 'EQUILIBLISTA' PAS-SAR!
?
'AGOLA' SEI COMO AS 'MULHELES' PODEM 'DE-SEQUILIBLAR' UM HOMEM!

Monica's first appearance in Jimmy Five's newspaper strip on March 3rd, 1963.
Even if you don't speak Portuguese, you can see the start of this comic rivalry!

Monica and friends have been together in comics for a long time—over 50 years, in fact. Cartoonist Mauricio de Sousa was inspired to create the cartoon Monica by his then-young daughter the real-life Monica, a stubborn little girl with a temper and a plush rabbit. He introduced her in the pages of his comic strip (pictured above) and she quickly became incredibly popular—with fans demanding to see more of this exciting and lovable character. Her series of comicbooks have been continuously published now for over 50 years, and millions of her comics are sold every month in Brazil. MONICA is a true, bonafide phenomenon.

The young Monica and her friends continue to star in their own comic, but a teenage Monica has a series of her own, as well. It's that series, called MONICA TEEN, that we're currently presenting here as this Charmz graphic novel series. Within these stories, you'll get a peek at the younger Monica and her friends in the flashback sequences. We'd love to publish the younger MONICA comics as a Papercutz graphic novel series…what do you think?

A SPECIAL MESSAGE FROM
MAURICIO DE SOUSA
THE CREATOR OF MONICA

There is a game that is played in almost every single comicbook production studio: adding "Easter eggs" and cameos to the books that are based on personalities of friends, colleagues, the boss, the directors, etc. Much like the way Alfred Hitchcock used to appear in his own movies. Or more recently, much like Stan Lee has been appearing in the latest Marvel super hero movies. In "Who Can Afford the Price of Friendship Today?", written by Flavio Teixeira, there are some examples of this game that serve as homages to his friends, colleagues, and so on. For the other individuals in the studio, this serves as a sort of improvised *Where's Waldo?* game, trying to find which of themselves or common friend of theirs made an appearance.

To the audience, sometimes, these small special appearances go completely unnoticed, so I am discussing this here so that I can help you enjoy a custom that we have at the studio; something to look out for and enjoy in future editions of MONICA ADVENTURES.

Just for you to get a clearer picture, in this edition the homages went to Osamu Tezuka (master of Manga, creator of Astro Boy), Kevin Smith (comics and cinema writer/director, comics store owner), Dik Browne (*Hägar the Horrible*), Paulo Back (another MONICA writer), Roberto M. Pereira (who sometimes likes to self-homage himself since he is the story's illustrator), Flavio Teixeira (the writer of this story), Rene Goscinny and Albert Uderzo (*Asterix*), Will Eisner (*The Spirit*), Sidney Gusman (Mauricio de Sousa Productions's editorial planner – in the story he was the owner of the comicbook shop), Silvia Back (Paulo's wife) and her many cats, George Lucas (*Star Wars*), and every once in a while another person peppered into different places in the story.

Editor Jeff Whitman (right), a Monica fanatic for years, had the pleasure of visiting Mauricio in his amazing studio in Brazil.

Photo credit: The *actual, real-life* **Monica**!

Some folks might feel inclined to believe that this exercise doesn't go with the "style" or "flow" of the story… I, however, am of a different opinion. I believe that these innocent and good-natured additions by the creators of the story only work to enrich the reality of our stories. In many ways, this serves as a tool to make the narration flow and the story more colorful and interesting. By adding different human voices and emotions we find ways to make the stories more attractive to our fans. So, with care and in the right way, we continue to do and allow these "games." In the future, I hope to tell you more details of how and why things happen in our stories and in real life… in the script and the lives of the creators.

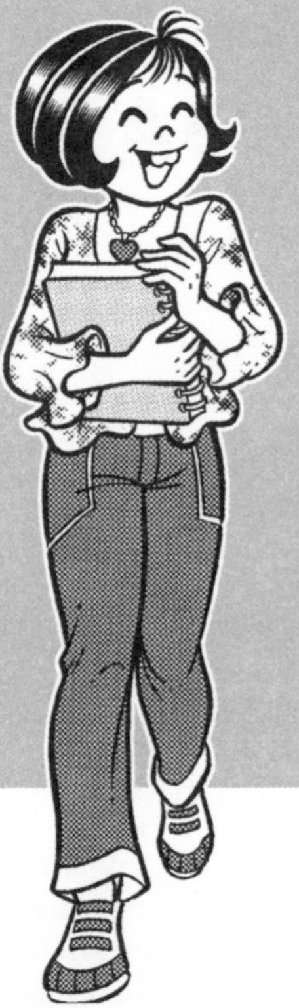

Mauricio de Sousa

Be sure to pick up MONICA ADVENTURES #2 "We Fought Each Other as Kids… Now We're in Love?!" available now wherever books are sold. Will Monica and J-Five finally have their chance together? Don't miss MONICA ADVENTURES #2!

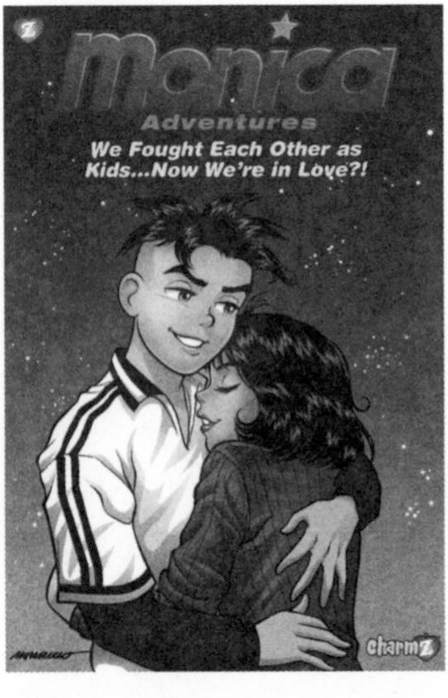
Monica
Adventures
We Fought Each Other as Kids...Now We're in Love?!
charmz

Want even more MONICA? Interested in seeing her and her friends's classic adventures? Well, write in and let us know!

STAY IN TOUCH!

EMAIL:	whitman@papercutz.com
WEB:	Papercutz.com
TWITTER:	@papercutzgn
INSTAGRAM:	@papercutzgn
FACEBOOK:	PAPERCUTZGRAPHICNOVELS
FANMAIL:	Charmz, 160 Broadway, Suite 700, East Wing, New York, NY 10038

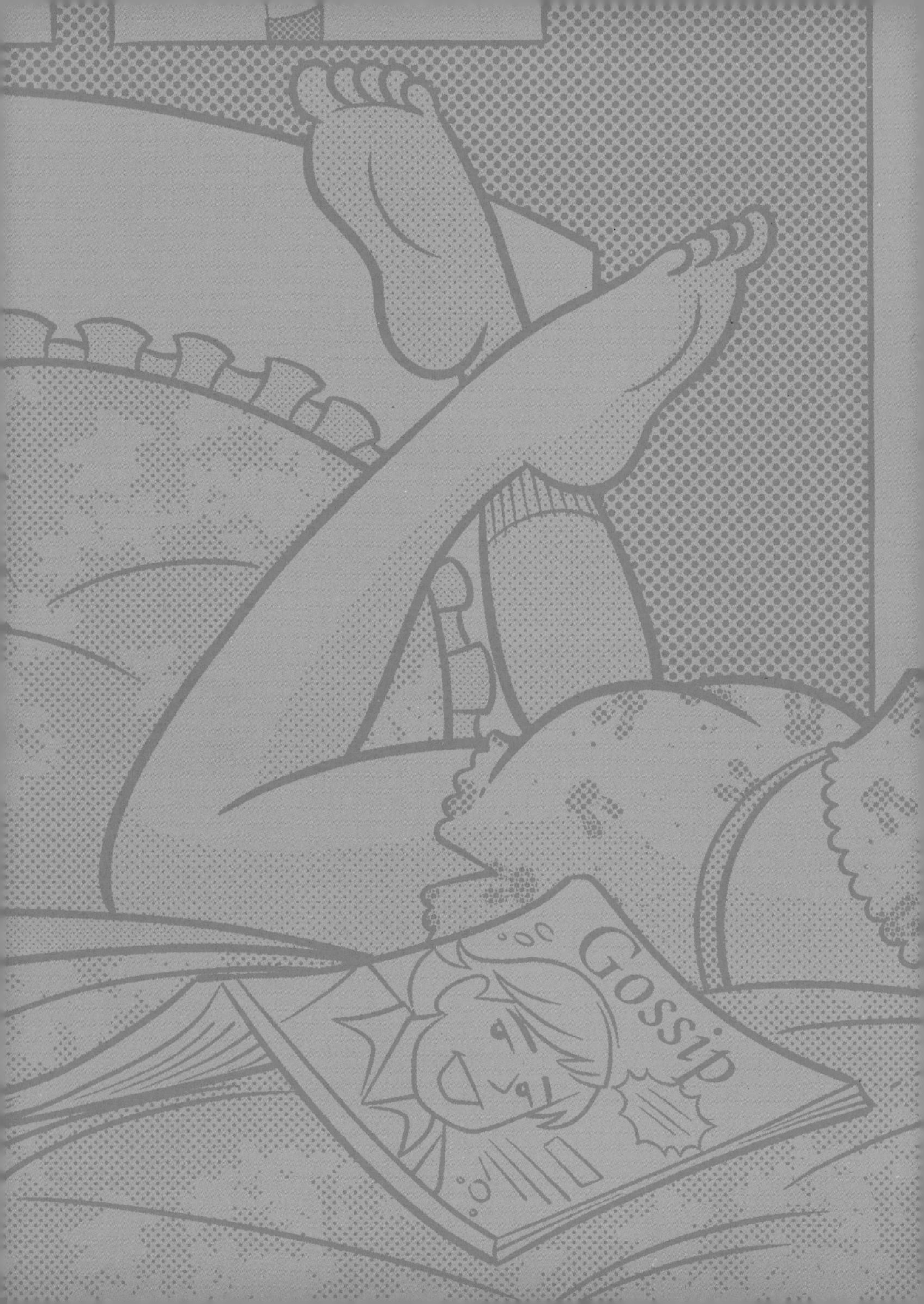
Gossip